a deadly shade of gold

JOHN D. MacDONALD

FAWCETT GOLD MEDAL • NEW YORK

A Fawcett Gold Medal Book
Published by Ballantine Books
Copyright © 1965 by John D. MacDonald Publishing, Inc.

ISBN 0-449-12770-2

Manufactured in the United States of America

First Fawcett Gold Medal Edition: February 1965
First Ballantine Books Edition: November 1982
Third Printing: October 1984

JOHN D. MacDONALD

NOW MEET HIS GREAT CHARACTER: THAT BIG LOOSE-JOINTED BOAT BUM, THAT SLAYER OF SMALL SAVAGE FISH, THAT BEACH WALKER, GIN-DRINKER, QUIP-MAKER—THAT MAN NAMED TRAVIS McGEE, IN THE FIFTH COMPELLING STORY OF A BRILLIANT SERIES BY

JOHN D. MacDONALD

one

A SMEAR of fresh blood has a metallic smell. It smells like freshly sheared copper. It is a clean and impersonal smell, quite astonishing the first time you smell it. It changes quickly, to a fetid, fudgier smell, as the cells die and thicken.

When it is the blood of a stranger, there is an atavistic withdrawal, a toughening of response, a wary reluctance for any involvement. When it is your own, you want to know how bad it is. You turn into a big inward ear, listening to yourself, waiting for faintness, wondering if this is going to be the time when the faintness comes and turns into a hollow roaring, and sucks you down. Please not yet. Those are the three eternal words. Please not yet.

When it is the blood of a friend. . . .

When maybe he said, Please not yet. . . . But it took him and he went on down. . . .

It was a superb season for girls on the Lauderdale beaches. There are good years and bad years. This, we all agreed, was a vintage year. They were blooming on all sides, like a garden out of control. It was a special type this year, particularly willowy ones, with sun-streaky hair, soft little sun-brown noses, lazed eyes in the cool pastel shades of green and blue, cat-yawny ones, affecting a boredom belied by glints of interest and amusement, smilers rather than gigglers, with a tendency to run in little flocks of three and four and five. They sparkled on our beaches this year like grunions, a lithe and wayward crop that in too sad and too short a time would be striving for Whiter Washes, Scuff-Pruf Floors and Throw-Away Nursing Bottles.

In a cool February wind, on a bright and cloudless afternoon, Meyer and I had something over a half dozen of them drowsing in pretty display, basted with sun oil, behind the protection of laced canvas on the sun deck atop my barge type houseboat, The Busted Flush, moored on a semi-permanent basis at Slip F-18, Bahia Mar, Fort Lauderdale. Meyer and I were playing acey-deucy. He was enjoying it more than I was. He kept rolling doubles. He looks like the diarama of Early Man in the Museum of Natural History. He has almost as much pelt as an Adirondack black bear. But he can stroll grinning down a beach and acquire a tagalong flock of lovelies the way an ice cream cart ropes children. He calls them all Junior. It saves confusion. He is never never seen with one at a time. He lives alone aboard a squatty little cruiser and is, by trade, an Economist. He predicts trends. He acquired a little money the hard way, and he keeps moving it around from this to that, and it keeps growing nicely, and he does learned articles for incomprehensible journals.

At reasonable intervals one of the Juniors would clamber down the ladderway, go below and return with a pair of cans of cold beer from my stainless steel galley. I always buy the brands with the pull tabs. You stare at the tab, think deep thoughts about progress, advertising, modern living, cultural advances, and then turn the can upside down and open with an opener. It is a ceremonial kind of freedom.

Just as Meyer got all the way around, blocked me out, and began taking off with exquisite care, smirking away to himself, humming, rolling good numbers, I heard my phone ring. It surprised me. I thought I had the switch at the off position, the position where you can phone out, but anybody phoning you thinks it is ringing, but it isn't. And that is another kind of freedom. Like throwing away mail without looking to see who it's from, which is the ultimate test, of course. I have yet to meet a woman who has arrived at that stage. They always have to look.

Perhaps if Meyer hadn't been making everything so disagreeable, I would have let it ring itself out. But I went on down to my lounge and answered it with one very cautious depersonalized grunt.

"McGee?" the voice said. "Hey, McGee? Is this Travis McGee?"

I stuck a thumb in my cheek and said, "I'm lookin affa things while he's away."

The voice was vaguely familiar.

"McGee, buddy, are you stoned?"

Then I knew the voice. From way back. Sam Taggart.

"Where the hell are you," I said, "and how soon can you get here?"

The voice faded and came back. "... too far to show up in the next nine minutes. Wait'll I see what it says on the front of this phone book. Waycross, Georgia. Look, I've been driving straight on through, and I'm dead on my feet. And I started thinking suppose he isn't there, then what the hell do you do?"

"So I'm here. So hole up and get some sleep before you kill somebody."

"Trav, I got to have some help."

"Doesn't everybody?"

"Listen. Seriously. You still ... operating like you used to?"

"Only when I need the money. Right now I'm taking a nice long piece of my retirement, Sam. Hurry on down. The little broads are beautiful this year."

"There's a lot of money in this."

"It will be a lot more pleasant to say no to you in person. And by the way, Sam?"

"Yes?"

"Is there anybody in particular you would like me to get in touch with? Just to say you're on your way?"

It was a loaded question, about as subtle as being cracked across the mouth with a dead mackerel. I expected a long pause and got one.

"Don't make those real funny jokes," he said in a huskier voice.

"What if maybe it isn't a joke, Sam?"

"It has to be. If she had a gun, she should kill me. You know that. She knows that. I know that. For God's sake, you know no woman, especially a woman like Nora, can take that from anybody. I dealt myself out, forever. Look, I know what I lost there, Trav. Besides, a gal like that wouldn't still be around. Not after three years. Don't make jokes, boy."

"She's still around. Sam, did you ever give her a chance to forgive you?"

"She never would. Believe me, she never would."

"Are you sewed up with somebody else?"

"Don't be a damn fool."

"Why not, Sam?"

"That's another funny joke too."

"She's not sewed up. At least she wasn't two weeks ago. Why shouldn't her reasons be the same as yours?"

"Cut it out. I can't think. I'm dead on my feet."

"You don't have to think. All you have to do is feel, Sam. She'll want to see you."

"How do you know?"

"Because I was the shoulder she cried on, you silly bastard!"

"God, how I want to see her!"

"Sam, it will tear her up too much if you walk in cold. Let me get her set for it. Okay?"

"Do you really know what the hell you're doing, McGee?"

"Sam, sweetie, I've been trying to locate you for three years."

He was silent again, and then I heard him sigh. "I got to sack out. Listen. I'll be there tomorrow late. What's tomorrow? Friday. What I'll do, I'll find a room someplace . . ."

"Come right to the boat."

"No. That won't be so smart, for reasons I'll tell you when I see you. And I've got to talk to you before I do anything about seeing Nora. What you better do, Trav, tell her I'm coming in Saturday. Don't ask questions now. Just set it up that way. I . . . I've got to have some help. Do it my way, Trav. I'll phone you after I locate a place."

After I hung up, I looked up the number of Nora Gardino's shop. Some girl with a Gabor accent answered, and turned me over to Miss Gardino.

"The McGee!" she said with irony and pleasure. "Let me guess. Something in a size eight or ten, lacy, expensive and, of course, gift wrapped."

"Nope. This time I want the boss lady. Gift wrapped. Instead of package delivery, I'll pick it up in person. About seven? Gin, steak, wine, dancing and provocative conversation."

"Oh God, I promised my accountant I would. . . ."

"Low lights."

"But this stuff is way past due now and I really. . . ."

"Close harmony."

"Seven o'clock then. But why? I'm pleased and so on, but why?"

"Because a McGee never never gives up."

"Wow, you're after me every minute, huh? Tireless McGee. Once a year, with bewildering frequency, turning a poor girl's head, never giving her a chance to catch her breath. But make it seven-thirty. Okay?"

I went back topside and lost my game, and the next, and

the next, while the Juniors cheered their Leader on. I lost $14.40. I paid off. The air was colder, and the heat was going out of the slanting sunlight. The Juniors were getting restive.

"Here," I said to Meyer. "Put it in something with a future. Jump the cultural trend. Electric hairbrushes."

Meyer smiled and surveyed his flock. "With your money, McGee, I'd rather be trivial. What I'll do, I'll send Junior off, when the time is ripe, to invest it all in bean sprouts, water chestnuts, almonds, candied ginger and wonton, and we'll choke it all down aboard this fifty-four feet of decadent luxury afloat, and play your fool records and all tell lies."

"Got a date."

"Mmmm," he said. He counted them. "Darlings, I see you are seven. Those of you who can be trusted to go round up one amiable young man each, respectful, attentive, light-hearted young men, raise your right hand. Three of you? Ah, four. Splendid. All of you take your little robes and slippers and beach bags and buzz off now, and get dressed, warmly and informally, and gather up your young men and we shall all meet at Bill's Tahiti at seven promptly."

They trooped off my boat, making their little bird noises together, smiling back at us, waving.

Meyer leaned on the sun deck rail and said fondly, "Darlings all."

"That's a pretty sloppy formation. Shouldn't you have them marching by now?"

"They are products of an increasingly regimented culture, my boy. Group activities give them a sense of security, of purpose, of adjustment. I am their vacation substitute for a playground director. Left to their own devices on vacation, they would become restless, quarrelsome, bitter, aimless. They would have a dreadful time. Now when they return to one of those dreary states which begin with a vowel, they will treasure the memory of being kept busy every minute. The western world, my dear McGee, is being turned into one vast cruise ship, and there is a shortage of cruise directors." He turned and gave me a somber hairy look. "After that phone call, you played even worse, if that is possible."

"An old friend."

"With a problem, of course. McGee, that expression is rapidly becoming obsolete too. In our brave new world there will be nothing but new friends. Brand new ones every day, impossible to tell apart, all wearing the same adjusted smile, the same miracle fabric, the same perfect deodorant. And they will all say exactly the same things. It will take all the stress out of interpersonal relations. From what I have been able to observe of late, I suspect that all the females could be called Carol and all the males could be called Mark."

He lumbered down my ladderway, refused an ultimate brew, and went trudging off toward his ugly little cruiser tied up to a neighboring dock. On its transom, in elaborate gold, was the name The John Maynard Keynes.

At the appropriate time I drove over to the mainland, across the 17th Street Causeway, and from there north to the back street where Nora Gardino lives in what was once a gardener's cottage for a large estate. Only that small corner of the grounds is unchanged, framed on two sides by the original wall, with the fierce ornamental iron spikes on top of it, screened on the other two sides by tropical growth, rich, thick and fragrant. As I drove in, tires crunching the brown pebbles, I wondered if, back in a world no longer comprehensible to us, my vehicle had ever called at the main house, now long gone, replaced by a garden apartment project. I drive a Rolls, vintage 1936, one of the big ones. Some previous owner apparently crushed the rear end, and, seeking utility, turned her into a pickup truck. Another painted her that horrid blue that matches the hair of a grade school teacher I once had, and I have named her, with an attack of the quaints, after that teacher. Miss Agnes. She is ponderously slow to get up to cruising speed, but once she has attained it, she can float along all day long in the medium eighties in a rather ghastly silence—a faint whisper of wind, a slight rumble of rubber. Miss Agnes was born into a depression, and suffered therefrom.

My lights made highlights on Nora's little black Sunbeam parked deep in the curve of driveway. I went up onto the shallow porch, and a girl answered the door. She was big and slender. She had a broad face, hair the color of wood ashes. She wore a pale grey corduroy jump suit, with a big red heart embroidered where a heart should be. I did not catch her name exactly, not with that Gaborish accent, but it sounded like Shaja Dobrak. She invited me in, after I had identified myself, and said that Nora would soon be ready. In her grey-blue eyes, above her polite and social smile, were little glints of appraisal and speculation. Two Siamese cats, yawning on a decorator couch, gave me much the same look, though slightly cross-eyed. The decor had been changed since that last time I was at the cottage. Now it was gold and grey, with accents of white and pale blue, a small, charming, intimate room. She made me a drink and brought it to me, and sat with her own in a chair facing me, long legs tucked under her, and told me she had worked for Nora seven months, and had been living at the cottage for four months. She was a grown-up, composed, watchful and gracious, and extraordinarily attractive in her own distinctive way.

In a little while Nora came hurrying out, and I got up for the quick small old-friends hug, the kiss on the cheek. She is a lean, dark, vital woman, with vivid dark eyes, too much nose, not enough forehead. Her voice is almost, but not quite, baritone. Her figure is superb and her legs are extraordinary. In spite of the strength of her features, her rather brusk and impersonal mannerisms, she is an intensely provocative woman, full of the challenging promise of great feminine warmth.

She was in a deep shade of wool, not exactly a wine shade, perhaps a cream sherry shade, a fur wrap, her blue-black hair glossy, her heels tall, purse in hand, mouth shaped red, her eyes sparkling with holiday. Her face looked thinner than I remembered, her cheeks more hollowed.

We said goodnight to the smiling Shaja, and as we went out Nora said, "I haven't had a date in so long, I feel practically girlish."

"Good. My car or yours?"

"Trav, you should remember that I would *never* slight Miss Agnes that way. She'd sit here and sulk." After I closed her in and got in beside her she said, "I hate to be a bore, but I left a letter on my desk that has to go out tonight. Do you mind?"

"Of course not." As I turned out of the drive I said, "I thought you were a loner."

"Oh, Shaja? She is a jewel. I'm in the process of setting the shop up so that she can buy in, a little at a time. She's the only one I've ever found I can really depend on. Or live with. She has a very precise sense of privacy, of fairness, of sharing. And . . . she reacts to things the way I do. We're men's women, both of us. No sorority overtones. No girlish giggles and confidences. And we're both tidy as cats. No hair in the sink, no crud on the dishes. So it works. She's married to a man years older than she is. She gets two letters a year from him. He's in a Hungarian prison. Four years to go, I think, and then the problem of trying to get him out of the country somehow, and get him over here, but she has a wonderful confidence that it is all going to work out. She is absolutely marvelous in the shop. If a woman is torn between something terribly expensive, and something quite suitable, Shaja has a little trick of raising one eyebrow a fraction of an inch and changing the shape of her mouth, and sighing in an absolutely inaudible way. We're doing just fine, and how are you doing, Trav, darling?"

"Medium well."

"You were away for quite a long time, weren't you? I tried to get to you for some little things that came up. I thought they'd amuse you."

"I've been back since Christmas. Emotionally convalescent, sort of. Ragged edges."

"Something rough?"

"I came out of it with a little money, and absolutely nothing else, except a case of the flying twitches."

"What in the world is that?"

"When you try to drop off to sleep and all of a sudden you leap like a gaffed fish and start shaking. So you have a drink and try again. But now I'm having play time. Months of it, Nora."

"Until the money gets low?"

"Is this going to work into the lecture about ambition, security, reliability, the obligation to use all the talents God gives you and so on?"

"No, darling. Not tonight. Not ever again. You are incorrigible."

I parked in the vast emptiness in front of her shop. She is in a superior shopping center, multi-level, with walks, planting areas, piped music, a sprinkling of nationally known retail names. The two feminine dummies in the shallow window were silhouetted against her night lights. In a slant of gold script on the display window was written Gardino. I went with her while she unlocked the door, and stood inside the door while she went back to her office in the rear to get the letter. In the still air was the scent of perfumes and fabric. Out of some mild ironic impulse I reached into the shallow window and patted the hard plastic curve of the sterile rump of the nearest dummy, covered by $89 worth of cotton. I thought of what Meyer had said, and I murmured, "I dub thee Carol."

She came swiftly and soundlessly back across the thick carpeting, the paleness of the letter in her hand and said, "I hate to be so stupid."

"What's the most expensive thing in stock?"

"What? We can get almost anything very quickly for special customers."

"I mean right here, right now."

"Why, dear?"

"Aimless curiosity, Nora."

"We have some absolutely lovely suits at nine hundred dollars."

"Would a woman buy one of those to please a man?"

She patted my arm. "Don't be an ass, Travis. A woman buys a nine-hundred-dollar suit to prove to the world at large that she has a man willing to buy her a nine-hundred-dollar suit. It gives her a sense of emotional accomplishment. Come along. You're a drink ahead of me."

As she checked the lock on the door behind us, I said, "How about the Mile O'Beach?"

"Hmmm. Not the Bahama Room?"

"Later, if we feel like it. But food and drink in the Captain's Room."

"Fine!"

It was a conversational place, a small dark lounge far from the commercial merriment, all black woods, dark leather, flattering lighting. We took armchairs at the countersunk bar, and I told Charles to bring us menus in about forty minutes, and told him what sort of table we would like. We talked very busily and merrily, right through the drinks and right into dinner, and then the conversation began to sag because there wasn't anything left to talk about except the way things once were. It brought on constraint.

I do not know if she ever actually realized, while things were going on, how it all was with me. Sam and Nora were so inevitably, totally, glowingly right for each other, that the reflected aura deluded Nicki and me into thinking we had something just as special. A habitual foursome can work that kind of uneasy magic sometimes. When Sam Taggart and Nora broke up in that dreadful and violent and self-destructive way, Nicki and I tried to keep going. But there wasn't enough left. Too much of what we thought we were to each other depended on that group aura, the fun, the good talk, the trusting closeness.

I waited until she had finished dinner and had argued herself into the infrequent debauch of Irish coffee.

Not knowing any good way to do it, I waited until one line of talk had died into a not entirely comfortable silence, and then I said, "Sam is on his way back here. He wants to see you."

Her eyes went wide and deep lines appeared between her dark brows. She put her hand to her throat. "Sam?" she whispered. "He wants. . . ." The color drained out of her face abruptly. She wrenched her chair sideways and bent forward to put her head between her knees. Charles came rushing over. I told him what I needed. He returned with it in about twelve seconds. I knelt beside her chair and held the smelling salts to her nostrils. Charles hovered. In a few moments she sat up, her color still ghastly.

She tried to smile and said, "Walk me, Trav. Get me out of here. Please."

two

WE WALKED on the dark grounds of the big hotel, among the walks and landscaping. In exposed places the wind was biting.

"Feel better?"

"Terribly maidenly, wasn't it? What did they used to call it? The vapors."

"I didn't do it very well. I sort of slugged you with it."

"How did he sound?"

"Exhausted. He'd been driving a long way."

"From where?"

"He didn't say."

"How did he sound . . . about me?"

"As if he's convinced you can never forgive him."

"Oh God! The fool! The damned fool! All this waste. . . . " She turned and faced me in the night. "Why should he think I couldn't ever understand? After all, a man like that is always terrified of . . . any total commitment. It was cruel and brutal, the way he did it, but I could have. . . . "

She whirled away and made a forlorn sound, staggered to a slender punk tree, caught it with her left hand, bent forward from the waist and began to vomit. I went to her, put my right hand on her waist to hold her braced and steadied, her hip pulled against the side of my thigh, my left hand clasping her left shoulder. As her slim body leapt and spasmed with the retching, as she made little intermittent demands that I leave her alone, I was remembering just how brutal it was, so all involved with that dreary old business of killing the thing you love the best. Because you are afraid of love, I guess.

Sam was a random guy, a big restless, reckless lantern-jawed ex-marine, a brawler, a wencher, a two-fisted drinker. He loved the sea and knew it well. He crewed on some deep water racers. He worked in boat yards. He went into hock for a charter boat, did all right, then had a run of bad luck

15

and lost it. He worked on other charter fishermen, and did some commercial fishing. A boat bum. An ocean bum. For a time he captained a big Wheeler for an adoring widow. He was a type you find around every resort port. Unfocused. A random, rambling man. After you knew him a long time, if he trusted you, you would find out that there was another man underneath, and a lot of the surface was a part he played. He was sensitive, perceptive. He had a liberal arts degree from one of the fine small colleges. He had a lot of ability and no motivation.

Then he met Nora Gardino, and she was that marvelous catalyst that brought all the energy of Sam Taggart into focus, into some sense of purpose. Nora gave him meaning. And it took a lot of woman to do that. She was more than most, by far.

At that time I picked up with Nicki and the four of us ran in a small friendly pack. Nicki and I got in on the planning phase. Her shop was doing well. Sam scouted a good piece of waterfront land. He wanted to start a marina from scratch, and he had sound ideas about it, and good local contacts. Once he got it started, they would be married. She would continue with the shop until too pregnant, and then she would sell out and put the money into the marina project. They designed the big airy apartment they would live in, right on the marina property.

Maybe he felt the walls closing in. Maybe he felt unworthy of all the total trust and loyalty she was so obviously giving him. Maybe he was afraid that, in spite of all his confidence, he would fail her in some way. By then he was earning pretty good money in a boat yard, and saving every dime of it. She had a dull little girl working for her at the time, plump and pretty, with an empty face. Her name was Sandra. Maybe, subconsciously, he wanted it to happen just the way it happened. Maybe, after he got drunk, it was just accidental. But it was cruel, and it was brutal, to have Nora, after a day and a night of searching for him, find him at last, see his blurred self-destructive grin as he stared at her from the tangled bed, with all the naked fattiness of Sandra snoring placidly beside him.

She turned on her heel quickly, closed the door with barely a sound, and went away from there, her heart breaking anew with every step she took.

By the next day he was packed and gone. I helped her try

to find him. She put a thousand dollars into agency fees without their finding any trace of him.

After a while you give up. Or maybe you never give up.

Nora straightened up at last, weak and dizzy, and held the slim tree with both hands and stood with her forehead resting against the soft silvery bark.

"I must be a very attractive date," she said in a half whisper.

"It's been three years."

"Not knowing if he was sick or dead or in trouble." She shivered visibly.

I patted her shoulder. "Come on. Go freshen up and we'll get away from here."

"When will he be here?"

"Saturday."

"What time?"

"I don't know."

"Will he . . . come to the shop?"

"Or phone you. I don't know."

"Does he know you've told me about him?"

"Yes."

"He hasn't found anybody else?"

"Neither of you have. For the same reason."

"I'm glad to have some warning, Trav. But I will be a complete wreck by Saturday."

I waited in the lobby for her. When she was ready, I drove to Bahia Mar. We could talk aboard The Busted Flush. Obviously she wanted to talk.

I turned the heat up. I made her a tall mild drink. She took her shoes off and sat on the far curve of my yellow couch in the lounge, her legs tucked up, her color better, her frown thoughtful.

"Damn it all, Trav, I just don't know how to handle it. Rush into his arms? I want to. But does he want me to? Or does he want to be punished? She was a dreadful little bit of nothing, you know. God, how I remember that whining little explanation." She imitated Sandra's immature little voice. " 'Miss Gardino, we just had a coupla drinks and you know, one thing led to another. Geez, I don't know where he went. I ast him and he pushed me away so hard I fell down. He just went.' "

"I don't know how he wants you to act."

"Boy, it was a real belt to the pride. My pride hurt so

badly, I didn't really know he was gone until he'd been gone a month. The wedding was a month away. We were practically living together. That was no secret. And it was such a wonderful magic, Trav. Every time was a promise of forever. Wasn't I enough for him? That's what made it such a terrible slap in the face."

"He was drinking."

"What started the drinking?"

"Fright, maybe."

"Of what?"

"A real live complete entire woman can be a scary thing."

"Did I come on too strong or something?"

"You have to be what you are, Nora. The complete package."

"Now I'm twenty-nine. Three lousy stinking wasted years. What did he *say?* Tell me some of his words."

"Quote God how I want to see her unquote."

She jumped up and went back and forth with panther stride. "What the hell did he think I was? A white plaster saint? A vision of perfection? Did he think I was so weak I couldn't handle a little ugliness? So okay! We'd have had a terrible couple of months. We'd have torn each other to ribbons. And I would have told him that if he ever did that to me again, I'd cut his heart out. But he didn't give me a chance! He didn't give us a chance. He ran, damn him!"

"After he gave himself the excuse to run, Nora."

She sat down abruptly and stared at me for a long time. "Sure," she said. "You can understand that better than I can, because you are one of those too, aren't you? One of those long distance runners. You wade around the edge, boy. But you never jump in. You go out on the end of the high board and bounce pretty and puff your chest, but you never take that big dive."

"That's reasonably accurate."

Her face twisted. "I'm sorry, Trav. I haven't got the right."

"Or maybe all the information. But no harm done."

She hit her knee with her fist. "I don't know how to handle it, meeting him."

"Don't plan anything. Play it by ear, Nora. Don't try to force any kind of reaction. It's the only thing you can do."

"I guess," she said. She gave me a shamefaced look. "This is idiotic, but I'm absolutely ravenous."

"Nora, honey, you know exactly where everything is, including the drawer where you'll find an apron."

"Eggs? Bacon? Toast?"

"All there. All for you. I'll settle for one cold Tuborg. Bottom shelf. No glass, thanks."

She brought me the beer. I heard the bacon sizzling out there. I looked over at the slim and lovely lines of her Italian shoes, one standing, one toppled. I wondered where Nicki was, and if she was making it the way she deserved. I heard Nora Gardino humming to herself. I sipped the cold beer. I turned on the FM and spun the tuner dial and found a Bach thing, a fugue, one of those that sounds as if the needle keeps getting stuck. Here, behind the thick opaque lounge curtains was that rare and special privacy obtainable in the middle of deserts and the middle of big marinas. Around me were the other craft, water slapping the hulls, gurgling around the pilings, little pressures of tide and wind creaking the lines.

She came out of the galley and said, "Why did he call you?"

"To find out if you were still around," I lied. "To find out if there were any chances left. To find out if it was too late to come home."

"It isn't too late. Believe me, it isn't too late."

three

SOUTH OF LAUDERDALE on U.S. 1 there are junk strips dating back to the desperate trashiness of the thirties. They are, as a governor of the state of Florida once said at a press conference, a sore eye.

Sam Taggart was in one of six cabins out behind a dispirited gas station that sold some kind of off-brand called Haste. The cabins were originally styled to look like little teeny tiny Mount Vernons. There was a field full of dead automobiles behind the cabins, a defunct Midgie-Golf on the left, a vegetable stand on the right. Sam was in number three, and I got there at four on Friday afternoon, twenty minutes after he phoned. The car beside the cabin was maroon and rust, a seven or eight year old Merc with bald tires.

A bed creaked as Sam got off it and came to the door. He let me in and hit me solidly in the chest and said, "You're an uglier man than I remembered."

"I compensate with boyish charm, Taggart." We shook hands. He motioned to the only chair in the room and sat on the bed. I had never seen him so dark. He was the deep stained bronze of a Seminole. His hand was hard and leathery. He wore faded khaki pants and a white T shirt with a ripped shoulder seam. He looked leaned down, all bones and wire. He had a crescent scar on his chin that hadn't been there before. He was missing some important teeth on the upper right. His black hair was cropped close to his skull.

"You know what I was remembering while I was waiting, McGee? That crazy time down at Marathon, and those big twins, Johnny Dow's nieces from Michigan. And we got in that game of trading punches, just for kicks. And every time, both those big old gals would scream. Finally I dropped you, and you stayed down so long I began to get nervous. Then you got up, a little bit at a time. I swear to God, it took you five whole minutes to get all the way up on your feet and you

20

stood there swaying and gave me a great big bloody grin and said, 'My turn, Sam.' That's what I was remembering. God, what idiots. How are things, Trav?"

"You mean with Nora?"

"Okay. With Nora. How did she take it?"

"First she got faint and then she threw up, and then she decided she loves you and wants you back."

"Boy, I come back like a hero, don't I? I come back in great shape."

"But you came back."

"She's a sucker for punishment, eh?"

"Why did you do her that way, Sam?"

He braced his arms on his knees and stared at the floor. "I don't know. I just don't know, Trav. I swear." He looked up at me. "How has she been? How does she look? How's she been making out?"

"She looks a little thinner in the face. And she's a little bit quieter than she used to be. She's made a good thing of the shop. It's in a new place now. More expensive stuff. She's still got the best legs in town."

"Coming back is doing her no favor."

"Leave that up to her, Sam. Unless you plan to do it the same way all over again."

"No. Believe me. Never. Trav, have there been any guys?"

"When you two get back together, you can decide whether you want to trade reminiscences."

"You know, I wondered about you and her. I wondered a lot."

"Forget it. It was a mild idea at one time, but it didn't work out. Where have you been all this time, Sam?"

"Most of the time in a little Mexican town below Guaymas. Puerto Altamura. Fishing village. I became a *residente*. Helped a guy build up a sports fishing layout, catering to a rich trade."

"You don't look so rich."

"I left real quick, Trav. Jesus, you've never seen fishing like we had there. Any day, you quit because your wrist is so sprained you can't hold a rod."

"How nice for you, Sam."

He peered at me. "Sure. Sure, you son of a bitch. When you don't think much of yourself, you can't think much of anything else."

"You said you're in trouble."

"You're still doing the same kind of hustling, McGee?"

"I am still the last resort, Sam, for victims of perfectly legal theft, or theft so clever the law can't do a thing. Try everything else and then come to me. If I can get it back, I keep half. Half is a lot better than nothing at all. But I am temporarily retired. Sorry."

"I've done some thinking since I talked to you. When I decided to come and see you, was I thinking about getting help, or an excuse to see Nora? I don't know. Everybody kids themselves. How can you tell. I knew I'd find out she's married, two kids by now. I could see the guy, even. One of those development guys, very flashy, speeches to the service clubs, low golf handicap, flies his own plane. A nice guy with thirty forty sports jackets."

"She's twenty-nine. She's not married. She should be."

"To me? To me, Trav? Take a good look."

His eyes moved away. He made a knotted fist and stared at it. I said, "Maybe you've gotten all the rest of it out of your system now. Maybe you're ready."

He sighed. "I could be. God knows I could be. I did some thinking. If there's a chance of her. If there's a good chance, then the thing that seemed so important to get your help on ... maybe it isn't all that important. Oh boy, they gave it to me good, friend. The stuff was mine, and they took it. You see, without Nora, it was a lot more important to get it back, or get half of it back, half to you. If you could do anything about it. Maybe not, even if you wanted to. This is not minor league."

"I don't have very much idea of what you're talking about."

"I suppose it's pride," Sam Taggart said. "Getting pushed around like a stupid kid. But it is better, I guess, to just get out of it with what I have." He stood up. "Stay right there. I want to show you something." He went out to the rusty car with the California plates. In a few moments he came back in. He sat on the bed and untied coarse twine, unrolled a piece of soiled chamois, reached and handed me a squat little figurine about five and a half inches tall. The weight of it was so unexpected I nearly dropped it.

It was a crude little figure, dumpy, a male representation like a child would make out of clay. It was startlingly, emphatically male. It was of solid metal, dull yellow and orange, blackness caught into the creases of it, shinier where it had been handled.

"Gold?" I asked.

"Solid. Not very pure. But that doesn't make the value of it. It's Pre-Columbian. I don't know whether this one is Aztec. It could be. It's worth a hell of a lot more than the gold, but nobody can say exactly what it is worth. It's worth what you can get a museum or a collector to pay for it. I imagine this one was some kind of a potency symbol. I had twenty-eight of them, some bigger, some smaller. Not all the same source or same period. Two were East Indian from way way back. Three were, I think, Inca. When they took the others, they missed this one because that night by luck or coincidence, this one wasn't with the others."

"They were yours?" I couldn't read his eyes.

"Let's just say there was nobody else they could have belonged to, the way things had worked out. Somebody might develop an argument on that, but when I had them, they were mine. A rough, a very rough estimate of the value of the whole collection would be three to four hundred thousand. Take the gold alone, it was two thousand, two hundred and forty-one point six ounces, discount that for impurities, it's still a nice bundle." He slowly rewrapped the figurine, knotted the twine. "Finding the right buyer for the whole works would be touchy."

"A question of legal ownership?"

"Who owns things like these anyway?"

"I'm not looking for a project, Sam."

"So you keep saying. And this one is too rough for one man. Some people have been hurt on this thing already. I thought it all over and I decided, what the hell." He bounced the wrapped lump of gold on the palm of his tough hand. "It scalds them they missed this one, not so much from the value of it, but because I could use it as a lever and give them a lot of agitation. If I wanted to give up any chance at any of it, and give this little fellow up too, I could raise political hell with them. So, earlier today, I made the decision to pull out with what I could salvage. I used most of the pennies I had left to stop along the road and make a couple of phone calls. They'd like to have this little fellow, and close the books. So I said fifteen, and they said ten, and it looks as if it will be twelve thousand five. They're sending a guy to close." He grinned widely enough to expose all the gap where the teeth

were gone. "At least I come back with a trousseau.
Twelve-five plus Nora is better than three hundred without
her. Lesson number one."

"It takes you a while. But you learn."

"Can I tap you for some walk-around money?"

I looked into my wallet. "Forty do it?"

"Forty is fine, Trav. Just fine."

"When are you going to see Nora?"

He looked uneasy. "After I get this thing closed out. God,
I don't know how to handle it. I don't know how to act
toward her. I ought to drop onto my knees and smack my
head on the floor. Tomorrow is the day. Three years of
thinking about her, and remembering every little thing about
her, and tomorrow is the day. I've got stage fright, Trav.
How should I set it up?"

"What you do, you hire fifty female trumpet players and
dress them in white robes and then you. . . ."

"Okay. It's my problem. Trav, how's Nicki?"

"I wouldn't know. She isn't around any more."

"Oh."

"When she left, we shook hands. What she really wanted
was a barbecue pit in the back yard, tricycles in the car port,
guest towels, daddy home from the office at five-fifteen. She
tried to be somebody else, but she couldn't make it. She
lusted to join the PTA."

He gave me a strange look. "So do I."

"You'll make it, Taggart."

"We'll have you to dinner every once in a while."

"I'll use your guest towels."

"We'll feed the kids first."

So I left him there and went on back to the boat, de-
pressed in a vague way. The plumbing facilities aboard The
Busted Flush are extraordinary. I heard that the Palm Beach
type who originally built her obeyed every whim of his
Brazilian mistress. The water tanks are huge. You could
almost set up a bridge game in the shower stall. One could
plausibly bathe a sizeable horse in the stainless steel tub.
Every possible area of the walls of the bath is mirrored.

When I had saved myself from extinction in that marathon
poker game by making a four heart flush stand up, the
houseboat chap showed an expensive tendency to see every
hand I had from then on. After I had all his ready cash and
his houseboat, as his friends gently and firmly led him away

from the game, he was trying forlornly to swing a loan on the Brazilian. With cash and houseboat gone, it would seem that his title to that particular asset was clouded.

I could guess that she had been a very clean girl. Other than that, she was either a very large girl or a very gregarious one.

I thundered hot water into the big tub, setting up McGee's Handy Home Treatment for Melancholy. A deep hot bath, and a strong cold drink, and a book on the tub rack. Who needs the Megrims? Surely not McGee, not that big brown loose-jointed, wire-haired beach rambler, that lazy fish-catching, girl-watching, grey-eyed iconoclastic hustler. Stay happy, McGee, while you use up the stockpiled cash. Borrow a Junior from Meyer for the sake of coziness. Or get dressed and go over to the next dock, over to the big Wheeler where the Alabama Tiger maintains his permanent floating house party and join the festive pack. Do anything, but stop remembering the way Sam Taggart looks with all the wandering burned out of him. Stop remembering the sly shy way Nicki would walk toward you, across a room. Stop remembering the way Lois died. Get in there and have fun, fella. While there's fun to have. While there's some left. Before they deal you out.

four

THE INSISTENT bong of the bell awakened me. I stared at the clock dial. Quarter after midnight. I hadn't gone out at all. I had read my book, gotten slightly tight, broiled myself a small steak, and baked myself a large potato, watched the late news and weather and gone to bed.

I put a robe on and went out through the lounge and put the afterdeck lights on. I looked out and saw Nora Gardino rehooking my gangplank chain. She came aboard and swept by me and into the lounge and turned on me, one fist on her hip, her eyes narrow. "Where is he?"

I yawned and rubbed my eyes. "For God's sake!"

"You know Beanie, over at the Mart."

"Yes, I know Beanie."

"She called me, over an hour ago. Maybe an hour and a half. She said she saw Sam about eight o'clock over at the Howard Johnson's. She was sure it was him."

"Can I fix you a drink, Nora?"

"Don't change the subject. Where is he? You said he wouldn't get here until tomorrow."

"So I lied."

"Why? Why?"

"Settle down, honey. He had a little matter to take care of first."

"I called you and called you, and then I decided you'd turned the phone off again, so I came on over. I want to see him, Travis."

"He wants to see you. Tomorrow."

She shook her head. "No. Now. Where is he?"

She stood there staring at me, tapping her foot. She wore flannel slacks, a yellow turtleneck sweater, a pale leather hip-length coat over the sweater, swinging open. She looked fervently, hotly, indignantly alive.

"Let him set it up his own way, Nora."

26

"I am not going to wait through this night, believe me. It's ridiculous. The time to have it out is right now. Where is he?"

"I don't know."

"Travis!"

I yawned again. "Okay, okay, honey. Let me get dressed. I'll take you there."

"Just tell me where."

I was tempted, but then I thought that Sam Taggart would be sore as hell if I let her go to that fusty little cabin without warning, bust in on him in the midst of that kind of squalor without warning. The best way I could retrieve it would be to have her wait out in the car and go get him and warn him and send him on out to her. As a matter of fact, as a penalty against myself, or a gesture of friendship, I could turn over The Busted Flush for the reunion, and stay in his little Mount Vernon.

I dressed quickly, woke myself up by honking into double handfuls of cold water, locked up, went out with her and woke up Miss Agnes. Nora sat very perky and alert beside me.

"What was it he had to take care of?"

"I'll let him tell you that."

"When did he arrive?"

"This afternoon, late."

"How does he look?"

"Fine. Just fine. He's in great shape."

I drove over to Route 1 and turned left. She was as rigid as a toy with the spring wound too tightly. When I glanced at her, she gave me a big nervous white-toothed grin in the reflection of the passing street lights. The gas station was dark. I parked on the asphalt beside the pumps and got out.

"In one of those crummy little cabins?"

"He isn't broke."

"I don't care if he's broke. I'll come with you."

"Nora, damn it, you stay right here. I'll send him out. Okay?"

"All right, Trav," she said meekly.

I walked around to the back. Cupid McGee. His car was beside his cabin. There was a pickup truck parked beside the end cabin on the left. The others looked empty. I rapped on his door. Night traffic growled by on Route 1. "Sam?" I called. I rapped again. "Hey, Sam!"

I tried the latch. The door swung open. I smelled musty linoleum, ancient plumbing. And a sharp metallic smell, like freshly sheared copper. I fumbled my hand along the inside wall beside the door. The switch turned an unshaded light on. The light bulb lay against the floor, on the maple base of a table lamp, the shade a few feet away. The eye records. The eye takes vivid, unforgettable pictures. Sam Taggart was on his side, eyes half open in the grey-bronze of the emptied face, one chopped hand outflung, all of him shrunken and dwindled by the bulk loss of the lake of blood in which he lay. A flap of his face lay open, exposing pink teeth, and I thought, idiotically, the missing teeth are on the other side.

They're sending a guy to close the account.

I heard the brisk steps approaching across cinders, and it took me too long to realize who was coming. "Sam?" she called in a voice like springtime. "Darling?"

I turned too late and tried to stop her. My arms were wooden, and she tore loose and took a step in and stared at what they'd left her of him. There are bodies you can run to. But not one like that. She made a strange little wheezing sound. She could have stood there forever. Lot's wife.

I had enough sense to find the switch and drop him into a merciful blackness. I took her and turned her slowly and brought her out. She was like a board.

In the darkness, with faint lights of traffic touching her face, she said in a perfectly conversational tone, "Oh, no. I can't permit that. I can't stand that. He was coming back to me. I can't have anything like that. I can't endure that. There's only so much, you know. They can't ask more than that, can they?"

And suddenly she began to hurl herself about, random thrusts and flappings like a person in vast convulsions. Maybe she was trying to tear herself free of her soul. She made a tiny continuous whining sound, and she was astonishingly strong. I wrested her toward brighter light and her eyes were mad, and there was blood in the corner of her mouth. She clawed at me. I caught her by the nape of the neck, got my thumb under the angle of her jaw, pressed hard against the carotid artery. She made a few aimless struggling motions and then sagged. I caught her around the waist and walked her to the car, holding most of her weight. I bundled her in on the driver's side, got in and shoved her over, and drove out of there.

By the time I walked her into her cottage, she was crying with such a despairing, hollow, terrible intensity that each sob threatened to drive her to her knees. Shaja wore a slate blue robe, her ashy hair tousled, her broad face marked with concern.

"I took her to Sam," I said. "When we got there he was dead. Somebody killed him. With a knife."

She said an awed something in a foreign tongue. She put her arms around the grief-wracked figure of the smaller woman.

"Do what you can," I said. "Sleeping pills, if you've got any."

"We haff," she said.

"I've got to use the phone."

She led Nora back to the bedrooms. I sat on a grey and gold couch and phoned the county sheriff's department. "A man has been murdered at the X-Cell Cottages, in number three, half a mile below the city line on the left. My name is McGee. I found the body a few minutes ago. I'm going back there right now."

I hung up in the middle of his first question. I went back to Nora's bedroom. Shaja was supporting Nora, an arm around her shoulders, holding a glass of water to her lips. A coughing sob exploded a spray of water.

"I'll be back later," I said. She gave me a grave nod.

When I parked at the gas station, a department sedan was already in front of the cottage. The cottage lights were on. Two deputies were standing outside the open door. A middle-aged one and a young one.

"Hold it right there!" one of them said.

I stopped and said, "I phoned it in. My name is McGee."

"Okay. Don't touch anything. We got to wait for the C.I. people," the middle-aged one said. "My name is Hawks. This here is Deputy DeWall." He coughed and spat. "Friend of yours in there?"

"Yes."

"When'd you find him?"

"A little after quarter of one. A few minutes after."

Cops do not have to be particularly acute. The average citizen has very few encounters with the law during his lifetime. Consequently he reacts in one of the standard ways of the average citizen, too earnest, too jocular, too talkative.

When someone does not react in one of those standard ways, there are only two choices, either he has been in the business himself, or he has had too many past contacts with the law. I could sense that they were beginning to be a little bit too curious about me. So I fixed it.

"God, this is a terrible thing," I said. "I suppose you fellows see a lot of this kind of thing, but I don't think I could ever get used to it. Jesus, as long as I live I'll never forget seeing Sam there on the floor like that with the light shining on his face. I can't really believe it."

Hawks yawned. "Somebody chopped him pretty good, Mr. McGee. The registration on the steering post says Samuel Taggart."

"That's right. Sam Taggart. He used to live here. He went away three years ago, just got back today."

The doctor arrived next. He stared in at the body, rocked from heel to toe, hummed a little tune and relit the stub of his cigar. Next came another patrol vehicle followed by a lab truck and by a Volkswagen with two reporters in it. A young square-shouldered, balding man in khaki pants, in a plaid wool shirt, and a baggy tweed jacket seemed to be in charge. Hawks and DeWall muttered to him as he stared in at the body. They motioned toward me. Everything was casual. No fuss, no strain. When a man with a hundred dollar car gets killed in a four dollar cabin, the pros are not going to get particularly agitated. The official pictures were taken. A reporter took a few shots. They weren't anything he could get into the paper. Tweed Jacket waved the doctor in. The ambulance arrived, and the two attendants stood their woven metal basket against the outside wall of the cabin and stood smoking, chatting, waiting for the doctor to finish his preliminary examination.

The doctor came out, spoke briefly to Tweed Jacket and drove away. The ambulance boys went in and wrapped Sam, after Tweed Jacket checked his pockets, put him in the basket, strapped him in and toted him out and drove away with him—no siren, no red lights. Tweed Jacket waved the lab crew into the cabin and I heard him tell them to check the car out too.

He came wandering over to me, the two reporters drifting along in his wake. He turned to them and said patiently, "Now I'll tell you if there's anything worth your knowing.

You just go set and be comfortable, if you can spare the time."

He put his hand out and said, "Mr. McGee, I'm Ken Branks. We appreciate it when people report an ugly thing like this rather than letting it set for somebody else to find, like when they come in the morning to tidy up. You come on over to the car where we can talk comfortable."

We got into the front seat of his car. He uncased a little tape recorder and hooked the mike onto the dash and plugged it into the cigarette lighter. "Hope you don't mind this. I've got a terrible memory."

"I don't mind."

"Now tell me your full name and address."

"Travis D. McGee, Slip F-18, Bahia Mar, aboard The Busted Flush."

"Own it or run it?"

"I own it."

"Now you tell me in your own words how you come to find this body."

"Sam Taggart used to live here. He went away three years ago. He got back today and called me up this afternoon, aboard the boat. I came right over and we talked for about an hour, about old friends and so on. I loaned him forty dollars. He said he was back to stay. I went on back to the boat. I spent the evening alone. I had my phone turned off. I went to bed and went to sleep. At quarter after twelve a woman came to the boat, a friend of mine. She used to know Sam. She said a mutual friend had phoned her and told her Sam was back in town. She thought I might know where he was. She thought it would be a good idea if we both paid him a visit. I got dressed and drove her over here. She left her car back at Bahia Mar. His car was here. I knocked and there wasn't any answer. I tried the door and it opened. I found the light switch. She came to the door and looked in at him too, and she went all to pieces. She used to be pretty fond of him. I took her back to her place, phoned in from there, and then came right back here. There's somebody to take care of her at her place. When I got back here, the two deputies were already here. So I waited around."

"Who is this woman?"

"She's a local businesswoman. It wouldn't help her any if it was in the newspapers that she was with me when I found the body."

"I can understand that, Mr. McGee. Who is she?"

"Nora Gardino. She has a shop at Citrus Gate Plaza."

"I know the place. Expensive. She knew this type fella?"

"I guess he didn't have much luck during the three years he was away."

"Where did he work and where did he live when he lived here?"

I remembered some of the places he had worked, and a couple of the addresses.

"Would the law around here have any kind of file on him?"

"It wouldn't be anything serious. Brawling, maybe."

"Who phoned Nora Gardino about seeing this man in town?"

"A girl called Beanie who works in the Mart, across from Pier 66. I don't know her last name."

"Do you know where she saw Taggart?"

"In that Howard Johnson's opposite the Causeway, about eight o'clock."

"Anybody with him?"

"I don't know."

"How long did you know Taggart before he moved away?"

"About two years."

"How did you meet him?"

"Through friends. A mutual interest in boats and the water and fishing."

"Where has he been living?"

"In California. And he spent some time in Mexico."

"And he came back broke?"

"He borrowed forty dollars from me."

"What do you do for a living?"

"I get into little ventures every now and then. Investments. Land deals. That kind of thing."

"It was sort of a gag, going to call on Taggart so late?"

"I guess you could call it that. She wanted to see him again, I guess."

"You didn't see anybody driving away from here or walking away from here when you drove up?"

"No."

"Was he the kind of fella goes into a bar and gets in trouble?"

"Sometimes."

"I'll have to check this out with Mrs. Gardino."

"Miss. She might be pretty dopey by now. Sleeping pills. It was a terrible shock for her to see anything like that."

"A knife is messy. There's no big rush about talking to her. How about Taggart's folks?"

"I wouldn't know. I think he has some cousins somewhere."

A man appeared at the window on Branks's side. Branks turned the tape machine off. "All clear, Ken. We got more prints than anybody needs, most of them smudged."

"How about that end cabin?"

"A farmer from South Carolina and a half wit kid. They didn't see anything or hear anything. No other cabins occupied."

"How about the owner?"

"He should be here any minute. He lives way the hell and gone out."

"Runs the gas station?"

"Yes."

"Check him on anybody coming to see Taggart. How about Taggart's gear?"

"I'd give you about twenty-eight cents for everything he owns, Ken."

"Have Sandy tag it and take it in and store it, and arrange to have that heap driven in to the pound."

The man went away. Ken Branks stretched and yawned. "He had a little over twenty left out of the forty, Mr. McGee. These things have a pattern. The way I see it, Taggart went out to do some cruising on your money. So he hit a few bars, and got somebody agitated, and that somebody followed him on back here and went in after him with a knife. In the dark, probably. Taggart did pretty good. The place is pretty well busted up. From the wounds, the guy was hacking at him, and got him a dozen times on the hands and face and arms before he finally got him one in the throat. So somebody left here banged up and spattered all to hell with blood. It won't be hard, I don't think. Leg work. Hitting all the likely saloons and finding where the trouble was, and who was in it. We'll pretty Taggart up for a picture we can use to show around here and there. Don't expect to see your name in the paper. Or Miss Gardino's. It won't get big coverage. The season is on, you know. Can't upset the sun-loving merrymakers." We got out of the car. He shook his head and said, "Some poor son of a bitch is out there tonight burying his clothes, throwing the knife off a bridge, trying to scrub the blood off his car seat, and it won't do him a damn bit of good. By God, nobody can get away with making a pass at *his* girl. She can drive up to Raiford once a month and pay him a nice visit. You can take off, Mr. McGee. If I remember something I should ask you, I'll be in touch."

As I drove away, my neck and shoulders felt stiff with tension. I was under no illusions about Mr. Branks. I remembered how he had maneuvered me into the light to give me a thorough inspection. And I had pretended not to see the flashlight beam as somebody had checked my car over while he was talking to me.

Branks would check me out with care and precision, and Nora too, and when his estimate of the situation did not pay off, he would go over us again.

A single lamp was lighted in Nora's living room. I saw Shaja, still in her blue robe, get up from the chair and come to unlock the door. I followed her into the living room. "How is she doing?"

"She fell to sleep, not so long ago." I noticed that she had brushed her hair, put on her makeup. "Such a wicked think," she said. "My hoosband, yes. One could expect, from a prison sickness. Some kind. Her Sam, no. Please to sit. You drink somesink, maybe?"

"If you've got a beer."

"Amstel? From Curacao?"

"Fine."

She went to the kitchen and brought back one for each of us, in very tall tapered glasses, on a small pewter tray.

"About him returning, she was so excite. So appy. It breaks my heart in two."

"Shaja? Is that the way you say it?"

"For friends, just Shaj. It comes from a girl in an old story in my land. For children. A princess turnink to ice slowly."

"Shaj, I had to tell the police she went there with me."

"Of course!"

"The way I told it, I made Sam a lot less important to her. I'll tell you exactly what I told them, and you remember it and tell her as soon as she wakes up. A man named Branks will come to see her. She should tell him exactly the same thing. It shouldn't be hard, because most of it is the truth."

She agreed. I repeated what I had said to Branks. She gave little nods of understanding.

When I had finished she frowned and said, "Excuse. But what is wrong to tellink this man she was in love with her Sam, all the three years he was gone? Is no crime."

"There is a reason for it. You see, there is something else too."

I saw a little flicker of comprehension in her eyes, product of a mind nicely geared to intrigue. "Somesink she does not know yet?"

"That's right."

"But you will tell her?"

"When she feels better."

She was thoughtful for long moments. She looked over at me. "You do not see her often, but you are a good friend, no?"

"I hope so."

"I am her friend too. She is good to me for a long time now. I can do all the work of the shop, completely. Those girls obey. What you will tell her, maybe it takes her mind from the work. But you should know, it will be no harm to anything."

"You're a nice person, Shaj."

She smiled, perhaps blushed slightly. "Thank you."

I leaned back into heavier shadow and sipped the beer. The light came down over her shoulder, backlighting the odd pale hair, shining on the curve of her broad cheek. This one had the same thing Nora had, such a total awareness of herself as a woman, such a directed pride in being a desirable woman, that every small fastidiousness was almost ritualistic, from stone clean scalp to glossy pedicure all so scented and cared for that, as is the case with the more celebrated beauties, the grooming itself forms a small barrier against boldness, against unwelcome intrusion.

Around us was the night silence ticking toward three in the morning. In a nearby bed slept the drugged woman, unaware for a little time of the depth of her wound. In that silence, which seemed more difficult to break with every passing moment, I felt the slow increments of awareness. That sort of awareness is an atavistic thing, a man-woman thing on a wordless level, and when it occurs in just that way, you know that she, in the cat-foot depths of the female heart, is just as aware of it as you are.

She lifted the glass to her lips, and I saw the silken strength of the pale throat work as she swallowed.

"What made the princess turn to ice?" My voice sounded too loud.

She stared across at me. At last she said, "Breakink a sacred vow."

"Was she forgiven?"

"Not at all. Her heart turns to ice. Her tears turns to ice. And where she is, on a high mountain, it then begins to snow, and forever, even in summertimes, the mountain there is white."

"It seems like a sad name to give a little girl."

"It is not my name."

"No?"

"My name is Janna."

"Where did you get Shaja then?"

"My hoosband call me that as a love name, because to him, in the beginning, I was of ice. But then not."

"Why do you call yourself that now?"

She came to her feet with a slow lithe grace. "Perhaps for rememberink at all times such a sacred vow. A vow to a man who throws at tanks little bottles of fire. Perhaps you should go and sleep a little, and come back here at almost nine when I must leave, because if she is not awaken then, she can sleep more and you can be here to tell her all those thinks, no?"

I agreed. No princess could have dismissed a peasant with a more gracious hauteur. She walked me to the door, turning on the hallway light.

"What was his work, Janna?"

"Please. You must not say that name for me. Not ever."

"What did he do for a living, Shaja?"

She shrugged. "A teacher of history. A man not quite as tall as me. A mild man, getting bald on his head in the middle. Just one year married. It was necessary, what he did. But then all of the world turned its back on our land. As you know. That is the shame of the world. Not his shame. Not mine. I came out because I was no use there. Not to help him there." She put her hand out. "Goodnight," she said. "Thank you."

It was the abrupt continental handshake, accompanied by a small bow, an immediate release of the clasp. As I walked to my car I looked back and saw her still standing there in the open door silhouetted against the hallway lights, hips canted in the way a model stands. We both knew of the hidden smoldering awareness. But there would be no breakink of vows, not with that one. It made her that much more valuable. Dobrak, the history teacher, bald on his head in the middle, mild slayer of tanks, had his hand on her loyal heart at all times. And she would wait out her years for him, unused and prideful.

As I drove back to Bahia Mar I wanted to hold fast to all the small speculations about her, the forlorn erotic fancies, because I knew that as she slipped out of my mind, Sam Taggart would take her place.

And he did, before I was home. I found a slot and then I shoved my hands into my pockets and walked across to the public beach. I walked slowly where the outgoing tide had left the sand damp and hard. The sea and the night sky can make death a small thing. Waves can wash away the most stubborn stains, and the stars do not care one way or the other.

It was a cheap and dirty little death, a dingy way to die. When dawn came, there would be a hundred thousand more souls alive in the world than on the previous day, three quarters of a million more every week. This is the virus theory of mankind. The pretentious virus, never knowing that it is a disease. Imagine the great ship from a far galaxy which inspects a thousand green planets and then comes to ours and, from on high, looks down at all the scabs, the buzzings, the electronic jabberings, the poisoned air and water, the fetid night glow. A little cave-dwelling virus mutated, slew the things which balanced the ecology, and turned the fair planet sick. An overnight disease, racing and explosive compared with geological time. I think they would be concerned. They would be glad to have caught it in time. By the time of their next inspection, a hundred thousand years hence, this scabrous growth might have infected this whole region of an unimportant galaxy. They would push the button. Too bad. This happens every once in a while. Make a note to re-seed it the next time around, after it has cooled down.

Lofty McGee, shoulders hunched against the cold of the small hours, trying to diminish the impact of the death of a friend.

But Sam was still there, in a ghastly dying sprawl on the floor of my mind. He wasn't going to make the PTA. They had closed his account. I squatted on my heels and picked up a handful of the damp sand and clenched it until my shoulder muscles creaked and my wrist ached like an infected tooth.

This time they had taken one of mine. One of the displaced ones. A fellow refugee from a plastic structured culture, uninsured, unadjusted, unconvinced.

So I had to have a little word or two with the account closers.

That was what I had been trying not to admit to myself.

It wasn't dramatics. It wasn't a juvenile taste for vengeance. It was just a cold, searching, speculative curiosity.

What makes you people think it's that easy?

That was the question I wanted to ask them. I would ask the question even though I already had the answer.

It isn't.

five

AT FIFTEEN-MINUTE intervals I went into the bedroom to look at Nora Gardino. In the darkened room, she was a curled girl-shape under a fuzzy green blanket, a black tousle of hair, a single closed eye, a very deep slow soft sound of breathing.

At ten thirty I heard a sound in there. I went in. She stood by the dressing table, belting a navy blue robe. I startled her. She stared at me, shaped my name with silent lips, then came on the run for holding and hugging, shuddering and snorting against me, her breath sour.

"It was a dirty dream," she whispered, and made a gagging sound. "Just a dirty wretched dream."

I stroked her back and said, "He never came back. That's all."

She pushed herself away. "You think you can make it that easy?"

"Not really."

"Don't try then," she said, and ran into the bathroom and slammed the door. I went back to the kitchen and poured myself some more coffee. I went back to the magazine article I was reading. A southern pusgut who fancied himself a liberal was patting the coons on their burry heads by asking them to live up to the responsibilities of conditional equality, the implication being that his white brethren were so doing. I would have liked to have sent that jolly racist crawling across bad terrain with a couple of skilled Negro infantrymen giving him covering fire. I decided that I wouldn't want to marry his daughter, and threw the magazine aside just as Nora came into the kitchen, taking small steps. I got the orange juice from the refrigerator and handed it to her.

She sat at the table and took several small sips and said, "I'm pretty flippy today, Trav. Don't listen too hard to anything I say."

"Shaj took off at quarter to nine. She said the shop is under control."

"Bless her. And you too, my friend."

She had not put on makeup. Her face had a new dry papery texture, as though it would crackle to the touch.

I told her about Branks. I gave her the same detailed report I'd given Shaj.

"Can you handle it?" I asked.

"I guess so. You mean, on the level that he was nothing more than a friend who'd been away. Yes. I can manage. But why?"

"Maybe I don't want him to know that we have a very intense personal interest in finding out who. . . ."

"Who killed him. Don't hunt for easier words. Use the brutal ones. Let them sting. Why shouldn't he know we have that personal interest, Trav?"

"Because we don't want him interfering with any looking we may want to do. If it is personal. If it is intense, we want a part of it, don't we?"

She put the empty juice glass down. "Do you know something about it?"

"I think so."

"Did you tell that man?"

"No."

I cannot describe the look on her face then, a hunting look, a merciless look, a look of dreadful anticipation. It reminded me that the worst thing the Indians could do to their enemy prisoners was turn them over to the women. "I want to keep it very very personal," she whispered.

"Then don't give Branks the slightest clue. He's a sharp man."

"If I thought there was no point to it, if it was just some murderous animal trying to rob cabins. . . ."

"More than that."

She locked icy fingers on my wrist. "Then what? The thing he had to take care of. What?"

"Later, Nora. It will keep."

I saw her accept that promise. I had polarized her, with one of the most ancient and ugly emotions. It was irresponsible of me, perhaps. I plead a shining motive. Without direction she had nothing but pain, loss, grief. I gave her a bullet to bite on while they amputated her heart. It is a temporizing world, fading into uncertain shades of grey, so full of complexities all worth and value are questioned, hag-ridden by the apologistics of Freud, festering with so many billions of us that every dab of excellence has to be spread so thin it becomes a faint coat of grease, indistinguishable from the Eva-Last plastics. In this toboggan ride into total, perfectly adjusted mediocrity, the great conundrum is what is worth living for and what is worth dying for. I choose not to live for the insurance program, for creative selling, for suburban adjustments, for the little warm cage of kiddy-kisses, serial television, silky wife-nights, zoning squabbles.

But what is the alternative? I know just enough about myself to know I cannot settle for one of those simplifications which indignant people seize upon to make understandable a world too complex for their comprehension. Astrology, health food, flag waving, bible thumping, Zen, nudism, nihilism—all of these are grotesque simplifications which small dreary people adopt in the hope of thereby finding The Answer, because the very concept that maybe there is no answer, never has been, never will be, terrifies them.

All that remains for the McGee is an ironic Knighthood, a spavined steed, second class armor, a dubious lance, a bent broadsword, and the chance, now and again, to lift into a galumphing charge against capital E Evil, his brave battle oaths marred by an occasional hysterical giggle. He has to carry a very long banner because on it has been embroidered, by maidens galore, The Only Thing in the World Worth a Damn is the Strange, Touching, Pathetic, Awesome Nobility of the Individual Human Spirit. The end of the banner trails on the ground way the hell behind his horse, and people keep stepping on it.

So, in polarizing the lady, I had at least given her a simplification she could live with and, if the need should arise, die for. But when I looked into the depths of her dark eyes, there was something there which made me wish I hadn't pushed that particular button. I had created something which perhaps I could not control.

Branks phoned at eleven-fifteen and came by at quarter to twelve.

She had dressed by then. Her heart said black, but she dressed in pink, a pleated skirt, an angora sweater, a mouth red for polite smiling.

Just a friend, she said. And it seemed like a kick to go visit him at such a crazy hour. But it was the sort of thing he would do. And Beanie had phoned her because she knew Nora used to run around with the guy sometimes. And McGee was an old friend too. It was just for kicks. Welcome home. You know. But, God, who ever thought we'd walk in on anything like that! Oh, yes, I went all to pieces completely. I never saw anything so horrible in my whole life, never. Maybe I should have stayed there, but I couldn't, really.

Branks thanked her and thanked me again. He said that Beanie had said Taggart was alone when she had seen him, eating at the counter. The owner of the cabins, who ran the gas station also, had seen Taggart drive out about seven and when he had closed at nine, Taggart had not returned.

"We'll find him," Branks said with absolute confidence. "You'll see it in the paper one of these days."

As he drove out, Nora's casual smile crumpled. She clung to me, asking if she had done all right. She got a case of hiccups. I patted her and said she had done fine. Just fine, honey. Slowly, with a labored effort, she pulled herself together, a nerve at a time. It was a valiant thing to watch.

"F-Find out about services for him, Trav. All that."

"Courtesy of the county."

"No!"

"Honey, just what difference does it make to Sam now?"

She lit a cigarette, her hand shaking. "I've been tucking money away, for the time when he'd come back. He came back. What do I do with the money? It doesn't mean anything."

"What do you want to do? Buy a plot? And bronze handles. Hire a hall? For two mourners?"

"I just . . . want it to be nice."

"All right. We'll do what we can, in a quiet way, like a hundred dollar way. On top of the county procedure, so that if Branks should ever wonder or ask, we took up a collection. Flowers, and a lengthier reading at the graveside, and a small marker."

I stalled her on the other until after the small ceremony. Six of us there, under the beards of Spanish moss blowing wildly in a crisp wind on a day of cloudless blue. Shaja, Nora and me, a pastor and two shovelers. The wind tore the old words out of his mouth and flung them away, inaudible. The single floral offering bothered me, a huge spray of white roses, virginal, as a huge bride might carry. Death is the huge bride, and the night of honeymoon is eternity. The stone would be placed later, one just big enough for his name, date of birth, date of death. We took her home, bleached with grief, moving like an arthritic. She was pounds lighter than on the night we had gone to see him.

Shaj hastened back to the shop. I set out a gigantic slug of brandy for Nora Gardino. Then I told her everything I knew.

Her numbness turned slowly to anger. "That is all you know? What does that mean? What can we do about that, for God's sake?"

"He wanted me to help him, and then because of you he changed his mind and decided to make a deal with them."

"But you've let me think it was ... somebody we could find right here, right now!"

"There's something to go on."

"But how far?"

"I don't know how far. I don't know until I try. If you don't like it, give up right now, Nora. I've gotten into things with less leverage than I have on this one."

"I'll never give up!"

"Do you want it all handed to you, wrapped and tied and labeled?"

"I didn't say that. You made me believe. . . ."

"That it would be easy? That doesn't sound like you."

"But. . . ."

"Nora, do you want to play or don't you? It can be long and expensive, and it can all come to nothing, or it could get somebody killed. I have a hunch two will work out better than one on this thing, less conspicuous. I'll pick up my end of the tab. But one thing clear, right now. You take orders. And if we make a recovery, of what Sam said was his, if we are convinced by then that it was his then we split it down the middle."

"That's what you're in this for?"

"Certainly. That's why I said no thanks, when Sam invited me in."

"I'm sorry, Trav."

"I can tell you one thing. From what we know right now, if we handle ourselves well, if you follow orders, we can get close."

Her right hand turned into a claw. "I would like that."

"Close is all I can promise. Remember this, Nora. Sam

was tough and quick and smart. You saw what he got out of it."

"Don't. But ... where is the starting point?"

"Finding out just what it was that he thought was his. That's my job. While I'm doing that, you get Shaj set up so she can run the store on her own."

Professor Warner B. Gifford was a fat, sloppy, untidy young man. He was not the tenant the architects had in mind when they had designed that particular building for Florida Southwestern. The building, I guess, was for dynamic scholastic living, for Communications courses, whatever they are, for machines to grade multiple choice questions, for that curious union of Madison Avenue, the N.A.M., foundation monies and the education of the pre-adjusted young which successfully emasculates all the factors thereof. It was a building to house the men who could turn out fabulous technicians with that contempt for every other field of human knowledge which only the truly ignorant can achieve. It was a place to train ants to invent insecticides.

But Warner B. Gifford was unaware of that. They had given him a weatherproof cube to work in, and he had managed to make it look and smell like the back room of a London hock shop. He goggled vacantly through thick lenses in frames mended with Band Aids. He committed all the small offenses he had no best friends to tell him about. He worked at a rickety little table amid piles of paper and unidentifiable junk, rank, scurfy, soiled and absolutely unconcerned with everything in the world except the expertise of taking one tiny fragment of the remote past and fitting it into another little fragment, and thereby filling that tiny gap in the continuity of the history of the human animal. If, in his total career, he could infect two or three other individuals with that same compulsion, I had the feeling he would be worth a round dozen of the tailored golfers who gave brilliant lectures which could have been printed intact in the *Reader's Digest*, and probably were.

It had taken two hours to thread my way through the labyrinth of exotic specialties and find my way to him.

"A what?" he said. "A what?"

I found myself raising my voice, enunciating clearly, as though he were deaf. I described the little golden figurine with greatest care, and he looked pained at my layman's language. He grunted up off his straight chair and went over to a corner full of books and got down on all fours, giving the impression of a large sad dog digging a hole. He brought a big book back, sat down, riffled the pages, turned it to face me and laid a dirty finger against a photographic plate. "Like this, possibly?"

"Very much like that, Professor."

He went into a discourse, pitched in a penetrating monotone, and it took me a long awed time to realize that he was still speaking English.

I stopped him and said, "I don't understand any of that."

He looked pained and decided he had to speak to me in Pidgin English. We both needed a course in Communications. With each other.

"Eight hundred years old. Um? Fired clay. National Museum in Mexico City. Gold is rare. Um? Spaniards cleaned it out, melted it into ingots, shipped it to Spain. Indian cultures moving, changing. Some used gold. Ceremonial. Open veins in mountains. Um? Low melting point. Easily worked. No damn good for tools. Pretty color. Masks, et cetera. Then conflict of cultures. Changed the meaning of gold. Cleaned them out, hunted it down. Torture, et cetera. Gold and silver. Um?"

"Then there isn't much left?"

"Museums. Late finds. Overlooked. Uh . . . less archeological significance than one would think. Have the forms in clay, carvings, bone, et cetera. Duplication. Um?"

"But a museum would be interested in the thing I described?"

"Of course. Highly. Not scholarship. Museum traffic. Publicity."

"What about a collection of twenty-eight little statuettes like that, some bigger and some smaller, all gold, and from different places? Aztec, Inca, some East Indian."

He shrugged. "Ancient man made little ceremonial figures. Handy materials. Ivory, bone, wood, stone, clay, gold, silver, iron, lead. Gods, spirits, demons, fetishes, from very crude to very elegant. Merely being of gold, it would not be a museum collection. A museum could assemble perhaps such a showing from other specific collections. Egypt. China. Not very professional."

"Then such a collection would be a private collection?"

"Possibly. Pack rats. Something shiny. No scholarship. Um? Acquisition. Most unprofessional. Hampers the work of professionals. Probably very valuable items all over the world, locked away. Valuable keys. Connectives. Take Egypt. Thieves looted tombs, sold to tourists. Same in Mexico. All changed now. But damage done. They should will collections to museums. Let the professionals sort them out."

"But such a collection would be valuable?"

"In money? Um? Oh yes."

"Who would know if such a collection exists, Professor?"

Again he went searching among the chaotic debris. He dug into a low cupboard. He took out correspondence files, put them back. Finally he extracted a letter from a folder, tore the letterhead from it and put it back. He brought me the letterhead. Borlika Galleries, 511 Madison Avenue, New York.

"They might know," he said. "Supply collectors. Hunt for things on assignment. Special items. Jades, African sculpture, ancient weapons, bronze artifacts, all periods, all cultures. Purveyors to pack rats. Sometimes they deal with museums, but not when they can get more elsewhere. Buy collections, break them up, sell items to the rich. Hunt all over the world. They might know. Business on an international scale."

He was bent to his lonely work again before I had reached the door of his office. My car was a quarter mile away, parked at the Administration Building. It was dusk on the big busy sprawl of campus. By now all the young heroes would be showering, savagely hungry, after all the intricate business of learning how best to drop an inflated ball through a hoop and net. The class day was over, and all the jolly business of the evening charged the air with expectancy. Gaggles of soft young girls hurried by, making little cawing sounds at each other. I marveled at the strange and tenuous link between them and Professor Warner B. Gifford. We are doing something wrong. We haven't found out what it is yet. But somehow we have turned all these big glossy universities into places which the thinking young ones, the mavericks, the ones we need the most, cannot endure. So all the campuses are in the hands of the unaware, the incurably, unconsciously second class kids with second class minds and that ineffably second class goal of reasonable competence, reasonable security, reasonable happiness. Perhaps this is the proper end product to people a second class world. All mavericks ever do, anyway, is make the sane, normal, industrious people feel uncomfortable. They ask the wrong questions. Such as— What is the meaning of all this. So weed them out. They are cultural mistakes. Leave the world to the heroes and the semi-heroes, and their rumpy little soft-eyed girls, racing like lemmings toward the warm sea of the Totally Adjusted Community.

Miss Agnes seemed glad to take me away from there. We made our stately way through snitty little clots of sports cars and Detroit imitations thereof, and were soon whispering toward home, through a hundred miles of cold February night.

SIX

GRIEF IS a strange tempest. Nora Gardino, her strong and handsome face becoming mask-like, bobbed about in her own storm tides, supporting herself with whatever came to hand. But she found that her sense of purpose provided the most useful buoyancy. And as I was the instrument through which she expected to achieve a bloody vengeance, she came running to me whenever she felt as if she were drowning. She thought my methods far too indirect. She wanted immediate confrontations. She had no patience with research. She wanted us to go at once to Puerto Altamura and start slamming around. She threatened to go by herself. I explained to her that it worked on television dramas and in muscular movies, but in the far drearier vistas of life itself, a man could pry nothing open unless he had a pry bar. And knowledge is that pry bar. Strangers do not suddenly open up because you confuse them. Confusion leads to a cautious silence. Strangers talk when they know that you have facts. They talk when it is in their interest to try to convince you your facts are wrong.

Shaja and I were partners in the cooperative venture of keeping her calm. She seemed like a pleasant child subject to temper tantrums, a child who might, unguarded, break every dish in the cupboard. There was a self-destructive aspect to Nora's urgencies. Soothed, she would pull herself together and give a plausible imitation of the way she had been before Sam had returned.

On the morning I was to fly up to New York, she drove me down to Miami International in her little black Sunbeam. We had time to spare, so we went to the restaurant atop the Airport Hotel and had coffee at a window table amid all those shades of blue, overlooked paved areas where the little yellow service vehicles sped back and forth in their ant-hill routines.

"I shouldn't be so impatient," she said. "But it just . . ."

48

"Look at it this way. You go charging at something, and nothing happens. Then you have to back off and try the vague chances, the off-beat things. By charging you may mess something up, and spoil all your chances. So armor yourself first. Later you may find out that the preparation wasn't necessary. But there's no harm done. This will keep, Nora. It's a case of whether you want an emotional release, or whether you really want to accomplish something."

"I want to. . . ."

"Okay. We do this my way. I had to learn the hard way. I had to learn patience and care."

They announced my flight. She went down with me. At the gate she gave me a sister's kiss, her dark eyes huge in her narrow face, eroded by loss. "As long as you're not just kidding me along, as long as we really will do something, okay then, Trav. We'll do it your way."

New York, on the first day of March, was afflicted by a condition a girl I once knew called Smodge. This is a combination of rain, snow, soot, dirt, and wind. The black sky squatted low over afternoon Manhattan, and all the store lights were on, traffic braying, the sidewalk folk leaning sullenly into the weight of wind. There is a tax loophole in recent years which makes it possible for men to acquire tax-free fortunes by putting up the cheapest possible office buildings. Like some hovering undisciplined anus, this loophole has excreted its garish cubes all over the Upper East Side. These are the buildings where they purposely build a roar into the heating and air conditioning systems to compensate for the tissue thickness of the walls. There, in a sterile and incomparable fluorescent squalor, in stale air, under low ceilings, are devised the creative ideas to amuse, instruct, guide, and convince an entire nation. This time I was in no mood for the newer, or pseudo-Miami hotel architecture, and took a single at an eerie little ugly old hotel I had stayed at long ago, the Wharton, on West 49th, in the first block off Fifth. Red stone, oak lobby, high ceilings and Victorian plumbing.

At two forty-five I ducked out of the sleety wind into the narrow entrance to the Borlika Galleries. The display window was a tasteful arrangement of small items of carved bone and ivory, some of it touchingly quaint. I hunted in my dust-bin mind for that word for that sort of work, and found it. Scrimshaw. Hobby of sailors on the old sailing ships.

I pushed the door open and went in, wondering if I was dressed for the impression I wanted to make. My suit and raincoat were too lightweight for New York in March. No hat. Seagoing tan. Shirt collar slightly frayed. Scuffed shoes, now slightly sodden.

A cluster of bells jangled as I pushed the door open. It was a long narrow place, meagerly lighted. It had the collection smell, leather and dust, sandalwood and age. In a long lighted display case was an ornate collection of cased duelling pistols. On a long table to my right was a collection of primitive wood carvings.

A young man came toward me up the aisle from the back, with bone-pale face and funereal suit. It was a hushed place and he spoke in a hushed voice.

"May I help you?" He had taken me in at a glance, and he spoke with precisely the intonation which fitted my appearance, a slight overtone of patronizing impatience.

"I don't know. I guess you sell all kinds of old stuff."

"We have many types of items, sir." He said the sir as though it hurt his dear little mouth. "We specialize in items of anthropological and archeological significance."

"How about old gold?"

He frowned. He was pained. "Do you refer to old coins, sir?"

"No. What I'm interested in is old statues made of gold. Real old. Like so high. You know. Old gods and devils and stuff like that."

It stopped him for a long moment. Finally he gave a little shrug. It was a long slow afternoon. "This way, please."

He had me wait at a display counter in the rear while he went back into the private rooms behind the store. It took him five minutes. I guessed he had to open a safe or have someone open it. He turned on a pair of bright little lamps, spread a piece of blue velvet, tenderly unwrapped an object and placed it on the blue velvet. It was a golden toad, a nasty looking thing the size of my fist. It had ruby eyes, a rhino horn on its head, and a body worked of overlapping scales like a fish.

"This is the only object we have on hand at the moment, sir. It is completely documented and authenticated. Javanese Empire, close to two thousand years old."

It had a look of ancient, sardonic evil. Man dies and gold endures, and the reptiles will inherit the earth.

"What do you get for a thing like this?"

He put it back in its wrappings and as he began to fold the cloth around it, he said, "Nine thousand dollars, sir."

"Did you hear me say I didn't want it, Charlie?"

He gave me a baleful glance, a murmured apology, and uncovered it again.

"Lovely craftsmanship," he said. "Perfectly lovely."

"How did you people get it?"

"I couldn't really say, sir. We get things from a wide variety of sources. The eyes are rubies. Badly cut and quite flawed, of course."

"What would you people pay for a frog like this?"

"That wouldn't bear any relationship to its value, sir."

"Well, put it this way, Charlie. Supposed I walked in off the street with this frog. Would I be one of those sources you said you use?"

It put the right little flicker of interest and reappraisal in his indoor eyes. "I don't quite understand, sir."

"Try it this way, then. It's gold. Right? Suppose somebody didn't want to get involved in a lot of crap, Charlie. Like bills of sale and so on. If he wants to make a cash deal, the easiest thing is to melt old frog down."

"Heavens!" he said, registering shock.

"But maybe that way he cheats himself a little."

"A great deal! This is an historical object, sir. An art object!"

"But if the guy doesn't want any fuss, Charlie?"

His eyes shifted uneasily. "I suppose that if . . . this is just hypothetical, you understand . . . if someone wished to quietly dispose of something on a cash basis . . . and it wasn't a well-known piece . . . from a museum collection, for example, something might be worked out. But I . . . ."

"But you just work here, Charlie. Right?"

He touched the toad. "Do you care to purchase this?"

"Not today."

"Would you wait here, please?"

He wrapped it up and took it away. I had a five minute wait. I wondered what they did for customers. A little old man came shuffling out. He had white hair, a nicotined mustache, a tough little face. I don't think he weighed a

hundred pounds. In a deep bass voice he said his name was
Borlika.

He peered up at me, his head tilted to the side, and said,
"We are not receivers of stolen goods, mister."

"Unless you're damn well sure they'll never be traced, old
man."

"Get out!" he bellowed, pointing toward the front door.
We both knew it was an act.

I put my hand on my heart. "Old man, I'm an art lover.
It'll hurt me here to melt all the beautiful old crap down."

He motioned me closer, leaned on the counter and said,
"All?"

"Twenty-eight pieces, old man."

He leaned on the counter with both arms and kept his eyes
closed for so long I began to wonder if he'd fallen asleep. At
last he looked at me and blinked as the gold toad would blink
if it could and said, "My granddaughter is in Philadelphia
today, doing an appraisal. In this area, you will talk to her.
Can she see the pieces?"

"That can be arranged later. After we talk."

"Can you describe one piece to me?"

I gave him a crude but accurate description of the sensual
little man. His eyes glittered like the toad's.

"Where can she find you this evening, mister?"

"I can phone her and arrange that."

"You are a very careful man."

"When I have something worth being careful about, old
man."

He wrote the phone number on a scrap of paper, told me
her name was Mrs. Anton Borlika, and told me to phone
after eight o'clock. When I got back to the hotel I checked
the book. The listing was under her name, an address on East
68th which would place it close to Third Avenue. With time
to kill, I got a cab and kept it while I made a tour of
inspection of the neighborhood. It was a poodle-walking area.
At about five o'clock I found a suitable place about two
blocks from her apartment. It was called Marino's Charade.
There was an alcove off the bar-lounge with a booth at the
end, perfectly styled for maximum privacy. The night shift
was on, and the boss waiter was happy to gobble up my ten
dollar bill and promise that he would keep it empty from
eight o'clock on.

Her voice on the phone, flat as only Boston can make it, had not prepared me for the woman. She was in her late twenties, black Irish, with blue eyes and milky skin, slightly overweight, dressed in a conservative suit, a big grey corduroy rain cape, droplets of the night moisture caught in her blue-black hair. As she walked along the alcove toward the booth I stood up and said, "Mrs. Borlika?"

"That's right," she said, slipping the cape off. I hung it up. "You made yourself easy to find, Mister . . . ."

"Taggart. Sam Taggart." I watched for reaction and saw none.

She smiled and smoothed her suit skirt with the backs of her hands and slid into the booth. "Betty Borlika," she said. "Have you eaten? I had a nasty sandwich on the train."

"Drink first?"

"Of course." The waiter appeared, took our drink order and hastened away.

"How were things in Philadelphia?"

She made a face. "I had three days of it. Thank God somebody else was doing the paintings. There must have been five hundred of them. Fifty years of miscellaneous collecting. Barrels, actual barrels of ikons. Temple bells. Chinese ivory. You have no idea."

"You know what all that stuff is worth?"

"Enough to give it an appraisal the tax people accept. I wouldn't say I missed it by far."

With all her friendly casualness, I knew I was getting a thorough inspection. I returned the favor. No rings on the ring finger. Plump hands. Nails bitten down. Plump little double chin. Small mouth, slightly petulant.

"You buy any of the stuff?"

"There are three lots we'll bid on, when it goes to auction. You see, Sam, a man with no taste and a lot of money and a lot of time will acquire good things when he deals with good dealers." It came out "acquah" and "dealahs." "I have a pretty good range," she said. "I have a museum school degree and seven years of practical experience." She sipped her drink, looking at me over the rim of the glass.

"Your husband do the same kind of work?"

"He used to. Before he died."

"Recently?"

"Three years ago. His father and his uncle are active in

the business. And his grandfather, of course. His father and his uncle are abroad at this time."

"Or I'd be talking to them?"

"Probably."

"I like it this way better."

"You won't get a better deal from me than you would from them."

"If we deal."

"Is there any question of that, Sam?"

"There's a lot of questions, Betty. Right now there's two real good gold markets. Argentina and India. And safer for me that way."

"Safer than what?"

"Than making any kind of deal with something... not melted down."

She scowled. "God, don't even *say* that."

"This stuff isn't hot in the ordinary sense. But, there could be some questions. Not from the law. Do you understand?"

"Possibly."

"Another drink?"

"Please."

When the waiter was gone, she said, "Please believe me when I say we are used to negotiating on a very confidential basis. Sometimes, when it's necessary, we can invent a more plausible basis of acquisition than... the way something came into our hands." She smiled broadly, and it was a wicked and intimate smile. "After all, I'm not going to make you tell me where you got them, Sam."

"Don't expect to buy them cheap, Betty."

"I would expect to pay a bonus over the actual gold value, of course. But you must consider this, too. We're one of the few houses in a position to take the whole thing off your hands. It simplifies things for you."

"The whole thing?"

"The... group of art objects. Did you say twenty-eight?"

"I said twenty-eight. Twenty-eight times the price of that frog would be...."

"Absurd."

"Not when you sell them."

"Only when you sell them to us, Sam."

In spite of all the feminine flavor, this was a very shrewd cool broad.

"If I sell them to you."

She laughed. "If we want to buy what you have, dear. After all, we can't buy things unless we have some reasonable chance of selling them, can we?"

"These things look all right to me."

"And you are an expert, of course." She opened her big purse and took out a thick brown envelope. She held it in her lap where I could not see it. She frowned down as she sorted and adjusted whatever she took out of the envelope.

Finally she smiled across at me. "Now we will play a little game, Sam. We take a photograph for a record of everything of significant value which goes through our hands. These photographs are from our files. There are fifty-one of them. So that we will know what we are talking about, I want you to go through these and select any that are among the twenty-eight you have."

"I haven't looked at them too close, Betty."

She handed the thick stack across to me. "Just do your best." They were five by seven photographs in black and white and double weight paper, with a semi-gloss finish, splendidly sharp and clear, perfectly lighted. In each picture there was a ruler included to show scale, and, on the other side of the figurine, a little card which gave a complex series of code or stock or value numbers, or some combination thereof. I made my face absolutely blank, knowing she was watching me, and went through them one at a time. I felt trapped. I needed some kind of opening. Somewhere in the middle I came across the same little man I had seen, squatting on his crude lumpy haunches, staring out of the blank eye holes. I did not hesitate at him. I began to pay less attention to the figures, and more to the little cards. I noticed then that, written in ink, on most of them, were tiny initials in the bottom right hand corner of the little code card. I leafed back to my little man and saw that the initials in the corner were CMC. I started through the stack again, looking for the same initials, and saw that they appeared on five of the photographs. The figurines were strange—some beautiful, some twisted and evil, some crude and innocent, some earthily, shockingly explicit.

I looked at her and said, "I just don't know. I just can't be sure."

"Try. Please."

I went through the stack and began putting some of them

on the table top, face down. You have to gamble. I put nine photographs face down. I laid the stack aside. I looked at the nine again, sighed and returned one of them to the stack.

I handed her the eight of them and said, "I'm pretty sure of some of these. And not so sure of others."

I tried to read her face as she looked at them. The small mouth was curved in a small secretive smile. She had to show off. She handed me back three photographs. "These are the ones you're not so sure of, Sam?"

I registered astonishment. "Yes! How could you know that?"

"Never mind," she said, and slid all the photographs back into the envelope and returned it to her purse. "One more drink and let's order, shall we?"

"Good idea."

"Mr. Taggart, your credentials are in order. But I didn't know he would have so many."

"Who would have so many?"

"Oh, *come* now!" she said. "Couldn't we stop playing games now? He bought from us. Of course, he would have other sources, in the position he was in."

"Put it this way, Betty. There was another party in the middle."

"You aren't acting as his agent, are you?"

"Why do you ask a thing like that?"

"I don't think you are completely the rude type you pretend to be, Sam. I can understand how, in the present circumstances, he might want to sell out through a clever agent. If you could prove you're his agent, we might see our way to being a little more liberal. After all, he was a good customer, long ago."

"If I knew his name, I'd try to convince you I was working for him."

"Politics creates a lot of confusion, doesn't it?"

"I don't even know what you mean by that."

"Then you are quite an innocent in this whole thing, and I shan't try to confuse you, Sam. Let me just say that I am personally convinced that the twenty-eight items are legitimate, and we would like to purchase them."

"For how much?"

"One hundred thousand dollars, Sam."

"So I melt them, Betty. Maybe I can get that for the gold

alone. Maybe more. I'm talking about a hundred and forty pounds of gold."

"A lot of trouble, isn't it, finding a safe place to melt them down, then smuggling the gold out, finding a buyer, trying to get your money without getting hit on the head?"

"I've had little problems like that before."

"This would be cash, Sam. In small bills, if you'd like. No records of the transaction. We'll cover it on our books with a fake transaction with a foreign dealer. It would just be a case of meeting on neutral ground to trade money for the Mente ... the collection, with a chance for both parties to examine what they are getting."

"What did you start to say?"

"Nothing of importance. You're very quick, aren't you?"

"Money quickens me, Betty."

"I too have a certain fondness for it. That's why I don't part with it readily."

"You won't have to part with a single dime of that hundred thousand."

"What would I have to part with?"

"Let's say twice that."

"Oh, my God! You *are* dreaming."

"So are you, lady."

"I'll tell you what. If the other pieces are as good as the five we know, I will go up to one twenty-five, absolute tops."

"The other pieces are better, and one seventy-five is absolute bottom. Take it or leave it."

We ordered. We haggled all the way through the late dinner. She was good at the game. Over plain coffee for me, coffee and a gooey dessert for Betty Borlika, we worked our way down to a five thousand dollar difference, and then split that down the middle, for an agreed price of a hundred and thirty-seven thousand, five hundred dollars. We shook hands.

"Even if you were his agent, I couldn't give you a penny more."

"You'll get a quarter of a million when you sell them."

"We might. Over a period of years. There isn't an active market in this sort of thing, Sam. You saw the jeweled toad. We've had that for over four months. We have considerable overhead you know. Rent, salaries, money tied up in inventory."

"You'll have me crying any moment."

"Don't cry. You drove a very good bargain. How would you like the money?"

"Used money. Fifties and smaller."

"It will take several days to accumulate it, Sam."

"I haven't exactly got the little golden people stashed in a coin locker."

"Of course not. From my estimate of you, they are probably in a very safe place. How long will it take you to bring them here?"

"You just get the cash and hang onto it and I'll phone you when I get back to town. How will we make the transfer?"

"Do you trust me, Sam?" I could not get used to being called that. I kept seeing those pink teeth.

I returned her smile. "I don't trust anybody. It's sort of a religion."

"We're members of the same sect, dear. And that gives us a problem, doesn't it? Any suggestions?"

"A very public place. How about a bank? Borrow a private room. They have them. Then nobody can get rough or tricky."

"You are a very clever man, Mr. Taggart. Now we can forget it all until I hear from you again. And could you order us a brandy? The deal is made. From now on it's social."

"Social," I agreed. Her eyes were softer, and her smile a little wider.

"You are a very competent ruffian, Sam. You give me problems. Did you know that?"

For the first time I could see that the drinks were working on her. "Not intentionally."

She frowned judiciously. "You know, I deal all the time with shifty shifty people. How many ways can a person be shifty? Not so many ways, Sam. It's like dancing. Ballroom dancing. It takes a few bars of music to get in step, and then you can follow every lead. But I stumble a little with you. You have contradictions, Sam. You look a little bit rough and sort of mild and sleepy and, excuse me, not too terribly sharp. I think I have you cased and then something else shows, and you go out of focus. Something quick and bitter and secretly laughing. Then I feel trivial and transparent. But I'm not!" She glowered at me. "Damn it, I'm not!"

"I know you're not, Betty."

I had seen the same thing happen with businessmen. The deal in process would sustain them, keep them alert and organized and watchful, and when it was settled, they would turn into softer more vulnerable mechanisms. The Betty Borlika of appraisals and bids, of dickering and expertise, had faded away. This was the woman of the bitten nails and the small petulant mouth, and blue Irish eyes slightly mazed, the young Irish widow, with a hidden uncertainty about the value of her goals and her attainments, driving loneliness underground with the pressures of her work.

I paid the check and helped her into her cape. The place was nearly empty. On the way out we stopped at the bar, at her suggestion, for another brandy.

"I came down here and got a small job," she said. "Betty O'Donnell, curator of practically nothing. Scut work at the Museum of Contemporary Crafts. I lived in the Village and dressed the part. Hairy stockings and ballet slippers. And I answered the Borlika ad. I worked there almost a year and then married Tony." She turned and stared up at me. "You see, my best professional asset is a hell of a fantastic memory, Sam. I can read an illustrated catalogue of a sale, and if five years later I come across something that appeared in that catalogue, I can recognize it, identify it, classify it, and remember what it brought at auction." She shook her head as though puzzled. "And I don't even have to work."

"What do you mean?"

"Maybe you read about it. It was such a weird accident it was in papers all over the country. High up on one of those crappy buildings they were building, a slab of some kind of imitation stone gunk came out of a sling and fell and hit a cornice and ricocheted across Park Avenue and smashed Tony dead. It was a nice day. He'd decided to walk. A lot of money came out of that, Sam. An awful lot. But I should work at what I'm good at, shouldn't I?"

"Of course."

She put her empty glass down. "It's such a family thing, you know. I'm a Borlika. I'm caught in it. Probably forever. At least it isn't, for God's sake, a chain of laundries. Beautiful things, Sam. Beautiful lovely things to buy and sell."

We went out. It was well below freezing, and the sky had cleared, the high stars weak against the city glow. The sidewalks were dry. We walked to her place, her tall heels tocking, her arm hooked firmly around mine.

"You don't say anything about yourself, Sam."

"Nothing much to say. I keep moving. I hustle a little of this and a little of that. I avoid agitation."

"When this is over, what will you do?"

"Bahamas, maybe. Lease a little ketch, ram around, fish, play with the play people. Drink black Haitian rum. Snorkel around the coral heads and watch the pretty fish."

"God! Can I sign on?"

"As cabin boy. Sure."

We arrived at her place. Three stone steps up to the street door. "Nightcap time?" she said as she got her key out.

"If it doesn't have to be brandy."

"Right. The hell with brandy."

The elevator was a little larger than a phone booth. It creaked and juggled and shimmied upward, taking a long time to reach the fourth floor. She had become very animated and chatty, posing her face this way and that as though I held a camera aimed at her, talking as though we were recording it all. Women act that way on television commercials.

Her apartment was big. She bustled about, turning on strategic lighting, tossing her cape aside. Modern paintings, lighted by spots, made big bright explosions on the walls. A complex wire sculpture on a low pedestal was lighted in such a way it threw a huge mysterious shadow form on a far wall.

"In spite of all the Borlikas," she said, "my personal tastes are contemporary. I happen to feel that . . . ." The phone started ringing. She excused herself, started toward it, then went into the bedroom and closed the door. The phone stopped. She came back out a few moments later, brisk and chatty.

She opened a small lacquered bar and scurried off to the kitchen to get cubes. I made us two tall highballs. She took me on a circular tour of inspection of the paintings and sculpture, lecturing like a museum guide.

Then she said, "I do have one little collection of eighteenth century art. Come along." With a brassy and forlorn confidence she marched me into her bedroom. It was more persuasively feminine than I would have guessed, canopied bed, pastel ruffles and furry rugs. She turned on a display light which illuminated a dark blue panel in the bedroom wall. In random arrangement against the panel were a dozen or so delicate little paintings, most of them round, a few of them oval, all framed in narrow gold, all a little smaller than saucers.

"French," she said. "Metallic paints on tortoise shell. It was a precious little fad for a time. They are quite rare and valuable."

"Very nice," I said.

"Look at them closely, dear," she said, with a mocking smile.

I did so, and suddenly realized that they were not what they appeared to be, not innocent little scenes of life in the king's court. They were not pornographic. They were merely exquisitely, decadently sensual.

"I'll be damned!" I said, and she gave a husky laugh of delight. She moved closer and pointed to one. "This is my favorite. Will you just look at the fatuous expression on that sly devil's face."

"And she looks so completely innocent."

"Of course," she said. Her smile faded as she looked at me. She turned and with exaggerated care placed her empty glass on a small ornate table with a white marble top. It made a small audible click as she set it down. She turned back with her eyes almost closed and groped her way into my arms, whispering, in a private argument with herself, "I'm not *like* this. I'm really not *like* this."

The physical act, when undertaken for any motive other than love and need, is a fragmenting experience. The spirit wanders. There is a mild feeling of distaste for one's self. She was certainly sufficiently attractive, mature, totally eager, but we were still strangers. She wanted to use me as a weapon against her own lonely demons. I wanted information from her. We were more adversaries than lovers. The comments of old Sam'l Johnson about the pursuit of women kept drifting into my mind. The expense is damnable, the position ridiculous, the pleasure fleeting.

But it went very well for her there in the faint night light under the yellow ruffles of the canopy, very well on a physical basis, which is perhaps, the least important part, sufficiently well to induce her, in the post-tempest euphoria, to give myriad little kitteny affections, a purring gratitude.

"This is the last thing I expected to happen," she said, with a luxurious stretching. "You're very sweet."

"Sure."

She took my wrist, guided my cigarette to her lips. When she exhaled she said, "Did you expect it to happen?"

"Let's put it this way. I hoped it would. Life is full of coincidences, Betty. Some of them are nasty. Some of them are fine. I guess they're supposed to balance out sometime. I suppose, in a sense, that guy brought us together."

"Who, darling?"

"The guy who collected the little gold people."

"Oh," she said in a sleepy voice. "Carlos Menterez y Cruzada."

"Who he?"

I made it a bored question, as indifferent as her response had been.

"Sort of a bastard, dear. A Cuban bastard. Very close to Batista. A collector. Those five you picked out, he bought them from us." She yawned, snuggled more comfortably against me and gave a little snorting sound of derision and said, "He collected me, too. In a sort of offhand way. I guess women were a lot more abundant than gold for Senor Menterez. I hated him a while. I don't any more."

"How did it happen?"

"Because I was a stupid young girl and he was a very knowing man. It was when I was working at the place, before I married Tony. We had two items he was interested in. I was on salary and two percent commission. He said he couldn't make up his mind. He had a suite at the Waldorf. He called up just before we closed and asked me to bring the photographs over. Drinks and dinner in the suite, of course. He was very charming, very amusing. He didn't make the mistake of begging or insisting or arguing. He just seemed to assume that I was going to go to bed with him, and that I wouldn't have come to the suite if I wasn't willing, and it all seemed to be so settled in advance, I just didn't know how to handle it. I couldn't seem to find the right moment to set my heels and pretty soon, there I was in bed, scared, confused and apologetic. A knowing man can manage it that way with a green girl."

"How old was he then?"

"Mmm. Eight years ago. Early forties. Twenty years older than I was."

"Nice looking man?"

"No. Not very tall. Sort of portly, even. Thin little mustache and going bald. Very nice eyes. Long lashes. Beautiful suits and shirts, and beautiful grooming. Manicures and facials and cologne and massages. A car and driver picked me up after work the next day too. He was in New York on business with several other Cuban businessmen, but he had the suite to himself. He bought me an absolutely beautiful gown. He wanted me to go back to Havana with him. He said he could set me up with a little shop of my own there. He had me in such a confused daze, I almost made that much of a fool of myself. I didn't even really like him. I couldn't understand why I kept doing exactly as he asked me to do. He didn't seem . . . very intense about me. Just sort of jocular and fond, like people are toward dogs."

"Was he married?"

"Yes. After he left it took me about two weeks to come out of the fog. You know, I had always wondered how reasonably attractive girls ever got themselves into entanglements like that with older married men. I just had a kind of anxious, earnest desire to please him. I didn't want him to be disappointed in me in any way. A vassal state. Then I woke up and knew it had been a very dirty business."

"What kind of business was he in in Cuba?"

She yawned. "I don't know. Lots of things. After the roof fell in on all those people down there, I used to wonder what happened to the Menterez collection. I suppose he got out with it. And whatever else he could carry. I wondered if we would ever hear. Or if he would show up to peddle it all back to us. But somebody got it away from him, and you got it away from somebody else?"

"Something like that."

"It doesn't matter does it, darling? Whether he's alive or dead. I'm so deliciously sleepy, dear. Let's sleep for a little while."

Something awakened me, perhaps the little tilt of the bed as she left it. I turned over, feigning sleep, and through slitted lids saw her, nude-white in the small amber of the night light, staring back at me, her body slightly crouched, the dark hair tangled across her pale forehead. After I took several deep breaths, she went plodding silently over to the chair where I had tossed my clothing. Though I could not see her clearly, I knew she was going through the pockets. She would find cigarettes, lighter, change and a thin packet of bills. All identification was back in the bureau drawer of my locked room in the Wharton. When she was through, she came stealthily back to bed, lay silently beside me for per-haps ten minutes, and then set about gently awakening me. When she dropped off into sleep again, I could sense that it was a very deep sleep. I tested it by shaking her, speaking her name. She made querulous little sounds that faded into a small buzzing snore. Ten minutes later I flagged down a hurrying cab on Third Avenue, in the first grey of a tomcat dawn. At the Wharton, I got my key at the desk and went up and took a shower.

After the shower, I sat on the bed and went through the envelope of photographs I had taken from her purse as I left her apartment. I took out the five pictures of the statues which had definitely belonged to Carlos Menterez y Cruzada and stowed them in my suitcase. I printed her name and address on the outside of the envelope in square block letters. It is an old caution, and the only way any person can completely disguise their own handwriting. Merely hold the pencil as straight up and down as possible, use all capitals, and base them all on a square format, so that the O for example, becomes a square, and an A is a square with the base line missing and a line bisecting it horizontally. No handwriting expert can ever make a positive identification of printing done in that manner, because it bears no relation to your normal handwriting. After I awoke, I would get it sealed downstairs, buy the stamps and mail it.

I slid between the hotel sheets and turned out the bed lamp. There was a brighter morning grey at the windows. I tried to sort out the facts I had learned. Facts kept getting entangled with textural memories of the woman, so gaspingly ardent. The facts and the woman followed me down into sleep, where the little gold figures came alive and one of them, an East Indian one, a woman with six graceful arms, made tiny little cries and fastened herself to my leg like a huge spider, bared little golden teeth and sank them into the vein while I tried to kick her away.

seven

I CAUGHT an early afternoon flight out of Kennedy, after phoning Nora from the terminal. She was waiting at the gate, and as I had just my hand luggage, we went directly to her little black car in the parking lot. It was a warm beautiful afternoon. She looked very trim and chic in a pale grey dress, a light yellow cardigan.

"You look better," I told her.

"Shaj took charge," she said. "It was a lovely afternoon, and I spent all of it in the side garden, soaking up the sun. I was beginning to look mealy. The sun exhausted me. I slept twelve hours, had my hair done this morning, and I had a drink while I was waiting for you, and I feel almost human for the first time in a long time. You didn't find out anything, did you?"

"A little bit."

"Really? What?" The sudden intensity gave her that hawk look, the dark eyes very fierce, the lips thinner, the nose predatory.

I drove out of the lot. When I was clear of the airport area, I said, "A rich Cuban, a buddy of Batista's, collected the figurines. He bought five of them from the Borlika Galleries. By the best luck you can imagine, one of the five he bought was the one Sam showed me. That gave me the break, and I did a little gambling, and it opened up very nicely. Carlos Menterez y Cruzada. Businessman, age about fifty now if still living."

"They told you all that? Why?"

"They got the impression I have the collection. Twenty-eight pieces. They don't care how I got them. We agreed on a price. A hundred and thirty-seven thousand, five hundred. Cash. A very quiet deal."

"Sam thought they were worth more."

"They are, if you can sell them in the open. They're worth

65

less on a back street. Anything is. I don't think Sam's title was exactly airtight."

"Did Sam steal them for Carlos Whosis?"

"That wasn't quite Sam's style."

"I wouldn't think so. Then how?"

"However he got them, Nora, it attracted the wrong kind of attention."

"All right. So you know who used to own them, you think. Does that really mean very much?"

"When we get to the boat I'll show you something."

I fixed her a drink and left her in the lounge. I took my bag into the master stateroom, changed quickly to slacks and a sports shirt, and took the pictures out and handed them to her. "The one on top is the one Sam showed me. The other four are from the Menterez collection."

She looked at them very carefully, lips compressed, frown lines between her heavy dark brows. She looked up at me. "They're strange and terrible little things, aren't they?"

"I keep wondering how many people have gotten killed over them. I saw a golden toad with ruby eyes in New York, two thousand years old. He looked as if he couldn't count the men he'd watched die."

She rapped the sheaf of cards against her knuckles. "This is something definite. This is real, Trav. I . . . don't know much about all the conjecture and analysis and so on. But something I can hold and touch . . . ."

I took them away from her and took them forward and put them in my safe. Any fifty-four foot boat has innumerable hiding places, and a houseboat has more than a cruiser. Once I turned a very accomplished thief loose aboard The Busted Flush. I gave him four hours to find my safe. He was a friend. I watched him work. He was very very good. When his time was up, he hadn't even come close.

"What will you do with the pictures?" Nora asked when I returned to the lounge.

"I don't know. They're bluff cards. And they'll come as a great shock to somebody."

"What do we do next?"

"Find out a little bit more about Menterez."

That evening, in Miami, it took me well over an hour to

locate my friend, Raoul Tenero. He is nearly thirty and looks forty. He was just beginning his career as an architect in Havana when Castro took over. I met him at some parties in Havana pre-Castro. When he got out of Cuba, he looked me up. I introduced him to some people. He worked for a time, and then went back in and was captured at the Bay of Pigs. He was finally exchanged with the others. His pretty wife, Nita, had a vague idea of his schedule. I finally caught up with him in a youth center building, part of the park system. It was one of their endless committee meetings, not on political action, not on invasion, but on how to fit their people into the Yankee culture, find the jobs, assist each other. It works. They have that unyielding, unending, remorseless pride. They are the objects of considerable resentment, as is only normal for the human animal when a big batch of people of a different heritage move in. But of all the ethnic groups in the Miami area, the *Cubanos* have the lowest crime rate.

I spotted him on the far side of the room in a small group of about nine men, chairs pulled into a circle. Raoul has the true Spanish look, the long chalky face, deep-set eyes, hollow cheeks, and elegant way of handling his body when he moves. He saw me and held his hand up, thumb and first finger a half inch apart in the universal Latin gesture of indicating just a little bit more time. Six or seven groups were in discussion. Some of them were very loud. I moved out into the night and leaned against the building and smoked a cigarette and watched the asphalt hiss of night traffic.

In about ten minutes he came out. "You all sewed up?" I asked him.

"No. I'm through in there. It's a resettlement thing. Winston-Salem. Ten families. Fifty-eight people. I took time off and flew up there and talked to the people who've been working on it. Nice people, Travis. Now it's all reassurance, prying them loose from here, from the Havana Annex. They think there's eight feet of snow all winter in North Carolina."

"I need some information and a drink."

"I'll watch you drink, Senor. While I have milk."

"Still messed up?"

He gave a mirthless laugh. "I gave my stomach for my country. Tried some rum a week ago. One drink. Broken glass would have been easier. That Havana Yacht Club

cruise, it was hard on the inside man. How'd you find me?
You see Nita?"

"She looks wonderful."

"How about her English? She's working hard."

"It's flawless."

"Oh boy. Hey, you follow me, okay?"

I followed his decrepit old Chev to a side street bar. The
clientele was a hundred percent Cuban. He was known there.
I went to a table in a far corner. He had to stop and talk to
half a dozen people. Finally he came to the table, a glass of
milk in one hand, dark rum on the rocks in the other.

"How's the work going, Raoul?"

He shrugged. "They trust me more now. The estimates are
close. They see me use a slide rule. It heartens them. Slowly,
slowly they are letting me do a little designing. But it is
strange, you know? They speak to me loudly, very distinctly.
My God, that's why my father sent me to Choate before the
University of Havana, to speak the language. It's going all
right, Travis. I shouldn't bitch. But my chance of a license,
the A.I.A.? I wouldn't give you a Castro centavo for that,
man. Hell, we had a closed shop over there too, you know.
An American architect coming in, the only way he could
work was team up with one of us, and the commission
double. Now I get it in the eye the same way. What's on
your mind?"

"I want to know something about a man. Carlos Menterez
y Cruzada."

Raoul stared at me. *"Hijo de* . . . . A long time since I
heard that name. A son of a bitch, Travis. A murderous
crafty son of a bitch. He is remembered. How long would he
last in Miami? With luck, twelve minutes. Where is he?"

"I don't know. If I can find out more about him, maybe I
can find him."

He leaned back. "I will tell you about that one. You have
to understand how it was under Batista. You people here
have never understood. He was, for my father, for other
successful men in Cuba, a fact of life. They all knew him.
They walked on eggs. They walked with great care. Circum-
spect. It is a question of honor. You are not such a great fool
as to try to fight such power, neither do you get too close to
a power which has a silent and secret side, sudden disappear-
ances, quiet confiscations. What you do, you give him and the
ones close to him no opening. How do businessmen survive

under Salazar, Franco, any of them? I am not being an apologist for my class. Perhaps we should have done something sooner, before the *communistas* came in with their perversions of freedom. How could we tell? It was a fact of life. My father lived with it. Other men lived with it. Without too great a cloud on their self respect. The men who lived with it, such as my father, too many of their sons have died fighting what replaced the old evil. And more will die, Travis. Ah, Menterez was totally at home in that situation. Very important, Menterez. Import, export, warehousing, shipping. Big home, big grounds. His specialty, my friend, was catching some man in a political indiscretion. Then he would say that only Carlos Menterez could give protection. Sell me just fifteen percent of your business for so many thousand pesos. Cheap. Then somehow would come litigation in corrupt courts, and finally Menterez and his cronies would own the entire business, with a suitable dummy ownership to cover the men in the government who had to have their share, of course. If a protest was too strenuous, the man might disappear. He was a barracuda, Travis. One little whiff of blood, and he would find a big meal. All honest men were afraid of him. He broke hearts and lives. No, he would not live long in this city. He got out in time, of course. But where did he go? I heard one rumor he is in Switzerland, another that he is in Portugal."

"What about his personal life ?"

"He had a wife, no children. A small silent woman, cowed by him I think. He was a womanizer. Always several mistresses in Havana. Many times they were foolish American girls he would keep there for a time. Big cars. A personal bodyguard. Another house at Varadero. A big cruiser. Also, a personal taste for gold. Gold fittings in cars and home and boats, gold accessories for himself and his woman, art objects of gold. A vulgar man, my friend. A dangerous and vulgar man, a kind we breed too often in Latin America."

"Not just there. Everywhere."

"But old Cuba was a place where such an animal can thrive. And the heart of it, always, is the corruption of the courts. Where justice can be purchased, animals like Menterez grow fat, and the common people despair. Then come the *communistas*, my friend. Look at the constitution of Panama. The president appoints the governors of the provinces for life. He appoints the justices of the Supreme Court, for life.

And those justices appoint the justices of the inferior courts, for life. Can you imagine a more fertile soil for corruption? But you are not here for a political lecture. What else can I tell you about Menterez? That he sucked the life out of one of my father's oldest friends? And my father could do nothing? That a woman died aboard his big boat under mysterious circumstances, and nothing was ever done about it? That celebrities from your country stayed at his house as his guests and thought him a fine charming man? That if he walked through that door, there would be a knife in his heart before he could take a second breath? They say you can't take it with you. Menterez screwed millions out of Cuba, and he took it with him. And sent plenty ahead. Good men were excessively polite to him. In a way that was ... an insult to which he could not take offense. His invitations would result in effusive and flowery apologies for not being able to attend. Let me see. What else? Oh, yes. He was a hypochondriac. Gold pill boxes in every pocket, and one week at the Mayo Clinic every six months. They say he was terrified of losing his virility. One understands that he had more than his share. He is on several lists. Many people would be delighted to diminish his virility. If you find him. Travis, promise you will tell me where he is. It would not be the same name, of course."

"If I find him alive, I'll get word to you, Raoul. But my hunch is that he is dead."

"Why do you think that?"

"Some day when there is some kind of an end to the story, *amigo,* some day when your stomach can take the booze, we will sit around and get stoned and I will tell you all of it."

He nodded, accepting that. "It has to be private and personal wars for you, eh?"

"I can understand the little ones. The big ones confuse me."

After a silent moment he said, "I have never asked you this before. Maybe I shouldn't ask it now. How close were you to coming on our little picnic at the Bay?"

"Very very close."

"I thought so. What stopped you?"

"A nervous little C.I.A. man with glasses and a rule book."

"Then it was very close."

"It occurred to him that I wasn't a Cuban."

He grinned. "Do you remember when you became an honorary Cuban, my friend?"

"At Rancho Luna?"

When the *soldados* made the lewd remark to your girl. The three of them there, standing by the sedan, waiting for the politico to finish his lunch. What a damn fool, Travis. Never, never will I forget it. You went smiling up to them and in that horrible kitchen Spanish, you asked that peasant idiot if you might examine his machine gun. You took it so gently and hit him under the chin with the stock, and in the same swing, chopped the other one behind the ear."

"And missed the third one, boy," I said, "and you powdered him just in time."

"And we ran like hell. And you were indignant because of all the people whistling. You didn't know it is a kind of applause there."

"I've never seen a pair of more terrified girls in my life."

"We comforted them, *amigo mio*," he said, and his smile was suddenly gone. "Yours was Teresa. She married. They waited too long. They tried to come out by small boat. Seventeen of them in a twenty-two foot boat. The motor quit. They drifted six days in August, near the keys. They were alive when they were found, and two of those died later. Teresa was one of the dead. Her husband lived. He went on our picnic, and he died there in the weeds and the swamp water."

"That makes my game with those soldiers sound pretty damned silly, Raoul."

"It was silly, of course. Idiotic, suicidal and foolish. I treasure it. The girls adored you for it. All Havana talked and laughed about it for weeks. One indignant tourist, armed only with rum, and three of Batista's soldiers with Thompson submachine guns, all for the honor of a pretty Cuban girl." He shrugged and sighed. "What made us think that was the most savage and dangerous of all worlds? Now it seems almost pure, something on a stage, with comedy uniforms."

"Can you people work your way back to something easier to understand?"

His mouth had a sour curve. "It depends, I think, on how long and how hard we can laugh." He looked around, then touched my arm. "I am getting signals from old friends. Do you have anything else to ask? No? Excuse me then. Come to our house soon, Travis. Nita will use the long words. She is in a strange limbo now, where neither Cubans nor Yankees can understand her. But she has become quite a good cook."

By the time I reached the door, I looked back and saw Raoul hunched in fierce argument with men who all seemed to be speaking at once, in fierce low tones. God only knows how it will come out for them. All over the world are the fringe peoples, pushed out of their countries for varied reasons, each group thinking it the most hideous inequity since the world began, the most shameful oppression. In every tiny span of recorded history, the exiles have huddled and plotted, schemed and starved and died. But perhaps it all used to be simpler to understand. Now the movements of nations have become like a huge slow solemn dance of the elephants, random power swaying in unpredictable directions, their movements obscured by a stifling rain of paper, pastel forms in octuplicate, programmed tapes, punch cards. Through this slow rain, in the shadowy patterns of the dance, scurry a half a billion bureaucrats, each squealing self-important orders. Beneath the wrinkled grey legs, ten thousand generals squat, playing with their war game toys. The billions of mankind sit in the huge gloomy reaches of the stands, staring without comprehension, awaiting the white blast that will char the dancers, end the act, and because tension and waiting can only be sustained so long, they make their own little games and charades in the stands, the charades of art, sex, money, power and random murder.

I went and sat in my old car of vulgar blue, and remembered the lovely, shy, mischievous face of Teresa, the night swim in a moonlight sea, the talk and the singing. I remembered her coming out of the sea in moonlight, combing her soaked hair back with her fingers, the phosphorescence twinkling around the wading thrust of her white thighs, seeing me waiting there, stopping, shielding herself for a moment with hands and arms, then lifting her chin and coming on toward me, boldly, making a single sound, deep in her throat, like a laugh. She loved her tropic sea and it had killed her dead, in the hot blazing days of August.

That's why they can never make it. They kill off the good ones. They gut their dreamers. Their drab stone discipline is a celebration of mediocrity. If we can restrain ourselves from killing off our own rebels, our doubters and dreamers, all in the name of making ourselves strong, then we can prevail. But if we use their methods, then any victory will be but the victory of one iron symbol over another, and mankind will have lost the battle whichever way it goes.

I drove north at a sedate pace, measuring the new reality of Carlos Menterez y Cruzada, collector of gold, of women, and of many kinds of pills. He seemed the type who would have a special talent for survival. Bombs kill their chauffeurs. They catch the last flights out. They change their money in the right places at a favorable rate the day before the currency collapses.

I was very tired. I went back to Bahia Mar. As I approached The Busted Flush, I heard sweet and cautious singing, and I found that it was coming from my topside sun deck. I stepped over the chain, went aboard, and climbed the ladderway. In the starlight and the random lights of the yacht basin, I saw Meyer with four of the little seasonal girls, all bundled in sweaters, sitting on the deck in a close circle, singing one of the old English rounds Meyer liked to teach them. They were always about maidens fair, deadly knaves, lonely death in the castle tower.

They ended on a sweet synchronous chord of girl voices and Meyer congratulated them extravagantly. "Excuse the invasion, my boy," Meyer said. "Junior here has a dull young man prowling around trying to create scenes. We're in hiding. This group is in very good voice. Lassies, if any of you do not know him, this is the crude fellow who owns the boat. His name is McGee. Excuse me a moment. Practice that last one again, please."

He took me over to a far corner of the sundeck. Behind us, the girl voices were heartbreakingly sweet and clear.

"A man named Branks was here, looking for you, Travis. He had some questions."

"Such as?"

"Your habits, your livelihood. Rather a clever fellow, I suspect. He leaps on any nuance, any mild hesitation."

"What kind of billing did you give me?"

"Why should I lie to him? I said you are a beach bum, a reasonably pleasant companion, that you seem to make a living from small speculative ventures, that you seem to enjoy practically anything, in moderation, in accord with your somewhat quaint standards of behavior."

"You two had quite a chat."

"It took a philosophical turn, the role of man in modern society, the decay of morals, the new permissiveness, group standards versus inner values. He said he would try to get in touch tomorrow."

"Did he seem hostile?"

"Not at all. Not at all. Quite amiable, and curious. I can depart with my little flock now, or, if you feel festive, we can all go below, for an hour of song and discussion."

"I don't feel that festive."

"Can I offer you a flower from my little garden? The one facing us, the alto, with the perfectly straight strawberry blonde hair?"

"Meyer, this is not like you!"

"She is more than old enough to vote, and she met you the other day and was curious about you, and she is in a horrid emotional state, on the verge of scampering off to commit untidy indiscretions with bad companions. Better a devil I know than several she doesn't know. I cannot keep her in my little gaggle of sweet geese much longer. She is disaster prone, compelled by a bruised heart. Otherwise . . . I would not step so far out of character."

I looked and saw the girl eyes intently watching me, the mouth making the round tones of the song, and was tempted. But any man who thinks of himself as therapy should not have a license to practice. If it could be guaranteed that she would remain a thing, a pleasure item, a recreation device —as recommended by *Playboy*, then the diversion would be so meaningless as to make the decision easy. But she would insist on being a person, a special soul hunting its own special agonies, and we would try to make those marks upon each other which prove that nothing is ever casual. I was wearing all the old marks I could handle, never having been quite able to play the recreation game, not for itself alone. So let her go find her own untidiness, her own bad companions, as I had done in my own seeking way. Any bandage presupposes a wound, and in these brave, hearty days there are more than enough wounds to go around. So take your strawberry hair elsewhere, dear. McGee's Clinic is closed for repairs.

"No thanks, Meyer."

"Too bad. She is in need of a rare additive. Kindness. Scientific tests show that with that special additive—KDS we call it—any woman fresh out of the show room, right out of dealer stock, will travel an additional eight hundred and seventy-one yards before stalling."

He repaired a shaky lyric, coached them in a chord, then trooped his little floc．: off and away, the girl voices calling their goodnights. One goodnight in a sad alto echoed in an empty corridor in my mind, and after I had at last fallen asleep in the vast custom bed in the master stateroom, I stood on a dream bridge and looked down and saw an open boat drift under the bridge on the black tide, full of a lost tumble of dead maidens, all with strawberry blonde hair, wide marbled eyes accusing.

Ken Branks, in yellow knit shirt, shapeless felt hat and racetrack tweeds, sat in my lounge and took cautious sips from the steaming mug of coffee and made small talk and watched me with clever eyes in a supremely ordinary face.

Finally he said, "You've been questioned a few times, McGee. Here and in Miami."

"I haven't been charged with anything."

"I know. But you seem to get a piece of the action on little things here and there. It interests me."

"Why?"

"Sam Taggart's death interests me too. It didn't check out the way I thought it would. We worked all the bars and came up with nothing. You know, I thought it was an amateur hacking, some guy working blind in the dark, drunk maybe, chopping at him, finally getting him."

"Wasn't it like that?"

"I thought maybe the murder weapon could have been ditched behind those cabins, somewhere in all those junked automobiles, so I had a couple people check it over. They found it. A brand new dollar-nineteen carving knife. Fifty supermarkets in the area carry that brand. There was some other stuff with it. One brand new cheap plastic raincoat, extra large. One brand new pair of rubber gloves. One set of those pliofilm things that fit over shoes. The stuff was bundled up, shoved into a car trunk, one with a sprung lid. Except for the blood, which is a match for Taggart's, the lab can't get a thing off that stuff. What does that all mean to you?"

"Somebody expected to get bloody."

"Somebody didn't like Taggart. They wanted it to last. They were good with a knife and they made it last. They wanted him to know he was getting it. Look at it that way, and study the wounds, and it was a professional job. Somebody played with him, and then finished him off. We traced

Taggart's car. It was bought for cash off a San Diego lot nearly two weeks ago."

"What do you want to ask me?"

"Who could take that much of a dislike to him?"

"He's been gone three years. He never wrote."

Branks scowled at his coffee. "You saw him that afternoon. You'd take an extra large size. Maybe he came back to find out if you were still sore at him. Maybe you got back to your boat minutes before Nora Gardino arrived there."

"If you could sell yourself that idea, you wouldn't be trying it on me."

His smile was wry. "You're so right. We're understaffed, McGee. We haven't got time to futz around with something that gets too cute."

"A man would get an extra large size to cover more of himself."

"Sure. I don't want pressure. I don't want newspapers howling about a mystery slaying. So I'm trying to keep it on the basis of a brawl, a vagrant, a dirty little unimportant killing. No release on the blood-proof clothing. I've asked California if they've got anything at all. I've checked him out three years ago here, and I don't find anything special. He had a job. He worked at it. He took off. What did the two of you talk about that day?"

"People we'd both known, where are they, how are they. Do you remember this and that. He said he was back for good, and he borrowed forty dollars."

"He was right about that. He's back for good. A man doesn't get burned that black in any kind of job except on boats."

"I got the idea that's what he'd been doing."

"Out of California?"

"Or Mexico. I told you before he said he'd spent some time in Mexico."

"You take a man on boats, and an international border, and you can come up with reasons for somebody getting killed. Smuggling. Maybe he was a courier, and he kept the merchandise and ran with it."

"He had to borrow forty dollars."

"Maybe he had something he could change into money. And somebody came after him and took it back. Maybe he tried to make a deal."

"Aren't you reaching pretty far?"

"Sure. Maybe there were two of them, and he didn't say anything to you about the other party. Maybe they couldn't agree on how to split it up. Maybe it was woman trouble, and the husband followed him. I can reach in a lot of directions, McGee. It doesn't cost anything. It's just that something like that, a man carefully dressing up to do bloody work, it bothers me. If he took that much care, he took a lot of other kinds of care too. I don't think my chances of unraveling it from here are very good. I can't believe anybody was waiting here three years to do that to him. They came with him or followed him, or agreed to meet him here. That's what my instinct says."

"I'd have to agree."

All the questions were about as welcome as a diagnosis of Hansen's Disease. He was noodling. Good cops have that trait and talent. The mediocre ones pick a theory that pleases them and try to make the facts fit it, one way or another. The good ones keep dropping a litle bit at a time, so that you have no way of knowing how much or how little they know, and then they watch how much effort you make to cover yourself regarding information you think they might know.

The best solution is to give them a little bit, particularly when you suspect they might already have it.

"I may have misled you about one thing, but I don't think it's too pertinent," I said.

"Did you now?"

"Maybe I understated the relationship between Nora Gardino and Taggart. I told you she was fond of him. I guess it was a little more than that. And I guess Sam had some business he wanted to take care of before he saw her again, because he told me to tell her he wasn't going to be in town until the next day, Saturday. I guess you could say they were in love with each other."

"And he went away for three years? Were they in touch?"

"No. It was a misunderstanding."

"So if this was a lover's reunion, what the hell were you doing there, McGee?"

"She didn't know where he was staying."

"So what made her think you'd know?"

"Well . . . I'd told her he was due back in town."

"Now how would you have known that?"

"He phoned me Thursday from Waycross, Georgia, to ask

me if she was so sore at him she never wanted to see him again. I said no."

"Couldn't he wait to get here to find out?"

"Maybe he wasn't even going to come here if I told him she was too angry, or married, or moved away."

"Okay, so why didn't you just tell her where she could find him?"

"Sam wasn't in very good shape, and that was a crummy place he was staying. And I didn't want him to think I'd tipped her off that he'd come in Friday instead of Saturday. I thought it would give him a chance to pull himself together, and go out to the car. It wasn't much of a setting for a reunion, you see."

"I can buy that. It ties up a few loose ends, McGee. Like the way she damned near passed out on Thursday night out at the Mile O'Beach."

"That's when I told her he was coming back. Did you think that's when I told her somebody was going to kill him?"

"The thought passed through my mind. I even wondered if last night in Miami you were trying to find the Cuban who did it."

"You're pretty good."

"I wondered if you went to New York to find out which Cuban to look for."

"You make me very happy I leveled with you."

"Did you?"

"And I intend to keep right on leveling with you. Nora is still pretty shaky about this whole thing. We're old friends. She has a gal who can run the store. I think it would do her good to get her away from here for a while."

He thought that over. "Mexico?"

"It might be a nice change at that."

"You are a brassy bastard, McGee. Don't push it too hard."

"Listen to me. I did not kill him. Nora did not kill him. Neither she nor I have any idea who did kill him. We would both like to know. You have a limited budget and you have a limited jurisdiction. And a lot of curiosity. And some anger about the way it was done. We're angry too. What do you know that could be any help to us? I trade that for my confidential report to you about how it all comes out. If you don't want to play, you won't get a chance to listen."

"My God, you *are* a brassy bastard! If there's anything

that turns my stomach, friend, it is the amateur avenger sticking his civilian nose into a rough situation, muddying everything up."

"I've seen it rough here and there, around and about."

He thought it over. He leaned back and looked at the lounge, tilted his balding head and gave me an oblique glance. "Just what is it you do?"

"I do favors for friends."

"Did Taggart want you to do him a favor?"

That damned instinct of his. "I don't know. Either he didn't get around to bringing it up, or he changed his mind."

"Nobody gives me the same story on you, McGee."

"I never exert myself unless I have to. A genuinely lazy man is always misunderstood."

"I even heard that you won this barge in a crap game."

"A poker game."

He waited, and then gave a long sigh. "All right. Except for this little morsel, I would have taken you in, just for luck. I don't think it's going to do me much good to sit on it. A bartender made him from the picture. A highway bar a half mile south of here. He came in about quarter of nine. He made a call from the pay booth. He sat at the bar and nursed beers. At maybe quarter after he got a call on that phone. He seemed jittery. A half hour later a well dressed man arrived, carrying a brief case. Dark, medium height, maybe about thirty. They seemed to know each other. They went back to a booth. They had a long discussion. They left together, somewhere around eleven. This was a handy bartender. Observant. The well-dressed type did not drink. He kept his hat on. Dark suit, white shirt, dark tie. The bartender said they seemed to be dickering over something, making some kind of a deal, and they didn't seem very friendly about it."

"It isn't very much."

"It's something, but not very much. It's enough to take pressure off you. He called somewhere and left a number. Briefcase phoned him back and he told him where to come. When Taggart thought he had the deal made, he took Briefcase back to the cabin. Assume Taggart was selling something. Two cars. Briefcase followed him. They make the deal. Briefcase leaves. He goes down the side road, parks by the car dump, puts on his blood suit, takes the knife and comes back, having cased the cabin. Maybe his orders were to make the deal, but rescind it good if Taggart gave him half a chance. Five dirty minutes used up in killing Taggart. Recover the money. Stash his costume in a junk car, drive away."

"In a rental car? Back to the Miami airport?"

He looked at me approvingly. "Maybe you're not a clown after all."

"But you couldn't check it out?"

"How many phone messages come in? How many cars are checked out? How many medium-sized, darkhaired guys, thirty years old fly in and out every day? Maybe it's an organization thing, and Briefcase is a local operator. It fades out into nothing, McGee. When it's professional, it always fades out into nothing, unless we get one hell of a break."

"What's so professional about hacking him up like that?"

"A professional with a personal interest, maybe. Or maybe that's the way he goes for kicks, when he has the time." He grinned. "I'm a pro too. That's why you're going to come along and sit in my car while I talk to Miss Gardino. It's the only way I can be sure you don't get on the phone."

He couldn't trick her or trap her. All he could do was break her down to the tears and the truth. And he left me there at the shop with her, back in the office, steadying her down. The big sobs were less frequent. Shaj stared in at us and gave a little nod and went away. I patted Nora's lean shoulder. Her dark hair smelled grassy, like summer grass and clover. She gulped against my chest, sighs between the fading sobs. The little office was functional, rubber tile, steel, electrical computation, posture chairs. Out in the shop the women were drifting in the buying glaze, touching fabric, pursing lips, standing hipshot and pensive, the chic skilled clerks in attendance, amid a readiness of mirrors, a piped music barely audible. The office girl lurked in one of the store rooms, in impatient diplomacy.

Nora launched herself back into self dependence, giving a little push at me to turn herself away, delving for tissue, honking into it and then trying to smile. "He hits the nerve, doesn't he?"

"He opens you up like a guide book. It's his trade."

"Trav, I didn't . . . let him make me say anything about . . . the gold."

"I didn't think you would."

"But he got the rest of it. The loving." That narrow, vital, ugly-lovely face twisted into a grimace that pulled the flesh against the bone, showing the skull shape, the tooth-look of death.

"So we can leave any time," I said. "As soon as you're ready."

She looked flustered. The eagerness was still there, but the actual fact of departure made her uncertain. "I ... I have a lot to do."

"As soon as you're ready."

eight

THE TRAVEL AGENT in Los Angeles was a darling fellow, in tight green pants, yellow shirt, green ascot, desert boots. At a distance he was still a sub-deb, but at close range he wore a thousand wrinkles, fine as cobwebs, and his eyes were as old as tombs. Nora and I sat on his moulded plywood chairs and talked to him across a pale pedestal desk. I had made it clear to him that it was Miss Gardino and Mr. McGee.

He looked pained and said, "If that is REALLY the sort of thing you have in mind, I think you would be TERRIBLY pleased with Mazatlan or Guaymas, or perhaps as far down as Manzanillo. Puerto Altamura is so DIFFICULT."

"In what way?"

"Transportationwise, sir." He studied the folder he had taken from the file, and went over to a large map of Mexico on the side wall. He put a manicured finger next to Puerto Altamura and said, "I could arrange some HORRID little flight into Culiacan, and from there you could rent a car and driver to take you to Pericos, and then over a DESPERATE little swamp road. Or perhaps a flight into Los Mochis, and a car over to Boca del Rio, and a rented boat from there. Or, I understand there is a little charter amphib at Navojoa. And then, of course, there is really only the one place to stay there . . . and suppose you are not comfortable?"

"It's supposed to be pretty good, isn't it?"

He shrugged, fluttered his hand. "The Casa Encantada. The literature always says they are luxurious. I've never been there, or talked to anyone who has stayed there. As you see here, sixty beautiful rooms, pool, beach, gourmet food, boating, fishing, tennis. . . . Really I can TRULY recommend a lovely place in. . . ."

"Puerto Altamura sounds pretty good to me," I said. "We'd like something . . . a little off the beaten track."

His eyes moved sidelong toward Nora, a reptilian flicker of understanding. He gave up. "I'll see what I can do, sir. It may take some time to arrange. Such perfectly GHASTLY phone service. I'll try to book you through by the most comfortable means, believe me, provided I can arrange reservations. How long would you want to stay there, sir?"

"A month. Six weeks."

"My word!" he said, aghast. "Uh ... two rooms, sir?"

"Please."

He looked at his watch. "I suggest you phone me in, say, an hour and I may be able to report some progress."

We went out into the milky overcast sunlight of the March morning. She looked up at me with a crooked smile and said, "Isn't he a dear?"

"He seems to know what he's doing."

"Could we just walk for a while? I feel very tense and restless."

"Sure, Nora."

I phoned him at noon. He said, "I'm doing MUCH better than I expected, sir. I have you reserved there, beginning tomorrow night. The manager, a Mr. Arista, assures me the accommodàtions are most pleasant. He suggested a way of getting there, and I have ticketed you through to Durango, leaving at nine-twenty tomorrow morning. I am working on the link from Durango to Culiacan, where a hotel vehicle will meet you. Suppose you stop by at three this aftermoon, and I shall have everything all ready for you."

The Aviones de Mexico prop jet made one stop at Chihuahua, and then flew on to Durango. About thirteen hundred miles all told. It was one-thirty when we got there. It was a mile in the air, wind-washed, dazzlingly clear, very cool in the shade. The men in the customs shack were efficient in an offhand way, armed, uniformed, officially pleasant. The one who spoke English phoned Tres Estrellas Airline for us, and ten minutes later an ancient station wagon appeared and took us and our luggage on a fast and lumpy journey to a far corner of the field. We waited a half hour for the third passenger to arrive, a young priest. The plane was a venerable Beechcraft. The pilot looked far too young. He wore pointed yellow shoes, a baseball hat, and a mad smile. Between us and the sea were peaks of up to ten

thousand feet, all jungled green with occasional outcroppings
of stone. It was over two hundred miles to Culiacan. He did
not waste company gas with any nonsense like climbing over
the peaks. He went through the valleys and gorges, the
tricky gusts tipping and tilting us, the treetops streaking by.
Nora's hand was clamped upon mine, her fingers icy. And
when at last we came out of the crumpled terrain, he followed
it downhill, building up more speed and vibration than the
aircraft was built to take. Finally, when we reached Culiacan, he achieved some altitude, merely for the purpose of
slipping it in, a very flamboyant gesture indeed, and set it
down without a bounce or jar.

At sea level the heat was moist, full of a smell of garbage
and flowers, and a faint salty flavor of the sea. It was nearly
four o'clock. There was a round and smiling little man there
in a bright blue uniform. It said Casa Encantada on his hat,
and it said Casa Encantada on the side of the bright blue
Volkswagen bus. He kept smiling and saluting. He would
load a piece of luggage and salute again. "Hello!" he kept
saying. "Ah, hello!" But he had no other English.

When I tried my broken Cuban Spanish, and Nora
tried her fragments of Italian, his smile merely became
slightly glassy. The back end of the bus was stacked high and
heavy with supplies. In his own way he was as fearless as our
pilot. He kept bouncing up and down in the seat, humming,
muttering, swaying back and forth trying to achieve more
speed. We whined north on Route 15 to Pericos, and there
he made a violent left onto an unpaved road. We had twenty
miles of it, part sand, part shell, part crushed stone, part
mud. The tropic growth was dense and moist on both
sides.

At five-thirty we came bouncing out of the jungle, climbed
a small ridge, and went dashing down into the town of Puerto
Altamura, a grievous disappointment in spite of the blue bay
and the low green of the tropic islands shielding it. Our
driver was shouting and waving at everyone, blowing his horn
as though he had just won the Mille Miglia. Unpaved
streets of mud and dust, some clumsy churches, a public
square with a small sagging bandstand, naked children, som-
nolent dogs, snatches of loud music from small cantinas,
scores of small weathered stalls, squatting street vendors,
ancient rickety trucks, a massive, pervasive almost overpowering stench composed of a rare mixture of mud flats, dead

fish, greasy cooking and outdoor plumbing. The village was a semi-circle on a curve of the bay, and between the waterfront building we could see rotting docks, a scrabbly beach, nets drying, crude dark boats.

"Paradise," Nora murmured.

We made a turn around the bandstand and headed south. The houses became a little more elaborate, and then stopped; the road curved and ahead of us, and a half-mile away, perched on a continuation of the ridge we had crossed, we saw the Casa Encantada, low and white and clean-looking, with many white out-buildings, all roofed with orange-red tile.

The driver beamed, nodded at us, pointed and said, "Hello! Hello!"

He drove into a cobbled front courtyard, banked with rainbows of tropical flowers, stopped with a great flourish at the broad steps leading up to the main entrance. Small boys in bright blue came hurrying to get our luggage. We got out. The hotel faced the sea. It was on a headland, projecting into the bay. We could see out through the broad pass to the southwest across water sparkling in the evening sunlight. There was a big pool down the slope to the south of the hotel, with a dozen or so people taking the late sun. In the small bay down beyond the pool, at the end of a long curving cement staircase was a small yacht basin, with a half dozen cruisers and sports fishermen gleaming bright down there, and space for twice as many more. Across from the small bay, on the opposite knoll, I could see several impressive-looking homes barely visible among the lush plantings.

"Paradise?" I said to Nora.

"It is absolutely unbelievably fantastic."

A bald brown mustached man in a white suit came down the few broad steps and said, "Miss Gardino? Mr. McGee? My name is Arista. I am the manager here. I hope your stay with us will be most pleasant."

"It's lovely here," Nora said.

"Was your trip enjoyable, Senorita?"

"Yes. Thank you."

We went in and registered. The lobby was small, with a center fountain, tiled floor, massive dark beams, bright mosaics set into the walls.

He said, "We are almost half full at the moment. Dinner is served from eight until eleven-thirty. We have our own water supply and it is tested frequently so do not be afraid to drink it. We generate our own electrical power and so, unfortunately, we halt all kitchen and bar service at midnight when we turn off the main generator and go onto the smaller one which handles our night lighting. It is switched back at seven in the morning. There are brochures in the rooms explaining the hours for everything and what activities are available. We are happy you are staying with us. Will you follow me, please?"

He snapped his fingers and the boys picked up the luggage. He took us down a long passageway, with room doors on one side and, on the other, open arches overlooking the sea. We were two-thirds of the way down that wing, in rooms 39 and 40. The interconnecting door was open, thus saving him the minor awkwardness of unlocking it for us. If we chose to close it and bolt it, that was our affair. Blue tile floors, plaster walls, broad low beds, graceful straw furniture, coarse draperies in crude bright colors, deep closets, low chests of drawers, small bright tiled baths, with tub and shower and geometric stacks of thick white towels.

"These rooms are satisfactory? Good." A shy brown broadfaced young girl in a blue uniform dress appeared in the doorway. Arista said, "This is Amparo. She will be your room maid while you are here. She has some English." The girl smiled and bobbed her head. She had coarse black braids tied with scraps of blue yarn. A wiry little man in blue with a face like braided leather appeared behind her, with gold-toothed smile. "And Jose is your room waiter," Arista explained. "You push the top button here for Amparo and the other for Jose. She will do laundry, pressing, sewing, that sort of thing. Please tip them at the time you leave us. I have given you table ten, and you will have the same waiter each day, so arrange the tip with him in the same fashion, please." He gave a little bow to each of us in turn. "Welcome to La Casa Encantada," he said, and left.

Nora selected number 39. Jose moved her luggage into that room. Amparo went in to help her unpack and Nora closed the interconnecting door. Jose unpacked my two bags. I took out the two items I did not want him to handle, the zipper case which contained the statuette pictures, and my slightly oversized toilet kit. When he was through, and had asked if I wanted anything else, and had bowed himself out, with golden smile, I checked the room for a suitable hiding place for the five pictures. I did not hope to find anything that would defeat a professional search. I just wanted to thwart amateur curiosity. One table lamp had a squat pottery base. I dismantled the fixture. The base was half full of sand for stability. There was ample room for the pictures, slightly curled, shoved down partway into the sand. I put it back together again. Now the leather folder contained misleading information, a sheaf of typed sheets of computations, percentage returns on real estate and investments, detailed recommendation for purchase of things I would never buy.

I took the toilet kit into the bathroom. It has a shallow false bottom, so inconspicuous as to be quite effective. I had debated bringing a weapon, and had at last decided on a flat little automatic pistol I had filched from an unstable woman's purse, a Parisian woman. It is a ridiculous little thing made in Milano, silver-plated, with an ivory grip, one inch of barrel, without safety or trigger guard. The six clip has a sturdy spring however, unusual in these junk weapons. It is 25 caliber. I'd brought a full clip and a dozen extra shells. At eight feet I could be reasonably certain of hitting a man-sized target every time. At fifteen feet I would be half sure. At twenty-five feet it would be better to throw stones. It is a bedroom gun, with a brash bark like an anxious puppy. Its great advantage is its size. It is very thin. The grip fits the first two fingers of my hand. I can and have carried it in my wallet, tucked in with the money. It makes an uncomfortably bulky wallet. I dumped the toilet gear out, pried up the false bottom and felt a little ridiculous as I looked at the toy gun. I had more faith in the other two items concealed there, the little vial of chloral hydrate, and the tin of capsules of a tasteless and powerful barbiturate, labeled respectively as nose drops and cold medicine. I checked the clip on the little gun and transferred it to the side pocket of my trousers. It was safe. It could not fire until I had jacked a shell into the chamber. I left my medicines and extra shells concealed.

After I had showered and changed, Nora rapped on the interconnecting door. I opened it and she came in, in an ivory linen dress that darkened her skin.

"Amparo is a jewel," she said.

"Nice rooms."

"Maybe the food will be good too."

"I hope so."

"Shall we walk around? Explore?"

"If you'd like."

"Why are we almost whispering?" she asked, and smiled nervously, her dark brown eyes glinting in the diminishing light of dusk.

"Before we go out, is there anything in your room, anything that ties you to him in any way?"

"You told me to be sure of that. I was. There's nothing at all, Trav. But . . . he could have talked to someone about Gardino and McGee. Old friends."

"There has to be a scrap of bait left out, a hint of bait, nothing definite."

"I have the feeling someone is listening to us."

"Not from this room. You'll feel that way all the time we're here. Until we know. Until we're sure."

"It isn't anything like I thought it would be."

We walked to the far end of our exterior corridor, away from the lobby and found a sun deck at the end, large, with an iron railing, with a short curved staircase leading down to a path that led to the apron of the pool. The sunbathers were gone. A couple swam, dived, the man full of the spurious peppiness of the mid-forties living up to the demands of a lovely young girl, making his youthful motions, keeping his belly tucked in, having a whee of a time. We walked to the far side of the pool and looked down at the little yacht basin. Two more sports fishermen had arrived, unloaded the customers, and the crew of two aboard each one was hosing down, oiling reels, slipping the canvas covers onto the boat rods, talking and laughing across the dock to each other.

We took a flagstone path through the flowers toward the main entrance, watching the orange sun slip down beyond the far islands which guarded the bay from the hundred and fifty mile sweep of the Gulf of California.

"We're almost opposite La Paz," I said. "I guess it's just a little south of us."

"You've been there?"

"Once upon a time."

"Trav, tell me why I feel so strange and uncertain and . . . unreal?"

"After we find the bar."

"Okay. After we find the bar."

It was on the level below the lobby, an upholstered little room hoked up with candles, nets, tridents, glass floats, but dim and pleasant enough. We got our drinks at the bar, took them to a banquette corner. Several tables had been pulled together to seat ten people, five couples—the men big and brown and beefy, and their women smallish, tough, leathery. I needed one glance for the whole story.

"Those are the big game fish buffs," I told Nora. "Names in the record books. Invitation tournaments. Except for the fox hunting crowd, they are the most insular, most narrow and arrogant and self-satisfied bores in creation. If you can't kill fish in proper style, you're vermin. They clutter up Bimini. They ought to be restricted to Cat Cay, where the only ruder people in the world are the Cat Cay dock hands."

"How about the four dark suit types in the corner?"

"Mexican businessmen. Maybe looking for another place to stick up a hotel."

"And those kids at the end of the bar?"

Three towering and powerful young men, and two slim sunbrowned girls, and a huge black dog. "That's tougher. I'd say scuba types, if this was a better area for it. I'll say it anyway. From the way they're dressed, they've got a boat here. Probably came down the coast of Baja California and around to La Paz and cut across to here and will end up in Acapulco. How about the gal clothes?"

"That simple little beach shirt on the blonde is a forty-dollar item."

"It would have to be a good hunk of boat. So it's that big motor sailor at the far dock out there. Fifty-something feet."

"And the couple just coming in?"

"Ah, the firm tread and the steady eye of shutter-bug tourists. Kodachrome and exposure meters, and hundreds of slides of the real Mexico."

She lowered her voice. "And the couple at this end of the bar?"

The woman was dark, hefty and handsome, glinting with gem stones. The man was squat and powerful, with an Aztec face and a gleaming white jacket.

"Just a guess. They're from one of the houses over there beyond the boat basin. Drinks and dinner at the hotel tonight, for a change."

"You're good at that, Trav."

"And often wrong," I said, and went to the bar and brought fresh drinks back.

She sat closer to me and said, "Why do I feel so strange?"

"Because on the other side of the continent it looked easy,

Nora. Now all you can see is closed doors, and no way of knowing if any of them will open. Baby, nothing is easy. Life comes in a thousand shades of grey, and everyone except madmen think what they do is reasonable, and maybe even the madmen do too. People don't wear signs, and being dropped into a strange area is like a starfish landing on a strange oyster bed. You don't know which one to open, or if you can open anything. On serial television it's easy. For superman it's easy. For Mike Hammer it's easy. But real people wander around in the foggy foggy dew, and never get to understand anything completely, themselves included. You put on your heroine suit, honey, and now you feel a little jackass in it. That's good for you. I brought you along as cover. A place like this, a man comes here with a woman, or comes after the fish. With you along they classify me harmless, as I did most of the people in this room. So keep your head close to me and glow at me. You had to come here or you'd never feel right about him, so it's good for you. But remember, we're standing at the plate blindfolded. They give us an unlimited number of strikes, so you swing until your arms get too tired, and hope you don't get hit in the head."

She leaned closer and said, "What kind of a lousy defeatist attitude is that?"

"It's the attitude that keeps me from getting anxious and careless. And dead."

Her eyes looked sick and I knew the vision of Sam dead had flashed in her mind.

"You're in charge," she said.

Table ten overlooked a sunken flood-lighted garden behind the hotel. The food was good. It was almost very good. The individual table lights made little cones of privacy in the expanse of the big room. Our waiter, Eduardo, was deft and diligent. We lingered long over coffee and brandy, and at ten o'clock we wandered down and sat in deck chairs by the lighted pool. The area had been fogged for bugs, a taint that spoiled the heavy scents of the night blooming flowers.

"Listen," she said.

I heard small music from the boat basin, a deep drone of the faraway generator, a distant competitive chorus of tree toads.

"It's so quiet here," she said.

"It would be good to be here for other reasons."

After a little while she said, "Maybe he would have brought me here some day."

"Cut it out, Nora."

"I'm sorry."

A few minutes later she stood up and said, "Goodnight, Trav. I'll try to . . . keep things under better control."

"Want me to walk you back?"

"No thanks. Really."

"Sleep well, Nora."

I watched her, slim and slow, her dress pale in the warm night, climb the stairs to the sun deck and disappear along the corridor.

After a little while I went back to the bar for a cold Carta Blanca. Aside from a young couple with a honeymoon humidity about them, sitting in the corner, the bar had turned into a men's club. The men at the bar gravely caught conversational fish, found them too small, explained how badly they had handled them, released them without regret. They lost decent billfish to the sharks, had reels bind at the wrong moment, frayed their lines, broke their tips. The occasional fisherman tells of triumphs. The compulsive ones relate only disaster. I listened, and picked up crumbs of information. The hotel owned four sports fishermen. One was hauled for repairs. "If you don't have your boat down here next time, Paul, the one to sew up is Mario. He'll keep you stern on, beautifully. He anticipates. George was out with him last year when he got that bruising son of a bitch of a blue. What did it go, Harry?"

"Four ten and a bit. Three hours, twenty minutes. Six thread. George swears by Mario. Pedro is second best."

"But Pedro's mate is a cretin entirely."

They got into a travelogue then. Fishing around the world. Zane Grey in Australia. Tarpon in the Panuca River as compared to tarpon in Boca Grande pass. They told each other stories of tragic disaster.

I like to fish. I like to fish absolutely alone, wading the flats, or casting from shore into the tide patterns. And when I catch something I like to eat it as soon as possible. I spent my slave time popping my shoulder muscles and bursting my blisters on tuna the size of Volkswagens. I gave it up, much the same way I gave up climbing trees, driving motorcycles, dating actresses and other equivalently boyish sports.

I tuned them out, and leaned on the padded rail of the

little bar and tried to relate myself to time and place. They haul you too far too fast, and unless you can think of the distances, unless you know distances from the brute process of walking them, sore-footed, scared and hungry, every place you go becomes a suburb of every other place. The screaming machines had whipped me from Florida to California and down into Mexico, and the soul had to follow along at its own pace, tracking me down. This was an ancient tropic coast backed by cruel mountains, and La Casa Encantada was an implausible oasis, Americanized by fish money. The people in the village of Puerto Altamura—a thousand of them? Fifteen hundred?—would find it even less plausible than the tourists could imagine. For all the years the generations of them, in the dust and the mud and sea smell, had lived and worked and died in this coastal pocket, the young always dreaming of going far away, and few of them making it. Then suddenly, down the beach, appeared the big hotel and the new homes of *los ricos*. What could make Puerto Altamura so attractive to people that they should come incredible distances? Fishing? But fishing was a brute dangerous business of nets and gambles and bad prices and the unpredictable and hostile sea, a fact of life. It brought in new money. Dozens of villagers had a new kind of employment. Insane *touristas* would walk into the village and buy things foolishly, and click click their cameras at the most ordinary and ugly and familiar things. But, on the whole, the change was less than the sameness. The old things continued, sin and salvation, sickness and death, work and school and fiesta, drinking and violence, drowning and dancing, politics and pesos. The sprained bus came waddling in three days a week, and the old ice plant clattered, and the trucks limped and groaned out over the bad road with the unending harvest of fish.

One thing was obvious to me. From what Sam Taggart said, he had spent an appreciable amount of time here. He had become a *residente*. He would be known. It was inescapable that he would be known, and known well. He said there had been trouble. So people would not want to talk. I had to find some way of unwinding it, of following the single strands to the marks he had left on this place and these people.

From the shadowy corner came the sound of the bride's febrile chuckle, and soon they walked out, obsessed with the legality of it all, the permissive access, and all the fishermen

at the bar turned slow heads to appraise the departing ripeness of her, and all seemed to sigh.

I signed my chit and went to my room. Amparo had
turned the bed down. Nora slept beyond the closed door. Or
lay restless and heard me come in, and wondered what would
happen to us here, among the flowers and fishermen.

nine

I SLEPT heavily, and longer than is my habit. Nora was not in her room. It bothered me. There was a quality of impatience about her which could get us in trouble, or slam all the doors before we could even begin.

I dressed quickly, but as I left the room, I saw her coming along the corridor in swim suit, pool coat and clogs, towel and swim cap in her hand, the ends of her dark hair damp. Her weight loss had not changed the impact of those excessively lovely legs, so beautifully curved, so totally elegant. For over two years, she had told me, she had made upwards of fifty dollars an hour modeling those legs for fashion photography in New York, had lived meanly, saving every dime, and then had gambled the savings on opening the shop in Fort Lauderdale. She was Jersey City Italian, her father a stone mason, and she had driven herself a long hard way and made it on her own terms, acquiring along the way that gloss and poise which hid her origins. She had a curious attitude toward those perfect legs. They had been a valued property, like inherited shares of stock. She was grateful to them, pleased with them, and utterly indifferent to any admiration from others. Too many lenses had stared at them, too many studio lights had been moved to illuminate them properly. The George Washington Bridge was a memorable sight. It carried traffic. Her legs were memorable. And they carried her around.

"I've been up forever," she said. "And I'm absolutely starving. Are you going to breakfast now? Tell Eduardo I'm practically on my way. It's a lovely pool. A lot of boats went out early. You were right about those kids on the motor sailer. They're checking tanks and things. Isn't it a gorgeous morning? I won't be long. What will I put on? What are we going to do?"

"Walk to the village. Skirt instead of shorts, I'd say. Flat heels."

By the time we reached the public square, we had adjusted to the rich odors of the town. The brown kids had flocked around us, demanding pesos, dollars, dimes, two beets, neekles, and in the face of smiling, polite refusal, had accepted the rejection cheerfully enough, somehow passed the word to other hopefuls, and let us go our way. The slightest unbending, the smallest gift, would have made any future trip to the village one vast annoyance.

We wandered, looked at the stalls, then sat on a bench in the square, where the inevitable pigeons pecked at the walks and the scrub grass. There were beads of perspiration on Nora's upper lip. We watched the people. Aside from the very few bureaucratic types in the ubiquitous dark suits, the men wore khaki and twill and denim, clean, faded with many washings. The women, the older ones, wore either skirts and white blouses, or shapeless cotton dresses. The young girls wore the bastard American clothes of the catalogue houses, the pastel pants to mid calf, brief tops and halters. They moved in flocks, chittering, slanting their dark glances. I had located the post office, the police station, the public market. These were handsome people, trim and muscular, with the broad faces, dusty black hair, liquid tilting eyes of the Indio blood. Not too many hundreds of years ago they had roamed these coasts in their dugout canoes, leaving mounds of shells at their camping places, weaving complex fish traps of tough reeds.

I thought of using the post office as a possible approach. Looking for an old friend. Yes indeed. Good old Sam Taggart. He still around here? But it seemed clumsy.

A young priest walked by us and glanced over and said, "Good morning!"

"Good morning, Father," Nora said meekly. I recognized him as the same one who had been on the Tres Estrellas flight. I watched him head toward the church on the other side of the square and disappear into the dark interior. And I had a little idea worth developing.

"Are you Catholic?" I asked Nora.

"If I'm anything. Yes. I don't work at it. But it sort of builds up . . . and then I go to mass. Twice a year, maybe. I had an awful lot of it when I was a kid. When I was sixteen I had a brother who died, terribly. Some kind of cancer. Big horrible lumps all over his body. He got immune to the drugs. Way down the street they could hear him screaming when he had to be moved, for dressings and keeping him clean. I wore my knees out and my beads out, praying for God to take him to end that agony. He was a sweet boy. He was the best of us, really. But he lasted and lasted and lasted, until you wouldn't think he had the strength to scream like that. But he did. Almost to the end. Why should a kid endure such torture? By the time he died, my religion was dead too. I had terrible fights with my family about it. But I wouldn't pray to anything my brother's death had proved didn't exist. Are you religious at all, Trav?"

"I think there is some kind of divine order in the universe. Every leaf on every tree in the world is unique. As far as we can see, there are other galaxies, all slowly spinning, numerous as the leaves in the forest. In an infinite number of planets, there has to be an infinite number with life forms on them. Maybe this planet is one of the discarded mistakes. Maybe it's one of the victories. We'll never know. I think the closest we can get to awareness is when we see one man, under stress, react in ... in a noble way, a selfless way. But to me, organized religion, the formalities and routines, it's like being marched in formation to look at a sunset. I don't knock it for other people. Maybe they need routines, rules, examples, taboos, object lessons, sermonizing. I don't."

"By the time I was twenty I saw that it was kind of shallow to blame God for what happened to my brother. I didn't go back to the church. The hold was broken by then. I go sometimes. It's kind of sweet. Nostalgic. There's a girl there I used to be, and it's the only way I ever find her again." She sighed. "How did we get onto this?"

"Check me on the routine. Any talk you have with a priest is privileged information, isn't it?"

"Up to a point. I mean if a person confessed a murder, the priest would have to tell the police. What are you getting at?"

"That priest might know some things that would help us."

She looked startled, and then she comprehended. "But ... how could I go about...."

"Ask for his help in a confidential matter. Wouldn't that keep him quiet?"

"I suppose it would."

"Tell him you were in love with the man, that you lived in

sin with him and he left you and you have been searching for
him for three years. I have the idea these village priests know
everything that goes on. And he speaks English."

"It would feel so strange . . . to lie to a priest."

"I hear it's done frequently."

"But not this way." She looked in her purse. "I have
nothing to cover my head."

We went to one of the sidewalk stalls. She picked a cotton
scarf. It was ten pesos, then five, then four, and finally three
pesos fifty centavos, sold with smiles, with pleasure at the
bargaining.

She gave me a tight-lipped and nervous look, and went off
toward the church. I watched her go. Blue and white blouse
in a diamond pattern, narrow white skirt, with a slit at the
side to make walking easier, blue sandals. I saw her go up
the worn steps, stop and tie the dark blue kerchief around
her head, then disappear into the interior, through the pointed arch of the doorway.

I went back to the bench. The broad leaves of a dusty tree
shaded me. Lizards flicked across the fitted stones of the
pathways. A strolling dog eyed me in unfriendly inquiry. Two
small boys wanted to shine my shoes. Two black and white
goats stopped and snuffled among wind-blown debris. A fat
brown man with one milky eye came smiling over and, with
fragmentary English, tried to sell me a fire opal, then an
elaborately worked silver crucifix, then a hand tooled wallet,
then a small obscene wood carving, and then, in a coarse
whisper, a date with a "friendly womans, nice, fat." He
sighed and plodded away. I had the feeling I was the object
of intense scrutiny, of dozens of people wondering how best
to pry some of the Yankee dollars out of my pocket. I knew
it would not have been that way before the hotel was built.
But now the village had begun the slow transformation to the
eventual mercilessness of Taxco, Cuernavaca, Acapulco. Too
many Americans had shown them how easy it could be. Greed
was replacing their inborn courtesy, pesos corrupting their
morals. The village cop, agleam with whistles, bullets and
buckles, strolled by, whapping himself on the calf with a
riding crop.

Nora was gone a long time. A very long time. Though I
was watching the church, I did not see her until she was
about twenty feet from me. Her color looked bad, her mouth
pinched.

"Let's walk," she said.

I got up and went with her. "Bad?"

"He's a good man. It got to me a little. Let me just . . . un-wind a little bit." She gave me a wry glance. "Mother Church. You think you've torn loose, but . . . I don't know. I lit candles for him, Trav. I prayed for his soul. What would he think of that?"

"Probably he would like it."

We headed back out of town, toward La Casa Encantada. After we passed the last of the houses, there was a path worn through grass down toward the beach. She hesitated, and I nodded, and we went down the path. The beach was the village dump, cans and broken bottles and unidentifiable metal parts of things. There was some coarse brown-black sand, and outcroppings of shale, and tumbles of old seaworn rock. We went down where the tide kept it clean, and after a hundred yards or so, came to an old piece of grey timber. She sat there and leaned on her knees and looked out. The big protective islands looked to be about eight miles offshore. An old fish boat was beating toward town, with a lug-rigged sail tan as lizard hide.

"He didn't speak very much English, Trav. Enough, I guess. When he realized who I was asking about, he became very upset. He said perhaps some people hoped Sam would come back here, but he hoped the man would never return. He said he had prayed that Sam would never return. Prayer answered, I guess. He kept getting excited and losing his English. He came here four years ago, at just about the time the hotel was finished. Sam showed up, he thought, over a year later. He arrived on a private yacht from California. He was the hired captain. There was some kind of difficulty, and Sam was fired. He stayed. The yacht went on. The hotel needed somebody to run one of the fishing boats for guests. They helped Sam get his workpapers straightened out, a *residente* permit. Then he . . . he lived with a girl who worked at the hotel, a girl from the village. Felicia Novaro. Then there was some trouble at the hotel, and he left and went to work for one of the families in one of those big houses beyond the hotel. Their name is Garcia. He abandoned Felicia for someone in the Garcia household. And there was trouble there. He left suddenly. I didn't get all of it, Trav. Federal police came after he left, and asked questions. It's possible that he killed someone. The priest was very cautious about that part. Trav...it didn't sound as if he was talking about Sam. He was talking about some stranger, some cruel, dangerous, violent man."

"What did he do for the Garcias?"

"Ran their cruiser, apparently, and perhaps something more. Several times he seemed on the verge of trying to tell me something, and then he would stop. Felicia Novaro doesn't work at the hotel any more. She works in town. She does not go to church. He takes that as a personal failure. She works at the Cantina Tres Panchos, and her family do not speak to her. Her people are very devout. She lives over the cantina, and he said she does foolish things, but if she comes back to God, He will forgive her."

"Will he talk to anyone about this?"

"I'm sure he won't."

I touched her shoulder. "We've got the starting place, Nora."

"Maybe I don't want to find out all these things."

"We can stop right here."

"No. I do want to find out. But I'm scared."

We walked up the beach until we came to too many big rocks, and then we picked our way through nettles and brambles and sea oats, back to the road.

In my room, I rang for Jose, and he said it was perfectly possible to have "ahmboorgers" served at poolside, with cold Mexican beer, and he would do it at once. I told him fifteen minutes would be better than at once. I changed to swim trunks and went down and found a white metal table shaded by a big red umbrella. Nora came down in her beach coat and her green sheath suit. The scuba kids and the newlyweds and two couples of young marrieds apparently traveling together were in and around the pool. Nora and I swam until we saw Jose coming with the draped tray, and then I climbed out and pointed out our table to him. The "ahmboorgers" came with crisp icy salad, and very small baked potatoes.

After lunch the pool boy got us two sun mattresses and I had him put them over on the far edge of the big apron, near the flowers and away from the other people. We stretched out under a high hot sun, with just enough sea breeze to make it endurable, a breeze that clattered palm fronds and rustled the wide leaves of the dwarf banana trees, and brought little creakings and groanings from a tall stand of bamboo on the slope leading down to the boat basin.

"So?" she said at last in a sun-dazed voice.

"So we don't rush things. We don't charge around. We give the folks a chance to label us."

"As what, Trav?"

"Furtive romance, woman. You had to show identity for the tourist card. Connecting rooms. We couldn't be Mr. and Mrs. Jones."

"I realize that! But I just . . ."

"Excuse me," a girl voice said. I sat up. It was one of the two scuba girls from the motor sailer, the blonde who had been in the bar in the expensive shirt. Now she was in a wet black tank suit that looked as if it had been put on with a spray can. She had the starlet face, bland, young, sensuously perfect, utterly unmarked with any taint of character, force or purpose. The lithe ripeness of her body had been tautened by the surfing, skin diving, water skiing and the beach games. This was the genus playmate, californius, a sun bunny.

She hunkered down, teetered, caught herself with knuckles against the concrete and said, "Oops," and settled into tireless balance, sitting on her heels like a Kentucky whittler, the webbed muscles of her brown thighs bulging against a tanned softness. She was mildly, comfortably stoned.

"What it is," she said, "it's a bet. How about two years ago, three years ago? You were offensive end with the Rams. Right?"

"Wrong."

"Oh shit," she said. "Excuse me. The loser, that's me, gets to go overboard and scrub the whole goddam water line with a brush. You looked like that guy, I can't remember his name. They'd throw it right into his hands, he'd drop it, but throw it off target, he'd grab it like miracles. Anyhow, you look the type. You play pro with anybody?"

"Just pro ball for a college."

"End?"

"Defensive line backer. Corner man."

She looked at me like a stock yard inspector. "You're big enough for pro."

"It wasn't such a big thing when I got out. And I had knee trouble off and on the last two years of it."

"Excuse me too," Nora said and got up and headed for the pool.

The sun bunny peered after her. "My asking you gave her a strain?"

"She just wants to cool off I guess."

"She's built darling for an older woman. I guess I got to get back and say I was wrong."

"Are you people moving on soon?"

"I guess so. Maybe tomorrow. Chip hasn't said. What we figured, we'd stay longer. It used to be there was always a brawl going on they say, one of the houses over there. None of us were here before, but Chip had a note to the people, a friend of a friend, you know, so we'd get in on the action, but he couldn't even get past the gate, and Arista says no parties this year up there, so that's it and it's pretty dead here. I want to go where there's good reefs. I just want to go down and cruise the reefs. It's the only thing I can't ever seem to get sick of. All the colors. Like dreaming it. Like I'm somebody else."

"What house was it, where the parties were?"

"Oh, the pink one furthest up the hill there. People name of Garcia. Real rich and crazy, Chip's friend said. Fun people, house guests and so on. Well, see you around." She stood up and trudged back to her friends, giving me a parting smile over a muscular brown shoulder.

Nora came back and toweled herself, saying, "Just think how many of them would flock around if you were alone, dear."

"She said you're built darling for an older woman."

"God, I couldn't be more flattered."

"Nora, even if I had sent for her, why should you get huffy?"

She looked angry and then smiled. "Okay. It was a reflex. The war between women. And that, you must admit, is quite a package."

"Not my kind of package."

"I'd say it was any man's kind of package."

"Take a look at the three gorgeous meatballs she and her girlfriend are slamming around with. They are the masculine parallel. Take your pick."

She looked over at them, and then back at me. "No thanks. Okay. I never thought of it that way. There wouldn't be anybody to talk to, would there?"

"Not after the first day. But she came up with something."

"I beg your pardon?"

I told her about the fine parties, now over. And then I

said, "What we're both thinking becomes pretty obvious after a while."

"Garcia. That's like calling yourself John Smith, isn't it?"

"Instead of Carlos Menterez y Cruzada."

"But wouldn't that be terribly difficult for him to arrange?"

"Expensive, maybe. But not too difficult. He had to scoot out of Havana nearly five years ago. A man like that would be thinking ahead all the time. Mexico is a lot less corrupt than other Latin American countries. But immunity is always for sale, if you have enough money, if you work through an agent who knows the ropes. He would be afraid of people wanting to settle old scores. A remote place like this would be perfect. Big house, wall and gate, guards. Enough money to last forever. But he'd want a chance to live it up. Raoul told me about his taste for celebrities when he lived in Havana. And for American girls. He could make cautious contact with friends in California. He'd be afraid to go where the parties are, so he'd have to bring them here. Big cruiser at the dock over there on the other side. Goodies shipped in. It probably would have been impossible for him to get into any kind of business venture in Mexico. Is he dead? Is he sick? Has somebody gotten so close to him he's had to slam the gates and stop the fiestas? Maybe the people who sold him the immunity have kept on bleeding him. Sam worked for Garcia. Sam got hold of the Menterez collection. And somebody knew he had it and took it away from him. We find that somebody by finding out what went on here."

"How?"

"We nudge around until we find somebody who would like to talk about it."

"Felicia Novaro?"

"Maybe. I'll try her, alone. Tomorrow night."

"Why not tonight?"

"I saw that cantina. It's just off the square. I want to do a little window trimming tomorrow afternoon. With your help."

"Like what?"

"I'll tell you as we go along. It'll be more convincing."

An hour later Nora got sleepy and went yawning back to her room to take a nap. With a vague idea I went down the steps to the boat basin. It was the siesta lull. I padded slowly around, looking at the boats. The dockmaster had a shed office and supply store at the end of the basin, beyond a gas dock. They looked as if they were set up to do minor repairs.

The sun was a palpable weight against my back, and I squinted into the water glare. Some fish I couldn't identify hovered close to the cement pilings. I went to the office. A man with red-grey hair and a perpetual sunburn sat sweating at a work table, copying figures from dock chits into a record book. He turned pale blue eyes at me and said, "Ya?"

"You the dockmaster?"

"Ya."

"Pretty nice layout you've got here."

"Something you want?" he asked. He had a German accent.

"Just looking around, if you don't mind. I live aboard a boat. In Florida. I wish I could get it over here, but there's no way, unless I want to deck-load it on a freighter."

"Big boat?"

"Barge type houseboat. Custom, fifty-two feet, two little Hercules diesels. Twenty-one foot beam. I've got a four hundred mile range at nine knots, but she won't take much sea."

"Not good for these waters. Better where you are."

"I guess so." I wandered over to the side wall and began to look at the pictures. They were black and white polaroid prints, scores of them, neatly taped to the composition wall. Boats and fish and people. Mostly people, standing by fish hanging from hooks from a sign saying La Casa Encantada, smiling, sundark, happy people, and limp fish. And I saw Sam Taggart. In at least a dozen of them, off to one side, grinning, always with a different group of customers, a raunchy yachting cap shoved back on his hard skull, his teeth white in his deep-water face. In most of them he was wearing a white, short-sleeved sport shirt, open down the front, the tails knotted across his waist.

The dockmaster had gone back to his records. He kept the office very tidy. I saw the books on a shelf, four of them, each labeled by year, each titled Marina Log.

"Mind if I see if I know any of the boats that stopped here?"

"Go ahead."

I took the one for three years back, and sat on a crate by the window and slowly turned the pages. The sign-in columns were for boat name, length, type, port of registry, owner, captain. I found it for July 11th, over two months after Sam had left Lauderdale. Quest IV, 62 ft, custom diesel, Coronado, California, G. T. Kepplert, S. Taggart, Capt. All in Sam's casual scrawl. It jumped out of the page at me. Business wasn't tremendous. Page after page was blank. I put it back and took down the more recent book and went through that and put it back.

"You get some big ones in here," I said.

"Anything over eighty feet, they anchor out, but it's a protected harbor."

I went back to the wall where the pictures were. A young Mexican in paint-stained dungarees came to the doorway and asked a question through the screen. The dockmaster rattled an impatient answer in fast fluent Spanish and the boy went away. He finished the accounts and closed his book and stood up. "Lock up here now for an hour," he said.

I had found the picture I wanted. "This man looks familiar to me. I'm trying to remember his boat."

He came over and looked at the picture. "Him? He had no boat. Look, he is in this picture, that one, that one, lots of them. No, he worked for me."

"That's funny. I could have sworn. Haggerty? Taggerty?"

"So! Maybe you did know him. Taggart. Sam Taggart. Yes, now I remember, he was in Florida maybe. He spoke of Florida. Yes. He worked for me here. Find the fish pretty good. Handled a boat too fancy, roar in here too fast, showing off. Hard fellow to control. But the people liked him. They would ask for him first. Maybe once he owned a boat, not when he was here. Maybe in Florida he owned a boat."

"That must be it."

He put his hand out. "My name is Heintz. You want some nice fishing, it's a good time for it now, and I reserve you a good boat, eh?"

"I'll think it over. McGee is my name."

"Five hundred pesos all day. The hotel packs lunch, Mr. McGee. A big man like you can catch a big fish, eh?"

"I can't imagine how Taggart happened to come work here. Is he still around?"

"No. He hasn't worked for me a long time. He took over a private boat. He's gone now."

I sensed that one more question was going to be one

question too many. I went out with him and he locked the
office door. He gave me an abrupt nod and marched away,
and I climbed the steps back to the pool level. Nobody was
in the pool. The brown bodies looked as if a bomb had
exploded nearby. I climbed on up to the sun deck. I looked
at the sea glitter, and then looked at what I could see of the
pink house, near the crest of the small tropic slope beyond
the boat basin, just a small pink peak, an angle of wall, a
fragment of white slanting roof.

Sometimes, when things are coming together, when fragments start to fit, you can get the dangerous feeling of
confidence that you are hovering over the whole thing, like a
hawk, unseen, riding the lift of the wind. Like all other
stimulants, it is a perilous thing to rely on. It makes you
reckless. It can kill you.

That night, at dinner and in the bar afterwards, Nora was
strange. She wore a slate blue dress so beautifully fitted it
made her figure seem almost opulent. She was very gay and
funny and quick, and then she would get tears in her eyes
and try to hide them with hard little coughs of laughter. At
last, in the bar, the tears went too far, and when she saw she
could not stop them, she said a strangled goodnight and fled.
I did not stay long. I took a walk in the night. I thought of
ways things could be done, ways that seemed right and ways
that felt wrong. Slyness has no special logic. Sam had done
something wrong. Knowing the shape of his mistake could
help me. I took the problems to bed, and they followed me
down into sleep.

But sleep did not take hold. I got hung up on the edge of
it, caught there by something just below the threshold of my
senses, too vague to identify. I was an Indian, and somebody
was snapping twigs on the neighboring mountain. I have
learned to respect these indefinite warnings. Once upon a
time I had been stretched out on a rock ledge watching a
cabin. Without thought or hesitation, I had suddenly rolled
away into a thicket of scrub maple, then saw the stain of
bright lead appear on the rock, heard the faraway smack of
the rifle, the banshee ricochet. We know that in deep hypno-
sis a good subject can hear and identify sounds far below his
normal threshold of hearing. Perhaps a customary state of
caution is a form of autohypnosis, and, without realizing it or
remembering it, I had heard the remote snickety-click-clack

of the oiled bolt as the man had readied himself to kill me.

I got up, barefoot on cool tile, and made a soundless circuit of the room and stopped at the interconnecting door and, holding my breath, heard the faint sound that was disturbing me, a tiny little smothered keening, the small frail noise of the agony of the heart.

I put my robe on and tried the door. It opened soundlessly into the other darkness of her room.

"Nora?" I said in a half whisper, so as not to alarm her. The answer was a hiccuping sob. I felt my way to her bed, touched a shoulder, thin and heated and shivering under silk. I sat with her. I stroked the lean firm back. She was down there in a swamp of tears and despair, where I could not reach her. Much of lust is a process of self delusion. If I stretched out with her, could I hold her more securely, could I make her feel less alone? If I gathered all this straining misery into my arms, tucked the hot fierce salty face into my throat, gave her someone to cling to in the night? These caresses were merely for comfort, were they not? They had absolutely nothing to do with the spectacular legs, and the clover-grass scent of her hair, and her lovely proud walk. This was just my friend Nora. And if all this began to turn into anything else, I had the character to walk away from it, didn't I? And certainly she could sense that seduction was the furthest thing from my mind, wasn't it?

But there was one place to stop, and then the gamble of waiting just a little longer, and just a little longer. She had long since stopped crying. Then another stopping place passed, and beyond that there was a slope too steep for stopping, a slope that tilted it all into a headlong run. After the peak of it for her, she said something blurred and murmurous, something I could not catch, and fell almost at once into a heavy, boneless, purring sleep.

Back in my own bed I said surly things to jackass McGee about taking rude advantage of the vulnerable, about being a restless greedy animal, about piling more complication on the shoulders of somebody who had enough trouble. I tried to tell myself this was no green kid. This was a mature, spirited, sensitive, successful woman, and grown up enough to do her own accepting and rejecting. But the intense wanting had come almost without warning, and together we had been more complete than I could have possibly guessed. Anxiety makes dreams all too vivid. In one that woke me up, I was in a small secret room, hot and murky as a steam bath, with a red battle lantern set into the ceiling. There was something there I did not want to find, but I had to look for it, knowing I was doomed if I could find it. I opened dozens of drawers and cupboards and they were all empty. I opened the last drawer, a great long low heavy drawer, and in there, wearing tall red shoes, were the severed glorious legs, side by side. As I stared at them, I knew the one with the knife was directly behind me, waiting for me to turn. I turned slowly, and Sam was grinning down at me out of his chopped face, and I lurched sweating up out of sleep.

At nine-thirty, showered and dressed, I wondered if I should knock at her door. I decided against it and went to the dining room. Eduardo said she had not yet arrived. Just as I finished the papaya, I glanced up and saw her approaching the table, walking with a slightly constricted demureness, her head a little on the side, her smile crooked. She wore dark green bermudas and a green and white striped blouse. I stood up for her, and Eduardo hurried to hold the chair for her. A flush darkened her face as she looked at me with eyes vast, dark and quizzical and said, "Good morning, darling."

"Good morning." Eduardo took her order. She ordered a huge breakfast. When he went away, I leaned toward her and lowered my voice and said, "Nora, all I want to say. . . ."

She leaned and reached across the small table very quickly and put two fingers against my lips, stopping what I had rehearsed saying to her. "You don't want to say anything, Trav. There isn't anything you have to say."

"Are you sure of that?"

"I know things. I know we are very fond of each other. And I know that words don't do any good. Words fit people into categories, whether they belong there or not. Then they have to keep explaining themselves. It was a lovely and beautiful accident, and I cherish it. Is that enough?"

"Yes," I said, "But I just wanted you to know that. . . ."

"Hush now."

There is no man so assured that he cannot be made to feel slightly oafish if a subtle and complex woman puts her mind to it. She wanted no sex lectures from Father McGee, no apologies, no explanations, no resolutions for the future. They have an awesome talent for the practical, for the acceptance of the inescapable, for almost instantaneous adjustment.

During our sun time and swim after breakfast, no sensitive observer could have been left in doubt about our relationship. She was not obvious about it. She merely related herself to me in an entirely different way, with a dark adoration of Mediterranean eyes, hanging on my every word in a way that turned me pontifical, making small affections, walking in a changed way for me, posing herself for me, her voice slower and heavier and furrier. She was focused on me like a burning glass in the sun. I was surrounded by her, and though the talk was never personal, never intimate, never explicit, we were carrying on a second dialogue all the time, in words unsaid. And when we went back to the rooms, she came to me sun-hot, eyes heavy and blurred, lips swollen and barely moving as she murmured, "No accident this time."

Later, when once again I succumbed to the dreadful compulsion to try to explain us to each other, she stopped me with fingertips on my lips. Hers was the better wisdom. Merely accept what had come to us. The emotional involvement was there, making it good. We were using each other as people, not as handy devices, and by making so forthright an advance, she had so evenly divided any guilt or blame, made herself an accomplice. I knew without being told that henceforth the aggressor role was mine. She had made her statement of acceptance, in a way more telling than words could have been. In her acceptance, I was in a surrogate role, which had a slightly unpleasant connotation. But, because we would not talk about it, it could remain slight, and thus not bruise male vanity.

Bed is dangerous country. The physical act is the least chancy part of it, requiring only health, maturity, and a reasonable consideration. It is the emotional interaction that makes it mysterious and perilous, turns it into something that mankind finds so endlessly interesting. Perhaps it is this simple. If, through the physical act, you are affirming emotions you believe in, then bed is cleansing, heartening, strengthening. But if the emotional context is greed, or the need for domination, or the yen to humiliate, or just the shallow desire to receive a pleasurable sensation, then bed diminishes, coarsens and deforms. The complicating factor is the great talent of the human animal to place a noble tag on ignoble emotions, intellectualizing something out of nothing, but the emotions are not deceived. They detect emptiness. Men use the available emptiness of the sun bunnies and call it a healthy release, and by so doing, over a period of time, reduce each other to a spiritless vulgarity. I wanted Nora for the sake of Nora, and her response was affectionate, joyous, and weighted with a sturdy practicality. She was saying, in effect, "Let's not talk about what it means until we know what it means. But it means something, or it wouldn't be like this."

While she was dressing for lunch, I tõld her I would see her in the lobby. I had noticed that Senor Arista was usually at his desk in the small area behind the registration desk during the hour before lunch.

I leaned on the registration desk and said, "This is a fine place, Mr. Arista."

He smiled carefully. "So glad you like it, sir."

"No complaints. Say, I was wondering about land around here. Like on the knoll over there where those houses are. Is it expensive?"

He got up and came over to the counter. "The land itself, by the square meter, is not too dear. But you see, the big expense is in construction. Skilled labor has to be brought in, as well as all the materials. And, of course, it is very awkward for a tourist to purchase land. One must have a change of status, to resident or immigrant. Are you really interested, sir?"

"Well . . . enough to want to talk to somebody about it."

"All that land to the south of the hotel, approximately two miles and half a mile deep, is owned by the same syndicate which established the hotel, sir." He got a card out of his desk and brought it to me. "This man, Senor Altavera, handles these matters for the group. This is his Mexico City office. The way it is handled here, there is the one road that winds up the hill, and the present houses, six of them only, are on that road, and they are connected with the hotel water and electricity. It would be a case of extending the road and the utilities, and there would be added charges for that, of course. But if you are genuinely interested . . ."

"Maybe you could give me some kind of an estimate of what the average house and land and so on would cost in dollars, total."

"I would estimate . . . let us say a three bedroom house, with appropriate servant quarters, walled garden, a small swimming pool, all modern fixtures and conveniences, I would say that for everything, it would be about one hundred thousand American dollars. One must use the architect the syndicate recommends, and build to certain standards of quality and size. I suspect that the same kind of land in the United States, and an equivalent house, would be perhaps as much as half again that cost."

"With use of the boat basin?"

"Of course, sir. And if one were to close the house for a time, an arrangement can be made with the hotel for care of the grounds, an airing of the house from time to time."

"There are five houses now?"

"Six."

"What kind of neighbors would I have?"

Arista looked slightly pained. "There is one United States citizen, a gentleman from the television industry. He is not in residence at this time, sir. And one Swiss citizen, quite an elderly man. The others are Mexican. It is not . . . a neighborhood in the social sense, sir. They are here for purposes of total privacy. You understand, of course."

"Of course. I wonder if any of the existing houses are for sale."

He hesitated, bit his lip. "Perhaps one that would be far more than the figure I . . . Excuse me. It is not at all definite. Really, that is all not a part of my duties. You should contact Senor Altavera on these matters. I am, of course, anxious that the property should be developed. It eases certain overhead expenses for the hotel operation, and it improves the hotel business."

"How about the local supply of people to work for you? Cook, gardeners, maids and so on?"

"Oh, these people are most difficult, sir. They are a constant trial. They learn well, and they have energy, but they have a fierce independence. Perhaps that is true of all peoples who are accustomed to make a living from the sea. They can give great loyalty, but they are very quick to take offense. And then they merely fail to come to work, and one must go in search of them. They are strong, as perhaps you have observed, and well formed. But they have many superstitions. It is one of my greatest problems, sir. It is not satisfactory to import help to this place because the local persons make them unhappy and they go away. Excuse me, it is not entirely black. With patience and understanding, these things can be managed." He smiled wanly. "One must be patient and understanding. When angered, these people can be very violent. At times there is murder done in the village, but somehow no one knows anything about it. Everyone is totally ignorant. I should say that for the people who own houses here, it is easier to have servants from the outside. They live at the houses and are in less contact with the village. We at the hotel are more at the mercy of the village."

Out of the corner of my eye I saw Nora approaching and I thanked him for all the information. He was wary, slightly skeptical, but willing to cooperate. I did not look like a man who would put up a hundred thousand dollar house in such a remote place, but he had learned not to judge Americans by looks. My woman was smartly dressed. The reservations had been made out of Los Angeles. I had the deep tan shared by the laboring classes and the leisure classes. It was best to be patient and polite. I guessed that compared to the size of the investment, La Casa Encantada was not yet showing a profit. The syndicate people might be slightly restive.

I followed Nora into the dining room, smugly and comfortably aware of the sleek flexing of elegant calves, taut swing of round hips under the linen skirt, the valuable slenderness of her waist. Possession always seems enhanced in public places, when the eyes of strangers follow the look of your woman, in secret speculation. She handled herself with the habitual grace of a model, and when I sat opposite her at our small table, her dark eyes were alight with our conspiratorial secrets, her mouth set in a different contour than on other days. The long days of strain, compression, despair had been eased for her. She had reached her breaking point and had endured through it and beyond it. Now her mouth was softened, personal, intimate—but still spiced with a small wryness, an awareness of the irony of our new relationship to each other.

ten

THE VILLAGE of Puerto Altamura lay steaming in siesta, insects keening of heat, the birds making small complaints in the dusty trees of the square, brown dogs puddled in shady dust, vendors asleep in their stalls.

The Cantina Tres Panchos was down the side street toward the sea, a few doors from the square. Three male heads were painted on the sign over the dark doorway, a crude drawing with garish colors, their mouths open in song. We went in, blinded by the change from bright sunlight to gloom. It was a bare, oblong room, about eighteen feet wide and thirty feet deep. There were two doors in the back wall. Between the two doors was an aged and silent juke box, dating from the pre-plastics era when they made them of wood and gave them a reasonably pleasing design. The walls were plaster, yellow-tan, streaked and blotched with mildew, pocked with marks of old violences. Calendar girls had been taped to the walls, frozen there in ancient provocative predicaments, caught halfway over barbed wire fences, caught on windy street corners with the leash of the poodle wrapped about one improbable ankle, caught on teetering ladders, caught midway in a fall into a swimming pool—all of them wearing precisely the same rueful, broad, inviting smile. The floor was of worn, scarred, uneven boards, the most recent green coat worn away in places, showing earlier coats of brown and grey and dark red. The bar was on the right, a tall scarred bar of dark wood, ornately carved. The brass rail was polished to a flawless brightness. The bartender was hunched over the far end of the bar, reading a newspaper. The chairs and tables were on the left. They were of the drugstore style of long ago, of sheet metal and twisted wire. The sole customer was at a table at the rear, sleeping with his head on the table, next to his straw hat. The hot still air was flavored with stale spilled beer, perfume, sweat and spiced cooking. I put Nora

112

at a table near the doorway and went over to the bar. The bartender had a flat, broad, brown, impassive face, tiny hooded eyes, and a huge sweep of curved black mustache. In too loud and too contentious a voice I ordered a beer, a Carta Blanca, for Nora, and a tequila añejo for myself. The imitation of drunk is nearly always overdone. To be persuasive, merely let the lower half of your face go slack, and when you want to look at anything, move your whole head instead of just your eyes. Walk slowly and carefully, and speak loudly, slowly and distinctly.

I went back to the table. In a little while the bartender brought the order over, bringing a salt shaker and wedge of lemon with my shot glass of tequila. In slow motion I took a wad of pesos out of my shirt pocket, separated a bill and put it on the table. He made change out of his pocket and picked it up. He went away. I left the change there. I had told Nora how to act, told her to sit unsmiling and look everywhere except at me.

I heard the clatter of heels. A girl came down the stairs in back and came out of the left doorway, a narrow, big-eyed girl with her dark hair bleached a strange shade of dull red. She wore an orange blouse and a blue skirt and carried a big red purse. She stared at us and went to the bar and had a brief and inaudible conversation with the bartender, and then went out into the sunlight, with one more glance at us, walking with a great deal of rolling and twitching. I hoped it wasn't Felicia. The girl had a look of brash impenetrable stupidity.

I signaled the bartender and pointed to my empty glass. Nora's beer was half gone. He brought me a shot and another wedge of lemon, took more money from the change on the table.

On cue, Nora said in a voice of dreadful clarity, "Do you really need that?"

"Shut up," I said. I sprinkled the salt on the back of my hand, the one in which I held the wedge of lemon. I picked up the shot glass in the other hand. One, two, three. Salt, tequila, lemon.

"Did you really need that?"

"Shut up."

She got up and hurried out. I sat there stupidly, and then I got up and lumbered after her. I left my change on the table.

"Hey!" I yelled. "Hey!"

She kept walking swiftly. I broke into a heavy run and caught up with her as she was walking through the square. I took her arm and she yanked it away and kept walking, toward the hotel, her chin high. I stood and watched her, and then caught up with her again.

When we were well beyond the village she looked behind us and then looked at me with a little nervous grin and said, "Did I do it right?"

"Perfectly."

"I still don't get the point."

"Credentials. I'm the big drunken Americano who's having trouble with his woman. I went away and left my money. When I go into town tonight, they'll have me all cased. I'll be the kind of a pigeon they can understand. Ready for plucking. I'll have a lot of friends when I go in there tonight."

I arrived at the cantina at about eight-thirty. The tables were full, the bar was crowded, the juke box was blasting. The room was lighted by two gasoline lanterns, rigged with some kind of heavy orange glass, casting a weird and lurid light. Most of the customers were men. There were a couple of fat women with the groups at the tables, and there were four girls in circulation, the one with the red hair and three others. A sparrowy withered little whitehaired man was the table waiter. My bartender was still on duty. There was a diminution of the dozen loud conversations as I came in. They made a small space for me at the bar. The bartender came at once and placed the forgotten change in front of me. He stared at me without expression. I carefully divided it into two equal amounts and pushed half of it across to him. He gave me a big white smile, and, with suitable ceremony, gave me a free tequila. We were closely watched. He made explanation to all, of which I did not understand a word, and the room slowly came back to the full decibel level I had heard as I walked in. I looked no more and no less drunk than before. My only change was a constant happy uncomprehending smile.

It took them about ten minutes to rig the first gambit. She edged in beside me, shoving the others to make room for herself, a chubby, bosomy little girl with a merry face, a white streak dyed in her curly black hair, a careless and abundant use of lipstick. "Allo," she said. "Allo."

I pointed at my glass and pointed at her and she bobbed

her head and gave the bartender her order. When it came I
pointed to myself and said, "Trav."

"Ah. Trrav. Si."

I stabbed her in the wishbone with a heavy finger and
looked inquisitive.

"Rosita," she said, and laughed as if we had made wonderful jokes.

"Speak English, Rosita."

"Af, no puedo, Trrav. Lo siento mucho, pero...."

I smiled at her, took her by the shoulders and turned her
away and gave her a little pat, then filled up the space at the
bar, my back to her. When I glanced back at her, she was
giving me a thoughtful look. I watched her make her slow
way through the crowded room and finally edge in near the
wall and bend over and whisper to a girl who sat with three
men. I could not see her very distinctly in the odd light, but
I saw her look toward me, shake her head and look away.
Rosita made her way back to the other end of the bar. She
beckoned to the bartender. He leaned over and she spoke to
him. He gave her a brief nod. A few minutes later he made
his way to the girl at the table and bent over her and
whispered to her. She shook her head. He said some more.
She shrugged and got up. A man at the table yanked her
back down into the chair. She sprang up at once. The man
lunged at her and the bartender gave him a solid thump on
the side of the head. There was a moment of silence, and
then all the talk started again, over the persistent sound of the
rrrrock and rrrroll. I saw the girl making her way in my
direction, and I saw that she was what they call *muy guapa*.
She wore an orange shift, barely knee length slit at both sides.
She was quite dark, and she was big. Her dark hair was
braided, pulled tight, coiled into a little shining turret on top
of her head. Her jaw was squared off, her neck long, her
mouth broad and heavy, her eyes tilted, full of an Indio
glitter. Her bare arms were smooth and brown, slightly
heavy. The shift made alternate diagonal wrinkles as she
walked, from thrust of breast to round heavy hip. She came
toward me with a challenging arrogance, the easy slowness of
a lioness. She was not pretty. She was merely strong, savage,
confident . . . and *muy guapa*.

Just as she reached me, there was a disturbance behind her,
shouts of warning, a shift and tumble of chairs. The bar
customers scattered, leaving the two of us alone in the empti-

ness. She turned her back to the bar, standing beside me. The man who had been thumped in the head crouched six or eight feet from us. He was young, and his face was tense and sweaty, his eyes so narrowed they looked closed. He held the knife about ten inches from the floor, blade parallel to the floor, winking orange in the light. He swung it slowly back and forth, the muscles of his thin arm writhing.

The bartender gave a sharp command. The young man bared his teeth and, looking at my belt buckle, told me exactly what he was going to do to me. I didn't understand the language, but I knew what he said.

The girl made a lazy sound at him, a brief husky message, like a sleepy spit. She stood with an elbow hooked on the bar behind her, her rich body indolently curved. Whatever she said, in that silence between records, was like a blow in the face to him. He seemed to soften. He sobbed, and, forgetting all skill, lunged forward, clumsily hooking the knife up toward her belly. I snapped my right hand down on his wrist, brought my left hand up hard, under his elbow, twisting his arm down and under, giving an extra leverage to his lunge that sent him by her in a long running fall into the tables and people as the knife clattered at her feet. I swear that she did not make the slightest move until she bent and picked the knife up. The next record started. The man thrashed around. People shouted. His friends got him, one by each arm, and frog-marched him out. He bucked and struggled, crying, the tears running down his face.

As they reached the doorway, the girl swung the knife back and yelled "*Cuidado, hombres!*" They gave her a startled look and dived into the night. She hurled the knife and it stuck deep into the wooden door frame. The populace whistled and cheered and stomped. A cautious hand reached in out of the night and wrenched the knife out of the wood and took it away.

She leaned on the bar again and turned toward me, a deep, dark, terrible amusement in her eyes, and in a clumsy accent, but a total clarity, said, "So what else is new?"

Then we were both laughing helplessly, and they applauded that too. She staggered and caught my arm for support, the tears squeezing out of her eyes. I bought her a drink. When we had stopped gasping, I said, "He would have killed you."

"He? No! He would stop. So close, maybe." She held up

thumb and finger, a quarter inch apart. "Or cut a little small bit."

"You are sure?"

She shrugged big shoulders. "Maybe."

"You didn't move."

"It is . . ." she frowned, "how you say it. Proud. I am not proud to run and fright from such a one. Ai, you are quick for so big a one. You can think he cuts me, no? How could you tell? Maybe this time he does. I say him a bad word. Very bad. Everybody hear it. Proud for him too. You unnerstan?"

"Yes."

She spread that big mouth in a warm approving grin. "Thank you for so brave, mister. Rosita say one man here wants a girl speaking English, but I say no. Then I say yes. Now I am glad. Okay?"

"Okay. So am I. What's your name?"

"Felicia."

"I am Trav."

She tilted her head slightly, a small memory nudging her perhaps. "So. Trrav?"

"No, dear. Trav. Trav."

"Trav? I say it right?"

"Just right, dear. Another drink?"

"Yes, please. You like some dancing maybe? Tweest?"

"No thanks."

"Okay here? Or a table is better?"

"Okay here, Felicia."

"Good!" Over the rim of her glass she looked at me with approving speculation. This was no wan foolish heartbroken village girl. She had a coarse, indomitable vitality, a challenging sexual impact. "You like the hotel?"

"It's a nice place."

"I was there. Kitchen work. Not any more."

"Hard work?"

"Not so much. But every day the same. You unnerstan?"

"Sure."

She leaned closer, breath heating my chin. "I like you, Trrav. You unnerstan that too?"

I looked down into the dark face, the soft-coarse pore texture, the unreadable darkness of her eyes. False jewels twinkled in her pierced ears. "I understand."

With a twisting and eloquent lift of her head she managed

to convey the idea of a place of refuge for us on the floor above. "You want to make some love with Felicia, Trrav? Two hundred pesos. Especial for you, uh? Much better than your skinny woman at the hotel, uh? I do this sometimes, only. When I like."

"Okay, dear."

She nodded, biting her lip. "What we do, you stay here ten minute, okay?" She was leaning close to me, leaning against me to be heard over the uproar. "Go out, go to the left, that way. Go beside this place to the back. To stairs. Up stairs is a door, unlock. Go in. Count three doors inside. One, two, three. Okay? It is number three door, mine." She dragged her fingernails down the back of my hand, squeezed her eyes at me, and then went away in that lazy, swaying, hip-rolling walk. She stopped at tables, talked to people, kept moving, and disappeared into the left hand doorway. I knew her departure had not gone unobserved. I hunched over the bar. I had the feeling that eight out of every ten people in that room knew how soon I would leave and where I was going. After a while I settled up, left a generous tip for the mustache and departed.

The alley beside the building was so narrow, my shoulders nearly brushed the side walls. There was a fetid smell in the narrow space. I stepped in something wet. After about twenty feet, it opened out into a small courtyard. I waited and listened. The noise from inside the place muffled the sound of anybody who might want to try something cute. The courtyard was littered with papers and trash. The stairway was open, with no guard rail. It creaked and sagged alarmingly as I went up it, brushing the side of the building with my fingertips. Mist had come with the night, haloing the few faint lights I could see.

I was careful about the door. Always be careful about doors. They can be the handiest surprise packages around. Do not carry your head inside just where it is expected to be, or at a predictable velocity. There was a clackety latch, the kind you push down with your thumb. It opened inward. I stayed against it as it opened, then moved swiftly sideways to flatten against the corridor wall. There was no sound close by that I could detect over the louder din from the room underfoot. No movement in the narrowing light as the door creaked slowly shut. When it was shut I had only a faint memory of the corridor. The blackness was total, except for a faint line of light ten feet or so away, close to the floor. I used my lighter, shading it with my other hand to keep from dazzling myself. One, two, three, with the thread of light under hers. It was the same kind of latch. I thrust it open abruptly and went in swiftly, and at an angle, giving her a dreadful start. She spun from her mirror, eyes and mouth wide.

I closed the door, saw a bolt lock and thumbed it over. With a definite effort I took my eyes from her and inventoried her small room. She had two fiberboard wardrobes overstuffed with bright clothing. She had one window, curtained with a heavy green fabric, a wash stand with pitcher and bowl, a dressing table fashioned of boards across crates, partially disguised with fringed green fabric, and loaded with a vast array of lotions, cosmetics, jars, perfumes. There were two kerosene lamps, one at either end of the dressing table, casting an even yellowish glow. She had a nylon rug designed to imitate a leopard skin, a tin kitchen stool in front of the dressing table, a stained old upholstered chair near the window, with stacks of comic books in the corner nearby, a big sagging old iron bedstead painted hospital white, with lidded chamberpot underneath it, and she had the walls covered with pictures, all of them taped there. Jesus and Mary and Elvis, sunsets and madonnas and pinups, Mexican movie stars, fashion drawings clipped from magazines, sailboats and saints, Mr. Americas, kitty cats and sports cars, an astonishing, bewildering array from baseboard to ceiling, like some fantastic surrealistic wallpaper. The size of the room, no more than ten by twelve, made it all the more overpowering. There was a slant of corrugated metal roof overhead, radiating the remembered sun heat of the day. In the heated air was a strong scent of a dozen perfumes.

She stood up from the stool as I looked at her room, and tossed the hairbrush aside. The orange shift had been draped over the footboard of the iron bed. She had undone the braids and combed her hair out. It came below her shoulders. She was naked. She stood there for me, obviously and properly pleased with herself. Her body, a half shade lighter than her face, was broad and rich, rounded, firm and abundant, the slender waist flowing and widening into the smoothly powerful hips. *Muy guapa* and *muy* aware of it. She made me think of one of P. Gauguin's women, framed against the Macronesian jungle. She came smiling toward me, two steps to reach me, arms lifting. She looked puzzled when I caught her wrists, turned her gently, pushed her to sit on the edge of the bed, near the footboard.

God, they were noisy downstairs, thumping and yelping. I turned away from her, took a fifty dollar bill from my wallet, turned back with it and held it out to her. Her eyes widened, and a look of sullen Indio suspicion came over her face. This much money might mean that something highly unpleasant was required.

"What for?" she asked, glowering.

"All I want to do is talk about Sam Taggart."

She sat motionless for perhaps two seconds, then came at my face with such a blinding, savage speed that she nearly took both my eyes with those hooked talons, actually brushing the eyelashes of my right eye as I yanked my head back. She followed it up, groaning with her desire to destroy me with her hands. I have never tried to handle a more powerful woman, and the heat in the room made her sweaty and hard to hold. I twisted in time to take a hard smash of round knee against my thigh instead of in the groin. I got her wrists, but she wrenched one free and tore a line across my throat with her nails. She butted me solidly in the jaw with the top of her head, and then sank her teeth into the meat of my forearm, grinding away like a bulldog. That destroyed any vestige of chivalry. I chopped the side of her throat to loosen her bite, shoved her erect and hit her squarely on the chin with a short, chopping, overhand right. She fell into my arms and I heaved her back onto the bed. I found a pile of nylon stockings on the lower shelf of the sash stand. I knotted her wrists together with one, her ankles with another, then bent her slack knees and tied the wrists to the ankles with a third, leaving about ten inches of play. Then I looked at the lacerated arms which had made the whole procedure slightly messy. I wondered if girl bite was as dangerous as dog bite. There was a half-bottle of local gin on the floor by the comic books. Oso Negro it was called. Black bear. I poured it over the tooth holes, and clenched my teeth and said a few fervent words. I looked at my throat in her mirror, and rubbed some gin into that too. I tore away a piece of white sheeting and bound my arm and poured a little more gin on the bandage. Then I tried the gin. Battery acid, flavored with juniper. I picked my fifty dollars off the floor and put it in my shirt pocket with the pesos.

She began to moan and stir. She was on her right side. I sat on the bed near her, keeping a pillow handy. Her eyes fluttered and opened, and remained dazed for about one second. Then they narrowed to an anthracite glitter, and her lips lifted away from her teeth. She had good leverage to use against the nylon, all the power of her legs thrusting down, all the power of arms and back pulling. She tried it. I do not know the breaking strength of a nylon stocking. Perhaps it is a thousand pounds. She closed her eyes, her face contorted with effort. Muscles and tendons bulged the smooth toffee hide. Her face bulged and darkened, and sweat made her body shine. She subsided, breathing hard, and then without warning, snapped at my hand like a dog. I yanked it away, and the white teeth clacked uncomfortably close to it. I saw her gather herself, and I picked the pillow up, and at the first note of the scream, I plopped it across her face and lay on it. She bucked and writhed and made muffled bleating noises. Slowly she quieted down. The instant I lifted the pillow, the scream started and I mashed it back down again, and held it until she was really still. When I lifted it she was unconscious, but I could see that she was breathing. In about three minutes her eyes opened again.

"What the hell is the matter with you, Felicia?"

"Sohn of a beech!"

"Just listen to me for God's sake! I wasn't trying to insult you."

"You wanna find Sam, uh?"

"No! I'm his friend, damn it. When I said my name, you had a look as though you heard it before. Travis McGee. From Florida. Maybe he said my name to you."

"His friend?" she said uncertainly.

"Yes."

"I remember he say the name one time," she said in a forlorn voice. Surprisingly the dark eyes filled, tears rolled. "I remember. So sorry, Trrav. Please tie me loose. Okay now."

"No tricks?"

"I swear by Jesus."

She had pulled the knots fantastically tight. I had to slice them with my pocket knife. She worked feeling back into her hands. As I started to get up, she caught my arm and pointed to her foot. She turned it so that the lamps shone more squarely on the broad brown instep. "See?" she said.

There were about a dozen little pale puckered scars on the top of her foot, roughly circular, smaller than dimes.

"What's that?"

"From the other ones who say questions about Sam." She pronounced it Sahm. "Where is he? Where he go? Where he hide. Sohns a beech!" She looked at me and firmed her jaw and thumped her chest with her knuckles. "Pain like hell, Trav. Not a cry from me. *Nunca palabra.* Fainting, yes. You know . . . proud."

"Who were they?"

She peered at my throat and made a hissing sound of concern. She slid off the bed and tugged me over to sit on the stool. She wiped my throat with something that stung, though not as badly as the gin, and put a Band Aid on the worst part of the gouge. When she unwrapped my arm, she said, *"Ai, como perra, verdad. Que feo!"* She had iodine. That too was less than the gin. She wrapped it neatly, taped the bandage in place.

"So sorry," she said.

"Put something on, Felicia."

"Eh?"

"I want to talk. Put on a robe or something."

"Some love maybe? Then talk? No pesos."

"No love, Felicia. But thank you."

"The skinny woman, eh? But who can know?" She stared at me, then shrugged and went to one of the cardboard wardrobes and pulled out a very sheer pale blue hip-length wrap. Before she slipped into it, she dried her body with a towel, and slapped powder liberally on herself, using a big powder mitten, white streaks and patches against bronze-brown hide. She knotted the waist string, flung her long hair back with a toss of her head and sat in the upholstered chair.

"So?"

"Who were the men who hurt you?"

"Two of them, burning, burning with cigarette, Trrav. *Cubanos* I think. One with the good English. Then they want love. Hah!" She slapped her bare knee. "With this I finish love forever for one of them I think. Screaming, screaming. He say to other one, cut the bitch throat. But the one, the one with the English, say no. Help his friend into car. Go away. Leave me there, seven *kilometros* from here. I walk on this bad foot back to here."

"When did this happen, Felicia?"

"Perhaps five-six weeks. Sam gone then. Gone ... three days I think. One night in this room. My friend is Rodriguez, with the fish truck going to Los Mochis. Sam walked before the day was light. Rodriguez, stop for him at a place on the road. I fix that. Every man thinks he is gone by boat. He ..." She stopped and frowned. "Sam said come here?"

"In a way."

"How is that—in a way?"

I sat on the tin stool, arms propped on my knees, and debated telling her. It is so damn strange about the dead. Life is like a big ship, all lights and action and turmoil, chugging across a dark sea. You have to drop the dead ones over the side. An insignificant little splash, and the ship goes on. For them the ship stops at that instant. For me Sam was back there somewhere, further behind the ship every day. I could look back and think of all the others I knew, dropped all the way back to the horizon and beyond, and so much had changed since they were gone they wouldn't know the people aboard, know the new rules of the deck games. The voyage saddens as you lose them. You wish they could see how things are. You know that inevitably they'll drop you over the side, you and everyone you have loved and known, little consecutive splashes in the silent sea, while the ship maintains its unknown course. Dropping Sam over had been just a little more memorable for Nora than for me. It would stay with her a little longer, perhaps. But I did not know how it would react on this one. He would be dropped over the side in this next instant. It would be brand new for her.

"Sam is dead," I told her.

She sat bolt upright and stared at me. "No," she whispered.

"Somebody followed him to Florida and killed him."

She made a gargoyle mask, the stage mask of tragedy, and it would have been laughable had it not been so obviously a dry agony. She thrust herself from the chair, bending, hugging herself, passed me in a stumbling run to throw herself face down on the iron bed, gasping and grinding into the bunched pillow. The rear of the little blue wrap was up around her waist, exposing the smooth brown slope of buttocks. She writhed and strangled and kicked like a child in tantrum. I went and sat on the bed near her. At my first tentative pat of comfort on her shoulder, she made a twisting convulsive leap at me, pulled me down in the strong warm

circle of her arms, making a great WhooHaw, WhooHaw of
her sobbings into my neck. I wondered how many women
were going to hold me and cry for Sam. I endured that close
and humid anguish, perfume and hot flesh and the scent of
healthy girl. The storm was too intense to last, and as it
began to dwindle I realized that in her little shiftings, changing, holdings, she was beginning to involve herself in seduction, possibly deliberately, but more likely out of that strange
and primitive instinct which causes people to couple in bomb
shelters while air raids are in process. I firmly and quietly
untangled myself, tossed a towel over to her and went and sat
in the chair near the window. I looked down and saw that the
comic book on top of one of the stacks was an educational
epic in the Spanish language. I guessed that she would call it
Oliver Tweest.

Finally she sat up in weariness, put a pillow against the
bars of the headboard, hunched herself back and leaned
there, ankles crossed. She swabbed her face and eyes and
blew her nose, and sighed several times, her breath catching.

"He was a man," she said in a soft nostalgic voice. I sensed
that she had wept for him, and would not have to weep
again.

"How did you meet him?"

"I work in the kitchen there. I have seventeen years, no
English, just a dumb kid. He is a boat captain, like Mario
and Pedro. A little room he has there, not in the hotel. Near.
Men and boys are after me, you know, like the dogs walking
fast, tongue hanging out, so, follow the she? Sam chase them
away, move me into his room. Ai, such trouble. The padre,
my family, everyone. But to hell with them. We have love. I
work in the kitchen all that time. A year I guess. More. Then
he works for Senor Garcia. Big boat. Lives there in the big
house. No so much time for love, eh? Time for the *rubia* . . . how you say . . . blonde. Yes. Blonde bitch in the big
house. I work a little time more in the kitchen. They make
laughs at me. Screw them all, eh? I am waiting like a mouse
for when he wants love? Hell, no. I come here. Sam find me
out. He beats me. Four-five times. Change nothing. He wants
the *rubia,* I do what I like. Okay? More trouble from the
padre, my brothers, everybody. Bad words. *Puta.* I have
twenty years. By God I do what I want. Pretty good room,
eh? Not so hard work. Dancing, *copitas,* making love. Sam
come here sometimes. Give me pesos. I rip them in front of

the face. I hear things about the big house. Trouble. Danger. Then he come in the night to hide. Marks from fighting. He is here all day. I fix with Rodriguez. Sam say he will send much money to me one time, so I am here no more. Such a fool! This is good place I think. Many friends. Then two man give a ride in a pretty car. Out the road and then into the woods, burning, burning the foot. Where is Sam? Then you are here. Sam is dead. In Florida." She made one stifled sobbing sound.

"Who is that blonde? Is she still around?"

"She is a friend with Senor Garcia. It is a hard name for me. Heechin. A thing like that, I think."

"Hitchins?"

"I think so. Many fiestas in that house. Very rich man. Very sick now, I think."

"Is the blonde still there?"

"They say yes. I have not seen."

"Felicia, what was going on at Garcia's house?"

"Going on? Parties, drunk, bitch blondes. Who knows?"

"Did Sam say anything?"

"He say he keep what he earn. Some big thing he had, locked. He was sleeping, I try to look. Very very heavy. Big like so." She indicated an object about the size of a large suitcase. "Black metal," she said. "With a strap he fix to carry. Only a strong man like Sam can carry far."

"He got to Los Mochis?"

"Rodriguez say yes."

"You were willing to help him, to hide him here?"

She looked astonished. "How not? He is a man. No thing changes that, eh? I am wife for a time. This stupid girl pleased him good, eh? He . . . we have a strong love. It can not be for all my life, with such a one."

"He never told you anything about what went on at Garcia's house?"

"Oh yes. Talk, talk, talk. Persons coming and going in big cars and boats. *Mucho tumulto.* What is a word? Confusion. I do not listen so much to him, I think. When he is close I do not want all the talking. I say yes, yes, yes. He talks. Then soon I make him stop talking. I think *misterioso y peligroso* that house and those persons. No man from here ever works at that house. Just Sam."

She got up from the bed and padded over and got a nail

file and took it back to the bed and began working on her
nails, giving me a hooded glance from time to time. The
downstairs hubbub was vastly diminished.

"Is now late, I think, Trrav," she said. "You can stay, you
can go. I think those two man find Sam, eh?"

"Perhaps."

"Shoot him?"

"A knife."

She made the Mexican gesture, shaking her right hand as
though shaking water from her fingertips. "Ai, a knife is a
bad dying. Pobre Sam. You look for them?"

"Yes."

"Because you are a friend? Maybe you are a clever man,
eh? Maybe what you want is in that heavy box."

"The box is why he was killed."

"Maybe you send me some money instead of Sam, eh?"

"Maybe."

"Down stairs you make me think of Sam. So big. Dark
almost like me, but white, white, white, like milk where the
sun is not touching."

"Felicia, please don't tell anyone what we've talked about.
Don't tell anyone he's dead."

"Maybe only Rosita."

"No one. Please."

"Very hard for me," she said, and smiled a small smile. I
took the fifty, folded it into a small wad, laid it on my
thumbnail and snapped it over onto the bed. She fielded it
cleanly, spread it out, looked content. As one is prone to do
with animals, it was a temptation to anthropomorphize this
girl past her capacity, to attribute to her niceties of feeling
and emotion she could never sense, merely because she was
so alive, had such a marvelous body, had such savage eyes
and instincts. She was just a vain, childish, cantankerous
Mexican whore, shrewd and stupid, canny and lazy. She had
done all her mourning for Sam Taggart, and had enjoyed the
drama of it. She was not legend. She did not have a heart of
gold, or a heart of ice. She had a very ordinary animal heart,
bloody and violent, responsive to affection, quick in fury,
incapable of any kind of lasting loyalty. Sam had not made
her what she was today. I suspect she was headed for the
rooms over the Cantina Tres Panchos from the time she
could toddle. Perhaps villages fill their own quotas in myste-

rious ways, so many mayors, so many idiots, so many murderers, so many whores.

"Not even Rosita," I said.

"Okay, Trrav."

I stood up. "I may want to come back and ask more questions."

"Every night I am down there. I am not there, you wait a little time, eh?"

"Sure."

She yawned wide, unsmothered, white teeth gleaming in membranous red, pointed tongue upcurled, stretched her elbows high, fists close to her throat.

"Love me now," she said. "We sleep better, eh?"

"No thanks."

She pouted. "Felicia is ugly?"

"Felicia is very beautiful."

"Maybe you are not a man, eh?"

"Maybe not."

She shrugged. "I am sorry about the biting. Good night, Trrav. I like you very much."

I let myself out into the blackness of the corridor. Downstairs a single male voice was raised in drunken song, the words slurred. I hesitated when I reached the mouth of the narrow alley. The street was empty. There were no lights at night in the village. But I had the feeling I was observed from the darkness. The American spent a long time with Felicia. I walked in the middle of the dusty road. A warm damp wind blew in from the sea. When I reached the outskirts of the village I could see the hotel lights far ahead of me.

As I crossed the small empty lobby, Arista appeared out of the shadows, suave and immaculate. "Mister McGee?"

"Yes?"

"There was some trouble in the village tonight?"

"What do you mean?"

"Over a village girl?"

"Oh. Yes, a young fellow started waving a knife around and I knocked it out of his hand."

"And you were drinking?"

"You are beginning to puzzle me, Arista."

"Forgive me. I do not want you to be hurt, sir. It would be bad for our reputation here. Perhaps you were fortunate tonight. Those men are very deadly with knives. Forgive me, but it is not wise to ... to approach the girls in the Tres Panchos. There has been much violence there. People tell me things, and the story worried me, sir. I believe a girl named Felicia Novaro was involved."

"People tell you very complete things, I guess."

"Sir, she is a wild reckless girl. There is always trouble around her. She worked for me here. Her ... behavior was not good. She cannot be controlled. And ... that is a squalid place, is it not, sir?"

"It seemed very cheerful to me."

"Cheerful?" he said in a strained voice.

I clapped him on the shoulder. "Sure. Local color. Song and dance. Friendly natives. Salt of the earth. Pretty girls. Man, you couldn't keep me away from there. Goodnight, Senor Arista."

He stared at my arm. "You have been hurt?"

"Just chawed a little."

"B-Bitten? My God, by a dog?"

I gave him a nudge in the ribs, a dirty grin and an evil wink, and said, "Now you know better than that, pal." I went humming off to my room.

eleven

AS SOON as I turned my room lights on, Nora came out of the darkness of her room, through the open doorway, wearing a foamy yellow robe with a stiff white collar. She squinted at the light, and came toward me, barefoot, looking small and solemn and strangely young.

"You were gone so long I was getting.... What's wrong with your arm?"

"Nothing serious. It's a long story."

I held her in my arms. After a little while she pushed me away and looked up at me, wrinkling her nose. "Such strange smells. Alcohol, and kerosene and some kind of terrible cheap perfume. And smoke and sort of a cooking grease smell ... Darling, you are a veritable symphony of smells. You are truly nasty."

"It is, in some ways, a nasty story."

"I am *particularly* curious about the perfume, dear."

"First I need a shower."

She sat on the foot of my bed and said, primly, "I shall wait."

When I came out of the bathroom, the lights were out, and she was in my bed. When I got in, she moved into my arms and said, "Mmmm. Now you smell like sunshine and soap."

"This is quite a long story."

"Mmmmhmmm."

"When I got there, that bartender with the mustache presented me with the change I left on the table when.... Are you listening? Nora?"

"What? Oh sure. Go ahead."

"So I split it with him. That was a popular gesture. He bought me a free drink.... I'm not sure you're paying attention."

"What? Well ... I guess I'm not. Not at the moment.

129

Excuse me. My mind wanders. Let me know when you get to the part about the perfume."

"Well, the hell with it."

"Yes, dear. Yes, of course," she said comfortably.

After breakfast, Nora and I walked up the winding road past the houses on the knoll beyond the boat basin. It was a wide graveled road with some kind of binder in it to make it firm. The drainage system looked competent and adequate. The homes were elaborate, and for the most part they were well screened from the road by heavy plantings, beautifully cared for. Each was so set on the hillside as to give a striking view of the sea. Gardeners worked in some of the yards. There were entrance pillars at the private driveways. There were small name plates on the entrance pillars. I made mental note of the names. Martinez, Guerrero, Escutia, in that order, and then Huvermann—who had to be the Swiss by process of elimination. Arista had said the Californian was not in residence, and I could see, in a graveled area, a man carefully polishing a black Mercedes, and a swimming pool glinting a little further away. The next one was Boody. There was a chain across the drive. The last one was Garcia, the big pink one at the crest of the knoll. The grounds were walled. I made Nora walk more slowly. The wall, better than ten feet high, curved outward in a graceful concavity near the top. At the top, glinting in wicked festive colors in the sun, I could see the shards and spears of broken glass set into cement. Any trees which had stood near the wall on the outside had been cleared away. The wall was cream white in the morning light, following the contour of the land. It did not enclose a very large area, perhaps less than the area Garcia owned. The beauty of it obscured the fact that it was very business-like.

I noted another interesting detail. The wall and the big iron gates were set back from the road, and the private drive, with a high cement curbing, made a very abrupt curve just before it reached the gates. No one was going to be able to get up enough speed to smack their way through in anything less than a combat tank. A man moved into view and stared morosely at us through the bars of the spiked gate. He wore wrinkled khaki, a gun belt, an incongruous straw hat—one of those jaunty little narrow-brim cocoa straw things with a band of bright batik fabric. He had a black stubble of beard.

I found his appearance promising. Guard morale is one of the most difficult things in the world to maintain. A long time of guarding against no apparent danger is a corrosive boredom, and is usually reflected in the appearance of the guards. When they are smart and crisp and shining, they are likely to be very alert.

In a low voice I told Nora what to call out to him. She turned to him and in a clear, smiling voice, called out, *"Buenos dias!"*

He touched the brim of the hat and said, *"Buenuh dia."*

Beyond the far corner of the wall, at a wide turnaround area, the road ended. "He's a Cuban," I said to Nora. "I didn't think he would answer me if I tried it."

"How can you tell?"

"They speak just about the ugliest Spanish in the hemisphere. You hear the best in Mexico and Colombia. The Cubans leave the s endings off words. They use a lot of contractions. They make it kind of a guttural tongue. A friend of mine said once that they sound as if they were trying to speak Spanish with a mouth full of macaroons."

We went back down the road. The guard looked out at us again, almost wistfully. He looked as if he wanted to walk down the road, go to the village and see how much *pulque* he could drink. But he had to hang around the gate in all the morning silence, listening to the bugs and birds, counting the slow hours of his tour of duty.

We were around a curve and out of sight of the Garcia place when we came to the Boody house. I stood by the chain and looked in. The hotel people weren't doing too good a job on maintaining the grounds. It looked scraggly. The drive needed edging. I stepped over the chain and said, "Let's take a look."

She looked a little alarmed, but came with me. It was a pale blue house, with areas of brick painted white. It was shuttered. Within the next year it was going to need some more paint. The pool area behind the house was, despite an unkempt air, a nymphet's dream of Hollywood. A huge area was screened. The pool apron was on several levels, separated by planting areas. There was a bar area, a barbecue area, heavy chaises with the cushions stored away, a diving platform, a men's bathhouse and women's bathhouse with terribly cute symbols on the doors, weatherproof speakers fastened to palm boles, dozens of outdoor spots and floods, a couple of thatched tea houses, storage bins, big shade devices made of pipe, with fading canvas still lashed in place. The pool was empty, the screening torn in a few places, the bright paint peeling and fading. It all had a look of plaintive gayety, like an abandoned amusement park. The effect was doubled when I remembered what had bought this hideaway paradise. Arista had said Boody was in television. Thus the armpits, nasal passages and stomach acids of America had financed this unoccupied splendor. In an L shaped building beyond the pool plantings were garages and servants' quarters. There was one red jeep in residence. We made our comments in hushed tones.

I took a closer look at the rear of the main house. An inside hook on a pair of shutters lifted readily when I slid the knife blade in.

"Are you out of your damned mind?" Nora asked nervously.

"I'm just a delinquent at heart," I said. The windows behind the open shutters were aluminum awning windows, horizontal, with the screen on the inside. I closed the shutters and wedged them shut with a piece of twig, and continued my prowl.

"Do you want to get in there? Why?"

"Because it's next door to Garcia."

"Ask a stupid question," she said.

It finally turned out that the front door was the vulnerable place. The big brass fittings were more decorative than practical. The sturdy plastic of a gasoline credit card slid the latch out of the recess in the frame. I invited Nora in. She shrugged and came in. Bright spots of light came through openings in the shutters. The big living room was persuasively vulgar, white rugs, white art-movie furniture, and some big oil portraits on the wall in kodachrome technique, of a jowly man looking imperious, a pretty dark-haired woman with a look of strain around her mouth, and two little girls in pink sitting on an upholstered bench with their arms around each other. The Clan Boody. There was a white concert grand piano, and as I passed it I ran a fingernail down the keys.

Nora started violently and said, "My God! Don't do that."

The basic plan of the house was pleasant. Big bedrooms, playrooms, studio, library, big kitchen and service area. It was moist and hot and still inside the house, with a smell of damp and mildew. The immediate procedure was to set up rapid access. She watched me rig the door at the side, a solid door opening onto the pool area from the bedroom wing. It was locked by an inside latch, and the aluminum screen door beyond it was latched. I unlocked them both. I found a piece of cord in the kitchen and tied the screen door shut. Anyone checking the house would find it firm. But if I wanted to come in in a hurry, all I had to do was yank hard enough to break the cord, then latch both doors behind me.

"I don't understand you," Nora whispered.

"The gopher acts like a very sassy and fearless beast, honey. But he is all coward. He spends a lot of time and labor preparing escape tunnels he hardly ever gets to use. But sometimes he needs one, and that makes him feel real sassy. Just settle down. You saw me try the lights and the water. If they were coming back in a hurry, they'd have them turned on, and the hotel would get the grounds in better shape and fill the pool and so on. Now let's check a couple of things."

I used my lighter to look at the cans in the storage pantry. "See, dear? Plenty of canned fruit juices. And stuff that doesn't taste too bad cold—beans, beef stew, chili. This is an advance base, next to unfriendly territory. Maybe we never use it."

She followed me to the library, staying very close to me, saying, "It just makes me so damned nervous, Trav." When I sat at the desk and began to look through the papers in the middle drawer, she sat on the edge of a straight chair, turning her head sharply from side to side as she heard imaginary noises.

"Claude and Eloise Boody," I said finally, "of Beverly Hills. Claude is Amity Productions. He is also Trans-Pacific Television Associates, and Clabo Studios, unless these are all obsolete letterheads."

"Can we leave now? Please?"

We went back out the front door. It locked behind us. She was a dozen feet in the lead all the way to the driveway chain, and she kept that lead until we were a hundred feet down the road. She slowed down then, and gave a huge lifting sigh of relief.

"I don't understand you, Trav."

"Carlos Menterez y Cruzada has or had a taste for the Yankee celebrity, show biz variety. He partied it up here. Boody would be a pretty good procurement agent. He lived next door. I wanted the California address. If things peter out here, it's another starting point."

"But still. . . ."

"The houses seem to have been done by the same architects. I wanted the feel of one of the houses, what to expect about the interior planning—materials, surfaces, lighting, changes of floor level. Garcia's is bigger and it will sure as hell be furnished differently, but I know a lot more about it now."

"But why should you. . . ."

"Tonight I'm going to pay an informal call."

She stopped and stared at me. "You can't!"

"It's the next step, honey. Over the wall, like Robin Hood."

"No, Trav. Please. You've been so careful about everything. . . ."

"Care and preparation can take you just so far, Nora. And then you have to make a move. Then you have to joggle the wasp nest. I'll be very very careful."

Her eyes filled. "I couldn't stand losing you too."

"Not a chance of it. Never fear."

I told her too early in the day. It gave her a bad day. She got very broody and upset. She toyed with her food. I knew what was happening to her. She was shifting to a new basis for her emotional survival. Maybe it was good, maybe it was bad. I couldn't judge her. The steam was going out of her. She was identifying more closely with what we were becoming to each other. God knows it could not have been a substitute for Sam. But they set the mad ones to weaving baskets, and it seems to help. Maybe the baskets become important—when all you have is a basket.

I left her by the pool in the afternoon while I walked into town and made some random purchases here and there. I had become some kind of a minor celebrity. I could tell by the way the kids acted. They didn't hustle me for coins. They followed me in a small and solemn herd, about twenty feet behind me. At one corner two bravos were squatting on their heels. As I went by, one of them spat across my bows. I stopped and stared at the pair of them, at two lazy smiles. One of them unsheathed a great ugly toadstabber of a knife and began cleaning his nails. I began to feel like the tortured hero of a thousand westerns, the fast gun, the one everybody wants to try their luck against. On that almost deserted corner I had the feeling I was being watched by many more eyes than just the round ones of my pack of children. I remembered an old trick I had learned the hard way, from some marines. They had used combat knives. Unless I gave these characters something to think about, there was a chance they might keep challenging me, and get a little ugly.

I went smiling to the man with the knife and held out my hand and said, in my hideous Spanish, "*Su cuchillo, por favor. Por un momentito.*"

He hesitated and handed it over. It was just barely long enough. I stuck it into the side of the building, shed my shoes and socks, and then stood out in the dust with the knife, facing the pair of them. I held the very end of the haft in one fist, and the end of the blade in the other, edge up. Then I jumped over it like over a jump rope, forward and back. You have to be reasonably limber and agile, but there is a very simple trick to it. You appear to hold the knife in your fists, but actually only the middle finger overlaps it. Then at the peak of the jump you turn the blade down by extending the index and middle fingers of each hand. You hold the knife between those fingers. It gives you more jumping room, and you are jumping over the dull side. As you land you curl your fingers back into fists, and this gives the knife the half turn back and brings it blade upward. It is very hard to detect, and even after you know the trick of it, it takes practice.

I put socks and shoes back on and presented the knife to its owner with a flourish, saying, "*Gracias, amigo.*"

They looked at me without expression. The knife owner got slowly to his feet and moved away from the building. He held the knife as he thought I had held it and looked questioningly at me. I smiled and nodded. People very seldom cut themselves seriously. The hands release the knife instinctively. Some of the most agile ones can go over the blade side even when held in the fists. He looked dubiously at the blade, moistened his lips, gathered himself and tried it. The knife flew through the air. He landed on his rear with a roar of dismay. The bright blood speckled the dust, and the children howled with laughter. His friend was rolling in the dust, helpless with laughter. A crowd began to gather, and I went on my way. Puerto Altamura was going to have an epidemic of gashed feet. I felt like a cruel bastard. I looked back. One of the children had acquired a knife and was gathering himself to make a try.

I roared at them and raced back. I took the knife from the kid. Slowly and carefully I showed them all the trick. Then the laughter was greater than ever. Men began practicing. Then all sound stopped and I saw the first man limping toward me, holding the big knife low. I had made a fool of him. It was a point of honor. He had the splendid idea of gutting me like a fish. I smiled and held my hand out to him and took a chance on saying, *"Su cuchillo, por favor."*

He stopped the advance and glowered at me. Then the corner of his mouth twisted. Then he grinned foolishly. And then he began to laugh. Everybody laughed. Arm in arm, in the midst of a pack of his buddies, we went across the square and into the Cantina Tres Panchos, and I bought a drink for the group. The hubbub was heard upstairs, and two of the girls came down, the one with dyed red hair Nora and I had seen, and Felicia. Felicia was a fantastic vision in purple stretch pants, a white canvas halter, and golden slippers with four inch heels. My new friend was hobbling about leaving bloody footprints on the floor. The kids were clotted in the doorway, staring in. All the men explained simultaneously to the girls, recounting the action with many gestures. One tried to demonstrate and gave himself a good slice on the bottom of a horny foot. The girls shrieked and got the two wounded over to a table and bound up their gashes. Felicia came over to me at the bar, and slipped an arm around my waist and hugged herself close to me. There was a small tentative silence and then it was accepted. I patted the taut purple fabric of a haunch and confirmed it. Somebody fed coins into the juke, and the narrow redhead began a solo twist. Felicia put her mouth close to my ear and said, "Goddam fool, you, Trrav. You get killed in my village one day."

When somebody led her off to dance, I gave Mustache enough money for another round for them all, and went off to finish my shopping. Mustache seemed to have become very fond of me. Maybe he hoped I'd come and jack up business during the slack hours every day.

After an after-dinner drink, Nora and I left the bar and went back to the rooms. She paced back and forth, complaining, while I improvised a grapnel. I had bought three monstrous shark hooks, some heavy wire and some cheap pliers. I bound the shanks of the hooks together to form a huge gang hook, using plenty of wire to make it firm and also give it a little extra weight. I had also purchased fifty feet of nylon cord that looked as if it would test out at about five hundred pounds breaking strength.

"If you insist on being an idiot, why go so early in the evening?"

"When people are moving around, a little extra noise doesn't mean too much."

"When people are moving around, where are you?"

"Watching them, dear. If everybody is asleep and all the lights are out, I can't find out anything, can I?"

"Do you expect to be invisible?"

"Practically, dear."

"How long will it take?"

"I haven't any idea."

"Honest to God, Trav, I don't see why...."

I put the pencil flashlight in my pocket and took her by the shoulders and shook her. "How did Sam look?"

The color seeped out from under her tan. "You cruel bastard," she whispered.

"How did he look?"

"My God, Trav! How can you...."

I shook her again. "Just say the word, honey. I'll put away my toys and we'll get into the sack. And then we'll go on back home anytime you say, and you can refund my split of all the expenses, and we'll forget the whole thing. Call it an interesting vacation. Call it anything you want. Or you can let me go ahead my way. It's your choice, Nora."

She moved away from me. She walked slowly to the other side of the room and turned and looked at me. Barely moving her lips she said, "Good luck tonight, darling."

"Thank you."

I had on dark slacks, a long sleeved dark blue shirt, dark canvas shoes. I had no identification on me. I had the silly bedroom gun in one trouser pocket, the pencil light and pocket knife in the other, the grapnel coiled around my waist. We turned the lights out. I opened the draperies and cautiously unhooked the screen, turned it and brought it into the room and stood it against the wall beside the window. I looked out, it was all clear. I turned back to her and held her and kissed her hungry nervous mouth. She felt exceptionally good in my arms, good enough so that I wished for a moment she had said the hell with it. Then I straddled the sill, turned, hung by my fingertips, kicked myself away from the side of the building and dropped. It was about nine feet down to soft earth. I had the right window marked by its relationship to a crooked tree. On my return, I would flip pebbles against the window to signal her. I would toss the line in and she would make it fast. If for any reason we could not anticipate, anyone had to come into the rooms, she would turn my shower on and close the bathroom door before answering the hall door.

She had the waiting. Maybe that was the hardest part.

twelve

IT WAS almost over before it began. It was almost over in one of the world's nastiest ways for McGee. I saw a man's body after it had happened to him that way, and it is one of my most persistent memories.

When I went up the road, the third of a moon was high enough to make the going easy. I stayed in the shadows. Halfway up I heard a car coming and saw lights and had all the time in the world to go down the slope on the sea side of the road and flatten out. It turned into the Escutia driveway, fifty feet before it got to where I was.

When I got to the Boody place, I stepped over the chain and went around to the side of the house opposite the swimming pool, and made my way to the Garcia wall through the Boody grounds. I stood by the wall a long time, listening, and heard nothing but the normal noises of the night, and the whining of mosquitoes looking for the meat of my neck.

After debating a moment, I decided to try a place where the top of the wall wasn't shadowed by the trees inside. I might be more visible, but I had that damned glass to fool with. I wanted the hooks to catch the inside edge of the wall. If they'd rounded it off, I'd have to try flying it into a tree. That made retrieving it more of a problem. I straightened the loops out and tossed the hooks over the wall. I heard them clink against the inside of the wall. I pulled them slowly, worrying about sawing the nylon against sharp glass. They caught, but when I put on a little pressure there was a tink of breaking glass, and a piece of glass and the hooks came back to me. After a third try, and more glass each time, I knew the wall was rounded off on the inside, another little touch of professionalism. I moved back away from the wall and moved along parallel to it, moving further away from the road, until I came to a tree I liked, growing on the inside. I held

139

the very end of the line in my left hand, the loops between thumb and finger, and swung the grapnel around my head a few times with my right hand and let it fly. It arched into the leaves with too much noise. I listened, then slowly pulled it tight. It was fast, and apparently on a good solid branch, because when I put my weight on it, there was only about a six-inch give. The angle of the line took it across my edge of the wall. At least it was out of the glass. I put my rubber soles against the white wall and walked up it, at an acute and unpleasant angle. The damned nylon was so thin it dug painfully into my hands. The concavity near the top was tricky, but I took a giant step and got one foot on the edge, and then the other, and pulled myself erect, wiggling my toes into areas between the shards of glass. Holding the line lightly for balance, I looked into the grounds. Off to my right I could see a faint light which I guessed was the gate light. I could see the lights of the main house almost dead ahead, between the leaves. I broke a few shards off, snubbing at them with the toe of my right shoe, and got myself a more balanced place to stand, then tried to yank the damned hooks free. They would not come free. All I did was make a horrid rustling in the leaves. I certainly could not go up such a thin line hand over hand to free it. As I decided it was hopeless, I gave a last despairing yank and it came free so unexpectedly that I did a comedy routine on top of the wall, my back arched, waving my arms wildly to keep from falling back outside.

When I had balance, I brought the grapnel up and fixed it firmly onto the outside corner of the wall at a place where the line lay between the sharpness of glass as it crossed the top of the wall. I lowered myself on the inside, and let myself down in the same way as I had climbed up. I knew I might want to find the line in one hell of a hurry. There were too many trees, and the wall was too featureless, the white of the line too invisible against it. Then I had an idea, and I fumbled around and found some soft moist earth and took it in both hands and made a big visible smear on the white wall. I knew I could find that in a hurry.

I started toward the house. I had not gone ten feet from the wall when I heard it. Something coming at me fast, with a little guttural sound of effort, a scrabble of nails skidding on the ground. It came into the silver of moonlight a dozen feet away, and made one more bound and launched itself up at me, a big black silent murderous Doberman. A killer dog is peculiarly horrible in the silence of the attack. A long time ago I sat with others on hard benches and listened to a limey sergeant talk about and demonstrate hand-to-hand assault and defense. They gave us three days of him. He knew all the nasty arts, and knew them well. We learned interesting little facts from him—for example, an inch or two of the tip of a knife high enough in the diaphragm, just under the breast bone, will cause an instantaneous loss of consciousness, whereas the whole blade into the chest or belly will give them time to bellow.

He spent about fifteen minutes on the guard dogs we might run into around enemy supply installations. He had a healthy awe of them. He said they leap for the throat, bowl you over like being hit by a truck, savage you to death in moments. The attack is so swift, a gun or knife is often useless. But he said there was one weak point in their attack. And you had to be very quick to take any advantage of it. Once the dog launches itself into its final leap, it is committed. He had his assistant sling an imitation dog at him, a canvas sack of sand with the two front legs sticking out of it. The man swung it close to the ground and hurled it at the sergeant's chest. The sergeant snatched at a forepaw, grasped it, pivoted and fell back, using the momentum of his fall and all the strength of arms and back to hurl the imitation dog on beyond him, in the same direction as its charge. He could throw it a startling distance. I remembered how it bounced in the dust. He said that in the leap the forepaws are relatively motionless. Snatch too soon and it can twist and tear your hands off. Wait too long and it is very hard to throw something that has hold of you by the throat.

He threw it a final time and dusted his hands and said, "Tykes the art out of im. Spoils is bloody leg for im. All you chaps do a spot of practice."

With that black shape launched at me, I wished I'd given it some more practice. Fear either freezes you or makes you eerily quick and strong. I was pivoting and falling as I felt my fingers of both hands dig into the corded forearm of the dog, with no memory of how I had managed to grasp it, an index finger hooked around the knob of the elbow. Unless I could impart enough centrifugal force to keep his head away from my hands, I was going to lose meat in a painful and ugly way, so I heaved as hard as I could, combining his leap, my backward fall, the pivot, into a single flight. I felt something give as I let go, heard a small whistling whine, a meaty thud as he struck the wall combined with a clopping sound as it snapped his jaws shut, a softer thud as he fell to the ground. I bounded up, feeling as cold as if I'd handled snakes. From the instant he bounded at me until he fell to the ground at the base of the wall, the total elapsed time was perhaps less than two full seconds. I wiped my hands on my thighs and waited for him. It is possible to age a year in two seconds. Animals that come at you in the night is one of the horror dreams of childhood. You never really get over them.

I moved to him carefully, screened the small pencil beam with my body and took a two second look. He was about eighty pounds of sinew, black hair and fangs—and he was quite dead.

It put an unknown limit on the time I could spend there. I had no way of knowing when they would call him. Perhaps they pulled in the human guard at nightfall and let the dog roam the grounds all night. He was too near my escape line. I waited until my eyes had readjusted to the night, then with a squeamish hesitation, took him by the hind paw and dragged him a dozen yards into a thickness of shrubbery covered with fragrant white blooms. Some variety of jasmine. Suddenly I wondered if they had a pair of dogs, and the thought nearly sent me hustling toward my escape line. I couldn't expect that much luck twice. Few men have ever given me as much instant fright as that dog gave me. And it was an unpleasant clue to the Garcia attitude about visitors. Uninvited visitors. Watchdogs trained to bark are a lot more common, and more civilized.

As I moved carefully toward the house, avoiding open patches of moonlight, listening for the slightest sound of a charging dog, I took note of direction and landmarks. I wanted to be able to leave at a headlong run, if need be, with a certainty of hitting the wall at the right place. When I had an unimpeded view of the big pink house, I stopped in the shadows and moved to one side and leaned against the trunk of a tree and hooked my thumbs in my belt and stared at it. By assuming one of the postures of relaxation you can trick your body into thinking things are perfectly under control. I was still shaky from the extra adrenalin the black dog had stimulated. I looked at the roof shape against the sky. There weren't many windows lighted. It was a big house, at least double the size of the Boody place. The complex of smaller buildings behind it was more elaborate, and there were lights showing there, too, and a faint sound of music from there.

I selected the next spot. There was a shallow patio with a low broad stone wall, the patio next to a wing of the house, parallel to it and up against it. Two sets of glass doors and two windows were encircled by the patio wall. The doors and window to the right were lighted. The light seemed to come through opaque white draperies. The doors and window to the left were dark. Once you decide, it is a strategic error to wait too long. Then it becomes like jumping off a roof. The longer you wait, the higher it looks. I had to cross a moonlit area. I bent double and moved swiftly, angling toward the dark end of the shallow patio. I went over the wall, moved close to the side of the house and lay on rough flagstones close against a low line of plantings. I listened. Now the fact of the dog was in my favor. Nobody was going to stay terribly alert, not with a monster like that cruising the grounds. When they've killed you, they stand and bay until somebody comes to congratulate them.

I wormed on over to the lighted doors, and found a place at the bottom corner I could look through. I was looking into a big bedroom with a sitting room area at one end of it, the end nearest the doors. A wall mirror showed me the reflection of the end of an elaborately canopied bed. A man sat on a grey chaise, turned away from me, so that all I could see of his face was a shelf of brow, curve of cheek. He wore shorts. One leg was outstretched, one propped up. They were pale legs, thick and powerful, fuzzed with a pelt of springy black hair. He was reading a book. His left side was toward me. Gold wrist watch and gold strap were half submerged in the curl of black hair on forearm and wrist.

I saw a movement in the mirror and then a girl came into view. She was walking slowly, barefoot, fastening the side of a green knit skirt, her head angled down so that a heavy sheaf of shining blonde hair obscured her face. She wore a white bra covering small breasts. Her upper torso was golden tan, with the narrow and supple look of youth. She fixed the skirt as she reached the foot of the chaise. She threw her hair back with a toss of her head, and stood and looked at the

man with a cool, unpleasant expression. It was a very lovely
face. I could guess that her earliest memories were of being
told how pretty she was. It was a cool and sensuous face. The
springing blonde hair, with a few tousled strands across her
forehead, fell in a glossy heaviness in two wings which
framed the sensitive and bad tempered face. I had seen her
before, and I groped for the memory, and finally had it. She
had stared very earnestly at me many times, looked deeply
into my eyes, held up a little squeeze bottle and told me it
would keep me dainty all day long. Despite all rumors to the
contrary, these huckster blondes are not interchangeable. I
knew this one because her eyes were set strangely, one more
tilted than the other.

She said something to the man. The curl of her mouth
looked unpleasant. He lowered the book, said something,
lifted it again. She shrugged and turned away and walked out
of my field of vision. I lay in controlled schizophrenia, split
between my interest in the lighted room, and my alertness
for any sound behind me in the night. When she appeared
again she was fastening the top half of the green knit two
piece suit and she wore shoes. She had that contrived walk of
the model, like Nora's walk but more so—the business of
putting each foot down in direct line with the previous step,
toeing outward slightly, to impart a graceful sway to the body
from the waist down. She was not tall. Perhaps five-four. She
made herself look tall.

She stopped at the right side of the chaise and perched one
hip on it, facing the man. She spoke to him. I could hear the
very faint cadence of her voice. She was intent, persuasive,
half-smiling. It was like a commercial with the volume turned
down. As she talked, he put two cigarettes between his lips,
lit them, handed one to her. She stopped talking and looked
expectantly at him. He reached and caught her wrist. She
sprang up and wrenched her wrist away, her face ugly with
sudden fury. She called him a ten letter word, loud enough
for me to hear it through the doors. She was no lady. She
strode out of range in the opposite direction, and I heard a
door slam.

She left with the look of somebody who was not coming
back immediately. There was no profit in watching a hairy
man read a book. I eased back and crouched in the moon
shadows and stood up slowly. From what I had seen of the
Boody house and what I could observe of this one, the dark

doors and window would open onto another bedroom unit. They were sliding doors, in an aluminum track. I tried the outside handle. Locked. It would turn down about an inch, and then it stopped. I stood close to it, got a good grip on it, then began to exert an ever-increasing pressure. Just as my muscles began to creak and protest, some part of the inner mechanism snapped with a sharp metallic sound. I waited and listened. I tried the door. It slid open with a muted rumble. I crouched, tensed up, ready to go. Burglar alarms seemed like a logical accessory to a killer dog. It didn't have to be a clanging. It could be a muted buzz at a guard station, inaudible to me. So I counted off six hundred seconds before I slipped through the eighteen-inch opening, brushing the draperies aside. I stood in the darkness in total concentration. We are given certain atavistic faculties which can be trained through use. You can stand in a dark room and after a time be absolutely certain there is no other person there. When I was quite certain, I used the pencil light, pinching the beam smaller between thumb and finger. It was a big bedroom-sitting room, less luxurious than the one I had looked into. There were no coverings on the two three-quarter beds. I went back and closed the door I had broken, and checked the three other doors. One opened into a roomy dressing room. One opened into a tiled bath, where an astonished cockroach sped into the darkness. The third opened onto a broad and dimly lighted hallway. There was a window at the blind end. The other end opened out into a big room as weakly lighted as the hallway. I could see the dark shapes of heavy furniture. Four doors opened onto the hallway. Two on each side. Four guest bedroom units, I assumed. The resident quarters would be in the other wing. I could hear no sound. I debated trying my luck with a quick and silent run into the living room at the end of the corridor, taking a chance on finding a dark pocket behind some of that heavy furniture. But there was too much chance of being cut off. I locked the bedroom door on the inside, and went back out through the glass doors, listened for a time, then left the patio and moved along the side of the house and around to the back, feeling more confident.

That is the familiar trap of course, the one that catches the cat burglars. They begin to feel invulnerable, and they push it a little further and a little further, until one day in their carelessness they wake up the wrong person—and then kill or are killed.

I sped through an area of moonlight, and crouched beyond the swimming pool, a layout almost identical to the Boody construction, near the building where the servants would be housed. Mexican radio was loud. Windows were lighted. The rooms were small and plain. I wanted a reasonable head count. The smell of cooking was strong. I saw a heavy woman walking to and fro in a small room, carrying a whining child, while a man sat alone at a table playing with a set of greasy cards. A screen door slapped. Somebody hawked and spat. I saw three men in a room, playing dominoes, placing them with large scowls and gestures, loud clacks of defiance. One of them was my wistful gate guard. A woman sat near them, stirring something in a large pottery bowl. A kitten mewed. The radio advertised Aye-low Shahm-boo. I looked through a gap in a sleazy curtain and saw, on a cot, under the bright glare of an unshaded bulb, in the direct blast of the music of the plastic radio, a muscular man and a very skinny woman making love, both of them shiny with sweat.

A quiet evening in the servants' quarters. I drifted away, and made my way back across to the big house, and came up to it at the rear, on the other side. I looked into a big bright white kitchen. A square-bodied, square-faced, dark skinned woman in a black and white uniform sat on a high red stool at a counter, polishing silver. A man leaned against the counter near her. A guard type, in khaki, armed, eating a chicken leg.

I passed dark windows. I came to a lighted one. I looked in. It was a small bedroom. A thin drab-looking, middle-aged woman sat there in a rocking chair without arms. She wore a very elaborate white dress, all lace and embroidery, strangely like a wedding dress. It did not look clean. Her hair was unkempt, strands of grey long and tangled. She had her arms folded across her chest. She was rocking violently, seeming to come close to tipping the chair over backwards each time. Her underlip sagged and her face was absolutely empty. There is only one human condition which can cause that total terrible emptiness. She rocked and rocked, looking at nothing.

As I moved along the side of the house I heard a woman's

voice. I passed more dark windows and came to three lighted ones in a row. They were open. As I crept closer I heard that she was speaking Spanish. And as it went on and on, I realized from the cadence of her voice that she was reading aloud. The accent seemed expert, as far as I could tell, the voice young and clear, nicely modulated. But she stumbled over words from time to time.

She seemed too close to the first window for me to take a chance, so I wormed on along to the last of the three lighted windows. I straightened up beyond it, and took a careful look. I saw a fat brown woman in a white uniform sitting on a couch sewing, her fingers swift and her face impassive. And off to the right, near the first window, I could see the blonde girl in the green knit suit, sitting on a straight chair beside a bed, her back to me, bending over the book she held in her lap. I could not see who was in the bed.

I waited there. She read on and on. Mosquitoes found my neck and I rubbed them off. I settled into the stupor of waiting. She could not read forever. Something had to change. And then I might learn something. At last she closed the book with an audible thump, and in a lazy, loving tone she said, "That's really all I can manage tonight, darling. My eyes are beginning to give out. I hope you don't mind too much."

There was no answer. She put the book aside and stood up and bent over whoever was in the bed. All I could see of her was the rounded girl-rump under the stretch of knitted green. The fat woman had stopped sewing and she was watching the girl, her eyes narrowed.

The girl made the murmurous sound of a woman giving her affection and then straightened. "Carlos, darling," she said, "I'm going to ask you to try to write your name again. Do you understand, dear? One blink for yes. Good."

She went out of my range and came back with a pad and pencil. She apparently sat beside him on the bed. I could see her slim ankles. "Here, darling. That's it. Hold it as tightly as you can. Now write your name, dear."

There was a silence. Suddenly the girl sprang up, and made a violent motion and there was the sound of an open palm against flesh. "You filth!" she shouted. "You dirty bastard!" The pad and pencil fell to the floor. The fat woman started up off the couch, hesitated, settled back and picked up her sewing.

The girl stood back from the bed, her body rigid, her fists on her hips. "I suppose that's your idea of a joke, writing a dirty word like that. God damn you, you understand me. I *know* you do. Try to get this through your head, Carlos. The pesos in the household account are down to damned near nothing. If you expect me to stay here and care for you and protect you, you are going to have to write your name clearly and legibly on a power of attorney so I can go to the bank in Mexico City and get more money. You have to trust me. It's the only chance you have, brother. And you better realize it. When the money stops, these people of yours are going to melt away like the morning dew, and you'll die and rot right here. Oh brother, I know how your mind works. You think I'm going to grab it all and run. If I did, you wouldn't be any worse off, would you? And what the hell good is money going to do you from now on? Listen, because I probably owe you something, Carlos, I swear I'll go and get the money and come back here and take care of you. I'll keep them from killing you. Don't you realize those men must have told somebody else before they came here to fix you? You think it over, my friend. You're not going to get too many more chances. I'm getting sick of this whole situation. Gabe and I may leave at any time. Who have you got left who could go for the money? Your wife, maybe? Your kook wife? We'll put wheels on her rocking chair. Jesus Christ, you make me sore, Carlos. Do me a personal favor. Have lousy dreams tonight. Okay."

She whirled and went out. She was a door banger.

I went back to the first window and took a look. The bed was directly under the window. Carlos Menterez was propped up on a mound of pillows. They'd dressed him in a heavy silk robe. With his bald head and his shrunken face, he looked like the skeleton of a monkey. The left eye was drooped almost shut, and the left side of his mouth and face fell slack, in grey folds. The look of severe stroke. But the right eye was round and dark and alert. In my interest, I had gotten a little too close to the screen. The good eye turned toward me, and suddenly became wider. His mouth opened on the good side, pulling the slack side open. He made a horrid cawing, gobbling sound, and lifted his right hand, a claw hand, as though to ward off a blow. I ducked down and heard the fat woman hurry to him. She made comforting sounds, patting and adjusting, fixing his pillows. Carlos made plaintive gobblings, wet sounds of despair. She worked over him for quite a while, and then she turned several lights out.

I went around the front of the house, completing the circuit. There was a light over the gate, but no guard. I could see that a heavy chain was looped through the bars of the gate. I wanted to get around and see what the blonde and Gabe were doing. I wondered how I could make myself a chance to hear what they were saying. It would be too much to expect that he might have opened the window. He hadn't. But as I lowered myself to look through the same place as before, I heard him bellow, "For Chrissake, Alma!" She was sitting huddled on the foot of the chaise. He was pacing back and forth, making gestures. He had a hard handsome face, glossy black hair worn too long.

Then behind me I heard a shrill whistle. A man yelled, "Brujo! *Eh, perro!* Brujo!" He whistled again. But Brujo had retired from the dog business. I went from the patio into the moon shade of the trees. I heard two men talking loudly, arguing. I saw lights moving beyond the leaves.

They both called the dog. And I made a wide furtive circle behind them as they moved, angling toward my escape line. I could sense that they were getting too close to where I'd left the dead dog.

There was a sudden silence, and then excited yelling. Then a shocking and sudden bam-bam of two shots rupturing the night. I was flat on my face before I could comprehend that they had not been aimed at me, that they were warning shots, fired into the air. More lights went on. There were more voices, raised in loud query. Suddenly at least fifty decorative floodlights went on, all over the pool area, all over the grounds. I guess I had seen some of the lights. They hadn't registered. I was in the cone of radiance of one of them. I swiftly pulled myself into darkness, momentarily blinded. Somebody ran by me, a few feet away, shoes drumming against the earth. All I had to do was wait for them to spot the smear on the wall, investigate, find the thin nylon rope, then hunt me down. Already they were beginning to fan out, five or six of them, shining flashlights into the dark places. And one was moving slowly toward me. He would have a gun in one hand and the light in the other. There was an unpleasant eagerness about them, as if they were after a special bonus.

I could not circle behind him. I would have had to cut

through the revealing lights. I moved back, came up against a tree, wormed around it, stood on the far side of it and went up it almost as fast as I can run up a flight of stairs. It had sharp stubby thorns sticking out of the trunk, and I did not pay them much attention at the time. I stood a dozen feet up, balanced in the crotch of a fat branch, holding the main trunk for support. Below me, the diligent fellow came through the lights and swept the light back and forth where I had been. I looked around. The others were just about far enough away. When he moved into the relative darkness under my tree, I stepped into space and dropped onto him, feet first, landing on the backs of his shoulders, driving him down to the ground. I rolled to my knees and snatched his flashlight. It had rolled away from him. I swept the beam over, saw his hand gun and picked it up. He stirred and I hammered him down again, laying the side of the revolver against the back of his skull. I stood, sweeping the light back and forth, as though searching.

A man thirty feet away rattled a question at me.

"No se," I grumbled. Avoiding the lights, I worked my way away from him. A few moments later, I reached the stain on the wall. I found the line. It was firm. In that instant all the lights flickered and went out, and I knew it was midnight. The big generator had been turned off. They called to each other, swinging their lights around dangerously. Somebody yelled, "Chucho? Chucho?" I guessed I had his gun and light. I turned the light off, then threw it toward the house as hard as I could, arching it up over the trees. There was a satisfying crash and chime of glass. As the shouts came, as they all began moving toward the house, I went up the line, stood on the wall, freed the hooks and jumped into the darkness. I landed on uneven ground, hit my chin on my knee and jarred my teeth, rolled over onto my side. I yanked the rest of the line over the wall, and hastened across the Boody grounds, coiling it as I went, the gun a hard lump between belt and belly. I could hear more shouts, and I wondered if they'd found Chucho. I wondered if he was the wistful one, the chicken eater, the lovemaker or one of the others.

When I rattled the first pebble into the room through the open window, she whispered, "Trav? Darling?"

"Get away from the window."

I tossed the hooks in. They clanked on the tile. She dug the hooks into the overlap of the wooden sill. I walked up the side of the building, caught at the edge, slid over the sill belly down, and spilled into the room. As I rolled over, she nestled down upon me, sobbing and laughing, smothering the sounds against my chest. "I heard shots," she said. "Far away, and I thought. . . ."

"There was some excitement while I was leaving."

She let me up. I pulled the line in. We went into the bathroom to inspect damage. The only room lights on the night circuit were weak bulbs in the bathrooms. Twenty-five watts. Those thorns had torn me up pretty good, puncturing and tearing the flesh on the insides of my arms and legs. Fear had been a marvelous anesthetic. I put the gun on the shelf above the sink and stripped down. It was a respectable weapon, a Smith and Wesson .38, a standard police firearm with walnut grips. It hadn't received tender loving care, but it looked deadly enough. And the damn fool had been carrying it hammer down, on the empty chamber, instead of hammer back with a fresh one in position.

Nora made little bleatings of concern when she saw how torn up I was. She hurried off and came back with antiseptic, cotton and tape. I took a cold shower first, bloodied a towel drying myself, then stretched out in the restricted area of the bathroom on my back so she could do a patch job. She bit down on her lip as she worked. She had trouble getting out of her own shadow. I could feel the exhaustion seeping through me. I told her there was a bad dog and I had killed it. I said I had been in the house. I had seen a few things, heard a few things, and I would tell her about them later. I had had to hit a man on the head to get out of there. It had been a little closer than I cared for things to be. The closeness of it made her weep, and then I had to make jokes to prove it had not been really that close.

Then we went to bed. She was dubious about my obvious intentions, but she was very very glad to have me back. And we had grown to know each other. It was no longer the mysterious business of strangers being too curious about the reaction to this or that, holding themselves in a kind of tentative reserve. Now I knew the arrangements of her, the strictures and the willingnesses, the fashioning of her for her needs and takings, so that I could lose myself in all that and become one striving thing with her, both of us all of one familiar flesh. There are anesthetics more wondrous than fear. In that time when past and future fade, when they are eclipsed by the reiterant now, I caught a receding glimpse of the man and the skinny woman under the bright bulb glare, felt an ironic aftertaste, then knew that all the differences which mean anything are subjective. In the drinking of a fine wine or a deadly poison, the mechanical functioning of elbow and wrist are identical. Whether the eye sees blood or roses, little sub-electrical impulses in the brain identify the color as red. I could fault us only on the grounds our coupling had a symbiotic tinge, a union keyed to survival of two discordant species. She had the wisdom to keep us from trying to explain that to each other. Her wisdom gave us the power to accept completely, using in place of value judgments the deep, ancient, rhythmic affirmations of the flesh.

thirteen

AFTER BREAKFAST I sat in umbrellaed shade while Nora swam, shirt and slacks covering the thorn wounds, my curled hand concealing the random stigmata, the girl-bite bandage also hidden under the long sleeves of the white shirt. I had some sore and creaking muscles, and a couple of bruises which felt as if they went all the way down into the bone marrow.

The revolver, sealed by a rubber band fastening into a plastic shoe bag, rested in the bottom of her toilet tank. The improvised grapnel was buried in the soft black dirt under a bush. I had rinsed the smeared stains of blood from my hands off the thin nylon rope, coiled it and stowed it in a bureau drawer. The ruined slacks and shirt were a minor problem. Nora had them stowed in her beach bag, tightly rolled. We could bury them at the beach.

She came out of the pool and returned to our table. She wore a sheath suit, vertical red and white stripes. She had explained the artifice of it to me. She said it was a suit for the underprivileged girl. The stripes were designed to be further apart at hip and breast, closer together at the waist, thus creating the illusion of more abundance than was there. She said that for some reason she could not understand, they had a most difficult time at the shop trying to keep very heavy women from buying them. I told her I hadn't noticed she was particularly underprivileged. She said a woman's ribs shouldn't resemble a xylophone, nor should hip bones be capable of inflicting a nasty bruise.

She toweled her face and shoulders, fluffed her dark hair, moved her chair into the sun and frowned at me. "What's the matter?" I asked.

"There was something between Sam and the blonde."

"If Alma's last name is Hitchins, and if Felicia is right, yes."

"Then she's been there a long time."

153

"Maybe. Back and forth is a better guess, I'd say. The intermittent house guest. For a nice long stay every time."

"Who is Gabe?"

"God knows. The relationship with Alma had a flavor of intimacy. But she seems to be in charge."

"Do you think she wants to get the money and run?"

"What else? Maybe Menterez was a lot of laughs before something gave way in his head. But what's there for her now? You know, she has it locked up pretty good. If anybody comes around who really wants to help him, she can keep them from getting past the gate. He is incapable of communicating with anybody. Speech is gone, but he can understand and he can write. I don't think that fat nurse understands English. I have the idea nobody gets into that room except Alma and the fat nurse. I don't think anybody else will get in there until he's ready to sign a power of attorney. I would bet the bulk of his fortune is in Switzerland, but he's likely to have a nice chunk of cash in a lock box in Mexico City. I don't think it would be on deposit. I'd lay odds it's in dollars or pounds. And he damn well knows she wants to clean him out. If she does, who can touch her? How far can he get by complaining to the Mexican authorities? I think I know what's eating her. She's afraid he'll have another one before she can soften him up. I think he's suffering the fate of all vultures. When they get sick, the others eat him."

"Don't be so damned vivid, Trav."

"I'd like to unravel that remark she made about some men having told somebody else where he was before they came here to fix him. They tried and they didn't make it, and evidently they didn't survive the experience. That was the inference. But if any kind of big dramatic violence went on around here, I think Felicia would have known about it and told me about it. How did Sam earn those gold figures? Who got all but one of them away from him? Honey, we're up to here in questions."

"What are you going to do about it?"

"Pry Alma open."

"You can't go back there!"

"Nora dear, I wouldn't go over that wall again for a thirty dollar bill. So we got to get sweetie pie out of there somehow."

"Is she another one of those ... what did you call them? ... sun bunnies?"

"Not this one. This one is bright and cold and hard and beautiful."

She gave a mirthless laugh. "Sam kept pretty busy."

"I think this one would have gone after Sam if she thought he could do her some good. And I think if she went after him, he wouldn't stand much of a chance. And I think her nerves are good enough to carry on another intrigue right in Menterez' house. This one has the cool sexually-speculative look, like the one who married the prince."

"Or like poor little Mandy? Christine's pal?"

"I think this one is a little more commercial than that."

"She and that Gabe are a team?"

"I don't know. He's a little too pretty. She'll cross him up when it comes his turn. I think he's just a stud she imported to liven the dull days of waiting. But I have the idea he knows what she's trying to do."

"I keep thinking of that black dog."

"Please. I keep trying not to think about him. How do we get her out of there?"

"Darling, the mail comes to the village by bus, and they bring the mail for those houses out here to the hotel. I . . . I might put a little note in there for her. My handwriting is obviously feminine. So is my note paper."

"Nora, you are a fine bright girl."

"I don't know what to say. But it should be something that. . . . She shouldn't be able to rest until she finds out the rest of it. Maybe I should phone her."

"There is one phone in this whole hotel, in Arista's office. I think there are two in the village. There are none on the hill."

"Oh."

"But the idea is superb. Let's give it a lot of thought."

"Shouldn't we make sure of her name? Wouldn't that help?"

"It would help indeed."

It seemed a difficult project, but like many such problems, it turned out to be extraordinarily simple. I found one of the hotel porters at a small table near the lobby door sorting mail, the mail he would carry up the hill and leave at the tenanted house. He was checking the addresses against a tattered, dog-eared sheet. The principal names had been typed. Other names in the household had been written under them in pencil. There was a long list under Garcia, well over a dozen names. Among them was the girl's name. She had phonied up the first name, as girls are inclined to do these days. Almah. Miss Almah Hichin. The porter was trying to tell me I would not find my mail in that batch. I misunderstood him. By the time Arista came over to straighten me out, I had what I needed.

Nora and I spent a long time composing a draft of a very short note.

"My dear Miss Hichin, I have heard so many things about you, I feel that I know you. ST told me many things, including one thing I must pass along to you in person. He said it would *deeply* concern you, and might change your future plans. It does not mean much to me, but from the sound of it I would judge it important. I am at La Casa Encantada, but for obvious reasons, that would not be a good place for us to meet."

"What obvious reasons?" Nora asked, scowling.

"If you don't have any, she will. Or she'll wonder what the hell your reasons are."

"Where should we meet?"

"I saw three cars up there. One is a dark red convertible Ghia. Say this: Drive the little red car down to the village tomorrow at one in the afternoon. Stop in front of the largest church. Please be alone. I shall be."

Her initials, NDG, were embossed in the top corner of the blue note paper. There was no address. I had her sign it with merely an N.

"What if she should know Sam is . . . dead?"

"She'll wonder what he said before he died."

"Do you think she'll come?"

"She'll have to."

"Tomorrow will mean the day after tomorrow. We can't get it to her until. . . ."

"I know. You'll give it to that old porter, with a lovely smile, and a five peso note."

"Then what do we do with her if she does come?"

"I'm going to take a long walk to find out, dear."

"Can I come?"

I did some mental arithmetic. A kilometer is six-tenths of a mile. "Can you manage ten miles in the heat?"

She could do better than that. She proved it. She became very mysterious, made me wait for her, came back full of suppressed amusement, then led me out to the back of the hotel, to the out buildings there, the supply sheds, generator building, staff barracks, back to a place where Jose, our room waiter, stood proudly beside a fantastic piece of transportation. It was an Italian motor scooter with fat doughnut tires, all bright coral, poisonous yellow-green and sparkling chrome. It had a single monster headlight, and two fluffy pink fox tails affixed to the handlebar grips. It had a radio antenna, but no radio, with a blue fox tail fastened to the tip of it. There was a broad black cycle seat, and behind that a padded black lid to the stowage compartment, a place for the passenger to sit. It was incongruous transportation for that severe, polite little man. He would not consent to rent it until he had checked me out on it. It had two speeds. I kicked it on and wheeled it sedately around the area, flatulently snarling. I comported myself with dignity and appreciation. I told him it was strikingly beautiful, and I would treat it with the greatest care.

When the deal was struck, Nora straddled the rear compartment, her dark hair tied in a scarf, and we took off for the village, Jose watching us with an enigmatic expression. There were little cleats for her to brace her feet on. She found that her best way to hold on was to hold onto my belt. She shouted that this experience had come to her about twelve years too late. With the soft tires and the heavy coil springs on the front fork, it was really quite comfortable on the rough road. In high gear, along a relatively smooth area, the speedometer showed a little over 50 kph, or something over thirty miles an hour.

Again I ruptured siesta by making three circuits of the public square. Brown dogs yapped and ran after us, then waited, gasping, for us to come around another time. Children shouted and imitated the art of jumping over an invisible knife. Dark faces grinned. I went down the road which headed in the opposite direction from the hotel, and found the ice plant and more fish docks, some old trucks at a loading platform, and more packs of kids and dogs. I discovered that the brake was tender. It had a tendency to lock the rear wheel. I made my turn, scattering a flock of white hens, and went back and made two more circuits of the square—to the cheers of the populace, and then turned inland over the crude road we had traveled in the blue bus.

After I was over the ridge and across the rocky flats and into the narrow road with the heavy growth on either side, I slowed it and stopped it, turned the key off and set it on the brace.

Nora was amused and indignant. "Really, Trav! My God, what were you trying to prove?"

"That we're nutty harmless Americans. Smoke screen, honey. Anybody who went over that wall couldn't possibly clown around in this gaudy machine the very next day. And I think the village damn well knows they had trouble up there last night. And what point is there in looking as if we had any special destination? When we come back, we'll bomb them again."

"It just made me feel so ridic . . ." Suddenly she began to make squeaking sounds and went into a wild dance, slapping at her feet and ankles. And at the same moment, one of them got me on the leg, a dark red ant with husky jaws and a sting like suphuric acid. We leaped onto the machine and escaped, slapping the persistent ones off while in transit. We bumbled along through sunny areas and through the jungly shadows where the trees met overhead. The previous mudholes were cracked and drying. I found that the most comfortable speed was about fifteen miles an hour. And it gave me time to inspect both sides of the road. Pebbles clinked off the festive mudguards. The fox tails rippled in the hot breeze of passage. Dust curled behind us. The woman clutched the back of my belt snugly. Once she shouted and pointed and I saw a flock of small bright parrots tilting and skimming through a shadowy green of the high trees.

We met a bus coming to the village. It came clanking and wheezing and shuddering along, going too fast for the condition of the road. The name on the front of it was El Domador. It blew a squawky horn at us as we waited in the shallow ditch for it to go by, and the passengers whooped. After it was gone, two hundred yards further, I found the place Felicia had probably been talking about. A smaller road, just a trace of a road, turned off to the left. It ended after about a hundred feet, in a little clearing which the jungle was reclaiming. I silenced our vehicle and we got off. The silence was intense. There had been a shack at the edge of the clearing. It had fallen in, and the tough vines were curled around the old poles of which it had been fashioned. We could have been a hundred feet or a hundred miles from any other road. In a little while the bird sounds began again, tentative at first. Then the bug chorus started. Nora peered carefully and rather timidly at the ground, looking for ants among the tough grasses.

There was an eeriness about the place that made it more suitable to speak in a half whisper.

"This is where they brought that girl?"

"Yes. Three days after Sam took off."

"Who were they?"

"Nobody from the house. Three days, it would be time to come in from somewhere else."

"And you want me to bring that girl here?"

"Yes."

"What are you going to do?"

"I'll be here when you get here with her. I'll have to walk it. I think her nerves are very good. I think she's tricky and subtle. So we have to plan it carefully, Nora. We have to make it look very good to her. So I'm going to give you some lines to say, and we're going to go over them, and then you're going to walk away from it, because I don't want to give her a chance to read you."

"Will she read you, dear?"

"I don't know. At least I know enough not to try to overact."

"What do you mean?"

"Sympathy and reluctance are a hell of a lot more impressive than imitation villainy, Nora."

I arrived at the clearing a little before one in the afternoon. I had cut across country rather than going through the village. I had had to take cover from only one vehicle, a burdened fish truck laboring out toward the markets. I had sweated the layer of repellent off, and I rubbed on more. I paced and I worried about Nora. If Almah Hichin showed up, if Nora did exactly as I had told her, as I had demonstrated to her, if she had tried no improvisation, and had kept her mouth shut, maybe it would work.

I paced back and forth in the clearing. I cut a reedy-looking thing and tried to make a whistle. The bark wouldn't slip. I kept stopping, tilting my head, listening. When I heard it, it seemed to merge with the bug whine and die away, and then it came back, stronger than before. Then it was recognizable as the doughty whirr of a VW engine. It turned into the overgrown trace. I saw at last the glints of dark red through the foliage. It came into the clearing and stopped, ten feet from me. Almah Hichin was at the wheel. She stared at me, frowning slightly as I walked over to the car. I reached in and turned the key off. The top was down. Almah wore a dark blue kerchief, a pale blue sleeveless silk blouse, a white skirt, flat white sandals. She looked up at me with respectable composure and said in a reasonable tone, "May I ask who you are, and what this is all about?"

"No trouble?" I asked Nora.

"None at all." She sat half turned toward Almah, holding my little bedroom gun six inches from Alma's waist. Almah's white purse was on the divider between the black bucket seats. I reached over her and picked it up and opened it. I saw her decide to snatch at it and then change her mind. Combination wallet and change purse, lipstick, very small hair brush, mirror, stub of eyebrow pencil. I took the bills out of the wallet. Three U.S. twenties, a ten, and three ones. A wad of soiled peso notes. I tossed the money into Nora's lap. I put the billfold back into the purse, snapped it, took a step back and slung the purse deep into the brush. I looked at the girl. Her eyes had widened momentarily. They were an unusually lovely color, a deep lavender blue, and their asymmetry made them more interesting.

"Won't somebody find that?" Nora asked on cue.

"It isn't likely." I knew how the inevitable formula worked in the girl's mind. Nobody expected her to be able to go look for it. I saw a slight twitch at the corner of the controlled mouth.

I took the coil of nylon line off my shoulder, separated an end and dropped the rest of it. "Clasp your hands and hold them out," I told her.

"I will not!"

"Miss Hichin, you can't change anything. All you can do is make a lot of tiresome trouble. Just hold your hands out."

She hesitated and then did so. Her wrists looked frail, her forearms childish. I lashed them together, swiftly and firmly. I opened the car door, gave a firm and meaningful tug at the line and she got out, saying, "This is altogether ridiculous, you know."

Nora slid over into the driver's seat and pulled the door shut.

"Enough gas to make Culiacan?" I asked.

She turned the key on and checked. "More than enough."

I reached and plucked the dark blue kerchief from Almah's blonde head and handed it to Nora. "This might confuse things a little."

She nodded. She glanced at Almah. "How about her blouse too?"

"I'll bring it along," I said. "You don't want any part of this do you?"

Her little shudder was very effective. "No, dear."

"Neither do I. Park it up there in the shade, just short of that last bend. Okay?"

"Yes, dear. Miss Hichin? Please don't be stupid about this. You see, we have a lot of time. The plane doesn't come until eight to pick us up. You're such a pretty thing. It will be very difficult for him if you . . . let it get messy."

"Are you people out of your minds?" Almah demanded.

"I'll handle this. You get out of here," I ordered.

She spun the little red car around deftly and headed back out again. The motor sound faded, and then it stopped.

I picked up the rest of the line and led the girl over to the spot I had picked, near the ruin of the shack. I flipped the line over a low limb, caught the end, took it over to another tree, laced it around the tree and then carefully pulled until she had her arms stretched high over her head, but both feet were firmly on the ground. I made it fast. I went to her and reached and checked the tension of the line above her lashed wrists. I wandered away from her and lit a cigarette and stood with my back to her, staring off into the brush.

"You're making some kind of fantastic mistake," she said.

"Sure," I said and went back to her. She looked sweaty but composed. Small insects were beginning to gather around her face, arms and legs.

"No need for you to be eaten alive," I said. I took out the 6-12 and poured some into the palm of my hand. "Close your eyes." She obeyed. I greased her face, throat, arms and legs with the repellent. I made it utterly objective, with no slightest hint of caress. She stared at me and moistened her lips. I knew that the small courtesy had shaken her more than anything which had gone before.

I walked away from her again. I wanted to sag against a tree and give a great bray of laughter. I had properly anticipated most of it, but not the comedy of it. The most wretched melodrama becomes high comedy. This was a little darling, a little lavender-eyed blonde darling, trussed up like a comic book sequence, and I could not harm a hair of her dear little head. And, of course, she could not believe it either. Nobody hurts the darlings. So our spavined act was balanced on that point which was just beyond our comprehension or belief. She was right. It was some kind of a fantastic mistake. Nora had bought it more readily than blondie or I could. Her Mediterranean acceptance of the violence just under the surface of life, perhaps.

I turned and looked at her. She stood sweaty and indignant and uncomfortable, reaching high, ankles neatly together. She was, of course, weighing me most carefully, estimating my capacity for violence, even though she could not believe this was real. It was a ponderous, embarrassing joke. She was angry and wary. She was trying to guess if I could hurt her. I saw myself through her eyes—a great big brown rangy man, wiry hair, pale grey eyes, broad features slightly and permanently disarranged by past incidents. I went close to her, and looked through the hypnotic impact of so much prettiness, and got a better look at the details of her. Caked lipstick bitten away, fingers narrow and crooked and not pretty, nailpolish chipped and cracked, the thumbnails bitten deep, a furzy little coppery stubble in her armpits, little dandruff flakes in the forehead roots of the blonde hair, slender ankles slightly soiled, pores enlarged in her cheeks and a blackhead near the base of the delicate nose, a tiny hole burned in the front of the pale blue blouse, a spot on the hip of the white skirt. She was lovely, but not very fastidious. It made her seem a little sexier, and more manageable. The signs of soil were slightly plaintive.

"You and that woman are going to get into terrible trouble about this," she said. "I'm an actress. A lot of people know me. Apparently you don't know who I am."

"I think you got mixed up in a lot of things, Almah, without knowing how serious they were. I guess it works sort of like the law. Ignorance is no excuse."

"You don't make any sense. I am a house guest."

"That's what Carlos Menterez y Cruzada called a lot of his shack jobs, I guess. House guests. But you'd be a little young for the Havana scene. Actually I guess you aren't any different than any of the rest of them. But you are the last one he had. And when he had no more use for you, in that sense, you should have gone back where you belonged. The big mistake was hanging around, Almah."

She stared at me as though she was peering at me through gloom, trying to identify me. She started to say something and stopped and licked her lips again.

"Who are you?" she asked.

"I'm just somebody who's been ordered to confirm a few things. Double check the details. They'll think you left when the going got rough. We sent some people in there last night to look around. It's all falling apart now. It's over for him, Almah. And it's over for you."

"But it isn't the way you think!"

"How do you know what we think?"

"You sound . . . you make it sound as if I'm there with Carlos out of some kind of loyalty or something. My God, it isn't like that! Honestly, I don't know anything about the political side of it. Listen, I came down here a lot, when there were parties and all. By boat a couple of times and private airplanes. For over two years, and I'd stay on for a couple of weeks or a couple of months. Okay, so I belonged to Carlos when I was here, and that was understood. Is that some kind of a crime all of a sudden? His wife is crazy. Ever since he built that house, she'd been out of her head. He liked me. He wanted me to stay there all the time, but I went back and forth. I mean I have a life of my own too."

"You should have left for good when you had the chance, Almah."

"You have to understand something. I lost some good opportunities on account of him. I mean they would have called me for more things, if I'd been handy all the time. A good series I could have been in. But they couldn't get hold of me for the pilot because I was here. So he owes me something. Right?"

"What are you driving at?"

"Look. There's a boy there with me. Gabe. Gabriel Day. You could check it out. He's a lawyer. He can't practice in Mexico, but he knows the right forms and everything they have to use down here. He's been down here for three weeks. I sent for him. You can check that out. Carlos is going to sign something for me, and people are going to witness his signature, and then Gabe and I can go get the money. It's in Mexico City. He's got over six hundred thousand dollars there. That's why I'm staying. It isn't political or anything like that. This is all some kind of a mistake."

"Sweetie, that's what they used to say in Batista's prisons and what they say now in Fidel's prisons. This is some kind of a mistake."

"I didn't have anything to do with the political part."

"No more than Sam Taggart did? He had enough to do with the political part so that it got him killed."

She stared. "Sam is dead?"

"Thoroughly."

"Gee, it's hard to believe. He. . . . He told me it was time to get out, when Carlos got the stroke and Sam couldn't get the money Carlos promised him. I guess they could have guessed it was Sam who . . . got rid of those people."

I sat on my heels, my back against the tree. I said, "I don't want to play psychological games with you, Almah. We know some of it, and there's some of it we don't know. But you have no way of knowing the parts we know and the parts we don't. I can't promise you anything, because there's nothing to promise. Suppose you just tell me the whole thing."

"And you'll let me go?"

"I want to see if you put in any mistakes."

"The way it started? All of it?"

"Yes."

"I guess you could say it started when Cal Tomberlin came down on his boat, with a lot of kids I know. That was about five months ago. Cal is sort of spooky. Maybe from having everything he ever wanted, and getting it right now. His mother was Laura Shane, from the old movies. And she put all the money she made into land. No taxes then. She got fabulously rich and Cal was the only child. He'd met Carlos one time in Havana, and they didn't get along, and he didn't know that Carlos was here calling himself Garcia. It made Carlos sort of nervous when Cal showed up. Carlos had three collections in the study, in glass cases. The gold statues and the jade and the coins. But Cal Tomberlin saw the gold statues and wanted to buy them. He couldn't imagine anybody saying no. When he wants something, he has to have it. And sooner or later he gets it. It can be a boat or a special kind of car or a piece of land or somebody's wife or those horrid little gold statues. They were here about five days and he kept after Carlos all the time, and it got pretty ugly.

Toward the end, Cal Tomberlin started making little hints, talking about what a nice hideaway Carlos had found for himself. But that just made Carlos more stubborn. Finally they left. Some of the kids stayed on for a while.

"About a month later, Cal Tomberlin came back on the boat again. What I think he was doing, he was just trying to put some pressure on Carlos to make a deal with him. Maybe he knew how much trouble he was causing. Maybe he was just trying to get even with Carlos for turning him down. But he brought a Cuban man with him, and the Cuban man stayed sort of hidden on the boat until there was a big party and Cal Tomberlin went down and got the man and smuggled him into the party. I was there when Carlos saw him. I thought he was going to have a heart attack. I didn't know anything could terrify Carlos so much. He never talked to me about such things, but that night in bed he had to talk to somebody, I guess. He said that he had been in a business deal in Havana with that man's brother. It had gone wrong somehow, and the brother had killed his wife and himself, and then their son had tried to kill Carlos and had been arrested and had died of sickness in prison. He kept saying he would have to leave Mexico and go somewhere else. But after a few days he quieted down. He stopped going outside the walls for anything. I guess he couldn't think of a place where he would be safer.

"About two weeks later, that boat came down, that Columbine IV out of Oceanside. It anchored out. That same man was on it, and two other men. They looked Cuban. I saw them in the village. They called me a filthy name. Carlos had Sam find out everything he could about them. The boat was chartered, and they were running it themselves. It was small enough so they could have tied up at the docks, but they anchored out. They didn't do anything. It made Carlos very nervous. He'd watch it with binoculars. The other two men were younger. I guess they could have been friends of the one who died in prison. They just seemed to be waiting for something. Then one night they tried to kill Carlos. When they ran, they left the ladder against the wall. They'd fired at him, he thought with a rifle, from the top of the wall, from a place where you could see into his bedroom. It ripped through his smoking jacket and made a little red line across his belly, and just barely broke the skin. Instead of going all to pieces about it, he got very calm and thoughtful. I said he should get the police, but he said there were political reasons why he couldn't ask for that kind of protection. He had to make do with the people he had brought from Cuba.

"I think it was two nights later he came to my room as I was going to bed and told me he knew all about me and Sam. He knew I'd been cheating on him with Sam from just about the second time I'd come down to visit. He said it had amused him. I made some smart remark and he gave me a hell of a slap across the face and knocked me down. He wanted me to work on Sam to get Sam to do what Carlos wanted him to do. He told me the lie he had told Sam. He had told Sam that the men on the boat were Castro agents, and that for several years Carlos had been financing underground activities against Castro, and those men were assigned to kill him so it would stop. I guess Sam never thought much about that sort of thing. I guess it would sound reasonable to him. He offered Sam a hundred thousand dollars in cash to get rid of those men on the boat. Carlos had it all worked out how it could be done. But Sam didn't want to kill anybody. It made me feel funny to think of Sam killing anybody. With Carlos not going out in his own boat any more, not since Cal had brought that Cuban man around, Sam didn't have much to do. The man who helped him on Carlos' boat is named Miguel. He's still at the house.

"When I was with Sam, it was usually on Carlos' boat, and sometimes in Sam's room. It wasn't anything important with us. It was just something to do. And I enjoy it. Unless there were parties, it was quiet around there. Sort of sleepy. Siestas in the afternoon. I don't like to sleep in the day. Maybe I'd be by the pool and Sam would give me a look and go away and I'd stay there and think about him, and then I'd have to go find him. I thought the servants probably knew. I didn't know Carlos knew. Anyway, I made Sam tell me about it, not letting on I knew, and then I worked on him to do it. I told him if he didn't have any guts, I wasn't interested any more. And besides, it was sort of patriotic. I said if he did it, I'd arrange to go away with him for a while. He was always a little more eager than I was. I guess guys always are. I didn't tell him Carlos had promised me a little money for talking him into it. And I wouldn't do anything with him until he said yes. I told him when he said yes, it would be the most special thing that ever happened to him. It did get me pretty excited, thinking of him killing those men in the way Carlos had it all figured out.

"They did it. Sam and Miguel. On the first calm dark night. They went out in the dinghy from Carlos' boat, I guess about three in the morning, making no sound at all. They went aboard barefoot. Sam told me all about it. He held onto me, shivering like a little kid. He was too sick to make love. Twice he got up and he went and he was sick. It wasn't like he thought it was going to be. One of the men was sleeping on deck. Miguel sneaked over to him and cut his throat. Sam said the man flopped and thumped around while he was dying. But it didn't wake the others. They went below. One of the men was easy. The other one put up a terrible fight. He knocked some of Sam's teeth out, hitting him with something. Sam strangled him. Then there was the woman. Nobody had known anything about the woman. She'd stayed below the whole time. There was some kind of little light on below. She came out of the front of the boat somewhere, and flew at Sam. He got her by the wrists. He said she was dark and pretty. He said that holding her, he could feel Miguel putting the knife into her back, and he could see her face changing as she knew she was dead. That was what made him so sick. He cried in my arms like a little kid.

"The dinghy was tied astern. They cut the anchor lines. Sam started the boat up and they went out the main pass, dead slow, without lights, heading south west. Once they were pretty well out, Sam put the boat on automatic pilot. Miguel had taken the other body below. Sam disconnected the automatic bilge pumps and opened a sea cock. He said Miguel had been scrambling around with a sack, getting money and watches and rings and cameras and things like that. He made Miguel quit and got into the dinghy. Sam closed it up below. He went to the controls then and yelled to Miguel to cast off, and he put it up to cruising speed, and ran and dived over the rail and swam back to the dinghy. They sat in the dinghy. He said they could see the boat for just a little while, and then they could hear it for a lot longer. When they couldn't hear it any more, they started the little outboard on the dinghy and came on back. They were about five or six miles out. They stopped the motor and rowed the last mile in.

"Sam said he estimated that the cruiser would run for maybe an hour before the bilge got full enough to stop the engines. Then it would go down pretty fast, and it would be nearly twenty miles out by then. About two or three days later we heard they were hunting for a boat. There were some search planes. Some men came and asked questions at the hotel. But all they could say was that the boat had left one night. That was about two months ago. After he did it, Sam wanted the money right away so he could leave. But Carlos stalled him. He said he had to make a trip to Mexico City to get it. He said he would go soon. I guess I was going to go with him. I don't know. Maybe I was partly to blame. He wanted to shove some of the blame off on me, so he could feel a little better about it.

"Then one morning Carlos was sitting by the pool and I was swimming. I heard a woman scream. I climbed out and I asked Carlos if he heard it. I was looking around. He didn't answer me. I looked at him again, and I realized he had made that sound. The doctor came up from Mazatlan by float plane. At first he thought Carlos would die. He was unconscious for four days. Then he was conscious, with his whole left side paralyzed and he couldn't talk. The doctor said there might be some future improvement, but probably not much. Dead brain cells don't come back. Sam was drunk for days. Then I found him in the study. He'd opened the glass case and he was putting those gold statues in the case Carlos had had made for them when he left Cuba. They go in little fitted places. He said he was going to get his money one way or another, and the whole thing made no sense at all unless he got his money. He said he was going to take them away and sell them to Cal Tomberlin. He said he'd earned them. I said they were worth more than what Carlos had promised him, that Cal had offered Carlos a lot more. He said then it would have to be a bonus, and the way he felt about it, the bonus could be for the woman. But maybe Cal wouldn't want to pay him as much as he had offered Carlos anyway. He told me I should leave with him. But he was acting sort of wild and unreliable. I didn't see how he could get those things across the border. He looked as if he was going to get into terrible trouble. And by then—I didn't tell him—I'd gotten into Carlos' wall safe, in his bedroom. He'd watch me with that one eye whenever I was in there. I looked everywhere and found the combination in his wallet, written on the edge of a card. I thought there would be a lot of money in there, but there was just some pesos, a little over twenty thousand pesos. And some bank books for accounts in Zurich, and the keys and records of the bank drawer in Mexico City. The money there is in American dollars.

"Sam left. That case was terribly heavy. He fixed it so he could sort of sling it on his shoulder. He wanted to take one of the cars. I didn't want any trouble to be traced back to Carlos. I told the men not to let him take a car, to let him take the heavy case, but no car. But before he could leave, two men came. They had been at the house before. Friends of Carlos, from the old days in Havana. When they would visit him, they would have long private conferences about money and politics. They didn't know Carlos had had a stroke. It made them very nervous. I took them to him and showed them how to talk to Carlos. He can blink his good eye for yes and no, and if you hold his wrist steady he can scrawl simple words on a pad. I wanted to stay there, but they shoved me out of the room and locked the door. At dusk—they were still in there—Sam decided that they were going to take over, and if they knew what he was going to take, they would stop him. So he left, and he told me to tell those men, if they asked, that he'd left by boat. He thought they would get around to looking for him.

"Those men spent a long time with Carlos. They talked to me about what the doctor had said. They spent most of the next day with him. I guess it was slow work, finding out things from him. Maybe he didn't want to tell them. That would make it slower. Once I listened at the door and heard Carlos make that terrible sound he makes when he gets frightened or angry. At last they knew all they wanted to know, from him. They found out I could open the safe. They made me open it. I'd hidden the keys and records for the Mexico City box. They didn't seem to know or care about that. They took the Swiss bank book. They said fast things to Carlos and laughed, and the tears ran out of his good eye. They took the jade and the coin collection too. They asked me about Sam. One's English was good, as good as Carlos'. They said Carlos had done a very stupid thing, and that Sam had been very stupid to obey Carlos' orders. They said that the friends of the people who had been on that boat would be told what had happened, so that nobody would start blaming the wrong people. And they said it would be very nice if they could turn Sam over to those friends, because that would satisfy them, and then the security of a lot of people living quietly in Mexico would not be endangered through political pressures. They said it would be nice if I told them every helpful thing I could think of about Sam, because if the authorities caught him with all that gold, and if Sam talked too much about where he got it, a lot of private and semi-official arrangements might collapse, and the newspaper publicity might make certain officials take steps they had already been bribed not to take.

"I made a sort of arrangement with them. I said I would stay on and sort of take charge of the household. They gave me some money. They said they would send me draughts on the bank in Culiacan to cover household expenses, plus a salary for me. Then when Carlos dies, they'll send people to arrange about disposing of the house, getting the staff resettled, getting Mrs. Menterez into an institution. And they said I'll get a bonus at that time. But I was to live quietly. No big parties and lots of house guests like before. They gave me an address in Mexico City to write to if anything happens. So . . . I told them all I knew about Sam, about how he planned to sell the statues to Cal Tomberlin. And I told them his village slut, Felicia, might know something. They went away in their car. After a few weeks I . . . thought of Gabe and sent for him. He's been here three weeks. Then yesterday I got that note . . . and I wanted to know what the message was. From Sam."

Her voice had gotten increasingly husky. Her head lolled. "Please," she said in a faint voice. "I'm getting awful uncomfortable." Perspiration darkened the blue blouse, pasting it to her midriff. I got up and stretched the stiffness out of my legs and went over and gave her three feet of slack and made the line fast in that position. She brought her arms down, moved in a small circle, rolling her shoulders.

"I've leveled with you," she said. "Completely. I've told you everything. Maybe it doesn't make me look so good. I can't help that. I know one thing in this world. If you don't take care of yourself, nobody else is going to."

"Have they sent you money?"

"Once. I guess it's going to come once a month. It wasn't as much as they said it would be."

"What are the names of those two men?"

"They never said. One was Luis and the other was Tomas.

They had a white Pontiac convertible, great big sunglasses, resort clothes, a very sharp pair. The other times they were here, they were very respectful to Carlos."

"Do you know the names of the people on the boat?"

"Just the one that Cal brought to the house, the older one. Senor Mineros. I don't know his first name."

"Where does Tomberlin live?"

"He has a lot of places. The only one I was at was a sort of lodge, way up near Cobblestone Mountain. I don't mind fun and games. But that got a little too rich for me, believe me. He had a lot of kids up there that weekend. I knew most of them. It got crazy up there. You couldn't walk without stepping on a jumbled up pile of kids and getting pulled down into a lot of messy fooling around. I got out of there."

She looked at me with delicate indignation, a righteous little snippet, asking my moral approval.

"How old are you, Almah?"

"Twenty-four."

Nora was having a long wait. I looked at the lovely and slightly soiled little blondie. I wondered what I would do with her if I really had the power to judge her and sentence her. Like the true eccentric, she thought she was just like everybody else. She was a cold mischief, with looks which had kept her from paying any penalties. In a small wind in the clearing, blowing toward me, she smelled of scent, of repellent, and a small sharp smell of nervous perspiration. She was too self-involved, in money hunger and pleasure hunger, to be the legendary femme fatale. She was a blunderer, but she would keep landing on her feet. She was never going to bring anyone any luck.

She had explained something I had felt about Sam Taggart. There had been a strangeness about him. During the short time I'd been with him, I'd felt—that we could never again be as close as we had once been. He'd traveled too far. That little boat ride had taken him a long long way. At the time he died, he was trying to come back, but he probably knew he could never make it all the way back. He could pretend for a time. But the act of murder was still with him. Nora would have immediately sensed that strangeness, that apartness. And she would not have rested until she learned the cause of it.

Little Almah Hichin, with her lavender eyes, and her slender girlish figure, and her greedy and available and random little loins, was going to go her way, making out, aiming for the money, spicing it with her kicks. As most of the people who would become involved with her would be as trivial as she was, she would probably do no great amount of human damage. A child of her times, running free as long as she dared, then setting herself to entrap some monied fool old enough so no childbearing would be asked of her. She felt herself to be infinitely sweet and precious and provocative. Enchantingly foolish sometimes. But talented and admirable. A lovely smile is really all a girl needs.

"Why don't you say something?" she asked.

Suddenly it didn't seem suitable to merely untie her. She would preen herself and pat her hair and tell me chidingly that I had been horrid to her. Her manner would be flirtatious and self-satisfied. I wondered if it would be possible to convince her of her own mortality, and if it would do any good. That cold little sensuous brain thought it would live forever.

"I guess I'm stalling. This isn't something I'm going to enjoy."

"What do you mean?"

I shrugged. "Chivalry or something, I guess. And when . . . a girl is as pretty as you are, Almah, it seems like such a hell of a waste. And, to tell the truth, I'm sort of an amateur at this. I've never killed a woman before."

Her mouth sagged and her eyes bulged. "Kill!"

"Sweetie, I told you I couldn't promise a thing."

"But I've told you everything! My God! You can't be serious! Look, I'll do anything you say. You could get in terrible trouble. People will look for me."

I pointed a thumb over my shoulder. "They won't look back in that jungle. I guess I'm not doing you any favor by stalling. I know I have to do it. But I feel squeamish about it."

She tried to smile. "This is some kind of a nasty joke, isn't it?"

"I wish it was. I'll make it easy on you. I won't hurt you."

"But I haven't done anything!"

"I have to do as I'm told."

I stared somberly at her. Her color had become quite ghastly. "Now wait a minute!" she said, her voice high and thin. "I'm going to get that money. Listen, you could come back with me and I could get you into the house. You could be with me every minute. You could come with me when we go to get the money. You can have half of it. You can have *all* of it."

"You can scream now if you want to. It might help a little. It won't make any difference, but it might help."

She had begun to babble, her voice high and thin and fast and almost out of control. "But you don't even know me. You've got no reason! Please! I can hide here. You can say you did it. Then I'll go wherever you want me to go. I can wait for you. Please. I'll belong to you. I'll do anything for you. Please don't do that to me!" She began to dash back and forth, yanking at the rope, making little yelping sounds of panic.

I went to the line and hauled it tighter than before, bringing her up onto tiptoe. Again I felt that urge to howl with sour laughter. Melodrama made me self-conscious. But I thought of what she had talked Sam into doing, and I wanted to make a lasting impression on her. I wanted her to feel death so close she could smell the shroud and the dank earth.

I took the pocket knife out and opened the ridiculously small blade. I walked up to her. Her eyes showed white all the way around the lavender irises. She had bitten into her underlip. There was a smear of blood at the corner of her mouth. She made a maddened humming sound, and her body spasmed and snapped and contorted in the animal effort to run. She looked at the knife, and the ultimate terror of it loosened her control over her bodily functions. Now she was beyond all pretense, perhaps for the first time since childhood. Sam's last duchess. Menterez' last blonde slut. As I raised the blade, she opened her jaws wide in a final yawning caw of despair, and I lifted it above her hands and cut the line.

She fell in a sprawling soiled heap, sobbing and shuddering, rolling her face against the earth. I looked down at her for a moment, pocketed the knife and walked out to the car. Nora started to say something, and looked at my face and stopped abruptly. She slid over and I got behind the wheel. I drove in silence to the hotel. Nora got out there. She said, "Are we going to leave?"

"Tomorrow."

"All right, dear."

"I think I'll go back and pick her up."

"Yes, dear."

fourteen

ALMAH HICHIN had taken a long time to free her hands and pull herself together enough to start walking west, toward the village. Felicia had walked it.

She was only about a hundred yards from the obscure entrance to the isolated clearing. She stopped when she saw the car coming. She looked small, lost, displaced in time and space. I went on by her, turned around in the road and came back, through my own drift of dust. I stopped beside her. She leaned on the closed door and gave a gagging cough. Then she looked at me with a hideous remnant of flirtatiousness, like the grin on a cholera victim, and said in a trembling voice, "Did you . . . want to give me a ride?" Her glance met mine and slid away, utterly humble.

"Get in."

She slid in, wary and apologetic and self-effacing. As I started up I told myself that something would have broken her sooner or later. She would have come up against something that couldn't be teased, cajoled or seduced. The ones with no give, the ones with the clear little porcelain hearts shatter. And in the shattering, some chips and splinters are lost, so that when, with great care, they are mended, the little fracture lines show. Did she, for God's sake, think she was going to be immune forever? The blackness is always a half step behind you, hand raised to touch you on the shoulder. Sam learned that. Carlos learned it. Nora learned it. Little golden girls cannot stay ignorant forever. But when you break a pretty thing, even if it is a cheap pretty thing, something does go out of the world. Something died in that clearing. And she would never fit together as well again.

I pulled over and stopped abruptly, short of the ridge where the village would be in view. She had ridden with her head bowed, her small fist and marked wrists cradled in her lap. I got out and said, "You can take it from here."

She raised her head slowly and looked at me through the sheaf of spilled blonde hair, her face crinkled and puzzled, like a child wondering whether to cry.

"Why?" she said. Her lip was badly swollen where she had gnawed it in her terror.

"Because you have to play these games with real blood and real people."

"Who are you?"

"Sam was my friend a long time ago," I said. "The woman on the boat was real. The knife was real. The blood was real. Sam died on that boat. It was just your turn to die a little."

"I'm just sick now. I'm just terribly terribly sick."

"So is Carlos."

She coughed into her fist. "You say crazy things. I don't mean to hurt anybody. You want to hurt people. You wanted to hurt me. God, I feel destroyed! What does that make you? Does that make you so great, scaring the wits out of me?" There was no real defiance. It was just a reflex, an habitual attitude, accompanied by that horrid little smirk I had seen before. Her glance moved swiftly away again, reminding me of the way a spiritless dog cringes when inviting a caress. She would have to learn how to imitate defiance. There wasn't any of the genuine article left. It had crawled off into the brush behind the clearing to die and rot. I wondered if she could sense how it was all going to be for her from now on. The jackals can always sense that kind of vulnerability. Imitations of defiance amuse them. They travel in packs. They would hand her around. She wouldn't last very well.

There was no answer I could give her. I began walking toward the village. After fifty feet I looked back. She was still on the passenger side. At the top of the ridge I looked back again. She was behind the wheel. A little later I heard the car start and come toward me. I played a little game, with a flavor of penance. As the car came up behind me, I listened for a sudden change in the motor noise, and I was poised to dive clear. If there was that much spirit left, maybe she wouldn't be jackal meat after all. Maybe there was a toughness I hadn't reached. The red car went by me, slowly, as far over on the other side as she could get it. She gave me a single empty look and went on, clutching the wheel at ten after ten, the blonde hair blowing in the dusty wind.

I went right to the Tres Panchos. It was a little after five. There were a half dozen fishermen in there, smelling of their trade. The juke was playing the brass *pasodoble* of the bull ring. I leaned into a corner of the bar, and made Mustache understand with bad Spanish and gestures that I wanted a glass of ice and a bottle of tequila añejo. *"Botella?"* he asked. *"La Botella?"* I reached and took it out of his hand. Twenty *pesos*. He shrugged and watched me pour the glasses and shrugged again and walked away.

I motioned him back and had him get himself a shot glass. I filled it from my bottle. I held my glass up and said, "Drink to me, my friend. Drink to this poisonous bag of meat named McGee. And drink to little broken blondes, and a dead black dog, and a knife in the back of a woman, and a knife in the throat of a friend. Drink to a burned foot, and death at sea, and stinking prisons and obscene gold idols. Drink to loveless love, stolen money and a power of attorney, *mi amigo*. Drink to lust and crime and terror, the three unholy ultimates, and drink to all the problems which have no solution in this world, and at best a dubious one in the next."

He beamed without comprehension, and said, "Salud!" We drank and bowed and I filled the glasses again.

I know that for a long time there was a respectful area of emptiness around me, even when the place had filled up. The Mexicans respect the solemn, dedicated, brooding *borracho,* and have an almost racial empathy for the motives which can send the soul of a man crawling down the neck of a bottle to drown. I know there was a purchase of another bottle. But from there on, memory is fragmented by a vast paralysis of the cerebral cortex. Chopped bright fragments of memory endure. McGee dancing—the feet very deft very tricky, so that I could look down with awe and watch them perform on their own. McGee, the soul of generosity, buying drinks for multitudes of friends. McGee leading a choral group in a song so heartbreaking it made him weep—Somewhere Over the Rainbowwwwwww ... And then a hilarious and giggling and cooperative process of getting the unwieldy bulk of McGee up a narrow staircase, some of the sweet gigglers pushing from behind, and some ahead, pulling him by the hands. Light of two yellow flames. Great blundering sprawl into a rickety clatter of bed, huge McGee guffaws—McGaw guffees?—mingling with the soprano jabbering, laugh-squeals, clothes-tugging. Later, in a heavy sweet humid blackness,

awakening to incomprehensible effort, a half-dream of holding someone, of trying to overcome, together, a great steady
remorseless beating, of trying to still and silence something as
implacable as the sea itself. Texture of dense hair, not clov-
ery, thick with perfume, taint of kerosene. A sticky chomping
next to my ear. Thin smell of spearmint mingling with the
rest. Guilt. Then a strange awareness of a sour justice in it—
This will cure that. This will end that. This will atone for
that. . . .

I awoke into suffocating heat, to barbed needles of light
which went through my eyes and into my brain, to a mouth
dry as sand, clotted teeth, and a headache that seemed to
expand and contract my forehead with each heartbeat as
though it were a red balloon a child was trying to inflate.
Tequila hangover, in a gagging density of perfume, under a
tin roof, on the sweat-damp sheets of a village whore. She
stood naked beside the bed, bending over me, looking at me
with melting concern, the heat in the room making her look
as if she had been greased.

"Leedle seek?" she said.

"Oh God. Oh God."

She nodded and shouldered into something pink and went
out the door. When she came back she had a tin pitcher of
ice water, a jelly glass, and some ice wrapped in a towel. I
drank water until my belly felt tight as a drum. Then I lay
back and chewed ice, with the chilly towel across my forehead and eyes, wondering where she had gone. She came
back and took the towel off my face and handed me a half
glass of reddish brown liquid.

"Drink fast," she said, making the gesture of tossing it off.

I did so. I think one could achieve the same result by
drinking four ounces of boiling tabasco sauce. I sprang up. I
roared and paced and wept. I sweated and gasped and wept
and held my throat. I ran back to the bed and opened the
towel and stuffed my mouth with ice and chomped it up like
Christmas candy. When the worst of it was over, I subsided
weakly on the bed. Felicia had watched the whole performance calmly, standing leaning against the door frame, her
arms folded. As I became aware of my headache again, I
realized it was not quite as bad. I mopped my face with the
cool towel. The cure reminded me of an ancient joke. A man
has all his teeth pulled and new plates put in immediately.

The dentist tells him they'll be uncomfortable for a while. Two weeks later he runs into the dentist. He is hobbling along on two canes. The dentist asks him what happened. He explains that he had gone fishing with his wife and she had fallen out of the rowboat. In diving overboard to rescue her, he had misjudged distance, and caught himself in the groin with an oarlock. He says, "You know, for about forty seconds there, Dock, my teeth didn't bother me a damn bit."

She went over to her dressing table, opened a box, and came back with my watch and wallet. It was five of eleven by my watch. She said, "Every goddam *peso* is there, Trrav."

She went over and filled the wash basin, laid out soap and towel and comb. She tossed her pink wrapper aside, searched one of the cardboard wardrobes and pulled out that orange shift I had seen her in before and pulled it on. She gave a couple of casual swipes at her hair with a brush, painted her mouth, yawned and said, "I am downstairs, okay?"

"Okay. I guess I was a damn fool."

She shrugged. "Pretty dronk, Trrav." She gave me a broad merry smile. "Almost too dronk for the love." She went out and closed the door.

Getting dressed was sad and enormous labor. A man in the grip of the remorses is a pitiable thing. You think of all the promise you once had, and what has become of you. A hundred different versions of yourself sit in the audience and applaud ironically. Your own body disgusts you. Alcohol is a depressant—physically and emotionally. And that final fermentation of the maguey seems to uncork the bottommost cask, where you have been hiding the black despairs of all the years.

When I found the inside staircase and went down, I was glad to see that only Mustache and Felicia were there. As I trudged toward the bar, Mustache uncapped a bottle of beer and set it on the bar with a flourish. He knew a glass would be superfluous. I held the bar with one hand and tilted it up with the other, and set it down when it was empty. I stopped him from opening another one.

Felicia took me by the wrist and tugged me over to a table. I told her I had to get back to the hotel. She said we had to talk first.

She sat opposite me and looked at me with a certain somber speculation. "One man from Garcia loves a hotel girl. I hear a thing. I wonder something. You go in there? Kill a dog? Almost kill some man too?"

"Me? No."

"Yesterday your skinny woman is in the red car with the Heechin *rubia*. Then you are alone in the red car. And one time you are in the car with your skinny one. And one time Heechin is alone, eh?"

"So?"

She slitted the anthracite eyes. "Felicia is not stupid. It is about Sam, eh? These things?"

"Felicia, those men who hurt you, they had a white car?"

"Ah, such a beautiful car, *sí*."

"How was Sam going to get to the States from Los Mochis?"

"He gets to Ensenada by little airplane, it is easy from there, Trrav. Many ways."

"Where no one will look in that heavy case he had?"

"Many ways. For a man who has some Spanish and some money." She closed her strong coppery fingers around my waist. "The hotel girl says one thing. There is one bad man at Garcia. One killer, eh? Miguel, I think. You are trouble to Garcia, maybe they send him. *Cuidado, hombre.*"

"Why would they think I'm trouble?"

"The *rubia* could think so, eh? Too many question, maybe? One thing. You have trouble, Trrav, you have friends here. Okay?"

"Okay."

"Miguel is most sad of the dog. His dog, Brujo."

"What does Miguel look like?"

"Tiny small skinny man with a sad face. Maybe forty years. Very quick."

"And he worked with Sam on the Garcia boat?"

"Ah, you know it too! On that boat, La Chispa. Very pretty. But not using it now a long time. Months, maybe. Garcia use it every day almost, long ago, many people, fishing, drinking, music. Nobody to run it now, unless Miguel." She patted my hand. "Have care, *amador*. Come back to Felicia."

"I think we are leaving soon."

She concealed a sharp look of disappointment with an almost immediate impassivity. She nodded. "Maybe this is not a good place for you."

I trudged the seven hundred miles to the Casa in my dirty shirt, feeling unwell. I had the cold sweats, and the residual twitches of alcoholic poisoning. And I had the guilts. You think that you have laboriously achieved adult status. Then you prove there must be an incurable streak of adolescence. I knew that Nora would be wild with worry. When I went to the desk for my key, I had the impression everybody knew exactly where I had been all night. Arista seemed blandly contemptuous.

He said, "At the lady's request, sir, I made flight arrangements for you. But you would have had to leave here at ten-thirty by bus. It is now too late. Please let me know if you want this arranged again for tomorrow. It is a considerable inconvenience to me when such plans are changed."

"Aren't you being paid to be inconvenienced, Arista?"

"In the case of valued guests, I would say yes."

For a moment I debated pulling him over the counter by the front of his spotless jacket, and running him down his front steps. But the effort would joggle my head.

"What kind of guest am I, Arista?"

He smiled. "We have discovered a small difficulty in the reservations. We shall require that your rooms be vacated by tomorrow, sir. I trust you will be able to settle your account in cash?"

"Or you will call the village cop?"

"I would not imagine you are entirely unacquainted with the police, sir."

I had difficulty in thinking clearly. I could not imagine what had so abruptly changed his attitude. Could Almah Hichin have made some kind of complaint? Had I been seen going in or out of my room window? Could he really be so prim about a night on the town?

"That's a dangerous smile, Arista. It tempts me to see if I can knock it off."

He took a hasty step back. "If you and . . . the lady leave quietly tomorrow, sir, I will not cause you any trouble. As you leave I shall turn over to you an object I now have in my office safe. It is not customary for tourists to bring such things into Mexico. The room maid reported that a toilet was not flushing properly. The maintenance man discovered . . . the hidden weapon and turned it over to me. I will give it back to you when you leave. I wish to operate . . . a quiet and respectable resort, sir."

I stood for a few minutes in thought. "I suppose your whole staff knows about this by now."

"It is the sort of thing that would entertain them."

"When was it found?"

"Yesterday, in the early afternoon. I expected you to deny any knowledge of it, sir."

"Why?"

"Possession of a weapon can be an awkwardness for a tourist, I would think."

I smiled at him. "Arista, it just grieves me that I can't ever tell you how stupid you're being. I might be able to tell the owners, but I can't ever tell you."

It was a childish counterattack, but it knifed him neatly. I saw his face go blank as he began to think of certain legitimate reasons why I might have a gun in the room. "But, sir, I can only go by what. . . ."

"Forget it, Arista."

"But . . . it could be possible that reservations might be rearranged so that. . . ."

"Forget that too. Set us up to get out of here tomorrow morning."

"Operating a place such as this is often a very. . . ."

"You have lots of problems," I said and walked away.

It was after twelve. The interconnecting door was closed. It was locked on her side. There was no answer to my knock. I took a tub, hot as I could stand it, and topped it off with a cold shower. I pared the sandpaper stubble from my jaws. All the thorn gashes were cleanly scabbed, and I got rid of the last of the little bandages. The gnawed place on my arm was healing well too, and did not look too much like tooth-marks, so I left the bandage off also. I dressed in fresh clothing, and looked at my face in the mirror. Eyes sunken and slightly bloodshot. Slight tendency toward cold sweat. A faint beginning of hunger. Small motor tremor of the hands.

Just as I was about to leave the room, I heard Nora stirring around on the other side of the door. I knocked and heard her call, "Just a minute!"

In a little while she unlocked the door and opened it and said, "Yes?" She wore a robe and a small and rather formal smile.

"I thought you might have wondered about me."

"Not particularly, Trav."

"Oh."

"I wandered out to the road and I saw Miss Hichin go by, alone, heading up toward the house, driving quite slowly. I thought you would come back and tell me what she had told you. I thought you might realize I was quite anxious to know. When it got to be dark, I sent Jose down to the village to find you, on his scooter. He said you were singing and dancing. I hope you had a jolly time. I made reservations, but. . . ."

"I know. I talked to Arista. He's making them again for tomorrow."

"I've been at the pool. I'll be going down to lunch in a little while."

"I don't think that would be a good place to talk to you."

"Why not?"

"It's public. You might be upset."

"I don't imagine anything can get me that upset."

"It upset me, Nora. I got pretty drunk."

"Evidently. You look it."

"I stayed there."

"More research, no doubt."

"You can't do much research after you pass out."

"Let me explain something to you. You don't have to justify yourself to me. I haven't put any strings on anything. You're a free agent, Trav. I expected a little more consideration. Not on the basis of anything between us, but just because . . . you know I was anxious to know what you found out."

"When you get dressed come in here and I'll tell you."

She came in when she was ready. I told her. Long after she kept denying that Sam could have done that, tears running down her face, I knew that she had begun to accept it. And I was certain when she began to blame Almah. I tried to explain to her how I had felt about the little broken blonde, but she could not comprehend that, because hers was a different kind of toughness. It wasn't the hard and fragile kind. Then I told her about Arista and the gun. She understood then why Arista had been rude and impertinent to her.

"There's something else about the gun," I said. "All the hotel servants know about it. They lost a gun up there the other night. It makes a pretty easy two plus two. But I don't think anybody will make a move. Menterez is helpless. The girl is demoralized. I don't think any of them want any police problems. Some girl that works in the hotel sees one of those Cubans. Word would get back that way, probably last night. Probably water swirling out of the tank moved the gun and it got in the way of the mechanism. One of those things."

"If those guards decide it was you, Trav, what would they think you were trying to do?"

"Friend of Mineros, maybe, coming to take another crack at Menterez. If they know about the gun, let's assume they know we're leaving. There's nothing more here, Nora. We go and try it from the other direction. Tomberlin and Mineros, the friends of Mineros."

"Why haven't those friends come after Carlos Menterez before now?"

"Maybe they have been around. Killing a man in that shape would be doing him a favor. And it would have to be a personal thing. Mineros could blame Carlos for the death of his brother, his brother's wife, his nephew. Maybe the people who knew what Mineros was trying to do, maybe they don't have strong reasons. This is remote. It's hard to get at him. And it's obviously dangerous. Maybe the two younger men who were killed along with Mineros are the only ones who would have had the push to make another try. Hell, maybe somebody is setting it up more carefully for the next attempt. We're in the dark, Nora."

"And the girl and that lawyer will get the money?"

"If she can get him to sign. If the bank accepts it. If somebody isn't waiting for her to walk out with it. If the cash isn't found at the border and impounded. Carlos Menterez must know exactly what she is. And he knows that's all he has left. Money he can't get to, and a girl who doesn't give a damn about him. A big house and a crazy wife and not much more time left. And a stranger's face at his window. Nora?"

"Yes?"

"Does it do any good to tell you I'm sorry?"

"It was probably a good thing, Trav. Maybe I was getting emotionally dependent. Maybe . . . things were getting too important." She tried to smile. "I guess it's a little bit like waking up."

I checked my watch. It was two-thirty. "Do you want lunch?"

"I guess not. Not now."

"What do you want to do?"

"Lie down for a little while, I guess." She went into her room. In a few moments she rapped and came back in and handed me the garish little bedroom gun.

"By the way, you handled that well," I told her.

She made a sour mouth. "I imagined her with Sam. I guess it made me pretty convincing. That plus a natural antagonism toward pretty blondes." The door closed.

I was able to get a sandwich at the hotel bar. Afterwards I wandered down to the boat basin and walked around to the other side reserved for resident boats. There were four tied up there. I would have expected La Chispa to have been one of the two bigger ones. But it was a flush deck cruiser, about 42 feet, twin screw, doubtless gas fueled. It was custom, with a big bow flare, outriggers, too much chrome for my taste. It had that look of neglect which a boat can acquire quicker than any other gadget known to man. The varnish was turning milky. The chrome was pitted. The white hull was black-ringed like a boardinghouse bathtub. Birds had left their tokens topsides. The mooring lines were chafed and bearded, and she looked a little low in the water, as if the pumps would have a long chore when somebody turned her on. The dinghy was upside down topsides, and named the Chispita. Sam's assault craft. The stupid son of a bitch.

I went back past the sign which said Owners and Guests Only, and hunted for Heintz and found him in the shed behind the dock office putting a new diaphragm in a complex looking fuel pump. I made some small talk, and when I thought I could do it casually enough, I said, "It looks like one of those over there is going to sink at the dock one of these days."

"Oh. La Chispa? The owner is sick."

"Doesn't he have anyone to look after it?"

"The man left when he got sick."

"I hate to see that happen to a boat."

"I know. One of these days, maybe, I'll see if I can get permission to fix it up."

"Pretty small to go anywhere from here, isn't it?"

"Just a local boat. He had it freighted to Mazatlan and brought up here. A long run for that boat, Mazatlan to here. You have to wait for good weather. If he wanted, he could run it over to La Paz, but nowhere from there except back. Not enough range. A damn fool maybe could get it up to

Guaymas, or maybe even down to Manzanillo, but that's the end of the line. The big motor sailers are what you have to have on this coast."

"I understand some pretty good-sized yachts get lost in these waters. I read about one a couple of months ago."

He tightened up the last bolts on the housing of the fuel pump before answering. "The Columbine. She was in here. She anchored off. A good sea boat. I would guess an eight hundred mile range at low cruising. Things can happen. It was chartered. Maybe bad maintenance. Dry rot. Bottled gas explosion in the galley. Maybe they set course for Cabo San Lucas and the compensation chart was wrong and they made a bad estimate of speed and passed it too far to the south. It's a damn big ocean out there."

He put the tools away and walked to his office. I walked along with him. He stopped suddenly and stared across the small boat basin. "Maybe we can both stop worrying about La Chispa," he said. I looked over and saw a swarthy little man in khakis trot out along the finger pier and leap nimbly aboard the boat, a cardboard carton under one arm, and a bulging burlap sack over the other shoulder. "That one worked as mate aboard," he said. *"Hola!* Miguel!" he called.

The man looked around the side of the trunk cabin. I could not see him distinctly at a hundred and fifty feet, but I saw the white streak of grin.

"Buena tarde, Senor Heintz!" he called back.

Heintz said about two hundred words at high speed, ending in an interrogating lift of his voice.

Miguel answered at length. Heintz laughed. Miguel disappeared.

"I told him he should be ashamed of the condition of the boat, and he said that if one works twenty hours a day, there is no time for playing with toys. Now he is ordered to put it in condition to sell it, very quickly and cheaply, and perhaps he will buy it himself and compete with the hotel for fishing charters. That was a joke. He's not that good with a boat, and you couldn't run that thing at a profit. I've been relieved not to have him around for a couple of months. He's a violent little man. He hurt two of my men badly. They were making loud remarks about the Cubans, for his benefit. If Taggart hadn't broken it up, he might have killed them both. He looked as if he wanted to. Taggart grabbed him and threw him off the dock."

"Was he taking supplies aboard?"

"Maybe. There'd be a better market for it in La Paz or Mazatlan. The owner will never use it again. But I wouldn't want to trust Miguel to get it there. I've seen him at the wheel. He tried to handle it like Taggart did. That is like letting a child drive a sports car."

After I had left Heintz, I went up to the pool level and sat at a shady table overlooking the boat basin and had a bottle of beer. I watched Miguel working around the boat and I felt curious and oddly uneasy about it. It made sense that Almah should try to pry loose all the money she could. Sell everything that wasn't bolted down. Maybe Carlos would sign the boat documentation, releasing ownership. And perhaps the title papers on the automobiles. But by doing that she would be delaying the day when she could force him to sign the bank papers. And from the look of him, she couldn't count on too much time.

I saw Miguel squatting and fooling with the dockside power outlet, trotting back and forth. Finally dirty water began to squirt off the bilge. Then, one at a time, I saw him lug four big batteries over to the office shed, where Heintz probably had a quick charger. Miguel went back and stood and studied the lines. It was well moored, with four lines and two spring lines. He took three lines off and coiled them, leaving the bow line, the stern line and the bow spring line on.

Then he went up the steps on the far side, and up the path and disappeared, moving very spryly. A few minutes later I saw a car going up the road, one of the three I had spotted while scaring hell out of myself. It was one of those Datsun things, the Nipponese version of a Land Rover. Carlos was fine for cars—the Datsun, the Ghia, and a big black Imperial. In addition to the steps and walk, there was a steep curve of narrow road which came down to the boat area. And I wondered why Miguel hadn't used that. He had the car for it. The Boody jeep would make it easily. And I wondered if Miguel hadn't been just a little too jolly in his long range conversation with Heintz. Also, he was doing nothing about dressing the boat up. Maybe she wanted to sell it in a hurry. That much of a hurry?

Ninety-nine percent of the things that ninety-nine percent of the people do are entirely predictable, when you have a few lead facts. Drunks, maniacs and pregnant women are the customary exceptions. Everyone has the suspicion he is utterly unique. But we are a herd animal, and we all turn to face into the wind.

I sat and tried to read that bloody little man from long range. I could presume he had been with Menterez a long time, and had done him many violent favors, and had had the protection of Menterez to hide behind. He had had years of exile from the homeland. He would know that Menterez was an attractive target. Assume a hell of a lot of pride. The shot which had nearly killed Menterez would have been a personal affront to Miguel. Possibly his duties aboard the boat were more as bodyguard than mate. Assume he had itched to take care of the men aboard the Columbine IV, and could perhaps have handled that part of it alone, but Sam had to be alone because it had to be done silently, and Sam would know just how to set up the controls to send them on their way. So it was done, and then the king was laid low when something burst in his head. The partner in murder took off.

Then there was the next affront, a bold invasion of protected ground, the treasured dog killed, a head broken. Perhaps the collapse of Menterez had made Miguel begin to feel a little insecure. He was, after all, a murderer. There can be an end to loyalty. This was not his country. Things were beginning to fall apart. The invasion would alarm him. And then, perhaps, he would see Menterez' woman come home, soiled and sick, dazed and broken. That special look would be meaningful to Miguel. tI would be something he had seen before. The marks on the wrists would be significant. And he would know she had known about the boat business. Chucho's revolver had been taken. A revolver had been found in the room of a hotel guest, a big brown man who looked as if he could come over a wall in the night. The same man had been seen in the red car with the dark woman who was at the hotel with him.

Loyalty must stop, and a small bloody man must start thinking of his own skin.

Once aboard the boat and clear, he had a lot of choices. Angostura. Topolobambo. A little brown spry man with a sad face, and some pesos in hand, abandoning the boat and melting into an alien countryside.

I shook myself out of it like a wet dog. Imagination is useful, but it turns treacherous if you depend too much upon it. But it was like a picture hanging crooked on the wall. I wanted to go over and straighten it. If that violent little man was leaving, I did not think he would leave quietly.

Nursing another bottle of beer, I waited and watched. A half hour later the Datsun came back and parked along the road at a place I could not see. Miguel came down the path, heavily laden, and pounced aboard. He had comported himself in that super-casual manner of someone who wishes to avoid attention by seeming to perform perfectly ordinary acts. He went and got the batteries, one at a time, and brought them back and spent enough time aboard so I was certain he had strapped them in and hooked them up. The cruiser rode higher. The bilge outlet was spitting dirty spray. He took his power line off the dockside connection and it stopped. He coiled the power line, knelt and tied it, and took it aboard. Again he hurried back up to the truck and went back up to the last house at the crest of the knoll.

What if Carlos' condition had suddenly worsened? Miguel would know it would make sense for him to take off the moment Menterez died. I could not imagine him being very close to the other Cubans in the compound. Those little deadly ones are loners, just as his dog had been.

I went to the desk and made arrangements about the bill. The fun-loving, sun-loving tourists were milling around. Arista was looking for an opening, perhaps to cover himself in the absurd eventuality that I had some sort of official status. I told him we would pay cash for breakfast, so he could have the account ready. The luggage would be ready to bring out at ten-fifteen. Yes, the bus would leave at ten-thirty, and make the air connection in Culiacan in plenty of time.

"I shall turn your property over to you upon departure, sir."

"What property?"

"Uh . . . the weapon, sir."

"I don't know anything about any weapon, Arista."

"But, sir, you admitted that. . . ."

"I don't know what you're talking about. You don't have anything of mine. If you think you have something of mine why you just keep it."

"But it was found. . . ."

"I'm not responsible for what other guests leave in the rooms."

When I looked back at him he was dry-washing his hands,

and I think his underlip was trembling. The rooms were empty. I went looking for Nora. I found her coming out of the bar. She was looking for me. She had changed. She wore a very simple sleeveless white dress with a sun back. She had flattened her hair, fastened it into severity. The white dress deepened her tan. She looked very composed. I steered her back into the bar, back to the far table where we had first sat. She wanted bourbon on ice, and I got two of them.

"Get some sleep?"

"No. I just . . . did a lot of thinking, Travis."

"Any conclusions?"

"A few. I felt very savage about Sam. It all seemed so black and white. Maybe that's my flaw, to see everything as totally right or totally wrong. But it isn't like that, is it?"

"You mean the bad guys and the good guys? No, it isn't like that, not when you know enough about it."

"I can't be some sort of abstract and objective instrument of justice, Trav, when I don't even know what justice is any more. I don't think I ever really knew Sam. I know that you brought me along as . . . as a disguise."

"And because you had to get it out of your system one way or another."

"One way or another," she said. She nodded. "Did you know that all that thirst for vengeance was going to sort of . . . fade away?"

"No. But I knew it was possible."

She took the last swallow, and the ice clicked against her teeth. She shook her head. "It's such a . . . such a lot of bloody confusion. And here I am, wandering around in it with my dime store morality. I feel like such an ass."

"It got to me yesterday. It shouldn't have. God knows I've been dry behind the ears for a long long time. But the little mental image of Sam holding the arms of the woman they didn't know was there, and that bloody little monster sliding up behind her with. . . ."

"Don't!" she whispered. "Please."

"I'd be better off without a little taint of idealism, Nora. Then I could accept the fact that man is usually a pretty wretched piece of work."

"You asked for conclusions. Okay. I'm dropping the dime store morality bit, darling. Yesterday you had it up to here. I don't care what you did. I don't even care if you slept with that Felicia. Maybe it would have been a kind of brutal therapy. I don't have any special privileges. I haven't asked for any or granted any. If you left me in kind of . . . an agony of suspense, I should have had the sense to know that whatever you had to tell me would keep. So I am still in your bed, if I please you."

"You do."

"Everybody is so damned lonely, you have to take what there is. And if there are any good guys at all, you're one of them."

"You'll turn my head."

"Further conclusion. When we leave here, I would be perfectly content to head all the way back. I'll reimburse you for everything, and I want no argument on that. But if you want to take it further, in California, and you think I'd be of any use to you, I'll go with you and do as I'm told. I can let it all drop right here. But I can understand that you . . . might feel as if you'd left something unfinished."

I went over and brought back two more bourbons. I thought it over and said, "I don't know. Tomberlin interests me. Maybe I better try the California thing alone. In one sense, he started the whole mess. In another sense, Menterez spent profitable years building it up to the ultimate mess, and it had to happen sooner or later. Let me think about it. The first thing we have to do is survive that airplane ride to Durango."

"If you hold my hand, we'll make it."

"You sank those nails in pretty good the last time."

"And we made it."

"Did you get any lunch at all?"

"No. Look. It's after five. I can last. I may get kind of glassy if you force another drink on me, but I can last. If you forced another drink on me, you could lead me off to the room and have your way with me, sir."

"Even without another drink?"

"One never knows unless one tries, does one."

fifteen

SHE WANTED to put on something else, but I asked her to put the white dress back on. I liked the way she looked in it. We went out onto the sun deck at the end of the corridor and sat where we could look down upon the pool people and, at the further level, the boat basin.

I told her about Miguel and the boat. Jose brought us drinks and a plate of little hot pastries with something baked into the center of each one—shrimp, steak, ham. She gobbled like a she-wolf, licking her fingers, making little sounds of pleasure not entirely dissimilar to the sounds the previous pleasure had elicited. The tautness was entirely gone out of her face, and she laughed more readily than ever before.

Then I finally realized that I had to do what I had been trying not to think of doing. The sun was low. The shadows were turning blue. And I told her I had to walk up the road and see if I could get a word with Almah. I said I would wear a disarming smile and stand well away from the gate and bellow Senorita Heechin por favor until the guard understood the message. I said I had to find out what shape she was in, and if she came out to the gate, I had a few questions about Tomberlin which might be helpful. I said that if there was any imminent ugliness, I would dive for the brush. It made her nervous for me to go up the road. She wanted to come along. I told her to stay and keep an eye on the boat. It was a make-work project, to make her feel useful.

When I started up the road, I looked back. I saw her going down the steps toward the pool, a slender distant figure in white. I stretched my legs and made pretty good time up the curves of the road. I was better than halfway to the pink house when I heard the pounding of running footsteps. An instant later the young lawyer appeared around the next curve. He wore pink shorts, a knit shirt, white sweat socks and tennis shoes. Those heavy white muscular hairy legs were not built for running. He was making a tremendous effort, but not covering much ground. The handsome face was mostly gasping mouth.

"Hay-yulp! Hay-yulp!" he bawled, and tried to point behind him and run at the same time. He ground to a stop in front of me, gasping hard, and said, "My God! He. . . . My God, the blood! Almah! My God . . . with a knife. . . ."

With a sudden rising roar, the Datsun came rocketing and sliding around the curve, and got a good grip and charged at us. I got the lawyer around the chunky waist and churned hard for the side of the road, with the tan vehicle aiming at us in a long slant. I scrabbled at the side hill beyond the ditch and almost pulled him clear, but the vehicle swerved into the ditch, bouncing hard, and one wheel caught his thick ankle against the stones in the ditch bottom and crushed it like pottery. He yelled and fainted. I left him there and took off after the vehicle. I came around a bend in time to see him pass the top of the path and brake hard and swing down the little steep side road to the boat basin. I swerved into the path. I was going too fast, slipped on loose stones, fell on one hip and skidded off into the brush. I got up and went on, running more slowly, and with a slight limp. When I got to the top of the steps, I could see the vehicle below me and see Miguel out on the finger pier, snatching the lines off and tossing them aboard. I raced down the steps and around the truck. I thought I might have a pretty good chance of running out and leaping aboard before he could get it started. He was aboard and scrambling toward the controls. Off to my right I suddenly saw Nora out of the corner of my eye, just past the sign saying boat owners and guests only, her hands clasped together, her eyes wide with alarm.

I didn't know how good an idea it might be to leap aboard with that desperate murderous little man, but I thought that if there was a handy boat hook, I might do some good.

The problem did not arise. A white blooming flower of heat picked me up and slammed me back against the side of the Datsun. I rebounded from it onto my face in the dust, too dazed to comprehend what had happened. Once upon a time I had been a hundred yards from a damn fool in a Miami marina when he had stepped aboard his jazzy little Owens and, without checking the bilge or turning the blowers on, had turned the key to start the engines. The accumulated gas fumes in the bilge had made a monstrous Whooompf. His fat wife was on the dock, and it had blown the sunsuit off her without leaving a mark on her. The owner had landed twenty feet away, in the water, with second degree burns and two broken legs. His crumpled beer cooler had landed on top of a car in the nearby parking lot. And what was left of the little cruiser had sunk seconds later.

This was no whooompf. This was a hard, full-throated, solid bam. It silenced that immediate portion of the world, and sent a thousand water birds wheeling and squalling. I picked myself up and fell. I saw Nora fifty feet away, trying to sit up. I started crawling to her. I stood up and took a dozen lurching steps and fell again and crawled the last few feet. She could not sit up. The white dress was not soiled. Her hair was not mussed. The only new thing about her was a crisp, splintery shard of mahogany. It looked as if it had been blown out of a portion of the rail. The rounded part of it was varnished. It was about twenty inches long. It was heaviest in the middle, tapering toward both ends. The middle of it was about as big around as her wrist. It was socketed into the soft tan hollow of her throat, at a slight angle so that the sharp splintered end stuck out of the side of her throat, near the back. She was braced up on one elbow, and with the fingertips of the other hand she touched the thing where it entered her throat.

She looked at me with an expression of shy, rueful apology, as though she wanted me to forgive her for being such a fool. Her lips moved, and then she frowned and coughed. She put her hand to her lips and coughed a bulging, spilling pint of red blood. She settled back. On hands and knees, I looked down into her eyes. She gave a little frown, as though exasperated at being so terribly messy, and coughed once again, and the dark eyes looked at me and then suddenly they looked through me and beyond me, and through the sky itself, glazing into that stare into infinity. She spasmed once, twitched those stupendous legs, and flattened slowly, slowly against the ground, shrinking inside that white dress until it looked too big for her, until she could have been a thin child in a woman's dress.

They said that things fell into the water for a long time, speckling the bay. They said that a broken piece of bronze cleat landed in the swimming pool. It blew the windows out of the office. They said that even flash-burned, with broken ribs and a sprained wrist, I kept four men busy getting me away from the body of Nora Gardino. They found some bits of Miguel. Enough for graveyard purposes.

The doctor who flew up from Mazatlan sprayed my burns, taped wrist and ribs. He treated the woman who had been so startled she fell down a short flight of stone steps. He did what he could with Gabriel Day's ruined ankle. I lay in bed and fought against the shot the doctor had given me. Then the first of the out of town police arrived, and after the first couple of questions, I stopped fighting the shot and let it take me under. It was easier down there.

With a hundred thousand U. S. citizens resident in Mexico, and with God only knows how many hundred thousand tourists wandering around, seeking access to the inaccessable, and with the economy waxing fat on tourist dollars, they are geared to swoop down upon any unpleasant happening and minimize it. We had special police from the state of Sinaloa. We had federal police and federal officials. And we had an influx of earnest young Mexicans in neat dark suits, carrying dispatch cases. They spoke fluent colloquial American.

I decided that I had better stay dazed for a while. I soon realized that they weren't looking for all the answers. They merely wanted something that sounded plausible. Something they could hand over to press association people as soon as they unlocked the gates and let them in.

As I saw the official version taking shape, I helped them along with it, and they seemed very pleased with me. I was just a tourist. Nora Gardino had been a friend of mine from Fort Lauderdale. I wouldn't want anybody to think, just because we had come down here together, that it was anything more than friendship. I had just taken an evening walk up the hill and ran into that fellow coming down, with some kind of a truck after him. I had done what I could, of course. What was he running from?

It made the men in the dark suits uneasy. But they had an official version for me. Mr. Day and Miss Hichin had been house guests of Carlos Garcia. Garcia had been seriously ill for many weeks, and Miss Hichin had stayed on to help care for him, as a gesture of friendship. She had asked Mr. Day to come and visit, with Garcia's permission. Now, to the consternation of everyone, they had discovered that Carlos Garcia was, in fact, Carlos Menterez, living in Mexico with falsified papers. He was a Cuban exile. Obviously, neither Miss Hichin or Mr. Day had known this. Apparently one Miguel Alconedo, also Cuban, a servant in the household, evidently emotionally unbalanced, had become infatuated with Miss Hichin. Perhaps he had made advances to her and she had rebuffed him. At any rate, poor Mr. Day had been walking toward the swimming pool to ask Miss Hichin if he could bring her a drink when he had seen the aforesaid Miguel Alconedo go up behind the chair where Miss Hichin was sitting, grasp her by her blonde hair, pull her head sharply back and slash her throat with such a ferocity the head was almost severed from the trunk. Mr. Day had hidden in the brush. He had seen Miguel run to the gates, speak to the guard there, and swing the gates open. In terror, Mr. Day had run through the open gates and down the hill. The demented murderer, after trying to run him down, and succeeding only in injuring him badly, had sought to escape on the boat which he had made ready for flight. But, as everyone now knew, there had probably been an accumulation of gasoline fumes in the bilge, a highly explosive situation. It was a tragic thing that Miss Gardino should have been killed by the bit of flying debris. It was fortunate that more people were not injured. In the reports it would be clearly indicated that the murderer of the lovely young actress was also in Mexico without proper and complete documentation. Now the authorities had stepped in, of course, and would see what could be done officially about the invalid and the rest of the household and staff.

I knew and they knew that Menterez had greased some palms, probably with the understanding that his cover would remain intact so long as he had no trouble. And they knew and I knew that it had been more than gas fumes. But the fun-lovers will not patronize a resort area where people go around wiring bombs into boats.

It had to be the Columbine IV, of course. Perhaps they had worked their dinghy ashore in the dark of night. It had acted like a six stick blast, plus the added push of all that gasoline. Based on the habits of the pre-stroke Menterez, such a device had a good chance of getting him. And hate can be so strong you cease caring whether you get some other people too. You can tell yourself the other people would be either his friends or his employees, and the hell with them.

It wouldn't have been hooked up after the stroke. No point. And the boat hadn't been used since the Columbine had been there.

The rest of the staff knew absolutely nothing, of course.

And there wasn't much danger of Nora getting much publicity. Not with an Almah Hichin and a young pretty lawyer to write about. The hotel had no legal responsibility in the matter, of course. After all, the lady was in an area clearly marked as private.

The wrist was a minor sprain. It throbbed when I let it hang. It was more comfortable if I walked with my thumb hooked over my belt. I had lost eyelashes, singed hair and eyebrows, lost the white sun-baked hair on hands and arms. I wanted to get to Mr. Day. Because his ankle was like a bag of marble chips, they were making complex arrangements about flying him to the nearest hospital with special facilities for that kind of work, in Torreon. They had him in room twenty. I got to him at ten in the morning. They were due to tote him down to the dock and slide him aboard an amphib at noon. He had a couple of the black-suited ones with him.

He looked at me as I came in and said in a mild drug-blurred voice, "You are the man who saved my life."

I asked if I could have a little time alone with him. They bowed and smiled their way out, like oriental diplomats. They liked us. We were being good boys. We had taken our indirect briefing like little soldiers.

I took the straight chair beside the bed. Staring out of all that hair and hard white meat and handsomeness were two ineffectual blue eyes.

"I lost my head," he said. "I would have kept running right down the middle of the road. They said your name is McGee." He put his hand out. "I'm very grateful to you." The handshake jiggled the bed, making him wince.

"What kind of law do you practice, Gabe?"

"Oh, theatrical mostly. Contract setups for independent producers. Special services contracts."

"Are you honest?"

"Of course!"

"Then how did you happen to team up with Almah Hichin in a conspiracy, boy?"

The pain-killer had slowed him. He blinked at me. "What are you talking about?"

"Almah's scheme to loot Menterez' lock box in Mexico City, boy."

"Whose?"

"Come off it!"

"Who are you anyhow?"

"I'm a tourist. Didn't they tell you that?"

He put the back of his hand across his eyes. "Jesus, I can't think. You . . . you have no idea how it was, seeing a thing like that. The way he jumped back, and all that blood. . . ."

"Was the money the big thing to you, Gabe? Over six hundred thousand in U.S dollars. And Menterez in no shape to lodge a complaint. You had the papers all set up, didn't you?"

He nodded. "Power of attorney. Doctor's affidavit."

"Was it the money?"

He took his hand away, but kept his eyes closed. "No. If she'd asked me to crawl through fire, I'd have done that too. She knew I was hooked. She knew I'd been hooked for a long time. When she could use me, she sent for me."

"It seems strange. You're good looking, and in a show biz area, and I'd think you could round up forty duplicates of her in one month."

He turned his head and looked at me. "Don't ask me to explain it, McGee. Infatuation. Sex. Put any word on it you want to. She was selfish and cruel and greedy. I know all that. She had a ring in my nose. And even when . . . it was the best for her, I had the idea it just happened to be me, and it could have been anybody. You know a funny thing? The closest I ever felt to her was the day before yesterday. She was out almost all afternoon. I don't know where she went. She didn't usually go out much at all. I didn't hear her come in. I didn't see her until she came out of the shower. She had a white robe on. She came to me and just wanted to be held. That's all. Just held close. She cried for a long time. She wouldn't tell me what was wrong. It was the only time . . . it was ever tender. He did it so quickly. He just yanked her head way back and. . . . Jesus, I am never going to be able to forget it. How could a man do a thing like that to so much loveliness?"

"How did you meet her?"

"Down here a year ago. I was at Claude and Ellie Boody's house, and the two house parties sort of got combined."

I wondered if I should tell him that his little cruel darling had been a big help in getting four people murdered, and that was why Miguel had finished her off before leaving. A last minute errand.

But Mr. Day had all he could manage. And I decided I might as well leave her one mourner.

Suddenly he realized what he had been saying. "There was no conspiracy involved, Mr. McGee. Almah was going to get that money out and bring it back to Mr. Garcia. That was the basis on which I agreed to help her."

"Sure, Gabe. They'll get a court order and open the box. A couple of bonded officials will discover about ten thousand dollars there, just enough to cover Menterez' hospital bills from now until he dies. But, of course, you didn't know his name was Menterez and his residency here wasn't entirely legal."

There was one knowing glimmer in the mild blue eyes. "I thought his name was Carlos Garcia."

"If we don't know our lines, they can make an investigation down here drag on forever."

"I . . . I'm sorry about that friend of yours, Mr. McGee."

I gave him a big empty glassy smile and got out of there. Later I watched them load him and his luggage aboard the amphib. They joggled him and he let out a very sincere yell. It taxied out and turned into the wind. There was a pretty good chop, and I could hear the distant sound of the aluminum hull going bang bang bang before they got up enough flying speed to lift off. Gabriel Day was paying for his sins out there.

I went back into the lobby just in time to be told my call had come through. It was my first chance to get through the heavy traffic on the single phone line. Shaja's voice was very faint. Apparently she could hear me all too well. It was the first inkling of disaster she'd had. Nora had been accidentally killed when a boat had blown up. Her people would probably want the body sent to New Jersey. There was a lot of red tape. No need for her to come down. I was all right. I would try to handle everything. I heard that faraway voice break into drab little heartsick fragments. I told her to inform Nora's local attorney.

The big league baseball players live by an ancient myth. Watch the next one get hammered in the shoulder muscle by a wild pitch, or get slammed in the meat of the thigh by a line drive. They believe that if you rub it, you make it hurt worse. The impulse is always to rub the place that hurts. They are very stoic. They walk around in little circles, moaning, but they don't rub it.

That was the only way I could handle Nora. I would get right up to the edge of taking a second look at that deadly shard of mahogany, and then I would walk off in my little circle, not rubbing it. I didn't want to get into all the ifs. You can kill yourself with ifs. If I hadn't had my little emotional tantrum which had dropped me into the tequila bottle, we would have been long gone. If I'd told her to stay the hell away from the boat basin. . . . If she had been standing three inches to one side or the other. . . . If my luck had gone bad long ago, I wouldn't have been around to bring her down and get her killed.

The ifs can kill you, and the never-agains can gut you. Never again to feel the smooth and eager musculature of that smooth narrow back. Never again to hear the smug and murmurous little pleasure sound. Never again to watch the lilt and swing of those marvelous legs as she walked with the guile of the trained model. Never again to make her laugh.

So what you do, if you have been down that road other times, is unhook the little hook and let the metal shutters bang down. When things have quieted down back there, you can lift them again. Time, divided by life, equals death every time. It is the deadly equation, with time as the unknown. I heard one of those heavy Germanic jokes one time. An enormously wealthy industrialist fathered an only son and, knowing death is often a matter of luck and circumstance, vowed to give the boy maximum protection. He was raised behind steel walls and shatterproof glass, breathed filtered air, was tended constantly by doctors, dieticians, tutors. He was permitted no toy or tool which could harm him in any way. On his twenty-first birthday, when they let him out into the world, the kid died of excitement.

Almah, Miguel, Nora. They had gone in quick succession like popcorn. And Carlos, the half-man, was still breathing. And his wife was still rocking.

I completed the necessary arrangements, with plenty of

official help. To the couple of wire service stringers who filtered in, I was a very dull party. I was the fellow who answered the first question with a half hour lecture on boating safety. Newsman have a very short attention span. It is a prerequisite in the business. That is why the news accounts of almost anything make sense to all ages up to the age of twelve. If one wishes to enjoy newspapers, it is wise to halt all intellectual development right at that age. The schools are doing their level best to achieve this goal. For the first time in history it is possible to earn doctorates in obscure professional techniques without upsetting the standard of a twelve-year-old basic intellect.

But after all the white-washers had moved along, back to other pressing PR problems, a little man moved in on me who was considerably more impressive. He was bald and wide and brown, and had a face like the fake Aztec carvings gullible tourists buy. He had an eye patch, and carried himself as if he were in uniform. His name was Marquez. I had been vaguely aware of him in the background, coming and going, keeping to himself. He came to me at the bar and suggested we go over to a table. He smiled all the time. He had a tiny gold and blue badge, and something that said he was Colonel Marquez, and something else that said he was in Investigationes Especiales for some kind of national bureau.

"That boat went up with one hell of a bang," he said.

I gave him my water safety lecture. He listened to it with total attention, and when I ran down, he said, "That boat went up with one hell of a bang, eh?"

"Yes it did indeed, Colonel."

"Down in Puerto Altamura, in the village, you're a pretty popular tourist, McGee."

"Every tourist should be an ambassador of good will."

"That Garcia house, it's like a fortress, eh?"

"Maybe they have sneak thieves around here."

"A man handles himself pretty well, and then he hides a gun in a john tank, for God's sake."

"Colonel, you skip around so much, you confuse me."

"This was the last place the Columbine IV was definitely seen."

"Was it?"

"How many women do you need for one little vacation, McGee?"

"Now look, Colonel."

"You pretend to be mad, then I'll pretend to be mad, and then we'll quiet down and play some more riddles, eh?"

He looked perfectly happy. I said, "Can I play a game?"

"Go ahead. But watch yourself. You're semi-pro. This is a pro league. Even if you're a pro in your own country, you're semi-pro here. We play hard ball."

"Let's just imagine that a rich man hides himself away here because it's a place where he's hard to get at, and he expects sharpshooters. He would expect some because they plain hate him, and some because they think he might be in a situation where they can pick some of the loot off him. I guess they've picked him pretty clean. There's one thing left, maybe, like a lock box in a Mexico City bank, with better than six hundred thousand U.S. dollars in it."

The smile remained the same size, but suddenly looked hemstitched. He got up and patted my shoulder and said, "Wait right here, please."

I had a twenty-minute wait. He came back. He signaled for a drink, and said, "I suddenly thought of a phone call which could prevent a little error in bookkeeping. I am enjoying your game."

"Thanks. We'll imagine a man comes down here after there's some trouble and tries to figure out who's been trying to do what to whom. The dust is settling, and he isn't too anxious to kick it up into the air again. How do we classify the little lady with the sliced throat? She brought along legal aid, so let's say she was after the loot. Maybe, along the way, she earned an assist on the Columbine thing, because she was anxious not to have anything drastic happen before she could get the loot."

"And what have you been after?" he asked.

"Just a little fun in the sun, Colonel."

"Like looking at the pictures on Heintz's wall? Heintz wants to be a company man, but he thinks it was a hell of a bang too. What if Taggart thought he would sleep better if Miguel for sure, and maybe the Hichin girl along with him, had one of those boating accidents you give the big talk about?"

The man had a very flexible and interesting mind. I checked his concept for about twenty seconds. Sam did have the opportunity. And it would be a horrid irony if the package he had prepared had waited right there until Nora was in range.

"No. It wasn't his style."

He shook his head sadly. "You spoil the fun. You tell me too much too fast, McGee. See what you told me? That you knew him that well and that he's dead."

"I've lowered my guard because I trust you, Colonel."

"My God, that is so unique, I don't know how to handle it. I seldom trust myself, even."

I was fascinated by the computer mechanism behind that Aztec face, so I put another little piece of data into the machine. "Of course, Miss Gardino knew him better than I ever did."

"So! An emotional pilgrimage. I'm disappointed in you, McGee. Or did I speak too fast, eh? Emotional for her? Loot for you?"

"Something like that."

"One little area of speculation is left. It will never be proved one way or another. I think these things entertain you too. Taggart and Alconedo do some very dirty work for Don Carlos. Certain people are getting too close to Don Carlos. Perhaps he has promised them much money for special work they have done. So he makes a sly scheme, eh? He will leave the house with Miguel and Taggart to go to the boat. His pockets are full of bank books, eh? Perhaps an old and trusted friend is at the hotel with a car. There is a hell of a bang, and the car drives away, with Don Carlos hiding under a blanket maybe." His smile broadened. "But it is so difficult to arrange, so intricate, so full of suspense, eh? With the strain, a little blood vessel goes pop in Don Carlos' head. How many times can a man successfully disappear?"

"Son of a gun!"

"It entertains me too. Taggart left with loot. What if he had left, or planned to, on that boat. Perhaps with Miss Hichin. The possible combinations are interesting. Ah, well. You are scheduled to leave tomorrow. You can leave."

"Thanks."

"You were discreet with those drab little news people. There is no need to kick up dust now. Let it all settle. The dead women are in transit. Don Carlos and his wife will be in institutions. We have the problem of those other Cubans. The land syndicate will find a buyer for the house. May I say a few things to you, McGee? On a personal level?"

"*Si, mi Coronel.*"

"My God, what a horrible accent! I think you are a reckless man. I think you are a mischievous man. But you have good intuitions. You have a sour view of yourself, eh? You are . . . I would say a talented amateur in these matters. But an adult, I think. One finds so few American adults these days. To you, the village Mexicans are people. Not quaint dirty actors we supply to make the home movies look better. I have some problems I work on. Tampico, Acapulco, Mexicali. Three kinds of nastiness. If you're bored, we could have some fun. I can give you no official protection. I would use you, and pay you very little out of some special funds they give me. I would throw you into those situations, and see what happens."

"I'm flattered, but no thanks."

"No temptation at all?"

"Not very much. I guess I get into things, Colonel, because I get personally and emotionally involved."

"The stamp of the amateur, of course. But why set up an order of which has to come first, my friend? Because you have the soul of an amateur, you will find that personal emotional involvement after you get into these things. You will always bleed for the victims. And always have the capacity for terrible righteous anger. This recruiting is very irregular, McGee. But when you are in the business of using people, it is hard to let a special person slip away."

"Give me a great big medal for what I accomplished here, Marquez."

"Don't be bitter about the woman. If she wasn't willing to accept risk she wouldn't have come here. She could stand there unharmed while a thousand boats blew up. This was the thousand and first."

"You are over-valuing me, Colonel."

"Maybe you mean this thing is not over for you yet."

"Possibly."

He put his hand out. "When it is over . . . if you survive it . . . if you have some curiosity, write me at this address. Just say you are going to visit Mexico and would like to have a drink with me. By then I will know much more about you than I know now. But I don't over-value you, McGee. The affair of the knife at the Tres Panchos was very swift and competent. One day I would like to know just how you managed the dog. And before leaving, do not forget the interesting photographs in the base of the lamp."

"Colonel, you are showing off."

He made a sad face. "That is the flaw in my personality. Vanity. And your flaw is sentimentality. They are the flaws which will inevitably kill us both. But let us enjoy them before the time runs out, eh? *Buena suerte, amigo.* And good hunting. And God grant we meet again."

sixteen

UPON RETURN to this country from any quiet corner of a foreign land, the most immediate impression is that of noise, continuous, oppressive, meaningless noise. Highway noise —from the labored snarl of the big rigs shifting on the grades to the pneumatic whuff of fast passenger traffic. The bell sounds of wrenches dropped on cement garage floors. Diesel bray. Restaurants all clatter and babble like huge cocktail parties, the sound rising above that stupefying placebo of Muzak, which is like cotton candy being stuffed into the ears. Sound trucks, brash snatches of radio music and TV laughter, shuffle and tick-tock of sidewalks full of people, rackety clatter of machines filling out paper forms, horn blatt, brake squeal, yelps of children, shrieking passage of the jets.

There is a spurious vitality about all this noise. But under it, when you come back, you can sense another more significant and more enduring vitality. It has been somewhat hammered down of late. The bell ringers and flag fondlers have been busily peddling their notion that to make America Strong, we must march in close and obedient ranks, to the sound of their little tin whistle. The life-adjustment educators, in strange alliance with the hucksters of consumer goods, have been doing their damnedest to make us all think alike, look alike, smell alike and die alike, amidst all the pockety-queek of unserviceable home appliances, our armpits astringent, nasal passages clear, insurance program adequate, sex life satisfying, retirement assured, medical plan comprehensive, hair free of dandruff, time payments manageable, waistline firm, bowels open.

But the other vitality is still there, that rancorous, sardonic, wonderful insistence on the right to dissent, to question, to object, to raise holy hell and, in direst extremity, to laugh the self-appointed squad leaders off the face of the earth with great whoops of dirty disdainful glee. Suppress friction and a machine runs fine. Suppress friction, and a society runs down.

As I holed up in the City of the Angels, I was also aware of a comforting feeling of anonymity. In the world's biggest third-class city I could pass unnoticed. I spoke the language. I was familiar with the currency. I could drink the water. I could almost breathe the air, late April air, compounded of interesting hydro-carbons.

I wanted transient accommodations, of a very special kind. I did not want to sign in anywhere as McGee or anybody else. I did not want to impose on old friends and get them implicated in anything. I did not want to be within that strata subject to routine police checks. I wanted anonymous transportation and freedom of movement. I wanted to be the nearest thing to an invisible man I could achieve. It might turn out that all such precautions were unnecessary. But I had to follow my hunch. The hunch said that this might get messy before it was over—or, more accurately, might continue to be messy.

I got in at six in the evening. By seven I was prowling the area where I hoped to work something out, the trash end of Sunset Boulevard. My luggage was in a bus station coin locker. By nine o'clock, in several assorted bars and lounges, I had surveyed several groups, ingratiated myself with a few and then given them up and gone on. By ten I had a promising group in a crowded corner of a place called The Pipe and Bowl. Extremely local cats, in the restless middle twenties, overdressed and slightly stoned, trying to look as if they hadn't spent their week in insurance agencies, department stores, dental labs and office buildings. They accepted the amiable stranger, with the usual reservations, indirect challenges, the waiting to see if there was any angle, any kind of hustling. I did my verbal card tricks, and struck the right attitudes, and bought my share. I was Mack, a boat chauffeur by trade. They shuffled me around to one of the two free lassies, perhaps on the basis of a girls' room conference, and amalgamated me into the group. Her name, unfortunately, seemed to be Junebug. She had a round merry face, a lot of gestures and animation, cropped brown hair. Her figure, as revealed by a little beige stretch dress, was quite pretty, except for a potentially dangerous case of secretarial spread.

She was careful to tell me her boy friend was an engineer working on some kind of rugged project up in Canada.

From time to time, according to mysterious signals, we all left and piled into cars and went to other places which seemed to be identical to the ones we left, the same music, the same drinks, the same faces at the bar. We had drop-offs, and we picked up some new recruits. By the third stop I had become an old-time buddy. At the fourth stop, well after midnight, I had her trapped in a dark corner and made my pitch.

"Junebug, I've been living a little too much tonight. This check will take me down to cigarette money."

"Gee, Mack, I've got a few bucks in my purse if. . . ."

"It isn't only that, honey. What happened, this isn't home base for the boat I was running. And I got fired today. It's no real sweat. The owner got a wrong idea of me and his wife. I've got money coming. And no problem about a job. The man said get off my boat, and I got my gear and got off. But now I am definitely hung up for a place to stay. My gear is in a bus locker."

She moved as far away from me as she could get, which was about six inches, and she stuck her underlip out and said, "If you think you're going to shack with me, buddy boy, if this is one of those cute ideas, I haven't had that much to drink. No sir. Oh-you-tee. Out."

"Honey, believe me, you are a very exciting woman, but that wasn't my play. I want a place where I can hole up until the money comes through. That's all. Not your place. I thought you might know of a place. As soon as the money comes through, I'll pay you a going rent."

"So how long is that supposed to be?" she asked with great skepticism.

I unstrapped my watch and handed it to her. "This is a solid gold case. You can check it anywhere."

"No. I don't want it. Look, I just thought you were trying to make it cute. Okay? Maybe one of the guys has an open couch."

"As a last resort. But maybe if somebody is away. How about your engineer?"

"No. He lives with his folks in Santa Barbara. Let me think."

She sat and pulled at that protruding underlip and scowled into her drink. Then she glowed with inspiration and went off to phone. She came back and wedged herself in again and in a conspiratorial tone said, "Bingo. And we're neighbors yet. The girlfriend I phoned was sore as hell at being waked up at all hours. But she's the one Francine left her key with. And she'll go over and put it in my mailbox, she said."

"Who is Francine?"

"Oh, she's away on this thing. What it is, the executives where she works, they take this trip and go to a whole mess of regional offices and have sales meetings. She's gone every year for a month about this time. It's pretty nice, going in a company plane and all, and they ball it up pretty good. She sacks out for days when she gets back, believe me. She shouldn't be back for another couple weeks anyway."

When the group decided to hit one more place, we broke away. Junebug had a little grey English Ford. She drove it with slap-dash efficiency. When I came out of the bus station with my bags and put them in the back seat, she said, "You know, Mack, I damn near drove off. I was thinking, this is pretty stupid, not knowing you or anything."

"I wondered if you would drive off."

"What would you have done, baby?"

"Had some naps in the bus station."

"Am I doing something real stupid?"

"I think you're smart enough to have a pretty good idea of whom you can trust."

"Well . . . I guess that's the way it has to be."

The place was off Beverly Boulevard, not too far from City College. It was one of those depressing little residence courts, small attached bungalows, about thirty of them, in a hollow square, facing a common courtyard. You drove in through an ornamental arch, from which hung a sign saying Buena Villas. There was a weak night light and a dead fountain in the middle of the court. Cars were parked in front of most of the bungalows. The bungalows all had shallow porches, one step up from minuscule yards with low iron fences.

She parked in front of hers. Number 11. While I got my gear out of her car, she went onto her porch and got the key from her mailbox. Then we went diagonally across the court to number 28.

After she put the key into the front door lock, she turned and whispered, "Honey, honest to God, you got to promise me you won't make me regret this. I mean no big phone bills, or messing the place up, or breaking stuff or stealing stuff. I told Honey it was a girl friend I wanted it for. Even so, she dragged her heels."

"You have no cause for alarm, Junebug."

We went in. She found the lights. Living room, bedroom, kitchen and bath. Quick tour of inspection. No side windows. It would be depressingly dark by daylight. And Francine was a miserable housekeeper. Junebug found beer in the small noisy refrigerator. I agreed to replace anything I used up. We sat on the couch in the living room. She was mildly, apprehensively flirtatious. She expected the pass, and I knew she could react in only three possible ways—rebuff, limited access, or totality—and I had not the slightest curiosity about finding out. Perhaps she wanted a chance to dizzy herself then bravely retreat, for the sake of the engineer. When I sensed she might get a little bolder, I cooled the situation by asking friendly questions about the engineer. Finally we said our polite goodnights, with thanks and reassurances, and she left.

I poked around my new domain. Francine had left dirty sheets on the double bed. I found fresh ones in a narrow cupboard in the bathroom. She had left long blonde hair in all the expected places. I got rid of those, and the ring in the tub, and the hardened fragments of cheese sandwich on the kitchen table. I am a confirmed snoop. I went through the living room desk and found out she was Mrs. Francine Broadmaster. Divorced. Age 27. I found some treasured little packets of love letters from several males. They were semi-literate, and so shockingly clinical they awed me.

I found myself conducting a search for whatever it was she would hide away. Everybody hides things. They think they have dreamed up the most perfect place, but it is always a very ordinary place. Hers was a brown envelope Scotch-taped to the underside of a bureau drawer with the flap paper-clipped shut. She had three one-hundred-dollar bills in there, and six fifties, all crisp and new. And she had twenty or so polaroid pictures in there. Evidently she or her boyfriend had a polaroid camera with a timing device. She was featured in them. She was a medium-sized blonde, with more than her share of jaw and breast. The boyfriend was a burly rascal. In the pitiless glare of the flash bulb they looked toward the camera, whenever possible, wearing that dazed blind nervous grin typical of all amateur pornography. I could imagine nothing of a more ghastly sadness than these little souvenirs.

After I had gathered up her stray garments and shoved them onto a closet shelf, I did the minimum of unpacking for myself and went to bed.

I had become a city rabbit and found a burrow.

In the darkness, stretched out in Mrs. Broadmaster's play pen, aware of the late mumbles of the city, I took a tentative rub at the place that hurt. "Forgive me," her dying eyes said. "Forgive me for being such a bloody mess."

And the black anger came rolling up, turning my fists to stones, bunching the muscles of arm and shoulder. Don't go away, Mr. Tomberlin.

At eight in the morning the people of Buena Villas started going to work. The court made for considerable resonance. Apparently standard procedure was to bang every car door at least three times, rev up to 6000 rpm, then squeak the tires and groan out in low low. I could have sworn half of them drove back in and did it all over again. By nine it had quieted down, and I got another hour of sleep before the phone started ringing. I began counting the rings, waiting for it to quit. It was beside the bed. It was a white phone. It had lipstick on the mouthpiece. After twenty-seven rings I knew who it had to be, so I reached and picked it up.

"Boy, you sleep pretty good," Junebug said.

"I wanted to make sure it wasn't for her."

"I was beginning to think you cleaned out the place and took off."

"What would I steal, honey? Dirty underwear? Eddie Fisher records? That beautiful refrigerator?"

"Look, is everything okay? Honey didn't come over to check on who I borrowed it for before she went to work?"

"No callers."

"Baby, you want to get in touch with me, you ask for Miss Proctor. You got something there to write down the number. I'll give you both numbers, my place and here. You got plans for after I get off today?"

"I'm not sure yet."

"What I'll do to keep from waiting so long next time, I want to phone you, I let it ring once and hang up and dial you right back. Okay?"

"Fine."

After I got dressed I checked the emergency reserve in my

money belt. I had eight hundred there, in fifties. I moved half of it into my wallet. I had a Lauderdale account I could tap at long range, but I still didn't want to have my name on anything. I imagined the car in front of the bungalow belonged to Francine. It was a sand-colored Falcon. It took a ten minute search to turn up the keys. They were in a bowl on the table by the front door, under some old bills and circulars.

It was one of only four cars left in the court. The battery sounded jaded, but it started in time. After I was out of the neighborhood, I filled the tank and had a soft tire pumped up. I found a breakfast place, and then looked in a phone book and found no listing for Calvin Tomberlin. I reviewed what I knew about him. Loads of money from his mother's real estate investments. Several residences, including a lodge up near Cobblestone Mountain. A boat big enough to go down the coast with. A persistent buyer of art objects, perhaps. And unlisted phones.

It wasn't a difficult problem. There are dozens of ways. My problem was to find a way which would leave no trace. I did not want anyone remembering the invisible man. Money can buy a lot of fences. Try phoning Howard Hughes sometime. Tomberlin could be on the other side of the world. He would find that wasn't far enough. But I hoped he was nearby. I had a pretty good hidey-hole. He had enough money to be wary of anybody with cute ideas, like selling him back to himself. Almah had called him spooky.

I started phoning the expensive retail establishments. I hit a vein on the third one, Vesters on Wilshire. I got a Mrs. Knight in the credit department and said, "This is Mr. Sweeney of Sweeney and Dawson, Mrs. Knight. We're doing an audit on Mr. Calvin Tomberlin's personal accounts. Could you please tell me his present credit balance with you?"

"Just a moment, sir."

I waited. If she thought to look in the yellow pages, she would find the accounting firm of Sweeney and Dawson listed therein. If she was bright, she would have suggested she call me back.

"It's just under eight hundred dollars, Mr. Sweeney. I imagine you want the exact figure. Seven hundred and eighty-eight twenty."

"Thank you. Could you give me your billing address on that, please?"

"Yes sir. Care of the trust department, First Pacific National Bank."

I thanked her for her cooperation, not heartily, but with the little touch of ice she might expect from diligent auditors.

I got First Pacific and asked for the trust department, and asked for the person handling the Tomberlin retail accounts. After some delay a very cool and cautious young voice said that she was Miss Myron.

"Miss Myron, I hate to bother you with this sort of a problem. This is Mr. Harmer in the credit department at Vesters. We show a balance in Mr. Calvin Tomberlin's account of seven hundred and eighty-eight twenty. Would it be too much trouble for you to check that for me, please?"

"One moment, Mr. Harmer."

Sooner than I expected, she was back on the line, saying, "That's the figure I have here. These accounts are set up to be paid on the fifth working day of each. . . ."

"Good heavens, Miss Myron! I am certainly not pressing for payment on Mr. *Tomberlin's* account. We have a confusion on another item. I wanted to make certain you had not yet been billed for it. It was a phone order from Mr. Tomberlin late last month, and we had to special order it. You see, I thought that if you *had* been billed, your copy of our bill form would show delivery instructions. The sales person who took the order cannot remember which address to send it to. I thought of sending it along to the Cobblestone Mountain lodge . . . but you understand, we want to give Mr. Tomberlin the best possible service. It just came in and I *do* so want to send it to the right place. It took longer than we promised."

"He's at the Stone Canyon Drive house, Mr. Harmer."

"Let me see. I believe we have that number. Our records are in horrible shape. We're changing systems here."

"Number forty, Mr. Harmer."

"Thank you so much for helping us."

"No trouble at all."

Her girlish caution had evaporated when the figure I gave her checked with hers. We had become companions then. We shared the same arithmetic. And we were both eager to be of maximum service to Mr. Calvin Tomberlin. He used that handy tool of the very rich, special services from the trust department of a bank. All his bills would go there and they would pay them all, neatly and promptly. At the end of the year they would make up a detailed statement, take a percentage of the total as a service charge, send the statement to the tax attorney handling Tomberlin's affairs.

I had to buy a city map to locate Stone Canyon Drive. It angled west off Beverly Glen Boulevard, a winding road like a shelf pasted against the wall of a dry canyon. The houses were very far apart, and so were the numbers. Ten, twenty, thirty, forty. Everybody had a nice round number. I came to 40 after the canyon had gradually turned north. But the house was invisible. A smooth curve of asphalt flowed down around the rocks. Where it entered the main road, a small sign on one side said "40" and the sign on the other side said "Private". There was a rubber cable across the asphalt. I could assume that the weight of a car set off a signal somewhere.

I had to keep going. There was no place to pull off. After I passed a house—or rather a driveway—with the number 100 on it, I came to a turnaround, and there was no place to go but back. It was three and a half miles back to the boulevard. Ten houses in three and a half miles is reasonable privacy. I went back to Sunset and over to Sepulveda, and wiggled my way around through some semi-pretentious little areas, trying to work back toward Stone Canyon Drive. At last I found what I thought was a pretty good view of the ridge that formed the west wall of the canyon. The houses were set along the reverse slope of the ridge. They weren't going to burn in tandem. There was too much bare rock up there. But each house was in a private oasis of green, or I should say near one, or perched over one. Various architects had hung them up there like strange little toys. Other ridge areas, lower and brushier, were clotted with houses. According to demand, I could imagine that each of those far houses was taking up at least a million dollars worth of barren real estate. In a sane world it would be 50¢ an acre, but there it is, status-symbol land, rocks and brush, ridges and gulleys, fires and mud, all the way to Pacific Palisades. The highest houses get to see the pizza signs, and the night sea beyond. Perhaps the only greater idiocy is visible in Beverly Hills where, on the older roads sit, jowl to jowl, on small plots, huge examples of the worst architectural styles of the past two hundred years, from Uncle Georgian to Casa-blanca Moorish. When San Andreas gives a good belch, they can start again at 50¢ an acre.

All I had learned was that if I was going to get any closer to C. Tomberlin, I was going to have to walk in. Or get him out of there.

At three o'clock, guessing I could catch Raoul Tenero at home in Miami, I loaded up with quarters and made a station to station call from a booth. Nita answered. I asked for Raoul. She carefully worked out the tense and construction and said, "I am calling him now soon to be here with the phone, thank you."

Raoul came on, chuckling. "Yes?"

"No names. This is the hero of Rancho Luna, boy."

"You have something to tell me? Maybe I heard it."

"Maybe you did. The man we talked about is alive, but if he had the choice maybe he wouldn't want to be."

"There have been some discussions about that. We wondered if it was the sort of story he could arrange to circulate, to take the pressure off."

"I saw him."

"Then I'll tell the others. We'll have a drink to that tonight. We'll drink to a long life for him."

"Now for a name. Mineros."

"Yes?"

"Can you fill me in a little? Background?"

"Of all the men in the world, perhaps he had the best reason to want to find the first man we were talking about. He disappeared, aboard a chartered boat."

"I know. Who was with him? I could check old newspapers, but this is quicker."

"Rafael Mineros. Enrique Mineros, his eldest son. Maria Talavera, who was at one time engaged to Rafael's nephew, who died in a Cuban prison. Manuel Talavera, her brother."

"They are dead."

"Presumed dead?"

The operator came on and told me to buy another three minutes. I fed the quarters in, and then said, "Definitely dead. The man you are going to drink to—he gave the orders."

"God in heaven, what a disaster that man has been to the Mineros family!"

"You can tell from the money how far away I am."

"I have a pretty good guess."

"Raoul, I need one contact here. Somebody I can trust. Trust as much as I trust you. Is there any kind of organized group here?"

"My friend, when two Cubans meet, the first they do is organize a committee. Out there, it is not like here. Comparatively few, but mostly a hell of a lot richer. There are several kinds of cats out there. Some of them cashed up and left six, seven, eight, ten years ago. Some at the right time, some scared out by Mr. B, or his buddies, who wanted what they had to leave behind. Then there are the ones who cashed up and got out when the brothers C looked as if they were going to make it down out of the mountains. Then there are the disenchanted, who stayed and saw red. There are other exiles too, South America, Central America—from old friends of little Eva to reasonably genuine patriots. But I don't have to think a long time to think of a man out there. Paul Dominguez. I have it here in the book. Just a moment. 2832 Winter Haven Drive. Long Beach."

"Thanks. How do I let him know I have your blessing?"

"Hmmm. Tell him he still owes me a pair of boots. If that isn't enough, he can phone me."

"He is sensible?"

"More so than you or I, amigo. And as much man as the two of us."

I found Dominguez in the book. A woman with a young and pleasant voice said he would be home about six. There wasn't enough time left to go down to Oceanside and find out who had chartered the Columbine to Rafael Mineros. I looked the name up in the book and found a Rafael Mineros in Beverly Hills and an Esteban Mineros in the Bel Air section.

I got back to Buena Villas at four thirty. About ten cars had come home. I parked in front of 28. As I got out of the Falcon, a woman came striding toward me. She looked like the young George Washington, except that her hair was the color of mahogany varnish. "Who are you and what the hell is going on?" she demanded at ten paces. She wore a Chinese smock and pale blue denim pants.

I let her march up to me and stop and wait for the answer. "Are you Honey?"

"Yes. What the hell is Junebug trying to pull around here?"

"Maybe you can solve my problem, Honey."

"I'm the one with the problem. I'm responsible. Turn over the house key and her car key and clear the hell out of here."

I extricated one fifty-dollar bill and said, "My problem is do I give this to Junebug? Do I leave it on the desk in there for Francine? Or do I turn it over to you?"

Her eyes wavered and her belligerence diminished. "What do you think you're buying?"

"A quiet place. No fuss, no muss, nothing to upset Mrs. Broadmaster."

"You know her?"

"I've seen quite a bit of her. Should I give this to Junebug?"

"I've got a responsibility."

"In a few days you get the key back. And Junebug gets another of these."

Her hand, faster than light, snapped the bill away and shoved it into the pocket of the oriental coat. "I look after the place for Fran. I can see she gets this. But you shouldn't use the car. It's not right you should use the car. It should be more if you use the car. Did Junebug say it would be so much, like making a deal with her?"

"I don't think she realizes I intended to pay for it. I'll tell her the kind of deal I've made with you."

"Why bother? It's my responsibility isn't it? Fran left the key with me. Maybe I'll have to go in and clean up when you leave. Junebug wouldn't do that, and you know it. So it can be between us. What Fran said, if I want to put somebody up, okay. A favor for a favor. But it should be more for the car."

"How much more, Honey?"

"Well . . . the same again?"

"You know, if it was that much, I'd have to ask Junebug if she thought I was being taken."

"You know, I don't have to dicker with you. You can get out."

"Give me back the money and I'll give you the keys."

"If you need a place, you need a place. How about twenty?"

"Twenty is fine."

"Suppose you do this for my protection. You get a key made and give me hers back. Then . . . if somebody is looking for you and they find you. . . ."

"That's fair enough."

She looked around, checking to see if anybody was looking at us. "After dark, you put the regular key in my mailbox tomorrow. With that twenty dollars like we agreed. You won't bust the place up or anything?"

"I want to live quietly."

"You tell Junebug I came over and we got along, and I said any friend of hers. Okay?"

"Fine."

"Fran is back May tenth."

"Oh, I'll be long gone. Don't you worry."

"I worry about everything all day long and half the night. I worry about things you never heard of," she said. She went scuttling away, up the line, and went into a bungalow four doors from mine.

Junebug rapped at my door at twenty after five. I got up and let her in. She hadn't been in her place yet. She wore her office outfit, a tight dark skirt and a white nylon blouse. She grinned a significant grin with her little comedy face, and squinched her jackolantern eyes, and hugged up for a big kiss of hello. Then she went stilting around on her office heels in a proprietary manner, and exclaimed at how I had neatened it up, saying I'd probably make a good husband even if I didn't look it. I told her Honey had been to call.

She looked stricken. "Oh dear Jesus," she said.

"What's the trouble? We got along fine. She said any friend of yours is a friend of hers. She gave me Francine's car keys and told me to drive carefully."

"You're kidding!"

I showed her the car keys.

"I will be damned," she said. "Who would have thought? Well, it just goes to show you never know, do you? Mack, dear, I'm just sick about not thinking of something. I got paid today and when I cashed my check I thought of it. You poor dear, what have you done about food? Gee, I could have left you a few bucks, you know. Did you get your money yet?"

"I looked a guy up and got a small loan. I'm okay."

"Well, thank goodness for that. Can I loan you some more?"

"No. I'm fine, thanks."

"What do you want to do tonight, honey? I like to swing a little on Friday because I can sleep in."

"I have to go see a man."

"About a job?"

"Yes."

She gave me a sultry glance, with some contrived eyelash effects. "Well, *that* won't take all night will it?" The glance matched the unanticipated kiss of hello at the door. Obviously she had been thinking about the situation, and had come to specific conclusions. The engineer was in Canada. I was the stranger, on my way through, and the place was perfectly safe, without likelihood of spying or interruption. She had found me presentable. She had done me a big favor. She wanted a little pre-marital fling. But it had to go by the rules. I could guess what her rules would be. Once she had induced me to make the pass, then she could dramatize, perhaps shed a few obligatory tears about not wanting to betray the man she was going to marry. After token resistances, enough of them to lay a firm foundation for the rationalizations she would need later on, she would find herself—to her horror and astonishment—seduced. After the enjoyment thereof, she could wallow in a delicious guilt, the dramatic agony of betrayal, with tears and protestations. The image would be preserved, and it would be a practice session for the infidelities after marriage, when Engineer was in Yucatan or Kenya and the babies were in their beds.

She was a reasonably ripe and lusty-looking little woman, but in my adult years I have lost my taste for soap opera intrigue and highschool solutions. I knew exactly what she would say, and exactly what she would expect me to say. The two of us would be able to convince her, after the fact, that she was truly virtuous, that it had been just one of those things redblooded people can't help. Doomed to that vapid kind of communication, there could be no real contact between us, and no importance to it. I had to make the pass or we would never get to the corny dialogue. So I did not make it, thus saving herself from herself, or me from her, or something, and managed to leave such a tiny scratch on the surface of her pride any Miracle Cleanser would make it invisible in a moment.

I drove to a pay phone and called Paul Dominguez. His accent was very slight. I didn't tell him my name. I merely said that I needed help, and Raoul Tenero had said to remind him that he still owed Raoul a pair of boots.

After a thoughtful silence he asked me where I was, then told me to meet him at eight o'clock at the bar at Brannigan's

Alibi, a place near the Long Beach Municipal Airport. He said to look for a man with two packs of cigarettes on the bar in front of him, stacked one on the other. He named the brand. It was a very tidy little identification device, and I knew I would remember it and perhaps use it myself one day.

I got lost and arrived at ten past eight. It was one of those sawdusty places with joke signs on the wall, doing a good neighborhood trade. I went to the bar and looked around and saw the two packs in front of a man who stood alone at the far end of the bar. He was tall and quite slender, with a tanned and almost bald head, a youthful face, big, powerful-looking hands. He wore slacks, a white sport shirt and a pale blue jacket. I moved in beside him and said, "Hi, Paul."

He gave me a quick look of inventory, smiled and greeted me, and then looked beyond me and gave a little nod. I turned and saw two men get up from a booth near the door. One finished the dregs of his beer, put the glass down and followed the other one out.

I got myself a beer and we carried them over to a booth.

"Precautions?" I asked.

He shrugged. "I phoned Raoul. I got the description, McGee. Maybe somebody had you place that call to him. If somebody else had showed up, it would have turned out to be a different thing. Old habits, I guess. But I don't think they'd take the trouble over me, not after all this time. How is Raoul, actually?"

"His stomach is getting better. He's busy. He's making out."

Dominguez smiled. "We never knew it was going to turn out like this, neither one of us. We were so goddam idealistic, you know. Up in those goddam mountains, sitting at the feet of our leader. You don't know whether to laugh or cry. The great democratic revolution. Raoul and I were galloping idealists. Havana Yacht Club idealists. We grew the club beards. Three months after the triumphal march into Havana, we knew we'd been had, McGee. Dupes of the first order. When they started shooting our friends, we got out. That makes us traitors to the new order. So I take precautions."

"What was it about the pair of boots?"

"Raoul and I were specialists. We called ourselves the ordnance supply corps. We had a group of ten. We'd raid small army posts. Homemade bombs. Lots of fire power.

Sneakers, blackface, absolute discipline. Hit hard, grab weapons and high tail it the hell out. Raoul was very proud of a pair of paratrooper boots he had. I said one guard area was clear, and Raoul went in, but I missed one of them. The son of a gun must have been asleep behind a bush. He cut loose with a weapon on full automatic, and as Raoul dived for cover, one slug tore the heels off both boots and stung his feet so badly he thought he'd been hit. From then on he wore sneakers like everybody else on our little team."

We had measured each other. I liked the way he had explained the boots. He had the look. I can't explain what it is. Raoul has it, in smaller measure. Sam Taggart had it, also in lesser degree. This Paul Dominguez was so slender as to look almost frail, but no sane man who'd had a good long look at him would try pushing him around. It isn't class. It isn't a special style. It isn't anything in the eyes. Perhaps you can call it the smell of a man who lives by absolutes. If you take him on, you have to be prepared to kill him, because there is no other way of winning. I realized that Felicia Novaro had that flavor too—and his eyelashes were as long as hers.

"Raoul says you used to play those games too," he said.

"In a different war. You didn't go on the picnic?"

He shrugged. "I went over there to a training area. Man, I didn't like the way it was shaping up. First, it was too soon. The big sell was still working. Full bellies and new schools. In the second place, it was too holy grail. A nice clean mission against the infidel, banners waving. Like the Children's Crusade. In the third place, too many different people were promising too many different things. And there were dog fights between the groups going in, with no guarantee of any decent communication between the invasion and the working underground. I'll go back. I'll go back when it is going to be bloody and professional and smart, like forty simultaneous landings of small infiltration groups coordinated with massive sabotage from within. I'll go in when we accept the fact it will take a year to make a good dent in the worker's paradise, land of peace and freedom. Nobody is going to have to trade me for four cases of headache remedies. I'll trade myself for about two dozen red hot reds. Big talk, huh? In the meanwhile, McGee, I sell sports cars. If there is anything I can help you with, let me know."

I started it. I had intended to let him in on bits of it, the pertinent little parts of it. But doing it that way made me sound like a bystander buzzard, watching death, waiting for the tidbits. And I found myself wanting his approval, even though I didn't have very much self-approval in this thing. He had that way about him, to make you seek his understanding. So I backed up and started again. It took a long time. When I got to the end of Nora, it uncorked a little more emotional involvement than I had intended to show, hoarsening my voice.

When I had finished, he got up without a word and brought two more bottles of beer back to the table. "My youngest kid," he said, "the other day he fell off a chair. He jumped up and gave that chair such a hell of a kick, he nearly broke his toes."

I saw what he meant. "It isn't like that, Paul. Tomberlin had something to do with it. He took Mineros down there. He lit the fuse."

"It was already an unstable situation. Carlos Menterez was too sociable. Sooner or later somebody who wanted him dead was going to find him. Once he had to leave Cuba, Menterez was an embarrassment to everybody, even to the little wolf pack of crypto-fascist exiles in Mexico City who think they can rebuild a Batista-type regime in Cuba when a power vacuum occurs after a successful invasion. God knows they funneled enough money out to finance it, but they don't realize how fast the world is changing. Those boys you talked about, in the white car. Luis and Tomas. They would be with that group. And those people know that their crazy dream would need the good will of families like the Mineros. So they would have to get the word back that what happened was all Menterez' doing. They would have to disavow Menterez, and explain how it had happened. If they could have found your friend Taggart and killed him, it would have been a good will gesture."

"To whom? Who is left, for God's sake?"

"Senora Mineros, the matriarch. In Cuba she lost a son, a daughter-in-law and a grandson to Menterez. In Mexico she loses the other son and another grandson. There are left, I think, two more grandsons, the younger sons of Rafael. They are about fifteen and sixteen. And the other daughter-in-law, Rafael's widow. Remnants, and tradition, and a hell of a lot of money. The family still exists. There would be property claims in Havana, a basis for cooperation. Oh yes, and there is another one too. Her brother. Esteban Mineros. An old man."

"So you can assume word got back to the family about Taggart."

"Yes, word that he would get in touch with Tomberlin to sell him what he had taken from Menterez, the statuettes Tomberlin wanted. Then it would be necessary to make some arrangement with Tomberlin so they could get their hands on Taggart. From what you say they got the gold, all but one piece of it, and missed the man."

"When I talked to Sam, he at first wanted me to help him get the gold back. Then he decided to sell the one piece he had left. He seemed to think he was in a good bargaining position. He said something about being able to raise political hell."

"All kinds of hell, man. Figure it out. The Mineros mystery. The Menterez collection in Tomberlin's possession. An anonymous letter to any good reporter out here could create an international incident. The Castro propaganda machine could have a lot of fun with it."

"So who killed Sam?"

"Rhetorical question? If he'd died easy, I could make up a list of names. But it sounds like a very personal execution. There were three young Talaveras. Two died on that boat. Maria and her brother, Manuel. There is a third brother, a little older. Ramon. Not only Maria's brother, but a very good friend of Enrique Mineros. It surprises me he was not with them."

"He would use a knife?"

"He is a very intense man. And he would consider it an obligation."

"You know all these people?"

"I used to know them well. Just as Raoul used to know them well. Upper class Havana was a small community, McGee. But now there is . . . a considerable financial difference between us. Raoul and I came out later. It is the Castro equation, my friend. The later you left, the cleaner you were plucked. So we no longer travel in the same circles."

"What does Ramon Talavera look like?"

"Slender. Dark hair. Medium height. Pale. A quiet man. Unmarried. Do you think he should be punished—if he is the one? Do you see these things in such a cloudy way, my friend?"

"No. But if he did, he was pretty damned cold-blooded about it."

"Somebody, for hire, kills his brother, his sister and his best friend with a knife. Man, you can expect a certain amount of indignation."

"It all comes down to Tomberlin."

"The way my kid kicked the chair."

"But he does have the gold."

"It isn't his. Okay. Is it yours?"

"I'll ask you a question. Maybe it was Ramon Talavera who decided it wasn't just that Sam should keep on living. Is it just that Tomberlin should be the only one who winds up ahead?"

"Greed or justice?"

"A little of both. Plus curiosity."

He smiled. "That's an answer I like."

"Do you know the man?"

"I met him once. At a banquet at a big hotel. One of the rare times when the latino guest list is so big, it includes Pablo Dominguez. He is a grotesque. He likes the Spanish-Americans. I think it is a taste for our women. Apparently he can be depended upon to give money to certain causes. I think he is tolerated. I think he is a man who would have to buy his way into any kind of group."

"How do I get close to him?"

Dominguez leaned back and ran his hand over his bald brown pate. "It's an interesting problem. He is suspicious of strangers, I understand. I heard some gossip about him. His personal habits are not very nice. He buys his way out of trouble from time to time. He has a look of corruption. A rancid man, I think. And a very acquisitive man. A collector. Let me think about this, McGee. I must ask a few careful questions. I think if you try to make contact carelessly, you'll spoil any future chance. Can you meet me here tomorrow night at the same time?"

"Of course."

seventeen

AGAIN I managed to get lost and again I was a little late. Paul Dominguez was sitting in the same booth, dressed much as before. He stood up and introduced the woman. She was attractive in a flamboyant way. She was big. Big shoulders, big hands, a big and expressive wealth of mouth and eyes. She was swarthy, with heavy black brows. Her hair was expertly bleached to a cap of soft silver curls. Her eyes were a pale yellow-green, feline, mocking and aware. Her voice was a baritone drawl, with an edge of Spanish accent. He introduced her as Connie Melgar. And he gave my name as John Smith.

Her hand was warm, dry and strong. Dominguez hesitated, then slid in beside her and pulled his drink over. I sat facing them.

"Constancia is Venezuelan," he said. "Very rich and very difficult."

Her laugh was vital and explosive. "Difficult! For whom? For you, Pablo, with all that machismo?" She winked at me. "I throw myself at his head, and he calls me difficult."

Dominguez smiled. "I told her the problem," he said.

"Your problem, Mr. Smith—certainly that cannot be your name—is to find a way to approach Calvin Tomberlin. I can arrange that, of course. Certain groups always have access to that gentleman. But I think it would be very pleasant if I could be assured that you will not waste the opportunity, Mr. Smith."

"In what way?"

"If you can do him some great harm, I will be delighted."

"If things work out, I hope to make him reasonably unhappy, Mrs. Melgar."

She looked at me for five long seconds, her head tilting, then exhaled and patted Paul on the hand and said, "Thank you, dear. Mr. Smith and I can get along very nicely."

224

Paul looked at me in interrogation. I nodded. He stood up and said, "When you see our friends, give them my best wishes."

"Thank you for the help."

He nodded and bowed to Connie Melgar.

After he had left, she said, "He is such a very cautious man. But a very good man. Do you know that?"

"I met him through a friend. I like him."

"He has asked me this favor, Mr. Smith. I owe him several favors. He told me not to ask you questions. That is a terrible burden for me, not to ask questions. And this is not a *simpatico* place to talk in any case. There is an animal at the bar who leers. You have a car here? Why don't you follow me?"

She drove a Mercedes 300 SL, battleship grey, with great dash and competence. I had to keep Francine's little car at a full gallop to keep her taillights in view. She stopped on a dark street and I pulled in behind her and parked. She had me get into her car, and we went another half block and down into the parking garage under a new high rise apartment house. She left it for the attendant to put away, and led me back to a passenger elevator, punched the button for ten. In her high heels she stood a vivid and husky six feet. She smiled and said, "You are damn well a big fellow, Mr. John Smith. You make me feel almost girlish and dainty. That is a rare thing for me. But not so rare in California as other places."

Her apartment was 10 B. It was huge, with dark paneling, massive dark carved furniture, ponderous tables, low ornate lamps with opaque shades. As she opened the door, a little maid came on the run to take her wrap. Constancia rattled off a long spate of Spanish which seemed to be half query and half instruction. The maid bobbed and nodded and gave small answers and went away. An older, heavier woman, also in uniform, made an appearance, and stood stolidly while more orders were given.

Connie Melgar led me to the far end of the room, on a higher level, to a grouping of giant chairs and couches. She said, "The way it was here, it was like trying to live in a doll house. I had it all torn out and paneled in honest wood, and had the furniture shipped up from my house in Caracas, then I had to have walls changed to make two apartments into one. But still I feel cramped here. I like the ranch much better. I have a nice ranch in Arizona."

"This is very nice here, Mrs. Melgar."

She fitted a cigarette into a holder. "I own the building," she said. "As Pablo said, I'm filthy rich. I've been riding the winds of change by slowly liquidating at home and reinvesting here. I don't like what's going on at home. It scares me. Could you fix us some drinks, please? That thing there is a bar when you open the door. Dark rum on ice for me, please."

As I fixed drinks I said, "Apparently you don't feel friendly toward Tomberlin."

"I don't like the man. I have no idea why I keep seeing him. Perhaps it's some manner of challenge to me. I have one horse at the ranch I should get rid of. His name is Lagarto. Lizard. Hammer-headed thing with a mean eye. He is very docile, right up to the point where he sees a good chance to run me into a low limb or toss me into an arroyo. He may kill me one day."

I took her the drink, and as she started to raise it to her lips, I said, "Maybe I want you to get me close enough to Tomberlin so I can kill him."

The drink stopped an inch short of her lips. The yellow eyes watched me, and then the drink moved the rest of the way. She sipped and lowered it. "Was I supposed to scream?"

"I don't know you well enough to make any guesses."

She studied me. "If that's what you want, I would assume you have a reason. If you want to do it, you will do it in some way which will not implicate me. But he is not that kind of a nuisance."

"How do you mean?"

"He's just a rich, sick, silly man. He might be killed by some other silly man. But a serious man would know he is not worth so much risk. He is an insect."

I sat at the other end of the gigantic couch, facing her. "What sort of insect?"

"You don't know him at all? He is a political dilettante. He supports strange causes. Each one is going to save the world, of course. He gives money to ugly little fringe groups and makes them important, and then he loses interest. He collects exotic things, and many of them are quite nasty. Antique torture instruments. Dirty books and films and pictures.

Sickening books. Shocking bits of sculpture. He's impotent, apparently, and he is a voyeur. Bugged bedrooms, and two-way mirrors and group orgy, that sort of boyish amusement. A sad and tiresome case, really. Sometimes he can be quite charming. Many people who get too closely mixed up with him seem to get into very sticky trouble. But Cal goes on forever. There is something mildly dangerous about him. Perhaps it's a sense of mischief. I don't really know. He is an intuitive blackmailer. He generally gets exactly what he wants out of people. He gets indignant when he can't have his own way. He loves to find some way of pressuring people to make them do things they had no intention of doing. It is an almost feminine taste for intrigue. He loves to make dark hints about all kinds of conspiracy going on, all kinds of nastiness. His latest cause is that Doctor Face."

"Who?"

"Doctor Girdon Face, and his American Crusade. Oh, it's very big lately. Lectures and tent shows and local television and so on. And special phone numbers to call any time of day or night. The liberal-socialist-commy conspiracy that is gutting all the old time virtues. It has a kind of phonied-up religious fervor about it. And it is about ten degrees to the right of the Birchers. The president is selling the country down the river with the help of the Supreme Court. Agree with us or you are a marked traitor. You know the sort of thing, all that tiresome pea-brained nonsense that attracts those people who are so dim-witted that the only way they can understand the world is to believe that it is all some kind of conspiracy. The most amusing thing about it is the way Dr. Face keeps plugging for virtue and morality. He wants to burn everything since Tom Swift, and he is not too certain about Tom. He wants a big crackdown on movies, books, plays, song lyrics, public dancing. And he wants to be the one to weed out the evil. If he ever was turned loose in the west wing of Cal's house up there at Stone Canyon, he would have a stroke. Cal keeps his various fields of interest quite well compartmented. It is a little frightening though, to think how quickly his little Dr. Face has established a huge eager following."

"I heard Tomberlin gives money to Latin American projects too."

"They tap him every chance they get. But he is most

generous with the militant right, the savage little groups who want to buy arms and smash the peons right back to where they belong. He's not a moderate, my friend. What should I call you? I want you to call me Connie."

"John Smith is a little too much, I guess. Mack Smith?"

"You want to play it close, don't you?"

"The name might mean something to Tomberlin."

"How about the face?"

"It won't mean a thing. When can you set it up?"

"Tomorrow evening. We'll go to his house. He seldom goes out. There'll be the usual group of sycophants hanging around him. I'll invent some excuse for dropping by. You'll have to play a part, Mack Smith."

"Who will I be?"

She stretched her long and opulent body and said, "I think the proper designation is Connie's Latest, if you don't mind too much. I shan't kid you, my dear. It is the best protective device you could imagine. I am the complete bitch, and it doesn't bother me a bit. I have a very rational approach to my needs and desires. I am thirty-five years old, darling, and I shall never marry again, and there is no reason why, with my looks and my money, I should settle for an empty bed. My nerves get a little flippy when I do. But I also treasure my emotional independence. So I am notorious for averaging about three young men a year. They are usually somewhat younger than you, but built along the same lines. My God, this California has the world's greatest supply of huge, healthy, beautiful young men. Tomorrow night you must act as they always do in the beginning—earnest and humble and anxious to please. That is when they are very nice, seeing to drinks and cigarettes and wraps, and holding doors, and looking so humbly grateful and happy. After a few months, when they begin to take too much for granted, then they get tiresome and I have to boot them out. Mack, my dear, I would look naked in public places without one of my young men at my side. I got rid of the last one over two weeks ago, and enjoying my little spell of spinsterhood, and I'm not yet ready to go prowling for the next. But Cal will be perfectly willing to accept you as the next one, the current one. Where did I find you?"

"I was running a boat for some friends of yours."

"Perfect. I was up at Monterey last week. Their name is Simmins. Gordon and Louise. I hired you away from them because I am thinking of buying a boat. But Cal won't be particularly curious." She held her glass out and I made her a fresh drink. She brushed my hand with her fingertips and said, as she took it, "Are you going to suggest that we might as well have the game as well as the name?"

I sat closer to her and said, "It would be normal to think about it, Connie. You are pretty spectacular, and you know it. But I don't think it is a very good idea."

"That is what I was going to tell you. If you suggested it."

"What are your reasons?"

"My dear, my young men think they are so bold and wild and free. But they are so easily tamed. And it is to my taste to have them tame. They respond to reward and punishment. So there is no emotional involvement. They are a charming convenience. Can you understand why I want it just that way?"

"I think so."

"You and I would be another thing, my friend. It would take us too long to find out who is winning, and in the process I might lose. I would not want that. It would diminish my personal liberty. I fought hard for it and I enjoy it. I am a violent, petulant, spoiled woman, and I wouldn't suit you unless you could dominate me and teach me manners, in and out of bed. I can sense that in you. And the money does not impress. I can sense that too. So I would not have that weapon either. No, I don't play the games I can't win, Mr. Smith, Mister Mysterious Smith. But what were your reasons?"

I smiled at her. "It would feel a little too much as if I had been standing in line, Connie."

Her eyes changed to narrow slits of gold and her lips lifted away from her teeth. Then suddenly she gave that huge laugh and gave me a punch on the shoulder that made my hand go numb. "See? You would beat me with that sort of talk. One day I would find myself weeping and begging your forgiveness. Like a woman. My God, we might be good enough together to take the risk. But no. Maybe five years ago. Maybe. Not now. I am too old to be physically beaten, and that is one of the things you would find it necessary to do. Because I am insufferable. I know it. Come with me."

She took me into a study which was also a trophy room. African game. Some very good heads. Leopard, lion, buffalo. There was a case of fine weapons behind glass. There were

framed photographs of her, younger, slimmer, just as vital,
standing by the dead elephant, rhino, great ape. "My guns,"
she said. "My dear dead animals. I took my sainted husband
on safari five years running, thinking it would turn him into
enough man for me. He killed like an accountant signing a
ledger. He bent over a bush to pick a flower for me and a
snake struck him in the throat. He was dead before he could
fall to the ground. If it was permitted, I would have his head
in here, mounted like the others. And the heads of all the
young men. Now you know me better, Mack Smith. You
might be enough man for me. I think I will always wonder
about that. It's bad luck we're past the years of finding out.
Be here at six tomorrow. We will use my car. Good night."

I found my way out. I heard that laugh as I was leaving. I
wondered if she had laughed the same way after downing old
jumbo, the tusker, shown in the framed glossy, recumbent
beside Mrs. Melgar in her safari pants, her smile, her big
bore weapon at port arms.

I do not like the killers, and the killing bravely and well
crap. I do not like the bully boys, the Teddy Roosevelts, the
Hemingways, the Ruarks. They are merely slightly more
sophisticated versions of the New Jersey file clerks who
swarm into the Adirondacks in the fall, in red cap, beard
stubble and taut hero's grin, talking out of the side of their
mouths, exuding fumes of bourbon, come to slay the fero-
cious white tail deer. It is the search for balls. A man should
have one chance to bring something down. He should have
his shot at something, a shining running something, and see it
come a-tumbling down, all mucus and steaming blood stench
and gouted excrement, the eyes going dull during the final
muscle spasms. And if he is, in all parts and purposes, a man,
he will file that away as a part of his process of growth and
life and eventual death. And if he is perpetually, hopelessly
a boy, he will lust to go do it again, with a bigger beast.

They have all their earnest rationalizations about game
control. It is good for animals to shoot them. It may serve
some purpose to gut shoot them with a plastic arrow. We
have so bitched up the various ecologies in all our areas,
game control is a necessity. But it should be done by professionals paid to do it, the ones who cherish the healthy flocks,
the ones who do not get their charge out of going bang at
something with thrice the animal dignity they can ever attain.

I do violate my own concepts by slaying the occasional fish. And eating him. But spare me the brotherhood of the blood sports, the hairy ones, all the way from Macmillan and his forty grouse a day to some snot kid who tries to slay every species of big game in the world, with the assistance of his doting daddy.

There is one thing which strikes me as passing strange. Never have I met a man who had the infantry memories, who had knocked down human meat and seen it fall, who ever had any stomach for shooting living things. I could not imagine Paul Dominguez ever shooting even a marauding crow. He would need no romantic fantasies about himself. His manhood would need no artifical reinforcing.

Now I was momentarily associated with a killer female. Perhaps with her too it was a search for balls. She tended to scare the hell out of me. In fact, she reminded me of that horse she mentioned. If I got involved, she would feign docility for the chance of heaving me into an arroyo or crushing me against a stone.

A hard rain came smashing down as I ran for Mrs. Broadmaster's tiny front porch. It was a little after ten. Ten minutes later Junebug knocked at my door. She said she had seen the lights. She wore a transparent rain cape with hood over a fuzzy yellow jump suit. She carried most of a bottle of scotch in her hand. She'd had a couple of belts to build boldness. She said she'd come for a cozy nightcap. She was like a sad and anxious little yellow chicken in that jump suit. It was raining hard, and she was spanking clean and smelled soapy and fresh, and she was touchingly nervous about her earthy intentions, and I did not want to prove that most females were not as overwhelming as Mrs. Melgar, and I had the hunch that the slightest touch would slip her out of that jump suit like a squeezed grape, and afterward she could have a nice little cry about Poor Engineer. But it was not my night for Junebugs. I played dense, evaded small traps, and finally managed to send her off home with just a few small scratches on her pride.

I felt virtuous as all hell. I took a hot bath in Francine's pebbly tub. But suddenly as I was sweating it out, and sipping a strong nightcap, I felt a sudden slide into depression. It was compounded of the old scars on my legs, of the garishness of the bathroom light, of the lingering soreness in my ribs from being hurled against the Jap truck, of the look of Francine's plastic tile, and a douche bag hanging on the back of the bathroom door, and the scrawniness of the pink towel I would have to use to dry off for bed. I felt the brute rejection of my apartness in this world, of too many losses and too few gains, of too much of the dirty underside of things, of too much vulnerability. It had all the sour tang of that post-coital depression which occurs when something hasn't meant enough. On the floor of my mind splintered mahogany floated in the puddled metallic blood. Connie had talked of the empty bed. But I still weaseled it. I left it to chance. I put a robe on and let the Junebug number ring once before I hung up. I left the door ajar and sat in the dark living room. She pushed the door open cautiously and said, "Was that you?"

And she was a warmth to cling to, to keep from drowning.

I had a drink in Connie's apartment while she finished dressing. She came out with the happy walk of a woman who knows she will be approved. She wore a dark sheath dress of some kind of knitted material. She was almost but not quite too big for knitted fabrics. Her shoulders were bare and honey-brown, smoothly muscled and magnificent.

"You're very elegant, Connie."

"Thank you. Wear that same look all evening, dear, and you'll fit the category."

"Drink?"

"The same as before. Please."

She went to the phone and called the basement and told them to bring her car around front. She came back and took her glass, touched it to mine. "To whatever you're after, Mack Smith. Mysterious Mack Smith. Your eyes intrigue me, Mr. Smith. Are pale-eyed people cruel? Your eyes are the color of rain on a window in the early morning. At first glance last night, I thought you looked quite wholesome. That's a deception, isn't it?"

"I have wholesome impulses."

"Kindly keep them to yourself. You know, I think you are just as violent as I am. But your control is better. What are you after?"

"A close look at Mr. Tomberlin."

"That's all?"

"I might bend him a little."

"What did he do to you, dear?"

"Let's say he set something in motion and it didn't work out very well for anybody except him."

"Who did you last work for?"

"Gordon and Louise Simmins of Monterey. Why?"

"Am I a better employer?"

"The relationship is a little more personal."

"My dear, the people at Tomberlin's will be a mixed bag. Fragmented groups spread about the place, serviced by his Hawaiian army. Circulate at will. I phoned him today. He is leaving in two or three days. He likes to go down to Montevideo this time of year. He has a beach house down there. It's autumn there. Tonight is part of the series of little parties he gives himself before he leaves. He'll stay in Uruguay a few weeks, then go up to Canada for part of the summer, then back to his Cobblestone Mountain lodge for the rest of the summer and into the autumn here, then back into the big house October through May. That is the overall pattern, but he is forever whipping off on mysterious little trips. He has the boat, of course. And one big bastard it is, some sort of a converted Canadian cutter. And a small airplane. But he has never learned to drive a car. Do you want to know these things about him? He drinks iced tea, gallons of it a day. Strangers think he is belting strong highballs, but it is always iced tea. He designs his own clothes and has them made, and some of his outfits are very strange. He has these enormous living expenses, and platoons of accountants and tax attorneys in the background somewhere, but he is very cheap about odd little things. The liquor will flow freely this evening, but it will be the cheapest you can buy. He never carries any money with him, and he's never been known to grab a check anywhere. His drivers have to buy those strange kinds of gasoline that nobody has ever heard of."

She put her empty glass down and said, "Are we ready?"

I draped the pale fur over her shoulders, a broad stole about ten feet long, big enough for a big woman. She wore cat's eye studs in pierced ears, and a single ring, a narrow oblong emerald that reached from knuckle to knuckle. She brought no purse. She loaded me with her cigarettes, lighter, compact and lipstick—typical burden for the captive male. She led me like a small parade. Down in front the doorman handed her into the car with humble tender ceremony. He gave me one glance of knowing appraisal. I got behind the wheel, identified the right gadgets, and stomped the car off into the bright evening.

eighteen

THE TILTED rocky area immediately surrounding the Tomberlin place was enclosed by a high wire fence. The gate was open. A broad little uniformed man with a merry Chinese face intercepted us, peered in at Connie Melgar, then backed, grinning, touching his cap.

There were at least twenty cars in the parking area, ranging from a glossy Bentley to a scabrous beach buggy. The big house was spilled down the rock slope. The garages were on the highest level, at the brow of the slope, with what seemed to be servants' quarters off to the right. We went down a broad stone stairway to the left of the house, sheltered by a cantilevered roof affixed to the side of the house. The house was of bleached grey wood, pale stone, glass, aluminum and slate. It was like three sizeable houses, each on stilts, each on a different level down the rock slope, all butted against each other. If there was an architectural unity about it, one would have to get a long way off to see it. The middle house was over a swimming pool big enough to extend half of itself out into the last of the evening sunlight, where there was a wide apron and a garden. Our staircase crossed the pool and continued on, I saw, ending at a huge deck in front of the lowest portion of the house, a deck overlooking a steep drop and a broad and lovely view. But Connie turned off down a narrow branching staircase that brought us down to poolside under the middle segment of the house. Some sleek young things were enjoying the pool, swimming back and forth from sunlight to shadow. We climbed a curve of staircase into the middle portion of the house, into a vast room vaguely reminiscent of a Miami Beach hotel lobby, but in better taste. People stood in chatting groups. Tawny little men in white coats brought their drinks to them. Chunky little Eurasian girls in uniform circulated with trays of little hot meats and pastries. The guests seemed like glossy people, filling the room with a cocktail buzz, a controlled laughter. Eyes slanted toward us in swift appraisal, and I adjusted my mild and fatuous smile.

A slender blonde woman detached herself from her group and came hurrying over to us. She was slightly long in the tooth, but she had carefully preserved a lot worth preserving. She gave little coos of pleasure and she and Connie exchanged a small kiss of greeting and told each other how marvelous they were looking.

"Rhoda, dear, may I present Mack Smith. Rhoda Dwight, one of my oldest and dearest friends." There was a dirty little emphasis on 'oldest'.

Rhoda beamed at me, squeezed my hand. "Connie, darling, where have you been hiding such a beautiful man?"

"Mack is helping me find a nice boat, dear. When we find one, he's going to run it for me."

"What *fun!* I hope I'll be asked to come cruising with you, dear. But don't you get quite horribly seasick, Connie?"

"We may never take it away from the dock, darling. How is Norm, by the way?"

"Who? Norm? But why in the world should you ask me how *he* is? Shouldn't I be asking you?"

Connie gave her a tiger smile. "Now isn't that strange! I haven't seen the dear boy in months. It must be some mistake, darling. I was told you were seen with him in Santa Barbara just last week. Really, I didn't think anything of it. After all, you and Quenton both seemed to like the lad."

"I haven't been to Santa Barbara in decades, darling."

"There's no reason for you to be upset, Rhoda."

"Upset? What gives you that odd idea?"

A little man came up to take our drink orders. Connie began slapping at my pockets to locate her cigarettes. Rhoda gave us a glassy smile and drifted away.

"Bitch," Connie rumbled. "Scavenger bitch." Our drinks came. As she had promised, they were inferior. She touched my arm. "There's the man. Come on."

Calvin Tomberlin was in a small group. He was a grotesque. He was of middle size, fairly plump, and stood very erect. He was completely hairless, without brows or lashes. He wore a toupee so obviously fraudulent it was like a sardonic comment on all such devices. It was dusty black, carefully waved, and he wore it like a hairy beret. His eyes were blue and bulged. His face was pale pink, like roast beef. His lips were very heavy and pale, and they did not move very much when he spoke. His voice was a resonant buzz, like a bee in a tin can. He wore a pewter grey silk suit, with a boxy jacket, cut like a Norfolk jacket but without lapels. He wore a yellow ascot with it.

He greeted Connie with what I guessed was supposed to be warmth, gave her a little hug, and placed two firm pats on her ample knitted stern. But it was done in a curiously mechanical fashion, as though he was a machine programmed to make these social gestures.

Connie introduced us. His hand was cold and soft and dry. He looked at me as a butcher looks at a questionable side of meat, and turned away. I had a feeling a relay had clicked and my file card had fallen into the right slot. I was next to him, but in an identity where I could not establish contact. Stud for the Venezuelana. Ambulatory service station. I sensed the same recognition and dismissal in the others. They weighed me with their eyes, so much captive meat, and turned away. I did some drifting. Groups formed, broke, reformed, changed. I saw the pool people. I paced the big suspended deck. The lowest level was bedrooms. The upper level was lounge area, dining areas, a library. The day was gone, and the lights came on as they were needed.

I found Connie and, after a patient time, cut her out of the pack.

"What was that about a west wing or something?"

"Cal's little museum. Up the stairs and to the left. Locked tight."

"Any way to get to see it?"

She frowned. "I don't know. I can try. Hang around this area, dear. If it works, I'll be back to get you."

While she was gone a wobbly type came up to me, a big blond kid with a recruiting poster face. He looked ready to cry.

"You have some good laughs when she pointed me out, pal?"

"You're wrong. She didn't."

"I saw it, buddy. I saw it happening. You know what you got to do. You got to take her a damn big bug."

"A what?"

He wavered and held up a thumb and finger, a quarter inch apart. "There's a hell of a smart spider. A spider, no bigger'n this. When he goes to see the old lady spider, he wraps up a big juicy bug and takes it along, like an offering. He's one smart little old son of a bitch, because he knows that it's the only way he can have his fun and get away alive, because she gets so busy eating that bug she doesn't get around to eating him. You got the message, buddy boy? You take Connie a hell of a big bug, and remember I told you so."

"Thanks a lot. Take off."

He shook his head. "You're so smart, aren't you? You know every damn thing. She's worth millions, and she's the best piece you ever ran into, and you're set forever. That's the way it is, huh? Living high, boy. Well, brace yourself, because she's going to...."

"Chuck!" she said sharply. He swung around and stared at her. She shook her head sadly. "You're turning into the most terrible bore, dear. Run along, dear."

"I want to talk to you, Connie. By God, I want to talk to you."

"You heard the lady," I said.

He pivoted and swung at me. I caught the fist in my open hand, slid my fingers onto his wrist. He swung the other fist, off balance, and I caught the other wrist. He bulged with the effort to free himself, then broke and started to cry. I let him go and he went stumbling away, rubbing his nose with the back of his hand.

"Nicely done," she said.

"I am supposed to bring you a wrapped bug."

"Yes. I remember that little analogy. He got very fond of it. He did turn into a dreadful bore. Come along. Cal is waiting. I told him I wanted to see how you'd react."

"How should I react?"

"Suit yourself. It gives me a funny feeling."

He was waiting for us, mild as a licensed guide. He unlocked a very solid-looking door, closed it and locked it again when the three of us were inside. Lines of fluorescent tubes flickered and went on. There were little museum spotlights. The room was about twenty by forty. There were paintings and drawings on the walls. There was a big rack of paintings and drawings. There were pieces of statuary on pedestals and on bases, and set into glassed-in niches in the walls. There were display cases. It was all very tidy and professional and well-organized. The windows, two small ones, were covered with thick steel mesh.

"I have here, and in the next room," he said in that buzzing voice, "what is probably the most definitive collection of erotica in the world today. It has considerable historical significance. The historical portion of the collection, the library of over two thousand volumes, the ancient paintings and statuary, are available for the use of qualified scholars by appointment. Because so many of these things are irreplaceable, I could not venture a guess as to the value of the collection."

Each major piece of art in that tidy room was shocking. There was a curious clinical horror about it, a non-functional chill. I had the odd feeling that walking into this room was precisely like walking into Cal Tomberlin's mind. I glanced at Connie. Her eyes were narrow and her rich mouth compressed.

He showed us the cases of ancient instruments of torture and ecstasy. He turned a ground glass easel on, took large Ektachrome transparencies from a safe file and showed us a few of them, saying, "These are studies of the Indian temple carvings at Konarak and Khajuarho, showing the erotic procedures which were always a part of the Hindu religion."

He put them away and said, "Beyond here we have the special library of books and films, a small projection room and a small photo lab. A recent project has been to duplicate the Konarak carvings, using amateur actors and period costuming. Stills, of course."

"A project?" Connie said. "Really, Cal! You make your own diseases sound so terribly earnest."

He looked at her blandly. "Connie, my dear, any time you wish to lend your considerable talent to any of these little projects. . . ."

"I would look a bit out of place among your poor hopped-up little actors and actresses, darling."

"You are wonderfully well preserved, Connie."

I wandered over to the side wall. The individual niches were lighted. I had counted one area of thirty-four of them. The gold statues were behind glass.

"Are these real gold, Mr. Tomberlin?"

He came up behind me. "Yes. I recently had more space

made for these. Most of these were a recent acquisition. As you can see, many of them do not fit in with . . . with the general theme of the entire collection. But I decided not to break the collection up. Strange and handsome, aren't they?"

I moved over and got a close look at the squatty little man. Borlika Galleries had sold him to Carlos Menterez y Cruzada. Carlos had taken him from New York to Havana to Puerto Altamura. Sam Taggart had taken him from Mexico to California to Florida. He had unwrapped him there and shown him to me. And somebody had come and taken him back to California. Now I had traced him down, and I imagined I could see an ancient sour recognition in his little eyes.

"Where would you go to buy stuff like this?" I asked.

"I purchased a collection, Mr. Smith. I haven't had them properly identified and catalogued as yet." He was bored. He had no interest in my reaction. He turned to Connie and said, "Would you like to see a new film, dear? It's Swedish, and quite extraordinary."

She shivered. "Thank you, no. Once was enough for all time. Show it to Rhoda, darling. She adores that sort of thing. Thank you for the guided tour. Let's all get back to the people, shall we?"

After we were alone again, she shivered again and said, "That's pretty snaky in there, isn't it?"

"He's a strange man."

She pulled me into a corner and put her hands on my shoulders. "Is it those gold things, dear?"

"Was I that obvious?"

"Not really. But it would be nice if it were those gold statues. He was so delighted to get them. He's had them only a few months. He must have made a very good deal. He kept chuckling and beaming. But, darling, it would be quite a project. That room is like a big safe. This place is alive with people at all hours. And I think he has burglar alarms."

"It presents a few little problems."

"Including the police."

"No. They wouldn't come into it."

"I beg your pardon?"

"They're not his. Twenty-eight of them aren't."

She looked amused and astonished. "Now don't tell me he stole them!"

"He sort of intercepted them after they'd been stolen."

"It's very confusing, my dear. And you are ... employed by someone?"

"Paul told you about asking questions."

"I remember something about that. Don't you trust me, my dear?"

"Implicitly, totally, without reservation, Constancia. But if you don't have any answers, you can't answer any questions."

"Will people ask me questions?"

"Probably not."

"Darling, do as you wish. I am the middle one of five daughters in a very political family, and we were all born to intrigue."

"The idea of there being five of you is a little disconcerting."

"Don't be alarmed. The other four are little satin pillows, surrounded with children. I am twenty-one times an aunt. Tia Constancia." She hooked a strong hand around the nape of my neck. "Be kissed by an aunt," she said. It was quick and pungent and most competent. And loaded with challenge.

"I think there'd be a nice place for me, just to the left of the lion."

"I would be more concerned about what your trophy room looks like, Mack Smith."

"It's very dull. You see, I don't go after the record heads. In fact, I don't go after anything at all. I'm not a collector, Connie."

"That makes you a little more dangerous. I understand collectors. You see, I.... What's the matter?"

"I just wondered if I know that man."

She turned and looked. "Oh, that's one of Cal's show business connections. A dreary little chap. Claude Boody."

There was no hint of the imperiousness the artist had put into the oil painting in Puerto Altamura. The jowls were the same. The eyes were sad, wet, brown and bagged, like a tired spaniel, and he walked with the care of a heart case.

"I guess he just looks like someone I knew once."

"He has some dreary little syndicated television things, and he buys old foreign movies and dubs the English and resells them to independent stations."

"You sound knowledgeable, Mrs. Melgar."

"I have some money in that, too. But not with him."

"Does Tomberlin have some business association with him?"

"Heavens no! Calvin cultivates a few people like Boody because they can always round up some reckless youngsters for fun and games. Poor Boody travels the world over scrounging properties, and he always looks tired. I guess he does well enough. He lives well. His wife is a neurotic bitch and his children are spoiled rotten."

We went back to the upper lounge where Tomberlin's hard-working staff had laid out a generous buffet. It was delicious, and we took loaded plates down to the big deck and ate like a pair of tigers. She licked her fingers, patted her tummy, stifled a belch and moaned with satisfaction. There is a direct relation between the physical approaches to all hungers. This great hearty woman would ease all appetites with the same wolfish intensity, the same deep satisfaction. She would live hard, play hard, sleep like the dead. Her strong rich body had that magnetic attraction based on total health and total use. She did not relate in any way to the sick subtleties, the delicate corruptions in Tomberlin's private museum. And I got the hell away from her before I had more awareness than I could comfortably handle.

I wandered again. The party kept shifting and changing, people leaving, people arriving, various states of various kinds of intoxication achieved, small arrangements made and broken, small advantages taken and rejected. Music boomed from hidden speakers when somebody turned the volume up. All evening it had been incurably, implacably Hawaiian. I heard the reason in a snatch of conversation. Tomberlin liked it, and would have nothing else.

I mapped the place in my mind. Then I rechecked my dimensions. I wandered outside and identified the windows and the relationship between them. I charted in the power sources. I wondered how many Hawaiians the damned man had. I wondered what kind of nippers would bite that wire, and how I would get up to the window, and how I would get back up to it from the inside bearing a hundred and a half of ancient gold, if I could get it out from behind those glass ports.

I went out into the darker end of the garden beyond the lights of the now empty pool, and sat on a pedestal, sharing it with a welded woman perched upon one steel toe. I smoked a cigarette and felt again the monstrous dejection which had nearly foundered me in Francine's tub. There can be a special sort of emotional exhaustion compounded of finding no good answers to anything. Too much had faded away, and the only target left was a grotesque pornographer with a voice like a trapped bee, and he seemed peripheral to the whole thing. Too much blood. Too much gold and intrigue. Too much fumbling and bumbling. It was like taking a puzzle apart and having the pieces disappear the instant they came free. From the talk with Sam, all the way to the hard tasteless gallop in Francine's bed, I had handled myself like an idiot, suffering all the losses, enjoying no gains.

And, except for Nora, the whole thing had seemed like a long bath in yesterday's dish water. The house lights faded the stars, but I looked up at them and told myself my recent vision of reality had been from a toad's-eye view. The stars, McGee, look down on a world where thousands of 4-H kids are raising prize cattle and sheep. The Green Bay Packers, of their own volition, join in the Lord's Prayer before a game. Many good and gentle people have fallen in love this night. At this moment, thousands of women are in labor with the fruit of good marriage. Thousands of kids sleep the deep sleep which comes from the long practice hours for competitive swimming and tennis. Good men have died today, leaving hearts sick with loss. In quiet rooms young girls are writing poems. People are laughing together, in safe places.

You have been on the underside of the world, McGee, but there is a top side too, where there is wonder, innocence, trust, love and gentleness. You made the decision, boy. You live down here, where the animals are, so stay with it.

I got up and went back to the party. A new batch of faces had arrived and some had fallen off. A dusty little man in his middle years, with fierce eyes and a froggy bassoon of a voice was standing orating in the big room, surrounded by a mixed group of admirers and dissidents. He wore a beret and a shiny serge suit and he had a great air of authority. I drifted into the edge of the group and heard an earnest woman say, "But Doctor Face, isn't it part of our heritage for anyone to be entitled to say what they think, right or wrong?"

"My dear woman, that is one of the luxuries of liberty, not one of the definitions thereof. And it is traditional and necessary in war that we forego the luxuries and concentrate on the necessities. My posture is that we are at war, with a vile, godless, international conspiracy which grows in strength every day while we weaken ourselves by giving every pinko jackass the right to confuse our good people. I ask you, my

dear. Who takes the fifth? Known hoodlums and fellow travel-
ers. Our so called traditional liberties provide the bunkers in
which these rascals hide and shoot us down. I say we must
work together. We must silence all the divisionist voices
among us. If we are to be strong, we must impeach all traitor
justices of the Supreme Court, give greater powers to the
investigating committees of the Congress, decentralize our
socialistic central government, institute wartime censorship of
all mass media, expand the counterespionage efforts of the
FBI, smash the apparatus of the Communist Party as it exists
within labor unions, the NAACP, the CLU, and the hard
core of sympathizers on all college campuses, both students
and faculty. We are engaged in a bitter war for the hearts
and minds of men, and our enemy is without soul or mercy.
To be strong we must silence, once and forever, every jackass who tells the people that we can win through weakness
rather than strength. Over twelve thousand people have
signed up as Crusaders. We're tough. We're smart. We're
wary. And we mean to save this country in spite of itself."

The delivery was effective. It radiated sincerity, concern,
earnestness. But he had it all down just a little too pat. He
had said it too many hundreds of times. And as I stood there
I had a curious feeling I had been there before. It took me a
time to remember. Then I recalled it, lifetimes ago, as a small
kid in a Chicago park, hanging onto the big hand of the
daddy, listening to this same dusty little man with his
smeared lenses and the same general impression of dirty underwear. Not the same man, of course, but the same mechanical
messiah approach. And that duplicate little man of long ago
had been calling upon all decent men to arm themselves
against the dirty capitalistic conspiracy, bread for the work-
ers, break the chains, unite, save America.

I moved away, to a different level of the house where, over
the goopy strings of the grass skirt music I could hear his
occasional clarion phrase "... ninety miles off our door-
step ... sense of purpose ... show them we mean what we
say ... bleeding hearts ..." but I could not follow the
strange line of his reasoning. There are a lot of them running
loose these days, I thought, fattening themselves on the sick
business of whipping up such fear and confusion that they
turn decent men against their decent neighbors in this sad
game of think-alike.

It seemed an odd business for Tomberlin to be backing,

but I have long since learned that the very rich specialize in irrational causes. Insulated from the brute reality of the money drive, they expand into the unreality of Yoga, astrology, organic foods and marginal politics. Tomberlin was immersed in the mismatched fields of erotica and the clanking of crypto-Fascist right. Next year it might be voodoo and technocracy. It was the search for importance, and the ones who could recognize that could con him very nicely and profitably.

I found that one of the strategic little bars had a fair brand of domestic brandy, so I got three fingers and one lump of ice and sat on a corner couch and looked across to where a group of young were sprawled up the side of some wide stairs. Some of them were the pool people. They had their private jokes, and their cool-eyed apartness from the rest of the party. They were a swinging little pack, with a flavor of tension and disdain.

There is one typical characteristic of both nightmare and delirium. Both these conditions of mind involve the grouping of people from random points in the past. A dead childhood companion will appear with last month's girl. A man who once tried very earnestly to kill you dead will show up and tell you symbolic things about your dead brother's wife. When there is an inexplicable association of people during a waking and rational moment, it inevitably recaptures that faint and eerie flavor of nightmare.

Suddenly one of the little blonde cupcakes on the stairway jumped into focus as though I was using a zoom lens. It was the nameless sun bunny from the pool at La Casa Encantada, the one who had come over tipsy, sat on her heels with brown thighs muscularly flexed, wanting to know if I'd been an end with the Rams. She wore a little white linen dress and had her hair piled high and wore considerable eye makeup, but it was the same one. I felt as if I could not take a very deep breath. I looked at the others. There had been five of them on that motor sailer, three young men and two girls. I found one of the men, a big dark hairy one, the one who had seemed to be in charge of the scuba outing. What had she called him? Chip.

I could accept the presence of Claude Boody. A mild coincidence. But I could not accept the presence of the sun bunny. It was a little too much. And so nothing had been as I had imagined. I had to let the structure fall down and then try again. I had to find a new logic. I was frightened without knowing why I should be. It was fright with a paranoid flavor. All I needed was for Heintz or Arista or Colonel Marquez to show up, humming a Hawaiian melody.

I knew the awareness was mutual. The bland, sensual little pug-face made automatic smiles and grimaces at the things people said to her. But she would angle her eyes at me now and again. Never a direct look, but only when her head was turned. It was unconsciously furtive. I could not read her big hairy friend. He was further up the stairs and seemed totally involved with a little brunette who squirmed and giggled and squirmed.

I moved casually away, but not entirely out of range. I was considerably more alert. I had an uncomfortable feeling. Like a herd animal, shuffling along with the group, and gradually beginning to wonder what that faint thudding and screaming means, way up at the head of the line. I was growing points on my ears and walking softly on my toes. I found Connie talking to a big broad balding fellow with tiny eyes and a large damp mouth and considerable affability. She introduced him as George Wolcott, introduced him in a way that told me she did not know him and found him boring.

"What kind of a boat are you going to help this lovely lady find?" he asked me, chuckling though no joke had been made.

"Just a comfortable day cruiser of some kind. Displacement hull. A good sea beam. Nothing fast or flashy."

"I suppose you got all the licenses to run one. Heh, heh, heh."

"To run a charter boat for hire, with Coast Guard blessings, Mr. Wolcott."

"Good. Heh, heh, heh. What kind of a boat do the Simmins have?"

"It is a great big gaudy vulgar Chris Craft," Connie said. "It's called the Not Again! Excuse us please, Mr. Wolcott."

He chuckled his permission. His loose smilings did not alter the dead bullet look of his eyes. I was getting hyper-sensitive. When we were far enough away from him, I asked her who he was.

"Oh, he's part of that Doctor Face deal. Chairman of arrangements or rifle drill or some goddam thing."

"He asks a lot of questions."

"I think it's just Dale Carnegie. Show an interest. Keep smiling. Remember names. Darling, how much of this can you take? My God, this music is hurting my teeth. I'd much rather take you home to bed."

"Give me another half hour here."

I turned her over to Rhoda Dwight for some more infighting, and wandered on. The sun bunny appeared at my elbow, showing teeth that looked brushed after every meal. But she seemed uneasy.

"I never was with the Rams," I said.

"I know. Look, I have to tell you something. Not here. Okay? Go down to the deck and over to the end, to the right as you go out onto the deck."

Without waiting for my answer, she walked away. Suspicion confirmed. There can only be so much coincidence in the world. So I went where requested. I had that end of the deck to myself. I looked at the night view. She hissed at me. I turned and saw her looking out of a dark doorway. I went to her. "This way," she said. It was a wide corridor in the bedroom area, a night-light panel gleaming.

She opened a corridor door and said in a low voice, "I didn't want to be seen talking to you. We can talk in here."

She walked in first, into darkness. I hesitated at the doorway, and went in. But I went in at a swift sidelong angle, and something smashed down on the point of my right shoulder, numbing my arm. I went down and rolled to where I thought the girl would be. The room door slammed. I rolled against her legs and brought her thrashing down, got an arm around her throat and one hand levered up behind her and stood up with her just as lights came on. Claude Boody stood with an ugly gun aimed toward us, and I turned the sun bunny quickly into the line of fire. But there was the faintest whisper of sound behind me, and before I could move again, a segment of my skull went off like a bomb and I fell slowly, slowly, like a dynamited tower, with the girl underneath. I was vaguely aware of landing on her, and of her strangled yawp as my weight drove the air out of her, and of tumbling loosely away.

I was not out. I retained ten percent of consciousness, but I could not move. The room was at the far end of a tunnel, and the voices seemed to echo through the tunnel.

"Oh God," a girl whined. "I'm all busted up inside. Oh God."

"Shut up, Dru."

"Both of you shut up," an older male voice said, enormously weary. "You let him get a look at me. It's a brand new problem."

"I'm hurt bad," the girl moaned.

Hands fumbled at my pockets, shifting and hauling. Down in my trauma drowse I had the comfy awareness they would find nothing. I was entirely clean, just in case. My cheek was against a softness of rug. They hitched and tugged at my clothing.

"Nothing," the tired voice said. "This stuff must belong to the Melgar woman."

"It's a Miami label in the suit. That mean anything?"

"Chip, I could be dying! Don't you care?"

"Lie down on the bed, Dru. And shut up, please."

Chip, Claude and Dru. Three voices from far away. I heard the click of a lighter. A moment later, I felt a little hot area near the back of my hand.

"What are you doing?" Chip asked.

"Let's see how good you got him. Let's see if he's faking."

Heat turned into a white stabbing light that shoved itself deep into my brain. Pain was like a siren caught on a high note. Pain cleared away the mists, but I would not move. I caught a little drifting stink of my own burned flesh.

"He's out," Chip said. "Maybe I got him good enough so there's no problem."

"Or a worse one, you silly bastard," Claude said. "Depending on who he is."

"Isn't *anybody* going to do *anything?*" Dru wailed.

They were kneeling or squatting, one on each side of me, talking across my back. The girl was further away.

"You slipped up on this one," Claude said. "I don't mean here and now. I mean down there."

"I told you, I wondered about him down there. So I had Dru check him out. She's no dummy. She has a feeling for anything out of line. You should know that. She threw the Garcia name at him and didn't get a thing back. He was with a woman down there. Gardino. And that was what it looked like, to be there to be with the woman and she looked worth it. And that was the same woman who had the bad luck. Honest to God, it was a one in a million chance, but she caught it. I'm still sick about that. It seemed like a hell of a big charge to me when I wired it in, but your expert was supposed to know what he was doing when he put it together. We were long gone by then, but still that woman didn't have any part of. . . . "

"Shut up! The problem is finding out who this bastard is and what he wants."

"Honest to God, Claude, when Dru spotted him and pointed him out to me about forty minutes ago, you could have knocked me over with a pin."

"Shut up and let me think. This is beginning to go sour. I don't like it. He's no fool. Coming here with the Melgar woman was almost perfect cover. And he made some good moves in this room. He nearly got out of hand. And he had good cover down there too, good enough to fool you and Dru, boy. So who is he working for? How did he trace it back to here? I thought we closed the door on that whole operation. I thought everybody who could make any connection was gone—Almah, Miguel, Taggart. But now this son of a bitch comes out of nowhere. I don't like it."

"And you know who else isn't going to like it."

"Shut up, Chip, for God's sake!"

"Why don't you drop it in his lap?"

"Because he doesn't like things fouled up. Let's come up with some kind of answer before I tell him."

"One answer," Chip said, "is to make this character talk about it. The name he used down there was McGee. Tonight it's Smith. God knows what it really is."

The girl made a groan of effort, as though struggling to sit up. "Jesus, he ruined me. Chipper, you get him tied up and let me get at him with that little electric needle thing, and I'll make him talk about things he never heard of."

"Shut her up," Claude said.

There was a sudden movement, a solid and meaty slapping sound, and then the girl's muffled and hopeless sobbing. "Goddam you, Chip," she sobbed.

"Hasn't he been trying to work out something with the Melgar woman?" Chip asked.

"Just to get some shots of her in action. Send them down to Venezuela for mass distribution."

"Why?"

"Use your head, you silly bastard. They know her face down there. Two brothers-in-law in the government. Notorious heiress having fun in the United States. But he hasn't been able to trap her."

"Did he give up?"

"Chipper, baby, he *never* gives up. Some day he'll juice up a couple of her drinks, and she'll go wobbling in there like a lamb, with spit on her chin, and give a hell of a performance."

"So if she brought this guy here, why not now? Two birds with one stone. Like the time with that state senator and that ambassador's wife."

After a silence, Claude Boody said, "We certainly got mileage out of that little session. You know, sometimes you show vague signs of intelligence. What he'll want done is keep this character and the Melgar woman stashed until the last drunk leaves. If he approves."

"I don't see how he has too much choice."

"I should get to a doctor," Dru said plaintively. "Every breath is like knives."

"What I'll do," Claude said, "you sit tight here and I'll go lay it on for him, which I think we should have done in the first place."

"He makes mistakes too."

"How often? How big?"

"Look, he can punish me. He can give me the Melgar broad."

"You're very very funny."

I gave a weak, heartbreaking groan and moved very feebly. I needed to manage a sudden change in the odds. And I couldn't do it face down.

"He's coming out of it," Chip said.

I writhed over onto my back, then started up suddenly. They stood up and moved back. I got halfway to a sitting position, eyes staring, then fell back with a long gargling sound, held my breath, let my mouth sag open, left my eyes half closed.

"Jesus H. Christ!" Chip whispered.

"You hit him too goddam hard with that thing!"

I wondered how long they would take. I hadn't oxygenated, but I thought I could manage two minutes of it. They moved in again, squatting close. I felt fingers on my wrist. "He isn't breathing, but his heart's still going good," Claude said. He released my wrist.

I snatched Claude by the windsor knot, and I hooked a hand on the back of Chip's neck, and slammed their heads together as hard as I could. I had fear and anger and a desperate haste working for me. It was like using a simultaneous overhand right and a wide left hook. Bone met bone with quite a horrid sound, much like smacking two large stones together underwater. Bone met bone hard enough to give a rebound that sent them both spilling over backward, settling slowly into the floor, both heads split and bleeding. I glanced at the girl, slapped at Claude, pulled the weapon out from between belt and soft belly. It was oddly light for such a large and ugly caliber. She had pushed herself halfway up, and she stared at me, eyes and mouth wide open. We were in a sizeable and elegant bedroom. I let her look down the barrel and she said, "Wha-wha-what are you going to do?"

I moved back to the door, stepping over new acquaintances. There was an inside bolt and a chain. I fastened them. There was a vent, a continuous whisper of washed air. The windows were closed and looked sealed. I had the idea sound would not travel far from that room. My conversational acquaintances hadn't seemed concerned about it. If any did get out of the room, it would have to fight that ubiquitous Hawaiian cotton candy music.

There was an object in the side pocket of Chip's green blazer. I took it out. I imagine our limey cousins would term it a home made cosh. It was an eight inch section of stubby pipe wrapped with a thick padding of black friction tape. I put Boody's hand gun in my jacket pocket and went over to the bed and sat on the edge of it, facing the sun bunny. Her eyes were puffed and apprehensive, her bland little face tear-stained.

"What do you want anyhow?" she demanded with false bravado.

I gave her a light touch across the ribs with the piece of pipe. She gave a thin whistling scream, the noise a shot rabbit will sometimes make. She lay back and said, "Oh, don't. Oh, golly, there's something all broke. I can feel it kind of grind. You fell with your whole weight on me."

"I have a headache, Dru, and a nasty burn on the back of my hand, and you were very anxious to play around with some sort of an electric needle. I lost a very marvelous woman in that clambake down there, and I am going to ask questions. Whenever I don't like the answer, I'm going to give you another little rap; with this."

"What if you ask something I don't know?"

"You get a little rap for luck. Chip wired the explosive into Menterez' boat. Why?"

"To kill Alconedo. Miguel Alconedo. He'd goofed somehow. I don't know how. You see, we took down his orders for him. He was supposed to kill Almah, then take the boat up to Boca del Rio, ten miles off shore, where he thought we'd be waiting for him. He thought it was all set so we could take him someplace where he could go from there back to Cuba and be safe. But there wasn't any intention of that. The other three kids aboard, they didn't know anything about anything. Chip sneaked off the night before we left, after midnight when a lot of the lights went out, and fixed the boat."

"Who did you think I might be? Why did you try to check me?"

"Chip wondered about you. You sort of didn't look like a tourist. You see, Almah couldn't be trusted any more. She told Taggart too much about things. And she got too anxious about getting that money. She was okay up until the time of the Mineros thing, and then she started cracking up. They thought that if she told Taggart too much, maybe she told somebody else too, maybe the wrong people, and maybe some C.I.A. was down there. Chip thought that's what you might be. Who are you anyhow?" She attempted a small shy friendly smile.

"Who got Taggart?"

"Gee, I don't know. I mean I'm not sure. I heard them making a joke about it. About the monkey's paw. It could have been a man named Ramon Talavera. They laughed a lot about Taggart. I know they picked him up before he had made any contact. They knew where he was. So when they made a date with him, to make arrangements about selling those statues to them, nobody showed up at the meeting place and when he went back all the others were gone, and all he had left was the one he'd taken along to prove he really had them. Then they got the last one back too, after somebody killed him."

"Tomberlin gave the orders about Almah and about the explosive?"

"I guess he told Claude what to do and who to pick to do it. Nobody meant for that woman with you to be...."

"Why do you do what they tell you to do, Dru?"

"Me?" She looked astonished. "Golly, I guess it's about the

same with me as it was with Almah and a lot of other people. Those pictures of me, if they ever sent a print of even one of the cleanest ones to my daddy, I swear it would kill him. You don't know about the first pictures they take, and then they use those to make you do things for more pictures. Rather than have my daddy ever see me doing anything like that, his own daughter, I'd cut my wrists first. I'd do anything they ask. I think where Almah got out from under, her mother died while she was down there."

I remembered the untidiness of Almah Hichin, the look of soil and wear and carelessness. It was easy to see now why she had ceased to value herself. And it was an ancient gambit, using the threat of the most horrid scandal imaginable to tame people to your will and use. And the son of a bitch had so casually mentioned his photo lab.

"You know what Tomberlin is? And Claude Boody?"

"I can't help that. I don't think about that."

"Baby, you are going to have to think about it. You are an accessory to murder. And your dear daddy is going to have to know the whole filthy mess, and you are going to have to talk and talk and talk to save your sweet skin, sun bunny. Even so, you may spend ten years in a Mexican rest camp, living on tortillas and frijoles."

"Leave me alone, you son of a bitch! I think I'm bleeding inside. You can't do anything to me. I bet you can't even get back through the gate out there."

I turned and looked at the two slumberers. Chip was still bleeding. Boody had stopped, though his gash looked bigger. I had a sudden idea about him. I went over and put my ear against his chest. When I was still a foot away from him, I realized there wasn't much point in it. I was aware of the girl moving from the bed to go and bend over Chip. I listened to utter silence. All I could hear was my own blood roaring in my ear, like listening to a sea shell. Boody didn't live in there any more.

As I slowly got to my feet, there was a sharp brisk sound, like somebody breaking a big dry stick. The sun bunny had backed over toward a dressing table. She had a little automatic in her hand, a little more weapon than my shiny bedroom gun. She held it at arm's length, aiming it at me. She was biting her lip. She had one eye closed. The small muzzle made a wavering circle. It cracked again and I felt a little warm wind against my ear lobe.

"Cut it out!" I yelled, fumbling for Claude's gun, tugging it out of my pocket. She fired again, and I knew she was going to keep right on, and I knew she couldn't keep on missing at that range, particularly if it occurred to her to stop trying to hit me in the face. The third shot tingled the hair directly on top of my head, and Claude's pistol was double action, and I tried to get her in the shoulder. It made a ringing deafening blam, and the slug took her just below the hairline on the right side of her head, and the recoil of that light frame jumped the gun up so that it was aiming at the ceiling.

The slug slammed a third of the top of her skull away, snapped her neck, catapulted her back into the dressing table, smashing the mirror, soiling the wall, leaving her in a limp, grotesque, motionless backbend across the dressing table bench. The silent room was full of the stink of smokeless powder. I made a sound that was half retching and half hysterical giggle. Hero McGee wins the shootout. He's death on sun bunnies. Stomach contents rose in an acid column against the back of my throat and slowly subsided. Dear daddy wasn't going to make out too well after all. Bits of mirror still in the frame gave fragmented reflections of her. No more the bikinied prance, thigh-swing, hair salt, gamin sun bunny smile—no working hips or droll wink or busting with fun, no loads of love to daddy from your loving Dru, no surfer teeter on the dipping board, or the slow greeny world down by the coral heads with the fins scooting her along. Her bright dreams and visions, stilled into paste, were clotted onto a bedroom wall. I wondered if she had really known that it was all real. When she had been popping that little gun at me, perhaps she had still been one step removed from the trueness of it, seeing herself as a TV second lead making up the script as she went along, seeing both me and herself as symbol figures in one of the dramas that would always end with everybody sitting around having coffee before the next take. I hoped she was taken dead so quickly she was given no micro-second of the terrible reality of knowing that she was ended. I stood tense, half on tiptoe, trying not to breathe, listening, listening. I moved to the door, listening. I could not risk opening it. Not yet.

The little gun was under the dressing table bench. I managed not to look at her as I retrieved it. I had assembled a rude script for my own survival, and I went through the motions like a wooden man, with everything but the necessities of the situation blocked out of my mind. I took the little gun over and stood over Claude and fired one slug down into his dead heart. I took the gun back and put it into Chip's hand and curled his fingers around it. I knelt beside him and gave him a solid blow on the side of the head with the length of pipe, to keep him sleeping. And, in the event he woke up too soon and wanted to rearrange the scene to fit some other pattern, I used the pipe to give him a knee that would keep him still and bother him as long as he lived. I folded the bigger gun into Claude's slack hand. I saw where the three times she had missed had put raggedy little holes into the panel meat of the door. I stood and looked at the scene. I knew I was going to wear it for a long long time, right in there on one of my back walls, with studio lighting. I tasted blood and realized I had nibbled a small piece out of the inside of my under lip.

I was still so rattled that I came dangerously close to wiping the door hardware clean. That is like leaving a signal flag. I recovered and smeared it, using the heel of my thumb, bases of my fingers. I had to leave the room light on. I opened the door an inch. The corridor was silent. I heard steel guitars. I slipped out and pulled the door shut and went to the end of the corridor. The deck was empty. I went out there and closed the corridor door. Somebody had left half a drink on the rail. I picked it up. My right arm ached. There was a very tender area behind my right ear and slightly above it, but the skin was not broken. I fixed my tie and took deep breaths of the night air. I had the length of pipe in a trouser pocket. I ambled back to join the party.

I had the eerie expectation of finding everyone gone, chairs overturned, drinks spilled, signs of hasty exit. But the groups were still there, unsteadier now. Some of the kids were on the stairs, and others were dancing. Dr. Face still brayed disaster at his captive circle. I looked at my watch. It had all happened in about twenty-five minutes. I saw mine host in pewter silk standing in a group, his dull black wig sitting trimly on his naked skull, iced tea in his right hand, his left hand mechanically honking the buttock of a slender woman who stood beside him, like a child playing with an ancient auto horn. No one paid me any attention. I searched for Connie without haste, and found her down by the sheltered part of the pool, sitting on a bench, talking real estate tax laws with a slight young man with a mild face and fierce mustache. The young man, after the introduction, excused himself to go off and find his wife.

Connie stood up and said, "*Now* can we go back to my place? My God, darling, this is turning into one of the dullest evenings of my life."

I hauled her back down onto the bench and she was a little off balance and came down too solidly.

"Hey? Are you tight?"

"Listen one damned minute, Mrs. Melgar. Listen to a suppose. Suppose you got a little foolish and reckless one night, and you got a little drunk, and you went back into that studio or whatever he has beyond that jolly museum of his, and somebody took some very unwholesome pictures of you. . . ."

"That may be his little hobby, dear, and he may have scads of friends who are sick enough to play, but it leaves me absolutely cold. He has made his oily little hints. For God's sake, you heard him. I may be lusty, dear, but I'm not decadent, not in any exhibitionistic sense."

"So suppose he sets you up sometime, with something in your drinks, and he picks a couple of choice negatives and sends them to somebody in Caracas who will make a couple of thousand prints and distribute them. What would happen then?"

Her big hand clamped my wrist strongly. "Dear God!"

"Two of your sisters are married to men in the government. What would happen?"

"My grandfather and my dead husband's grandfather were terrific men. They're sort of folk heroes now. It didn't help very much, having me leave for good. A thing like that would. . . . It could be put to terrible frightening use. What are you trying to tell me? That Cal would do a thing like that? But, my dear, it doesn't make sense! Everybody knows that Cal helps a lot of people fight the sort of people who would put pictures like that to political use. He gives loads of money to people who are fighting Communist influence in Latin America."

"What if he strengthens the groups who are going about it in the wrong ways, in ways that merely help rather than hinder."

"But that would mean he. . . ."

"He is a grotesque. He loves intrigue. Maybe he hates his own class, and particularly himself. Maybe he hides behind this facade of . . . political gullibility and this collection of erotica. Maybe he is not quite sane."

"For goodness sake, he is just Calvin Tomberlin, a dull, self-important, rich, silly, sick little man."

"I don't like wasting time with these questions, but I have to ask them. Was Rafael Mineros doing anything effective about the Cuban situation?"

In the shadowy reflections of the pool lights, she looked startled. "He asked me to come in with them. Maybe I was too selfish. Maybe I didn't have his dedication. He had organized a group of wealthy people, about half of them from Cuba and the others from sensitive areas, Guatemala, Venezuela, Panama. They formed a syndicate to try to stifle trade with Cuba. They weren't working through governments, with sanctions and embargos and things like that. They were dealing directly with the businessmen in Japan and Greece and Canada, the ones who wanted to buy from Cuba and sell to Cuba. They would line up other sources and other markets, and then put in enough money to make the deal more attractive than if they'd dealt with Cuba. It was his idea that if they could hasten the economic collapse of Cuba, they would be hastening the fall of the Castro government. He showed me where they could prove they had stopped forty-three ships from taking cargoes to Cuba and bringing Cuban goods out, just by locating other deals elsewhere. I guess it wasn't very dramatic and exciting, like buying little airplanes and hiring madmen to drop little bombs on refineries, but I imagine it is dull negotiations like that which do a lot more damage. Rafael was completely tireless and dedicated. I think he was flying a million miles a year. It is probably all falling apart now. It was an expensive project. His son Enrique and Manuel Talavera were his aides, and Maria Talavera did a lot of the office work. Now they are all gone."

I took her by the upper arms and shook her. "Now listen to me. Listen to two things. Make it three things. One. Tomberlin had that group killed. And then he had the people killed who had killed them. He used his collector's mania as window dressing. Two. I told you precisely the plan Tomberlin has in mind for you. Three. In one of the bedrooms of this house there are two very dead people right now, dead by violence, and this whole situation may blow up in our face at any moment. But there is too damned good a chance that Tomberlin can cover the whole thing up. He has too many personal pictures of too many people in his files. His big levers are money and blackmail. I didn't want to get you too involved. But now there isn't much choice. You can still say the hell with it. Or you can help. It depends on how much any of this means to you."

She huddled her big shoulders. "I . . . I've never been what you would call a p-patriot. But the way they think about my family . . . that's a precious thing. And . . . Rafael was a good man. What do you want of me?"

"Let's get him back into that museum."

"How?"

"Be a little drunk. Tell him you want your picture taken. Tell him it has to be with me, and it has to be now, before you change your mind."

"What are you going to do?"

"You said that layout is built like a safe. Nobody is going to get in and upset anything. Let's see what happens."

nineteen

IT TOOK her about fifteen minutes to set it up. The party was now visibly dwindling. Tiresome drunks were in the majority of the diehards still left. I noted with approval that when we went in, Tomberlin locked the heavy door. Connie was doing a good job of simulating a constant high foolish giggle. I was unsteady on my feet, and wore a vacant, lecherous, fisheating grin. Tomberlin was very soothing, and kept turning a quick broad smile off and on as though he were hooked up to a repeating circuit.

He took us back through a library to a small studio. There was a shiny jungle of lighting equipment. A technician was fiddling around with cameras. I had not anticipated his presence. He was a little old fellow, a mixture of oriental blood lines, part Japanese.

"As I explained, my dear, you will have absolute privacy," Tomberlin said. "I wouldn't want you to feel too restrained. Charlie will get the cameras set up and then we'll leave you alone."

The equipment was interesting. There were three 35 millimeter Nikon cameras, still cameras with automatic drive and oversized film carriers. One was locked to a track directly over the low broad couch, aiming down. One was on a high sturdy tripod at the foot of the couch, slanted down. One was on a low tripod beside the couch. Charlie led the drive cables over to jacks in a timer box. He adjusted lights, one a direct flood, but softened and diffused, and the other a bright bounce light from the white ceiling. Charlie turned the timer on. One camera clopped, and after about six seconds another one clopped and buzzed, and at the same interval the third one fired. Charlie turned the timer off and nodded.

"The film will last about fifty minutes, dears," Tomberlin

said, wiping his pale lips on the back of his hand. "Do try not to be too dull and ordinary."

"What are you going to do with these pictures, Cal?"

"Darling, it's just a fun game, that's all. We can go over the contact sheets together and see what we have worth enlarging. I'll give you all the negatives. You'll have some very interesting souvenirs, Connie dear. The lady in her prime. Don't be too quick, dears, and waste all that film."

"Is anybody likely to walk in?" she asked.

"There's not the slightest chance."

"Where will you be?"

"I might rejoin the party and come back in an hour."

I rambled over to the timer box and turned the switch on. The little old fellow hissed at me and slapped my hand away and turned it off. I'd wasted one exposure.

"Please don't touch the equipment," Tomberlin said.

I went grinning over to where he stood. Bashful guy. The old Hank Fonda in a farm picture. Shucks. I studied my fingernails, head bent, and said, "There's one thing about all this, Mister Tomberlin."

"Yes?"

I pivoted a half turn. I had screwed my legs down into the floor, and I pivoted with thighs, back, shoulder and arm, to see if I could drive my fist all the way through softness above his belt, right back to the backbone. The wind yawffed out of him and he skidded backward, bowing low, spilling tripod and camera, hitting the couch with the back of his knees, rolling up into a kind of curled headstand on the couch before toppling over onto his side. Even though I started moving the instant I hit him, I still almost missed the old man. He had the speed of a lizard. I got him by the back of the collar just as he went through the doorway and hauled him back. He began to jump up and down and whoop and bat at me with his hands. He was too hysterical to listen to anything. I held him at arm's length, got the length of pipe, timed his leaps, and with due regard for the long fragile look of his skull, bumped him solidly right on top of the head. His eyes rolled out of sight and I lowered him to the floor. I don't think he weighed a hundred and ten. Within moments he was snoring heartily. They do that quite often.

Connie stepped out of my way as I went over to the couch. Tomberlin was on his side, his color dreadful, knees against his chest, semi-conscious, moaning softly with each breath. I shook him and said, "Greetings from Almah. And Sam. And Miguel. Rafael, Enrique, Maria, Manuel. Greetings from the whole group. Dru is dead too. And so is Boody."

"Boody!" Connie gasped. "Claude Boody?"

"World traveler."

I shook Tomberlin but I couldn't get through to him. I'd given him too much. He was going to be out of touch for a long time. I tore one of the cables loose and wrapped him up. I wondered if I should stuff his mouth. The black toupee peeled off with a sticky sound and I wedged it into his jaws. It muffled his moans. Connie stared at me with a wide and horrified grin, wringing her big hands.

"N-Now what?"

I took her out and we found his photo files. It was an extensive and complex system, with thousands of negatives cross indexed to proof sheets and print files. There was another complete filing system for color, and a third for movies both black and white. It wasn't a collection you could burn in a wastebasket. Connie was fascinated by the files of finished prints. She kept dipping into them, looking for familiar faces, gasping with a mixture of horror and delight when she found them. I set her to work emptying all the files, dumping everything into a pile in the middle of that small room which adjoined the photo lab. I went back out into the museum part. The glass covering the gold statue niches was set permanently in place. I could see no clue that the niches were hooked up to any alarm system. It took three solid blows with the pipe to open up each niche, one to shatter the glass, two more to hammer shards out of the way so I could pull the heavy images out. I remembered the two big cushions on the couch and went back to the little studio. I ripped the covers off, and had two sizeable sacks. I divided the statues evenly between the two sacks. I took the whole thirty-four. The Menterez collection had grown. The sacks weighed close to a hundred pounds each, though the contents were not bulky. They were all jumbled in there, like jacks in a child's game. I bound them with twine. Little Santy Claus packs for good children. I lifted them carefully, one in each hand. The stitches held. I put them back down again.

I went back to the file office. Connie had finished her work. It was spilled wall to wall in the middle of the room, about three feet high at the peak. She was pawing through it, still looking at things.

"You have no *idea!*" she said. "My God, some of these people are so proper! How in the world did he ever.... "

"Listen to me. I've got Tomberlin's keys here. Take them. I think this one unlocks the museum door. I've got things to carry. Now get the sequence. We take Tomberlin and the little guy out into the museum. I unwrap Tomberlin. I come back and get this stuff burning. We'll have to wait a few minutes to be certain it is going real good. Then we unlock the door and go out, yelling fire. Because there is going to be a nice fire, there is going to be considerable confusion. You head for the car as fast as you can. I'll be right behind you. We go to your place and split up. My car is there. You are going to pack quickly and get out quickly and take a little vacation."

I saw fifty questions in her eyes, and then she straightened her shoulders and said, "Yes dear."

It nearly worked. It came within inches and seconds of working. She was trotting ahead of me, the ends of the big stole flying out behind her, a rather hippy and bovine trot but she was making good time. We were almost at the car when the voice of authority called "Halt!" I risked a glance. It was George Wolcott, of the little leaden eyes and the large damp mouth.

"Keep going!" I ordered Connie.

"Halt in the name of the law!" he yelled with stentorian dignity and precision, fired once in the air as the book says, and fired the second one into my back, without a suitable pause. I was fire-hot-wet in back, and fire-hot-wet in front, without pain but suddenly weakened. I wavered and stumbled and got the gold into the car with a vast effort, ordering her to take the wheel and get us out of there. I clawed my way in. She had it in motion the instant the engine caught, and she slewed it between and among the few cars left, then straightened and headed for the gate. The man there jumped out and then back, like a matador changing his mind about a bull. We went over a hump, screeched down the long curve of drive and onto Stone Canyon Drive, accelerating all the time. She slammed into curves, downshifting, shifting back, keeping the rpm well up toward the red, showing off, laughing aloud.

"Okay," I said. "Ease off. You're great."

She slowed it down. "My God, it's too much!" she said. "What a change in a dull evening! My God, that couch for a frolic, and those cameras clucking like a circle of hens, and those dirty pictures curling and steaming in that lovely fire. And the great Tomberlin with his mouth full of wig. And a lovely lovely madman smashing glass and stealing gold. And shots in the night. For God's sweet sake, I haven't felt so alive in a year. Darling, wasn't that that dull fellow, actually shooting?"

"That was that dull fellow."

"But why?"

"It didn't seem a very good time to ask. I'm glad it was a fun evening for you. There's a pretty little girl back there with the top of her pretty head blown off. And Claude Boody is dead. He's always good for laughs."

The edge of delight was gone from her voice. "So there is going to be a big and classic stink about all this?"

"Yes."

"But then I don't think it would be so very smart for me to go away, do you? I don't know very much. The little I do know, I can lie about. I think you had a little gun in my back. You forced me to do things. I don't know who you are or where you went."

"That's fine, if it's police questions. But Tomberlin will have some questions. He won't ask them himself. He might send some people who wouldn't be polite."

She thought that over as we waited for a light. "But if I am just ... absent, there'll be a stink about that, officially. I think the best thing is to ... report this myself. As an injured party. I can make a statement, whatever they want, and tell them I am going away, and be very careful and go quickly."

"That probably makes more sense."

"How will I ever find you again?"

"Maybe you won't."

"But isn't that a horrible waste? Don't you feel that way about it?"

"I can't guarantee the same kind of evening every time, Connie."

"Are you sleepy? You sound sleepy. It's a reaction, I guess."

"I parked around in that back street, the same as before."

She spotted the little English Ford and pulled up behind it.

I was assembling myself to get out. No pain yet. Just numb-hot on the right side, from armpit to hip. I had the feeling I was carrying myself in a frail basket. As with my care with the stitching on the pillow covers, I felt I had to stand up very slowly and carefully. I opened the car door. She put her hand on my knee. "Will you be all right now?" she asked. "You have everything all planned?"

"Nearly everything."

I got out, feeling as if I moved in separate parts and pieces. I felt as if the left side would work better than the right. I got one sack in my left hand and took the strain of it as I swung it out. Nothing seemed to tear, in the sack or in me. The sack weighed a mere thousand pounds. I marched slowly to the rear of the little car, put the sack down, found the keys, opened the trunk. I was cleverly constructed of corn flakes and library paste. Her car lights were bright on the trunk of the little car. I got the sack in and floated back to her car and got the other sack. I had dry teeth and a fixed grin. I put the second sack in and when I closed the back lid I folded against it for a moment, then pushed myself back up to my dangerous height. Her car lights went off and suddenly she was with me, a strong arm around me.

"You're hit!" she said.

"There's probably some blood in your car. Wipe it off. Go home. Make your statement. Get the hell out of this, Connie."

"I'll get you to a hospital."

"Thanks a lot. That's a great idea."

"What else?"

"Anything else. Because they'll nail me with some of the trouble back there. And make it stick. And I'd rather be dead than caged. So would you, woman."

I expected the moral issue then and there. Did you kill anybody? But she was the kind who set their own standards.

"Do you have a place to go?" she asked. "A safe place?"

"Yes."

She helped me to the passenger side of the little car, and helped me lower myself in. She wrested the car keys out of my hand. I made protest.

"Shut up, darling. I won't be long. Try to hold on. In case you can't, tell me the address now."

After hesitation, I told her. She hurried off. She didn't start her car for a few moments, and I suspected she was swabbing my valuable blood off her leather upholstery. She swung out and went up the street and turned into the underground garage. I undid my jacket, pulled my shirt out of my pants and looked at the damage in front, by the flame of my lighter. It was on the right side, in the softness of my waist. Exit holes are always the worst, unless it is a jacketed slug. This seemed about half dollar size, so the slug hadn't hit anything solid enough to make the slug mushroom very much. My posture kept the lips closed, and it was not bleeding badly. I tucked the soaked shirt tail back in and hugged myself. I wished I knew more anatomy. I wondered what irreplaceable goodies were within that line of fire. From the absence of pain I knew I was still in shock. There was just a feel of wetness and looseness and sliding, and a feel of heat. But there was another symptom I did not like. There was a metallic humming in my ears, and the world seemed to bloat and dwindle in a regular cycle. I hugged and waited, wondering if on the next cycle the world would dwindle and keep dwindling and be gone. If she was a very smart woman, if she came back and found me too far gone, she would do well to take me to the address I gave her, and walk away from it.

That son of a bitch had been too eager. The look of people hurrying away with a burden had gotten him terribly excited. The business shot had come about a second and a half after the warning shot. He sounded official. Maybe he was after a citation.

I hung on. I felt suspended in a big membrane, like a hammock, and if anything jounced, it would split and I would fall through.

Suddenly she opened the car door and bounced in. The bounce stirred the first tiny little teeth of pain.

"How are you?" she asked. She threw a small bag into the back seat. She had changed her clothes. She was breathing hard.

"I'm just nifty peachy dandy, Mrs. Melgar."

She got the little car into motion very swiftly, giving the little teeth a better chance to gnaw. She said, "Just as I was leaving, the phone rang. Men down at the desk. Police. I told the night man to send them right up. I went down the stairs."

"Fun and games. The romantic vision. Have fun, Connie."

"My friend, once you decide you want the animal to charge, and once he begins the charge, you cannot change your mind. You stand there and you wait until he is close enough so you can be absolutely sure of him."

"Grace under pressure. Kindly spare me the Hemingway bits."

"Are you always so surly when you're wounded?"

"I hate to see people being stupid for no reason. Get out of this while you have the chance."

"Darling, I will take every chance to feel alive, believe me."

The little man inside me decided that teeth weren't enough. He threw them aside and got a great big brace and bit, dipped it in acid, coated it with ground glass and went to work, timing each revolution to the beat of my heart. She parked in front of 28. I leaned against the side of the bungalow while she unlocked the door. She took me in. My legs were too light. They wanted to float. It was hard to force them down to the floor to take steps.

She managed the lights and the heavy gaudy draperies. She had changed to a dark pleated skirt and a dark sweater. I kept my jaws clamped on the sounds I wanted to make, and settled for the occasional snort and whuff. We got the ruined jacket and shirt off. I sat on a low stool in the bathroom, forearms braced on my knees, head sagging.

She said, "It's off to the right, in back, just under the last rib. You've got to have a doctor."

"I've lasted pretty good so far."

"You look ghastly," she said. "I think we can stop the bleeding, though."

She went scouting around and I heard her tearing something into strips. She found a sanitary napkin and fashioned two pads and bound them in place by winding the strips around my middle and knotting them. Now I felt as if I had a heavy bar of lead through me, from back to front, red hot. She found the bourbon and poured me a heavy shot. I asked her to leave the bathroom. I urinated, but it was not bloody. I could take a deep breath without any inner rattling or gargling. But something essential had to be messed up.

As I headed for the bed, I went down. Very slowly, protecting myself, bracing myself, rolling onto my good side. She helped me up and onto the bed. I stretched out on my back, but it felt better to keep my knees hiked up.

She looked down at me and said, "I'm going to use the phone."

"What are you thinking of?"

"Pablo Dominguez. He might have an idea. At three in the morning, he might have an idea, you know. But is that all right with you?"

"That's very much all right."

"Is it hurting a lot?"

"It didn't help it very much, falling down. This is a borrowed place."

"It looks it."

"And a borrowed car. I was planning on getting out of here without leaving a trace, without leaving people around with a lot of questions. Tell Paul that if he can manage it, if he can manage anything, getting out of here should be part of it."

"I don't think you should be moved any more."

"Tell him I have some interesting things to tell him."

I heard her on the phone, close beside me, but I couldn't keep track of what she was saying. Her voice turned into three simultaneous voices in echo chambers, overlapping into a resonant gibberish. I raised my hand to look at it. It came into sight after a long time, hung there, and then fell back into darkness.

I was jolted awake. Somebody was saying in a husky whisper, "Careful. Easy now!" They were trying to get my legs up over a rear bumper. It was a panel delivery truck. I had clothes on. There was a faint grey of dawn over Buena Villas. My gear was in the truck. There was a mattress in there.

I helped them. I crawled toward the mattress. I had been sawed in half and glued back together, but both ends worked. I saw Dominguez and Connie staring in at me. "There's one thing," I said.

"Don't try to talk, baby," Connie said.

I made her understand about the promise and the money, and she agreed that she would immediately put the key and the seventy dollars in Honey's mailbox, don't worry about it, the house is in good shape, everything's fine, don't worry. In the middle of trying to form the next question, my arms got tired of chinning myself on this bottom rung of consciousness, so I just let it all go.

When I awoke again it was hot. Light came into the truck,

dusty sunlight. I was being juggled and bounced. Connie sat on a tool box. It was a bad road. She looked tired. Her smile was wan. She said something I couldn't hear and felt my forehead. I saw my gear and her small bag and the two sacks of golden idols. I wanted to say something vastly significant, about a woman and gold and a wound, like those things you say in dreams, those answers to everything. But when I unlocked my jaw, all that came out was a bellow of pain.

She knelt and held me and said, "Just a little bit more, dear. Just a little bit more now."

I was on my face, in a rough softness, in a smell of wool and a sharper smell of medicine. They'd let something loose at me and it was eating its way into my back. I tried to roll over, but a hand came down on my bare shoulder and forced me back. I heard Connie in an excited clatter of Spanish, and a man's voice answering. Suddenly a huge pain towered shining white and smashed down on me and rolled me under.

I awoke slowly. I was in bed, I accumulated the little bits of evidence one at a time, with a great slow drifting care. I was naked. I was well-covered. I felt a stricture around my middle. I felt a wide, taut, professional bandage. It was dark where I was. There was a yellow light on the other side of the room. I turned my head slowly. Connie Melgar was over there, sitting, reading a book by a kerosene lamp, near a small open fire in a big fireplace. She seemed to be wearing pyjamas, and a man's khaki hunting jacket. There was a huge night stillness around us. I could hear the small phutterings of the fire.

"Connie?" I said, with somebody else's voice. A little old man's voice.

She jumped up and came over and put her hand on my forehead. "I was going to have to try to wake you up," she said. "You have pills to take."

"Where are we?"

"Pills first," she said. She went out of sight. I heard the busy ka-chunking of a hand pump.

She came back with two big capsules and a glass of chill water. Nothing had ever tasted better. I asked for more, in my little old voice, and she brought me another glass. She brought the lamp over and put it on a small table, and moved a straight chair near. I saw that I was in a deep wide bunk, with another above me, and a rough board wall at my left.

She lit two cigarettes and gave me one.

"Are you tracking, Travis? Do you think you can understand what I tell you?"

After a slow count of ten, I said, "Travis. My wallet?"

"That's the way a snoopy woman amuses herself, Mr. McGee. It is now midnight, my dear. You were shot about twenty-two hours ago. I am sorry we had to bring you such a terrible distance. I wouldn't have taken the risk. But Paul gave the orders and did the driving. You are in a cabin which belongs to one of Paul's friends. It is near the San Bernadino National Forest, and not far from Toro Peak, and it is five thousand feet in the air. You've been winking off and on like a weak light. You've had a doctor. He's a good doctor, but he doesn't have a license in this country. He also is a friend of Paul's. He works for a vet in Indio. He did a lot of prodding and disinfecting and stitching, and he put in some drains. He doesn't ask questions and he doesn't report gunshot wounds. He says you are fantastically tough, and you took the bullet in a very good place. If he had you in a hospital, he would open you up. And it may still come to that. We'll wait and see. He'll be back tomorrow. We have provisions, firewood, water and an old jeep. There isn't a living soul within six miles of us. You are not to move, for any reason. He gave you some shots. Paul went back. When you want the improvised bedpan, shout. It seems you might live. In the meantime, you are a big nuisance to everybody."

I closed my eyes to think it over. I drifted away and came back.

"Are you still there?" she asked.

"I think so."

"You can have some hot broth, if you think you can keep it down, and if I can make that damned wood stove work."

"I could keep it down."

She had to wake me up for the broth. She wanted to feed it to me, but after she got my head braced up, I was able to handle it.

"What about . . . have they said anything? Have you heard any news?"

"Strange news, Travis. Television executive slain in gun battle over beach girl, at millionaire's canyon home. Beauty contest winner slain by stray shot in bedroom gun battle.

Charles "Chip" Fertacci, skin-diving instructor, held in connection with the dual slaying, found unconscious in bloody bedroom. All very sexy and rancid, dear."

"No mystery guest sought?"

"And no Venezuelan heiress either, according to the news. But they could be looking."

"You can be damn well certain they are. What about Tomberlin?"

"Oh, he's in the hospital. Smoke inhalation and nervous collapse after successfully fighting a fire that broke out mysteriously in his photo lab. It seems he is a hobby photographer. The official diagnosis is that it was some sort of spontaneous combustion of chemicals. Minor fire damage. No report of anything missing."

"They don't tie it up with the other story at all?"

"Just that it was a coincidence it happened the same night at the same house, and that Tomberlin's collapse might be partially due to shock and learning of the murders."

"When is Paul going to come back?"

"He didn't say. But he'll be back."

I started to take the last sip of the broth, and without warning my teeth tried to chatter a piece out of the rim of the mug. My arm started twitching and leaping, and she reached and grabbed the mug. I slid down and curled up, wracked with uncontrollable chills. She tucked more blankets around me. Nothing helped. She went over and put logs on the fire, came back and took off the khaki jacket and came into the bunk with me. With tender and loving care, she wrapped me up in her arms, after unbuttoning the front of her pyjama coat to give more access to her body warmth. I got my arms around her, under the pyjama jacket, and held her close, my face in her sweet hot neck, shuddering and huffing and chattering. I was not a little old man. I had slipped back to about ten years old. I felt cold and scared and dwindled. This was the mama warmth, sweet deep musk of hearty breasts and belly, of big warm arms enclosing, and soft sounds of soothing, down in the nest of wool. At last the shudderings came less frequently. I was waiting for the next one when I toppled off into sleep.

I awoke alone in stillness, red coals on the hearth, a white of moonlight patterning the rough floor. I listened until I found the slow heavy breathing mingled with that silence, and traced it, and found it came from above me. At the foot of the bunk I could make out the rungs of the ladder fastened there. I swung my legs up and sat up. At the count of three I made it to a standing position. I held onto the edge of the upper bunk. She had her back to me, pale curls on pale pillow. The khaki jacket was on the straight chair. I was nine feet tall, and I had been put together by a model airplane nut. I got the jacket on, realizing it was not a case of gaining strength, but merely using what I had for what I had to do, before the strength ran out.

I made the door, opposite the fireplace. I leaned on the frame and slid the bolt over. It creaked as I let myself out. Porch boards creaked under my feet. There were no steps, just a drop of a few inches to stony ground. It was a pale landscape on the far side of the moon, sugar stones and a tall twist of pines and silence. Something far off made a sad sad cry. I braced my back against one of the four by fours that held up the porch roof. Huge and virile project for a hero. Relief in the night, a stream to arch and spatter, small boy's first token of virility. As I finished the porch creaked again and she said, "You fool! You absolute and utter idiot!"

"How high are we?"

"Five thousand feet. Come back inside."

"What makes that mournful sound, Connie?"

"Coyotes. Come back inside, you burro."

"I can make it."

But I probably wouldn't have. I put a lot of weight onto those big shoulders. She sat me down, took the jacket, swung my legs in, tucked me in.

"If you want anything, wake me! Understand?" She laid the back of her hand on my head. She made a snort of exasperation and climbed back up her ladder. She flounced around up there, settling herself down.

"McGee?"

"Yes dear."

"You are *muy macho*. You have to be the he-mule. Too much damned pride. That pride can kill you, the way you are now. Let me help you."

"I'm not going to die."

"How do you know?"

"I keep remembering how you cured my chill. If I was going to die, I wouldn't have that on my mind."

"God help us all. Go to sleep."

The little doctor came in an old Ford in the late afternoon, roaring up the final grade in low. He had a leathery frog-face, and it was part of the deal that he did not give his name. He asked questions about fever, appetite, elimination. He inspected the wounds. He made clucking sounds of satisfaction. He bandaged again. He left more pills. He said he would be back. He would skip one day and then come back.

On the following afternoon I was stretched out on a blanket in the side yard in my underwear shorts when I heard another car come up that last pitch. It sounded like more car than the little doctor had. Connie brought Dominguez and another man around the corner of the cabin and out to my blanket.

"See him?" she said. "Disgusting. He said weak men have to have meat. I drove that foul jeep to Indio. I bought four steaks. He ate two for lunch."

"How do you feel, *amigo*?" Paul asked.

"Perforated."

"Permit me to introduce Senor Ramon Talavera."

Talavera was a slim dark-haired man, with a Spanish pallor, a dark and clerical suit. I hesitated and then held my hand out to him. His hesitation was longer than mine, and then he bent and took it.

Paul turned to Connie. "If you don't mind, *chica*."

She plumped herself down on the corner of the blanket, affixed her stretch-pants legs Buddha style and said defiantly, "I sure as hell do mind. What do you think I am? The *criada* around here?"

Paul looked inquiringly at Talavera. The pale man gave a little nod of agreement. Paul got two fat unsplit chunks from the woodpile, and they used them like stools. Connie handed cigarettes around.

Paul said, "It could be a mistake, but from what Connie said to me, I thought it would be wise to bring Ramon here to talk to you."

I looked at the pale man and said, "You have my sympathy in the loss of your sister and your friends."

"Thank you very much, sir."

"I think I know what you want to know, Mr. Talavera. Tomberlin wanted to stop Mineros' activities. He knew that, because of past history, he could make Mineros lose his head if he could bring him face to face with Carlos Menterez. If Mineros killed Carlos and was caught, it solved the problem.

If Carlos killed Mineros, it solved the problem. Tomberlin had two people planted down there. Miguel Alconedo, on Menterez' staff, and Almah Hichin, his mistress. I imagine he got word to them to try to take care of Mineros. Tomberlin used the collection of gold figures as a smoke screen. He is a very devious man. Almah Hichin talked Taggart into helping Miguel kill those four people. Then Tomberlin began to worry, I think, about the reliability of Almah and Miguel. He sent people down—Fertacci and the beach girl—to deliver an order to Miguel to kill the Hichin woman and escape in the boat. They booby-trapped the boat. Tomberlin's orders were given through Claude Boody."

"Who is dead," Talavera said gently. "We got word that one of the men who killed them was on the way up from Mexico to sell things to Tomberlin. We approached Tomberlin. He did not know anything about anything, but he promised to cooperate. When he was contacted, he let us know at once. We tricked the man out of the gold, but we missed him. When he made contact to sell the last piece, I had the honor of being selected to go and deal with him." He looked into my eyes. "I understand he was your friend?"

"He was. He didn't know there would be a woman aboard. He had been sold an entirely false story about the whole thing. Almah Hichin was a sly woman. She made me believe she was telling me the whole truth by only telling me a part of it, in great detail."

"Your friend, Taggart, tried to tell me these things, but it was too late by then. A sister can be the most special person one can have, Senor McGee."

"He tried a bad gamble and it went wrong. There's been too much blood since then. It happened a long time ago, Talavera, and I have lost interest in it."

"Thank you. These other things you say, are they guesses?"

I held my hand out. "Boody burned my hand to be certain I was unconscious. But I wasn't. I listened to Boody talk to Fertacci about these things. I was able to fill in the blanks. I took a chance and knocked their heads together. I think Boody's heart gave out. The girl got a gun and started shooting at me. She missed with three shots from close range. I tried to knock her down with Boody's gun without killing her. But it threw high and to the right. So I disabled Fertacci and set the scene and let myself out. Neither Fertacci nor Boody nor the girl had the slightest idea who I could be. The

girl remembered seeing me at Puerto Altamura. It made
them very nervous. And I think that having Chip Fertacci in
custody is going to make Tomberlin very nervous."

"Bail was set at fifty thousand," Paul said, "and he was
released today. I have a strong feeling that young man is
going to disappear."

Talavera got up quickly and walked away. He went about
fifty feet and stood with his hands locked behind him, staring
at Toro Peak.

"The poor twisted son of a bitch," Paul said softly. "He
thought you would want to try to kill him. If it's any
consolation to you, McGee, you took a perfectly legal au-
thorized official bullet in the back. I have my little sources.
The gentleman who plugged you broke his cover by doing so.
He was assigned to infiltrate Doctor Girdon Face's organization. He had the idea that Face was using Tomberlin's dirty
pictures to extract contributions for the cause. When he
found there was a fire aboard, and saw you running with
sacks, he thought the fire was a coverup and you were taking
off with the files and records. It upset him because he was on
the verge of getting a search warrant. Even though I ... do a
little work on the side for the same organization, I am glad
that stuff got burned. It shouldn't sit in government file
cabinets."

"Pablo," I said, "now that we know where Tomberlin
stands, I get confused by this relationship with Dr. Face."

He gave a latin shrug. "Why should you be confused?
Reasonable conservatism is a healthy thing. But that kind of
poisonous divisionist hate-mongering Face has been preaching
is one of the standard Communist techniques. If you create a
radical right, their vicious nonsense pushes more people toward the radical left. Then when fear pushes people into
violence, or silence, the comrades enter and flourish. My
friend, any way that they can make Americans hate Americans helps the cause. They would like to make Rockwell
stronger too. That is the heart of contemporary propaganda,
amigo, to strengthen ignorant terrible men who believe themselves to be perfect patriots. Now Tomberlin's other activities
begin to seem most curious too. Suppose there are three
groups of Cuban exiles eager to hurt the Castro regime. Two
are plausible, sane and orderly. One is reckless and wild and
dangerous. Tomberlin strengthens the dangerous element, thus

dividing the cause. Perhaps he is under orders. Perhaps he is merely a dilettante. The effect is the same."

Ramon Talavera came back to the group.

He sat down and studied his knuckles and said, "I can promise one thing. I can make them understand that Rafael's program was so effective, it had to be stopped by them, one way or another. When they understand that, they will take heart. It will all be organized again, stronger than before. I promise that."

"Count me in," Connie said. "Count me in this time."

Talavera smiled at her. "Of course. I will squeeze money out of you, Senora." The smile was gone abruptly. "And there is that one small thing left unfinished, Mr. McGee. I would have thought, when you had the chance. . . ."

"I had no taste for it. Not after that girl."

"Of course. But I have made a personal vow. I shall not please myself by doing it myself. It was no pleasure, actually . . . that other time."

"It never is," Paul said gently.

"That man did not beg. I wanted him to beg. He merely fought. I think this might be a good time. While that man is still in the hospital. There is some sort of rupture of the diaphragm which they wish to mend. He has special nurses, of course. If one became busy on other matters, I believe a replacement could be arranged."

Connie shivered, though the sun was hot. "Shall we drop it right there?"

"Of course, Senora. Forgive me. I was merely saying that it is not remarkable when persons die in a hospital." He turned to Paul. "I will need help to continue Rafael's project. There can be money for staff salaries."

"Let's talk about that while we're driving back."

Connie walked off with Talavera. Pablo grinned at me. "So the adventurer has the woman and the gold and the healing wound, eh?"

"Thanks for the help. The place and the doctor. And the nurse."

"A little money was needed. I found it in your wallet and in your belt."

"Let's not say it's all roses, Paul."

"I did not imagine that it was. Is it ever? You add things in your mind and wonder where you are, and where you have been, and why. But you have much woman for a nurse, my friend. Sometimes a woman is a better solution than too much thinking. No one has yet tamed this one. But it is amusing to try, eh?"

"Are they looking for her?"

"Not seriously. What will you do now?"

"Mend. Send her home. Go back where I came from."

He shook my hand. "Goodby. I think you have done some good around here. I do not think you meant to do it. I think it was incidental to the gold. But some people will think of you with gratitude. Kiss Nita for me. And tell Raoul he is an ugly fellow."

I heard their car leave. Connie came back. She sat on the blanket again, cocked her head, stared at me and sighed. "Your eyes look sad, *querido*."

"I was doing some forlorn mathematics. Sam, Nora, Alma, Miguel, Dru, Boody, Rafael, Enrique, Maria, Manuel. Ten. And three to go."

"Three?"

"Carlos Menterez. Chip Fertacci. Calvin Tomberlin. Thirteen, Constancia."

"And almost you, darling. Two inches to the left, and it would be you too."

"But who are the good guys and who are the bad guys?"

"Darling, death does not make those distinctions. With your pale pale grey eyes, perhaps you are an angel of death. Perhaps you are the branch that breaks, the tire that skids, the stone that falls. Perhaps it is not wise to be near you."

"You can leave."

We glowered at each other, her eyes golden slits, her big mouth ugly, the cords of her neck tautened. She broke first, saying, "Ah, you are incredible. I have four and a half million of your dollars, and here I am cooking and sweeping, carrying wood, pumping water, making beds. Doesn't anything impress you?"

"Gentle, courteous, humble women always impress me favorably."

She stalked off, but as she went around the corner of the cabin I heard her laugh.

The veterinary's assistant came just at dusk the next day. He expressed delight. I did not give a damn about his delight. He removed the drains, pulled healing edges more closely together with criss-crosses of tape, provided separate and smaller bandages. I felt like a sad sick dog. I wanted no part of anyone's care and attention. When I went down into sleep, broken women grinned at me. Almah, Nora, Dru. And there were other faces, standing behind them, fragments of older memories, all grinning at their personal angel of death.

She went out with the little doctor and talked for a long time in the night before he went rattling down the slope in his old car. When she came in she was thoughtful, absentminded. I put a jacket on and sat in the old rocker on the porch while she cooked. She called me and we ate in front of the fire. A silent meal.

While she was cleaning up, I went back to bed as was the custom, after using the back lot privvy and brushing my teeth in the out of doors.

I lay with my back to the room and heard her getting ready for bed. She flipped my blankets up and slid in with me, fitting herself to my back, naked as a partridge egg.

"I didn't realize my teeth were chattering," I said.

"Perhaps mine are."

"What the hell is this, Connie?"

"I had a long talk with that nice little man. He couldn't help noticing how morose you are. I told him that some very bad things had happened, and you thought they were your fault, and you were brooding about them. He said there is a certain depression which one can expect as an aftereffect of shock and weakness. I proposed a certain antidote for his consideration. He was dubious. But he is a very practical little man, and I am a very practical woman. There is one thing, Senor McGee, that is the exact opposite of death. Now turn over here, darling."

That big husky vital woman was incredibly gentle. I don't believe that at any moment I bore more than five pounds of her enfolding weight. I do not think she expected anything for herself, but at the final time, she gave a prolonged shudder and sighed small love words in her own tongue and, after a little space of time, rested herself sweet beside me. *"Angel de vida,"* she murmured, *"de mi vida."*

I held her close, stroked that silver head, her curls crisp to the touch, damp at the roots with her exertions, her breath a sighing heat against my jaw and ear. It made me remember something from a long time ago, visiting the zoo man who had the half-grown lioness for a house pet. She had come to me in a tawny stalking, bumped the great beast-head against my thigh, made a furnace sound of purring, huffed that hot breath of carnivore, demanding that this stranger scratch her ears and ruffle her throat fur, tilting her yellow eyes at me in a kind of mocking amusement at this charade we played.

"Happier?" she whispered.

"Bemused."

"Sleep now, and we will awake singing. You will see."

"You'll stay here?"

"From now on, *querido*. For whenever and however you want me. I was not designed by the gods for an empty bed."

twenty

THE TEMPTATION was to stay there too long. I pushed myself to the limit each day. At first it was shockingly limited. A mile of walking, a few simple exercises, and I would get weak and sweaty and dizzy. When I had begun to improve, she left me alone for two days, went back to the city, and came back in the gunmetal Mercedes, bringing more clothes for herself, many gifts for me, games and exercise equipment and clothes and wine and target weapons. And she brought news. Chip Fertacci was being sought for jumping bail. After a minor hernia operation, Calvin Tomberlin had died in hospital of an embolism. The day after she returned, I went with her in the grey car to Palm Springs and brought back the jeep she had left there at the airport.

We had no visitors. We spread blankets and took the hot sun. She said it was foolish for her to do it, as she was already as dark as she cared to be. The hole in my back was healed first. I looked at it with an arrangement of mirrors, a shiny pink button, the size of a dime.

As I became fit again, able to split mountains of wood, jog my five miles up hill and down, do the forty pushups, and heartily service the lady, our relationship became ever more violent and disruptive. We brawled like wicked children over the competitive scores we made on our improvised shooting range, and she could yell Spanish obscenities that echoed in the stone canyons. Once in a fury over my comment about her having let vegetables boil dry, she sucker-punched me with an enthusiasm which split her knuckle and caused my knees to sag. I upended her and walloped her rear, trying to get some yelp of pain out of her, but the only sound was my own roar when she sank her teeth into my thigh. We took all the fierce and childish competitions of the day into the bunk at night, and there it became competition on a different level. I was sometimes fool enough to imagine I could sate her, and even managed to, a very few times. We had immediate and violent differences of opinion on everything from Freudian theory to how to cook beans. But there were the good times too, when something set off laughter, laughing until we wept, rocking and gasping, setting each other off all over again. It was good to laugh like that. It was another part of healing. I hadn't known laughter like that for years.

But we were tearing each other apart in the constant clawing for advantage. I have memories of her, naked by firelight, pacing back and forth, shaking her fist, yelling at me. Nobody sulked. Nobody walked away. We fought every fight right down to the bitter finish, and they all ended in a draw. We learned each other well enough to learn all the tender places, to be able to draw blood at each encounter.

The symbol of the end of it was the sizeable wooden packing case I brought back from the town, along with a dime store stencil kit and excelsior. I got a big enough case so the size to weight ratio would not be unusual. I packed the thirty-four gold images, fastened the top on with wood screws, labeled it as marine engine parts and addressed it to myself in Lauderdale. I had about a hundred and seventy-five pounds of gold and twenty pounds of crate, and I took a childish pride in making the effort look easy when I swung it into the back of the jeep.

I took it down alone and shipped it out and got back in the first cool of dusk. It was a quiet and thoughtful evening. We finished the wine. In the night I missed her. I got up and put something on and went looking for her. I found her beyond the road, throwing the gifts and games and toys one by one down into the rocky gully, hurling them with great force, crying as she did so. It was foolish and petulant and very touching.

I held her and, in the wrack of sobs, she kept saying, "Why? Why?"

She was asking, I suppose, why she had to be the person she was, and why I had to be the person I was, and why it was impossible for us to find any way to be at peace with each other. She knew it was time to end it, and she wanted to end it, but resented the necessity of ending it. I led her back in and made love to her for the last time. I guess it should have been symbolic, or a special closeness or sweetness. But we had already lost each other. Our identities had been packed in separate crates, with the lids securely fastened. So it was merely competent and familiar, while our minds wandered. It had all been reduced down to an amiable service.

She was bright and cheerful in the morning. We tidied the place, buried the perishables and left the rest, stacked wood high and scrubbed the board floor. On the way down in the grey car, we did not look back. At Los Angeles International I found a flight that would leave for Miami in ninety minutes. I checked my luggage aboard and then walked her back out to her car. There was no point in her hanging around, and she showed no desire to do so.

After she got behind the wheel, I leaned in and kissed that indomitable mouth.

"Come around for the next incarnation," she said. "I'll be a better one next time."

"I'd planned on being a porpoise."

"I'll settle for that. Look for me."

"How will I know you?"

"I'll keep the yellow cat eyes, darling. But I'll throw the devils out. I will be the sweet, humble, adoring girl porpoise."

"I'll be the show-off. Big leaps. A great fishcatcher."

She blinked rapidly and said, "Until then, darling. Take care." And she started up so fast she gave me a good rap on the elbow with the edge of the window frame.

There was no reason why I should not use the same name and the same hotel in New York. I came up with the golden goodies packed into two sturdy suitcases. I put them into a coin locker in the East Side Terminal. By three o'clock on that hot and sticky afternoon, I was settled into the Wharton as Sam Taggart. I used a pay phone to call Borlika Galleries. They said they expected Mrs. Anton Borlika back in about twenty minutes.

I had difficulty visualizing her until I heard that flat Boston accent, then I saw all of her, the Irish shine of the black hair, the whiteness and plumpness and softness of all the rest of her.

"It's Sam Taggart, Betty," I said.

There was a long silence. "I never expected to hear from you again."

"What gave you that idea?"

"Let's say because you left so abruptly."

"It couldn't be helped."

"It's been months. What did you expect me to think?"

"Do you need those pictures back?"

"The negatives were on file. Keep them as souvenirs. What do you want?"

"I thought we had a deal lined up."

"That was a long time ago."

"Maybe they're more valuable now, Betty."

After a silence she said, "Maybe there's more risk."

"How?"

"You bastard, I'm not that stupid. You took the pictures. You lined up the outlet first, and then you went after the merchandise. And it took you this long to get it. How do I know the whole thing won't backfire?"

"Betty, I had them all along. I was just busy on other things."

"I can imagine."

"But I did manage to pick up a few more."

"Of the same sort of thing?"

"To the layman's eye, yes. Six more. Thirty-four total. So it will come to more money. And I'm ready to deal. I told you I'd be in touch. There's only one small change. I've lined up another outlet, just in case. But because we had an agreement, it's only fair to give you the chance first. If you're nervous, all you have to do is say no."

It was one of those big pale banks on Fifth, in the lower forties, one of those which manage to elevate money to the status of religious symbolism. I arrived by cab at eleven, and toted my bloody spoils inside.

She got up from a chair in the lounge area and came over to me. She looked thinner than I remembered. There were smudges under her eyes. She wore a hot-weather suit, severely tailored and slightly wrinkled.

"Back this way please," she said.

We went through a gate and down a broad corridor. An armed guard stood outside a paneled door. When he saw her coming, he turned and unlocked the door, swung it open, tipped his cap and bowed us in. It was a twelve by twelve room without windows. When the door closed she smiled in an uncertain way and said, "Hello, Sam."

"How are you, Betty?"

"All right, I guess. I feel a little strange about ... the last time I saw you. It wasn't ... standard practice for me."

"I didn't think it was."

She lifted her chin. "I'm engaged to be married."

"Best wishes."

"I'm going to marry the old man."

"Best wishes."

"He's really very fond of me, Sam. And he is a very kind man."

"I hope you will be very happy."

She stared at me for a long moment and then said, "Well, shall we get at it?"

There was a long steel table in the room with a linoleum top. There were four chairs around the table. There was a blue canvas flight bag in one of the chairs. I put a suitcase on the table, opened it and began taking out the pieces. She hefted and inspected each one and set it aside. She did not make a sound. Her lips were compressed, her nostrils dilated, her blue eyes narrow. Finally all thirty-four were on the table. A little army of ancient spooks.

"Which six were not in the Menterez collection?"

"I have no idea."

"Where did you get the extra ones?"

"From a cave at the bottom of the sea."

"Damn you, I can't take the chance of. . . ."

"You will have to take a chance on my word that nobody misses them, nobody wants them back."

She said she would take the whole works for her original offer. I immediately started packing them away again. She asked what I wanted. I said two hundred. She laughed at me. She made a phone call. She offered one fifty. I came down a little. After two long hours of dispute, we settled at a hundred and sixty-two five. She had a hundred and forty in the canvas bag, fifties and hundreds, bank wrapped. She went out into the bank and drew another twenty-two five, while I packed the heavy little figures of ancient evil back into the suitcases.

There was room for the extra money in the canvas bag, after I had completed my count. She put her hand out and when I took it she laughed aloud, that exultant little chortle of someone who is happy with the deal just made.

"I'll use a porter and a guard to take these away," she said. "Perhaps you would like to leave first. I could arrange a guard if you like."

"No thanks."

"I didn't think so. Sam? Once you have this in a safe place, perhaps we could . . . celebrate the deal tonight?"

"And celebrate your pending marriage, Betty?"

"Don't be such a bastard, please."

I smiled at her. "Honey, I'm sorry. You just don't look to me like the kind to forgive and forget. I think you are itching to set me up somehow."

There was just enough flicker in the blue eyes for me to know it had been a good guess. "That's a silly idea," she said. "Really!"

"If I'm going to be free, I'll give you a ring at the apartment."

"Do that. Please."

A side door of the bank opened into the lobby of the office building overhead. I had marked it on my way in, so I went through in a hurry, got into an elevator and rode up with a back-from-lunch herd of perfumed office girls and narrow-faced boys. I rode up to twelve, found a locked men's room and loitered until somebody came out. I caught the door before it closed, and shut myself into a cubicle. The blue canvas bag was just a little too blue and conspicuous. I had the string and the big folded sheet of wrapping paper in an inside pocket. The blocks of money stacked nicely and made a neat package. I left the blue bag right there, walked down the stairs to ten, took an elevator back down.

A trim little gal with chestnut hair, wide eyes, a pocked face and not enough chin was just ahead of me. I caught up with her and took her arm and said quickly, as she gave a leap of fright, "Please help me for thirty seconds. Just out the door and head uptown talking like old friends."

I felt some of the tension go out of her slender arm.

"What do old friends talk about?" she said.

"Well, they talk about a man who'll leave me the hell alone if he sees me come out with a date."

"Big date. Thirty seconds. This must be my lucky day."

We smiled at each other. I did not look around trying to spot anybody. She came along almost in a trot to keep up with long strides. At Forty-fifth we had the light, and there was a cab right there waiting, so I patted her shoulder and said, "You're a good kid. Thanks."

As I got into the cab, she called, "I'm a good kid, tenth floor, Yates Brothers, name of Betty Rassmussen, anytime for thirty-second dates, you're welcome."

At nine o'clock on an evening in late July, Shaja Dobrak invited me into the cottage she had shared with Nora Gardino. Her grey-blue eyes were the same, her straight hair that wood-ash color, her manner quiet and polite. She was a big girl, and slender. She had been working at a gold and grey desk in the living room. The two cats gave me the same searching stare of appraisal.

"Please to sit," she said. "You drink somesink maybe?" She smiled. "There is still the Amstel, you liked last time."

"Fine."

She went to get it. She wore coral cotton pants, calf length, gold sandals, a checked beach coat. When she brought it to me, she stared frankly at me. "In the eyes I think you are older. Terrible thinks?"

"Yes."

She went to the couch, pulled her legs under her, grave and waiting. "You wish to say them?"

"I don't think so. You went up to the funeral?"

"Yes. So sad. Less than one year I am knowing her, Travis, but I loved her."

"I loved her too."

An eyebrow arched in question.

"Yes. It started sort of by accident. It was very good. It surprised both of us. It pleased us both. It could have lasted."

"Then I am so glad of her having that, to be happy that way a little time. Was it a hard dying for her?"

"No. It was over in an instant, Shaja."

"She was thinking she would die down there I think. There is this think of the will she made out. I have this fine house from her. Her family was given the store. But the way it is, I am in charge. The shares, they are in escrow. The bank, it is helping me run the store, and as I make money I pay it to her family and each time a little of the store is more mine, until finally all, if I have the luck and work very very hard. By the time my hoosband can come, everything will be safe and nice here for us two."

I had improvised my lie. "Shaj, she was so happy that she was certain something might go wrong. We talked about you. She was very fond of you. As you know, we had a chance to come out of this with a profit. She said that if anything happened to her, you should have her share for a special purpose. I have it in a safe place for you."

"A special purpose?"

"Something to do with a mild little man, getting bald on his head in the middle, a teacher of history, one year married to the ice princess before he threw the little bottles of fire at the tanks."

She leaned toward me, eyes staring, "What you say?" she whispered. "What you say to me?"

"These things can be arranged for money, can't they?"

"Ah, yes. Political things. Yes. A case of being very careful, of going to the right persons. I think it is done nicely with English pounds or Swiss francs or American dollars. About needing the exchange, I think. But it has to be *much much* money, and time to work so carefully."

"How much?"

She made a mouth of distaste. "They are greedy. An impossible amount. A hoondred thousand of dollars, maybe."

"Then that will leave you an extra twenty-five thousand for expenses, Shaja."

She did not move. Tears filled, spilled, rolled, fell. She turned and flung herself face down on the couch, sobbing. I went over and knelt beside her, patted her shoulder awkwardly.

When at last she raised her tear-stained face, I have never seen such a look in all my life, such a glow, such a lambent joy. "We will not be too late for children," she cried. "Ah, we will not be too late for them."

She pulled herself together. She tried to ask polite questions about Nora, but her heart was not in it. I knew I should leave her with her happiness. She went to the door with me. Her last question had an old testament ring about it. "The guilty have all been punished, Travis?"

"Yes. Along with the innocent."

She put her hands on my shoulders and kissed me on the mouth. "Do not have sick eyes, my good friend. My hoosband is once telling me this strange thing. We are all guilty. Also, we are all innocent, every one. God bless you."

I went back to The Busted Flush. I wanted to get very very drunk. I wanted to hallucinate, and bring back the women, one at a time, where I could see them, and tell each one of them how things had gone wrong, and how sorry I was.

But instead I got hold of Meyer and he came over with me

backgammon board and we played until three in the morning. I took forty-four dollars away from him. He said, upon leaving, that he didn't know where I'd been or what I'd been doing, but it had certainly given me a nice rest and improved my concentration.

As I was going to sleep I decided I would look up Branks and tell him that Sam Taggart had been killed by Miguel Alconedo, now deceased. And, indeed, he had been, just as surely as if he'd driven the knife into Sam instead of into the woman whose arms Sam had held as it was done.

And I wondered if Shaja would want help on her mission. It would be nice to see one splendid thing come of this, without accident. Good old Cal Tomberlin and good old Carlos Menterez had each chipped in, to bring back the history teacher. And there was some money to send down to Felicia . . . as Sam had promised her. . . .